Tess Mercury & the Crooked Pink

Eleanor Prophet

I0532819

An imprint of Diogenes Club Press

Worldly, Whimsical, and Weird Books

www.diogenesclubpress.com

Dallas, TX

DC Dreams, an imprint of Diogenes Club Press
8619 Reva St. Dallas, TX 74227
www.diogenesclubpress.com

The characters and events in this book are fictional. Any similarity to real persons, living or dead, is coincidental and not intended by the author.

ISBN: 9781622010110

Library of Congress Control Number: 2017955891

Chapter One

The air in the Devil's Fandango was fetid and sweltering. A raucous, drunken crowd pressed in upon us. A man in a threadbare, grey pinstripe suit and faded black felt top hat pounded out a spirited melody on a pianoforte on a makeshift stage in the center of the room. Saloon girls danced with weather-beaten wranglers and local big bugs in fancy suits. In the corner, a group of cagey-looking men clustered around a poker table, eyeing each other narrowly. A petite blonde woman in a red dress danced on a table in the middle of the saloon, kicking up her heels to the music. Around her, the patrons whooped and hollered.

I glanced at Vaughn perched on the stool beside me at the battered wooden bar. His face was expressionless. His coal black eyes rolled languidly around the room.

"Nice night," I remarked.

His thick mouth turned up slightly at the corners. "Yeah. Nice night."

"Hot."

"Real hot."

"Reminds me a bit of home."

He lifted a thick, black eyebrow. "Why?"

"Sense of impending doom. How long you reckon we got before Quim or Hazel blows it?"

Now his teeth flashed brilliant white against his ebony skin. "'Bout five minutes or so."

I gestured to the tall, burly old publican behind me. He narrowed his eyes slightly at Vaughn and me. I scowled at him and slapped a banknote on the counter.

"Get you somethin'?" he asked brusquely.

"Two whiskeys." He passed them across the bar as though he didn't want to give them up, but he snatched up my money fast enough. "Yeah, thanks." I handed one of the greasy glasses to Vaughn. "You'd think the war never ended sometimes."

"I don't think it's me he's got a problem with, Tess."

"Yeah, well, at least my money's good."

"You lousy, cheatin' son of a bitch!"

I sighed. "Damnit, Quimby. Can't go one night without startin' a fight."

Vaughn and I rose to our feet in one single motion. The men at the poker table were suddenly dead silent. They folded their hands in their laps and looked nervously at each other. A strapping, golden haired man leaned back in his chair and smiled around at them all with gleaming white teeth.

"I never cheat," Quimby Burton announced serenely.

A grizzled old man in a worn, tanned leather vest and a battered John B. shot to his feet. His hand hovered over the pistol on his hip. "You sharpin' me, pretty boy?"

"That's Bonny," Quimby replied proudly. "They call me Bonny Burton."

I paused beside the poker table. "Damnit, Quimby, no one calls you that."

"Is this really the time for this argument, Tess?"

"I don't care what they call you!" the old man growled. "You're a lousy, no-good, stinking cheater!"

Quimby shot to his feet so quickly, his chair crashed to the floor behind him. The other poker players froze, staring between the two men warily. "I don't cheat." Quimby's voice was deadly quiet. "I don't need to."

The old man hesitated, but then he puffed out his chest. "Ain't no one plays that good without an ace or two up their sleeve."

Quimby's brilliant blue eyes narrowed. "You want to fight me over it?"

"You bet I do!"

The grizzled old man leapt across the table at him. It splintered under his weight. Cards and poker chips went flying. Quimby and the old man tumbled to the floor in a heap of flying limbs. Around them, the poker players leapt up, whooping and hollering.

"Ah, hell," I complained.

The other pokers players jumped into the fray, throwing punches and smashing bottles indiscriminately. Vaughn and I stepped back from the angry, brawling crowd.

Vaughn sighed. "Every damn night."

A young, wiry man in a tattered black suit flew through the air over my head.

I ducked. "You gonna help him, Vaughn?"

"Nah. He got himself into this one. He can get himself out."

I shrugged and tossed back my whiskey in one gulp.

"At least he ain't ruin' Hazel's night."

The piano player seemed completely untroubled by the fracas. He pounded away enthusiastically on the keys. The small, curly-haired blonde woman in the red can-can dress continued to dance as though she hadn't noticed the brawl at all. In the midst of the mêlée, Quimby pushed to his feet in the center of the angry card players.

I sighed. "Here we go."

Quimby's guns were in his hands and aimed into the crowd so quickly, no one saw him move. The brawlers reared back, throwing up their hands in surrender. Quimby didn't fire. He should have. He lost his advantage as soon as the six other men realized they had their own guns and fumbled them from the holsters on their hips. Quimby's triumphant smile faltered as six guns pointed into his handsome face.

"Being the fastest don't always mean you'll win," Vaughn remarked.

"Hooooooeeeeeee!"

Vaughn and I exchanged a long-suffering glance. We ducked under a table.

Hazel whipped a big, bulbous, long-barreled pistol from under her red ruffled skirt. It hummed ominously over the lively piano tune. She raised it over her head and fired. A beam of toxic blue light flashed from the barrel. It blew a hole straight through the rickety rafters on the ceiling. Splinters of wood showered the suddenly rapt patrons in the bar. Hazel blew on the barrel and grinned around at us.

Quimby grinned. The brawlers around him dropped their guns and raised their arms into the air.

Damn. Not again.

* * *

"Now, I appreciate you folks coming out here to Copper Head," Sheriff McFly said politely.

The trail out of Copper Head, Arizona was barren, endless desert. Stars twinkled in the dark, cloudless sky overhead. Away from the bustling center of town, a chilling breeze swirled around us, blowing my long, black hair around my face. I drew my thick, woolen poncho over my arms and glared at Quimby.

"We always like new faces, but I reckon the rest of the townsfolk don't much care for particle guns and card sharps, if you know what I mean."

"You sayin' we ain't welcome anymore?" Hazel demanded indignantly. Her curly blonde hair floated around her head like a halo. Her large, dark eyes widened. She looked as young and innocent as an angel. A crazy angel.

Sheriff McFly drew his Stetson from his head and swiped a hand nervously across his gleaming baldpate. "Now, I ain't said nothin' of the kind. I'm just suggesting maybe you want to find another town to spend the night tonight. Rattle Snake Junction is just a couple miles up the main road there." He dipped his head and backed slowly away as though he was facing a dangerous animal. "You folks have a good night now."

"Yeah. A real good night," I muttered irritably. I glared sideways at Quimby as we mounted our horses. "Quim, you better hope Rattle Snake Junction has private bathrooms. I was really looking forward to a hot tin bath."

＊ ＊ ＊

A toxic green glow penetrated the thick darkness around us. It bobbed up and down as the small, radiant green globes bounced against our horses' flanks. Despite the tussles and chaos that broke out around her, Hazel did have her uses. Her gadgets were ace-high.

"I see light ahead," Vaughn said.

Rattle Snake Junction was quiet when we rode into town. Soft hanging lights twinkled on spindly trees in the small town square. Most of the storefronts were silent. Light and boisterous music flooded out of the door at the end of the narrow dirt thoroughfare.

"I don't even care about that bath anymore," I said wearily. "I just want to lie down and get some sleep."

The Grody Python Saloon was the only inn in town. Quimby peered longingly at the dancing girls and lively poker players in the small, crowded saloon, but Vaughn clipped him by the collar and dragged him toward the rooms upstairs.

"Hell no, Quimby," he said in a low, inarguable voice.

Quimby's thick, sensual mouth pushed out in a pout. I glared at him. "I ain't

6

spendin' the night out on the road again, Quim. Not when there's a warm bed to sleep in a few feet away."

Hazel poked him sharply in the ribs. "You ain't gettin' us kicked out of another town."

He opened his mouth in outrage. "Me? I'm not the one who shot a hole in the ceiling with a death ray."

Hazel lifted her chin haughtily. I ignored them and opened mine and Hazel's room. I moaned in ecstasy; it had a private bath. "Night, Vaughn. Night, Quim."

"Vaughn, you sure you don't want to—"

"I said no, Quimby."

I didn't emerge from the bath for several very long moments. A tin bath was a rare find, even in these civilized times. I didn't waste an opportunity to enjoy one. I sighed contentedly as I strode into the room, wrapped in a thick, yellow towel.

Hazel hadn't bothered to change out of the red dress, but her corset lay in a pile of laces on the floor beside her bed. She sat cross-legged on the threadbare patchwork quilt covering her mattress. She didn't look up at me as I entered. Large brass goggles covered her eyes. She bent in concentration over a small, metal wand with two sharp prongs on one end. The tip of her tongue stuck out of the corner of her mouth.

"What are you doing, Hazel?"

She looked up at me in surprise. Her eyes were hugely magnified behind the lenses of the goggles. "Huh? Oh. Hey, Tess. Just working out some kinks in this lock pick device."

"Lock pick device?"

"Hell yeah."

"Are you intending' to break into some places?"

"Come on, Tess. When did you become so sanctimonious? We pick locks all the time."

I chuckled and yanked a thin, white cotton nightdress over my head. I stretched out on the bed. "Yeah, all right. So we do."

Sparks flew between the two metal prongs on the device. Hazel cackled.

"Put that away, Hazel. I ain't up for one of your all-night mad science fairs. I want to get some rest."

"Just another couple minutes!"

"Hazel, I ain't interested in havin' my face blown off tonight. I'm tired."

"What's with you, Tess? You've been grouchy all day."

"I ain't been grouchy."

"Sure you have. You mad at Quimby, or somethin'?"

"Mad at Quimby? Nah. It's just his way. Life wouldn't be any fun without you two around to cause trouble wherever we go."

"You've been traveling with a big Negro for five years. I think you got into enough trouble on your own."

I smiled up at the warped wooden rafters. "Yeah. That's the truth. Least Vaughn never went looking for it, though." I sighed. "I'm feeling a little out of sorts, Hazel. I'm feeling like maybe we need another job. We've been living off our last bounty for the last couple weeks, and the idle life don't suit me so well."

She laughed. "Yeah, I think I understand. Bar brawls and benders ain't the way to be."

"I know Quim and Vaughn want some downtime, but I suspect they're ready to get back out on the road doing useful with themselves. I reckon they'd be happy enough to find us a new hunt."

"If not, what do we need those two for, anyway?"

I considered this. "Quim's fast gun and Vaughn's sense."

She scoffed. "We got sense enough between the two of us."

"Hazel, last week in Tombstone you were stinking drunk and tried to death ray a horse 'cause you thought he was talkin' back to you."

She scowled. "That bastard had a right filthy mouth on him."

"That was you cussin' back at yourself."

"All right, maybe you're right," she admitted. "I reckon it might be time to get back out on the road."

I settled back against the thin pillow. "I reckon we need a break from all this leisure time. I'm tired to the bone."

* * *

The men were quiet over breakfast. Quimby's right eye was already turning a garish purple. He prodded the bruise gingerly. He winced. "My beautiful face," he moaned.

"It's your own fault for sharpin' those old cowboys," I told him.

"But my face!"

"It'll heal. You've had worse."

"I ain't listen' to you two argue before I've had my first cup of coffee," Vaughn said in a low, melodic drawl. His coal black eyes glinted dangerously.

Quimby subsided and lifted his hand for the old, graying publican, whose watery green eyes looked tired. He'd been the one to hand out our rooms last night; I wondered if he'd gotten a break at all. "Garcon, some coffee over here, please."

The publican scowled, but he dipped his head in a nod. He returned moments later with four mugs of coffee. When we'd ordered our breakfast, I looked around at Quimby and Vaughn. "Hazel and I have been thinking, boys."

Vaughn's black eyebrows traveled up towards his sleek, gleaming baldhead. Quimby grinned. "I don't know that that's such a good thing; you two thinkin' on your own like that."

Hazel narrowed her dark eyes to slits. "Now, Quimby, what did I say?" Vaughn warned.

Quimby chuckled. "All right, go on, girls. What you been thinkin' about?"

I leaned back in my chair and sipped the thick, bitter black coffee. "We been thinkin' maybe it's time we found ourselves a new bounty to hunt. It's been a nice few weeks traveling the frontier and enjoyin' ourselves, but I think maybe it's time to start back up workin' again."

Vaughn sighed deeply. His dark eyes met mine. I grinned. Quimby huffed. "I've been liking the quiet life," Quimby said sullenly.

"Quiet life? You been gettin' into fights every night. If it ain't sharpin' cards, it's bedding some other man's wife."

"Well, it's quieter than chasing outlaws through the frontier, anyway."

"Not much, though."

Quimby sighed. He tilted back in his chair and stared at us silently for a long moment. Finally, he held up his hands in surrender. "All right, all right. I'll do it.

I reckon I'll be better off working."

"Yeah, you would. You've been on the shoot since we went on hiatus."

"Well, I'm just trying to have a little fun, is all." He winked at a pretty young barmaid as she passed our table. "Old Bonny Burton likes to have a good time."

"No one calls you that, Quimby," I said.

He grinned. His large, brilliant blue eyes crinkled at the corners. He closed one in a wink. "They will. Oh, yes. They will."

"All right, all right. I've had enough of your big fat head," Hazel put in irritably. "Can we get back to work, or what?"

Quimby pushed his lip out sullenly. "Yeah. All right. Post office, then?"

* * *

The local post office was swarming with mid morning customers. They stared at us as we entered, tinkling the bell over the door. Two well-dressed women in sunbonnets gasped at the sight of us. I was used to this sort of treatment, and I didn't really blame them. The appearance of a large black man and a handsome blonde-haired trick shooter with two scandalous women nearly always drew attention. The women bent their heads together and began whispering heatedly amongst themselves.

I tipped the brim of my Stetson to the ladies and tilted my head at my posse. Nah. I didn't blame them. I tucked my thumbs into the belt of my scuffed leather chaps and turned toward the wall papered with yellowing, dog-eared WANTED posters. There was a wall like this in every post office in every town in every frontier state these days. The good folks just had to deal with our kind ambling in to find their next meal ticket.

"How 'bout this one?" Quimby said after several moments. He pointed to the crudely sketched rendering of a burly man with tousled hair and a toothless grin. "$100, wanted for bank robbery in Montana."

"Ah, too easy," I complained.

"Too cheap," Vaughn added.

"He looks like a sissy," Hazel put in, curling her lip in disappointment. "It wouldn't take long to bring him in."

"Right," Quimby replied. "Easy money."

"I ain't looking for easy money, Quim," I told him. "I'm lookin' for a challenge."

"Since when did you pass up easy money?"

"I ain't in it for the money."

"Yeah, well, I am. Not all of us have rich dead husbands and daddies who own plantations in Savannah."

I scowled at him. "I ain't seen my daddy in five years. He ain't given me nothin'. He lost most of it in the war, anyway. And Jace didn't have nothin', I reckon, 'cause I ain't seen a dime."

"You ain't been home in five years," Vaughn put in. "He might've left somethin'."

"It don't matter. This ain't what we came here to discuss."

"I don't need the money, either," Hazel said absently. "My husband left me heaps of gold."

"That's real nice, Hazel," Quimby said, scowling at her. "We know you're only in it for the fun of it."

"Yeah. About that, how about this one?" she said. "Wanted for blowing up a Marshal duty station in Kansas. Hoooooeee! That sounds like a challenge if I ever heard one."

"You just want to see if you got better guns than he does," I said.

She cackled. "Yeah, you're right."

"This one," Vaughn interrupted in a low voice like warm honey. He reached out and plucked a poster off the wall. He held it up for us to read.

WANTED FOR MURDER

Ezekiel "Angel" Cooper

Dead or Alive

REWARD $500

"Who'd he murder?" Hazel asked.

"It don't say."

I tilted my head to study Angel Cooper. He didn't look like a murderer. He looked like a decent sort of guy. He had short, pale hair and even features. Round glasses sat on top of his long, patrician nose. I glanced at my posse and grinned. They grinned back at me.

"Whoever he murdered, they must want him bad," Quimby remarked.

"What say we give it a go?" I said.

Vaughn rolled up the poster and tucked it into his soft, tanned leather vest. He flashed brilliant white teeth around at us. "Guess we ought to head to Grand Junction."

Quimby whooped in delight. "All right. I love Grand Junction."

* * *

We hitched our horses to the post outside the U.S. Marshal duty station in Grand Junction, Colorado. The main thoroughfare was just awakening in the first rays of the early morning sun. Weary wranglers and carriages plodded along the dirt road, just in off the range, and the first shoppers of the morning emerged from their homes to conduct their daily or weekly business in town.

Quimby grinned at me. "I reckon you'd better wait out here, Tess. This could be delicate work."

I curled my lip. "You tell that lady I wouldn't touch you with a ten foot spike, Quimby."

He chuckled and ducked inside. He was only gone a few minutes. He popped his head out the door to peer at us with a smug look. His hat was slightly off-kilter, and there was lipstick on his collar. "All right. Sadie says you can come on in." He winked at me.

The duty station was quiet this early in the morning. A pretty, plump woman with long, thick auburn hair and sharp hazel eyes sat at the front dispatcher's desk. Beside her, a telegraph clicked and spit out strips of paper. She barely glanced at them as she addressed and filed them. She gave me a distasteful look. "You're looking rode hard and put away wet, Tess."

I smiled stiffly at the dispatcher. "And you're looking as tart as usual, Sadie."

Sadie Carter's thick, red lips tightened. "I think I might have changed my mind, Quimby."

He turned to me with an incredulous expression. I sighed. Sadie and I might not see eye-to-eye where old Quimby Burton was concerned, but she knew everything about anyone who was wanted by the Marshals. We needed her information. I swallowed my pride with a painful gulp and bared my teeth. "Pardon me, Sadie. You're looking as radiant as the early morning sun."

"That's what Quimby said when he walked in," she replied suspiciously.

I sighed. "Yeah. I heard 'im say it once." Sadie opened her mouth in outrage. Quimby waved his hands wildly. "About you, I mean. Of course. He was talkin' 'bout you."

Sadie smiled sweetly. "That was difficult for you, wasn't it, Tess?"

"Yeah, you know it was."

She looked satisfied. "All right. Who are you after now?"

"Angel Cooper," Vaughn said.

She lifted her eyebrows in interest. "Yeah?"

"What do you know about him?" Hazel asked eagerly.

"A lot, actually. And I'd tell anyone else not to bother hunting him down."

Vaughn's dark eyebrows traveled up his brow. "Why?"

"He's a big bug with the Pinkertons in Boston."

"He's a Pink?" I demanded.

"Yeah. Well, he was up until the other day."

"What happened the other day?"

Sadie's hazel eyes lit up. She loved to impart a scandal. "He was working a case for Silas Ratcliff, a legal clerk in Boston whose fiancé went missing a week or so ago. Word is Angel and Ratcliff knew each other from before. There might have been something going on with Angel and the fiancé."

"Did he figure out what happened to her?"

"If he did, no one knows about it, and no one's really fussed about it. A few days ago, a witness saw Angel come out of Ratcliff's house. The next morning, the housekeeper found Silas dead on the floor. Angel's glasses were there all smashed up like he was in a fight with Silas before he shot him."

"They sure Angel shot him?" Quimby asked.

"Sure as they can be. He was shot with a Colt .45 Peacemaker, same gun Angel uses."

"A lot of Pinks use that gun," I remarked. "You got anything else?"

She frowned at me. "I'm not the one who put out the bounty."

Quimby gave me a warning look. He stepped forward and took Sadie's hands. He smiled sweetly at her. "Tess don't mean nothin', Sadie. She's rough 'round the edges. Do you know anything else that might help us catch him?"

Sadie's expression softened. She smiled and fluttered her eyelashes at him. "He has a lot of contacts and friends in Boston, mostly Pinkertons and Marshals. They've checked them out already, but they haven't found anything. If he's still in Boston, he's hiding out well, and no one's been able to find him. He's just vanished."

"Is there anywhere else he might have gone to hide out?"

"He's got some family in Laramie, Wyoming, where he's from. The Marshals went by to see them already."

Quimby smiled radiantly. "That just means they'll be feeling pretty secure right about now." He pressed her hand to his chest. "You got anything else for me, Sadie?"

Her cheeks flushed slightly. "You know I do."

"You know what I mean."

She tittered. "He's good. Real good. He's one of the best the Pinkertons have got. He's smart, and he doesn't make a lot of mistakes. He's not your average outlaw. He never did a single wrong thing his whole life until this. He's been living on the straight and narrow. He never even so much as cheated on his wife, so far as anyone knows. Everyone liked him. We were all shocked."

"Have you met him before?' I asked.

She shook her head. "No, not in person. I heard about him, though. He's been around here working cases. He's run into some of the Marshals. They all speak high. If he did this, maybe he had a good reason. And he won't be easy to capture."

I grinned around at my posse. They grinned back. "That's exactly why we want to," I replied cheerfully.

"Well. Good luck, then."

Quimby looked at us pointedly. I lifted an eyebrow. He jerked his head toward the door. I sighed in disgust. "Yeah, yeah. Thanks, Sadie."

She only had eyes for Quimby. "You aren't leaving so soon, are you, Quimby? Sometimes I think you only come by to get information."

He winked at her. "It's not the only reason. You know that."

I rolled my eyes. "We'll see you outside, Quim. Nice seeing you, Sadie."

She didn't bother to offer an insincere reply. I spun and strode out of the duty station without pausing to see exactly what else she had for Quimby. Outside, the sun heated the streets. A gentle breeze rustled my hair and swirled the dirt on the ground into tiny twisters. I crossed my arms over my chest and scowled up at the brilliant blue sky.

"You know, I like that Sadie," Hazel remarked. "She knows what she wants."

I sneered. "Yeah, like every other damn woman west of the Mississippi."

"You jealous, Tess?"

I spun around to glare at Hazel. "Now why would I be jealous of Sadie?"

Quimby emerged from the duty station, carrying his hat in his hands. His golden hair was disheveled. He smiled smugly at us. I huffed.

"Oh, I think you know," Hazel replied slyly.

"I ain't."

"Okay. Don't jump down my throat."

I scowled at her.

"Y'all ready? Let's get a wiggle on," Quimby said. He winked at me.

"You're disgusting, Quimby."

"Yeah, but you like the results."

I opened my mouth in outrage. "What?"

He chuckled. "Come on. Laramie ain't that far away. We could make it in a few days."

Chapter Two

The road to Laramie was rough, but the weather was pleasant this time of year. We paused on a cloudless afternoon to water our horses on the bank of a quickening river in a deep, lush gully. I hopped down from my chestnut mare, Lady Jay, while my posse dismounted their horses around me. Jay didn't wait for me to direct her to the water. I followed her, dipping my hands into the clear, rushing blue current. The water was freezing despite the warmth of the day. I reached into my rucksack for my tin cup and scooped up the chilly water. It tasted fresh and clean. I sighed in contentment.

Vaughn crouched on the bank beside me. He cupped his huge hands and splashed the cool water on his face. He glanced at me and smiled. I grinned back at him. For a moment, he turned his face up to the sun, as if to dry the droplets of water in the warmth of its rays. I knew Vaughn still remembered what it had been like to be a slave. I knew, in moments like these, that he was just letting himself enjoy his freedom. I didn't interrupt him.

"Uh, y'all..."

I glanced up at Quimby. He pointed toward the cliffs above us. They hadn't made a sound, but dozens of Ute Indians stared down at us with their bows and arrows raised. I peered around at them with a sigh. Beside me, Vaughn rose slowly to his feet. There was no expression on his smooth features.

In one motion, my posse and I drew our guns from their holsters and aimed them around at the Utes. The mahogany-skinned men and woman on the ridge shifted slightly, but they did not draw back.

"We're just passing through to Laramie on business," Vaughn said in a smooth, carrying voice. "We have no fight with you. We don't want anyone to get hurt."

The Utes glanced warily at each other. After several long, tense moments, they lowered their weapons.

I glanced at my posse. "We'd better get a wiggle on before they change their minds," I said quietly.

They did not argue. We caught the reins of our reluctant horses and guided them on foot toward the flat, wooded opening of the gully. The Utes waited there, lined up in a silent gauntlet. They watched us cagily as we passed. I held my head high and avoided their gazes. The Utes were a generally peaceful tribe, but they did not like outsiders, regardless of their color, trespassing on their territory. I'd be happy when we were shot of them.

Ahead of me, Quimby tilted his hat and smiled brilliantly at a young, pretty Ute girl with long, black hair that glinted in the afternoon sun. The young girl smiled back, her cheeks coloring slightly. Beside her, a young, handsome man with high cheekbones and a broad, bare, hairless chest looked between her and Quimby.

I sighed in irritation and paused. My muscles coiled for a fight. Every damn time.

The young Ute man drew his bow and arrow from its quiver so quickly, it was aimed at Quimby in a blur of black hair and bronze skin. Quimby was faster. The long barrel of his gun was already pointed into the shorter, stockier Ute man's face.

The lot of us drew our weapons at the same time, aiming them around at each other.

"Well," I drawled, "this is sure awkward."

The Ute girl's man fired first. Quimby's return fire did not strike him; the bullet splintered the whizzing arrow in mid-air and lodged in the tree behind the Ute man's head. The young man's dark, almond-shaped eyes widened in shock.

His brothers let out a loud, angry war cry. Their arms drew back to fire their bows.

Quimby didn't give them a chance. He spun in a circle and fired off several shots in rapid succession. When the smoke cleared, the Ute men stared around at each other in surprise while their arrows lay in splinters at their feet. In a single motion, the Utes backed up away from us. Then they turned tail and fled, streaming over the hills and across the river.

I glanced around at my posse. They looked back at me. At the same moment, we began walking toward the trail again.

"Why you always gotta get us in trouble, Quimby?" I demanded gruffly.

"It ain't my fault! I was just being polite."

"Yeah, right. Next time you keep your bedroom eyes to yourself.

* * *

The Coopers' homestead was nestled between two foothills. The land around

17

the small, single-story wooden cottage was green and flat, but the mountains loomed up on every side in the distance. Even in the mid-afternoon, smoke billowed from the stone chimney. Several horses grazed in a corral on one side of the house. They didn't glance up at us as our mounts plodded along the winding dirt trail toward the house.

We hitched our horses to a post outside the front gate. The proprietors of the homestead didn't seem to hear our steeds snorting and whinnying or our hushed conversation as we approached the front door; no one came out to see who was tromping up to their front door.

"You think they'll talk to us?" Hazel wondered aloud.

I shrugged. "Probably not. You know how folks are."

"Mayhap you ought to hang back, Vaughn. This ain't exactly enlightened civilization," she remarked, glancing sidelong at the large black man.

He didn't seem troubled by this. "Sure, Hazel. 'Less you need me, I'll keep quiet."

"It never hurts to have a big Negro on your side when folks start to get reticent," Quimby added, smiling slightly.

I stepped forward toward the large, thick, polished wood front door. I rapped sharply. For several moments, nothing happened. Then a short, plump, wrinkled woman in a gingham apron opened the door. Her long, graying hair was wrapped up in a thick bun on the top of her head. She looked sweet and sympathetic. She glanced around at us warily. Her smile was brittle.

"Good afternoon," she greeted guardedly. "You folks with the Pinkertons?"

We looked at each other in surprise. "The Pinks? Nah. We ain't Pinks," I told her.

She looked slightly relieved. Then her eyes narrowed. "If you aren't Pinkertons, who are you? The Marshals have already been by here. We told them everything we know about Ezekiel. Who are you folks? Why are you here?"

I lifted an eyebrow. "I'm Tess Mercury. This is Hazel Harley, Quimby Burton and Vaughn Blair."

She looked at us shrewdly. "You working for the law?"

"We work for ourselves," Hazel told her proudly.

"What's that mean?"

"They're bounty hunters, Alice," a deep voice said behind her. A tall, balding man in coveralls and a wide-brimmed straw hat appeared in the anti-chamber behind her. He laid a hand on her shoulder.

"Bounty hunters?" Alice Cooper exclaimed. She frowned at me as though I had attempted to deceive her. I looked back at her innocently.

"When the occasion's right," Quimby told her smoothly.

Alice's husband frowned. "Well, in this case, it ain't."

"I beg your pardon, sir?"

"Our Zeke's innocent," Alice told him firmly.

We stared at her in silence a long moment.

"What are you folks doin' here, anyway?" Mr. Cooper demanded. "It ain't like you expect we'll tell you where he is, do you?"

My posse and I exchanged a glance. "In our experience, most parents do," Hazel told them helpfully.

"Is that so? That don't sound very loyal to me."

"It's not so much about loyalty as an uncontrollable urge to give your kids their just desserts," I put in. "The good ones, anyway. Ain't no good ever came of enabling an ill-behaved child."

Alice considered this. "I can understand that."

Her husband scowled. "That don't mean we intend to tell you anything. We won't help soldiers of fortune use our son to make a buck. He ain't a murderer or a criminal."

I eyed him in interest. I liked him. He was earnest, and he was loyal. I liked that in a man. You didn't see that much these days. "We just wanna talk."

Mr. Cooper scowled at me. "I don't know what to think about a woman who dresses like a man and does a man's work."

"Who says it's a man's work?" Hazel demanded heatedly. "It's work. We can do it as well as some men. Better than most."

This was counterproductive. Vaughn stepped forward. His massive form cast the rest of us in shadow. His voice was like warm, sweet molasses. "We're just looking for the truth, sir, ma'am. We don't intend to profit from anyone who don't deserve it. I reckon the Marshals and the Pinks didn't listen to your story."

He won Alice over instantly. She smiled up at him. "They didn't. No one listened. They just believed everything those lawmen in Boston said about Zeke. No one listened to his mother, but I know him better than anyone."

"We'll listen. We're bounty hunters, but we're the good guys. If your boy is innocent, maybe there's something we can do."

The rich, honeyed tone of his voice convinced even me. I glanced at Alice and her husband expectantly. Mr. Cooper narrowed his eyes at Vaughn, but he seemed so intimidated by his massive form that he didn't attempt to argue. "You won't just take him in?" he asked uncertainly.

"We're not in it for the money," Quimby assured him brightly. I managed to keep from rolling my eyes, and I was pretty proud of that. "We're in it to see justice done."

His handsome, charming smile seemed to work on Alice, anyway. Mr. Cooper ignored him. He only had eyes for Vaughn. "You were a slave?"

"Yes, sir. In Georgia. I was freed when the South lost the War."

"Terrible business," Mr. Cooper said in a low voice. "None of that came here. Some of our boys went to fight, but it didn't touch us much. We got enough problems."

"You want to tell us a little about your son Angel?" I asked gently.

Alice glanced at me. Her pale green eyes were slightly misty. I saw a lot of old women respond that way when people brought up Vaughn's history. It almost made me proud to be an American. "We don't call him that. His name is Ezekiel. The Pinkertons started calling him that 'cause he was named for one, I expect. Or because he was always such a good boy. He always did what was right."

"Why don't you folks come inside? We've got some coffee on the stove," Mr. Cooper said, stepping aside to gesture us in.

I glanced at Vaughn, but he did not return my gaze. We moved inside to perch on the threadbare paisley sofa and scuffed leather wing-backed chairs in the Cooper's old, cramped sitting room. Mr. Cooper stood watching us pensively by the fireplace, leaning against the mantle to smoke his pipe. His wife bustled past us into the small kitchen. She put a kettle on to boil.

"He was, you know," she said, turning to face us from the kitchen. "He was a good child and a good man, and he was good at his job. He could spot a criminal from a mile away, and he wouldn't stop until he got him."

"He liked his job?" Vaughn asked.

"He loved it."

"He'd never kill a client," Ezekiel Cooper's father added sternly. "It's just ridiculous. They said he might have been personally involved with the victim and his fiancé. That's just plumb crazy. Zeke would never do such a thing to Lenora."

"Lenora?" I asked.

"His wife," Alice replied.

"He might have met this Silas guy before he took the case, or the guy might have known him by reputation--"

"He was very well-liked and very well-respected."

"--but he had nothing to do with them. He's been framed."

Silence filled the room. We considered this a long moment.

"Why would someone want to frame him?" Quimby asked.

Alice sighed mournfully as she placed a tray of coffee mugs on the beaten wood coffee table before us. "We don't know," her husband said. He strode forward and seized a mug of coffee. He sipped it thoughtfully.

"We didn't know a lot about his life in Boston," Alice admitted. "Just what he told us in letters."

"He never should have left Wyoming," Mr. Cooper added, scowling.

"Why did he leave?" I asked.

"He loves Wyoming. He wanted to build a ranch here some day, but there wasn't a lot of opportunity to make big money out here, not for a nice country boy." He eyed us warily a moment. "At least in a traditional way. He went east to join the Pinkertons."

"He was always planning to come home," Alice said. "He wasn't much for the big city, our Zeke. He liked the quiet life."

My posse and I glanced at each other. "Any idea where Zeke might be now?" I asked.

His parents exchanged a glance. "No," Mr. Cooper said. I believed him.

"If he's on the run," his mother added, "no one will catch him."

Mr. Cooper puffed out his chest proudly. "He's a damn smart boy."

My posse let out a collective sigh. "Can you think of anything that might be helpful to us?" Vaughn asked them.

If anyone else had asked it, they might not have considered the question so earnestly. "Lenora's from Cheyenne," Alice told him. "Her family is still there. When Zeke was accused and went on the run, she came right home. She's been to see us."

"You think she knows where he is?" I asked her.

Mr. Cooper shook his head. "Nah."

"She's beside herself," Alice added. "What woman wouldn't be when her husband is accused of a crime he didn't commit?"

"She thinks he's innocent, too?" Hazel asked with dark, narrow eyes.

"'Course she does," Mr. Cooper replied scornfully. "She's his wife. What kind of wife doesn't stand by her husband?"

I felt a little hot around the collar at this. I glanced at Vaughn. He was looking right back at me.

"You could go see her," Alice offered helpfully. "Maybe she knows more about their life in Boston. She might know about who is trying to frame him up."

Mr. Cooper glanced around at us shrewdly. "That is, if you really want to know the truth. Otherwise, I reckon you'll be wasting your time 'round that way if you're trying to run Zeke in. He'd never put his wife in danger on account a' his own troubles."

"I reckon that sounds about right," Quimby said, glancing around at us.

"You want to take the main road toward Cheyenne," Mr. Cooper told us. "The back roads and trails are infested with Injuns. They don't care much for... well...folks that ain't red, anyway."

I smiled. "Thanks, Mr. Cooper. We'll do that."

* * *

Cheyenne was a dusty, bedraggled little town. The main thoroughfare was bustling in the early afternoon with local businessmen, shopkeepers, and ranchers just finishing their shopping as the local townsfolk emerged from their homes and filled the quiet, desolate streets. Painted ladies in intricate gowns and plumed hats strolled slowly arm in arm along the wooded sidewalk, eyeing the evening's potential clientele with interest.

Quimby drew every female eye on the boardwalk. Vaughn drew everyone else's.

"You ever feel invisible, Hazel?" I asked her in a low voice as we strolled casually toward Black Eyed Susan's, a loud, raucous wooden storefront from which the most noise could be heard, even so early in the day.

"Yeah. Pretty much all the time."

I glanced at her in interest, but she already seemed to have forgotten the conversation. She bounded forward to peer excitedly into a glass storefront window, behind which was a collection of gold, brass and silver goggles with multi-colored lenses and vials of eerily glowing liquids. I sighed.

There was an unusual clamor in Black Eyed Susan's. The patrons milled around in a strange, electrified tizzy, moving from group to group of wranglers, saloon girls, card players, and townsfolk. They all talked loudly to each other. We moved toward the barkeep immediately. They always knew exactly what was going on in a place like this.

"What's everyone so worked up about?" I asked the barkeep.

He was a tall, thin man with a gleaming baldpate and a high-necked, white-collared shirt. He barely glanced at us. He looked thoroughly preoccupied. "Jimmy Steele's called out Owen Spencer for a duel tonight at five o'clock."

"That so?" Quimby said. His eyes lit up in interest. "I do always like a duel."

"Who're Jimmy Steele and Owen Spencer?" Hazel asked, only half-interested.

"You folks from out of town, then?" the barkeep asked.

"You taken a look at us?" I asked, amused.

Finally, he did. For a moment, his expression lit in surprise. There it was. "I see. I reckon you ain't from around here."

"Nah. We ain't."

"Jimmy's a local boy. Works at the Triple Six just outside town. He's a horse trainer. Spencer--he owns the local general store."

"They're duelin'?"

"Yeah."

"I take it that thing ain't usual around here?" Vaughn asked.

The barkeep snorted with humorless laughter. "Nah. Don't happen much. Jimmy called out Spencer this morning."

"Why?" I asked, taking a seat at the bar.

The barkeep sighed deeply and poured four shots of whiskey. He pushed them toward us. "Jimmy accused Spencer of taking advantage of his intended, Clara Mills."

We looked at him in surprise. "Is it true?" Hazel demanded. Her dark eyes narrowed.

"Don't know. Maybe. Spencer ain't exactly a saint, but neither is Clara. No one knows how Spencer got the money to open the shop two years ago when he showed up here. He's got a bad reputation. I reckon no one really knows what he's capable of."

"If it's true, why aren't the Marshals arresting him?" I asked.

He chuckled humorlessly. "He's a big bug in town. Got lots of gold. You ask me, the Marshals round here ain't brave enough to go against money. Only Jimmy's been brave enough to face Spencer since he came to town."

My posse looked as interested as me. "Think he'll win?" Quimby asked.

The barkeep let out a long sigh. "No."

"Why not?"

"Spencer is a fast gun. Real fast. His money ain't the only reason no one wants to go against him. Jimmy isn't a gunslinger. He's a cattle wrangler. He's a good kid. He works hard, but he's not that bright. Poor Clara will lose more than her innocence in all this."

"Can't someone stop Jimmy from fightin'?" Hazel asked.

"Nah. He's got it in his head. He'll see it through."

My posse and I glanced at each other. "Maybe we should stick around for the duel," Quimby said.

Vaughn inhaled deeply and squared his shoulders. We all looked at him hopefully. He peered back at us with a bland expression. I sighed in disappointment. "We're here to talk to Lenora Cooper," he told us sternly. "It ain't the time to be watchin' gunfights. Every minute is precious in a bounty hunt."

We stared at him in silent incredulity.

He sighed. "All right. I think we can make it to Lenora's and back before the fight."

Quimby, Hazel and I cheered. I turned back to the publican. "You know where we can find Lenora Cooper?"

The publican paused. "You folks ain't lawmen, are you?"

"Do we look like lawmen?" Hazel asked.

His mouth turned up slightly in a smile. "Nah. S'pose not. Bounty hunters, huh?"

"We're not so sure this time."

He didn't look interested in what she meant by this. "Yeah. Lennie's been back a couple days. S'pose you know about her husband, Zeke, or you wouldn't be here."

"That's right. We just got some questions to ask her about him."

"She's beside herself. Her husband is on the run. You folks ought to tread lightly."

"Obviously, we always do."

He lifted a doubtful eyebrow. "Follow the main road out of the town center; you'll find a little cluster of houses. Lennie's parents live in the little blue one. There's a white fence around the house with a little black pony out front. Can't miss it."

"Thanks. See you back for the fight."

The barkeeper's description had been spot on. We found Lenora Cooper's parents house just a mile off the main thoroughfare. The cottage was small and painted a fresh, new sky blue with delicate white latticework around the doors and windows. A clean white fence wrapped around a tiny, well-chewed lawn where a small, black pony grazed nonchalantly on the grass. It didn't look up as we unlatched the gate and strode toward the front door.

Hazel tramped up to the porch with a spring in her step. I shook my head; she was too keen to see that gunfight. She rapped cheerfully on the front door. After several moments, a tall, thin young woman with a severe, mahogany bun dressed in a blue day dress and crisp, clean white apron answered the door. She matched the house perfectly.

"Hi there," Hazel greeted with an enormous, toothy grin. "We're looking for Lenora Cooper. You her?"

The woman stared at Hazel for a long moment, as though she weren't sure what to think of the small, chipper blonde woman. "No. I'm Ruth. The maid. Miss Lennie's in the garden out back."

"They have gardens here?" Hazel asked in interest.

Ruth peered at her. Then she looked past her at Quimby, Vaughn and me. Her thin lips tightened. "May I ask who you people are?"

I held my breath. Hazel's dark eyes twinkled. "Zeke's parents sent us."

Ruth's expression changed dramatically. She stepped back and gestured us in with a large smile. I felt a little bad about deceiving her. I didn't think Lennie Cooper would appreciate it when she found out who we really were. "I'll let her know you're here."

"Thanks."

She directed us to a small, clean sitting room. The furniture seemed strangely small, as though designed for abnormally little people. Quimby and Vaughn leaned against the mantle. Hazel perched on the edge of the settee, and I lowered myself into a narrow chintz armchair to await the crooked Pink's wife.

In moments, a short, thin man in cut-off trousers and rolled up shirt sleeves strode into the room. He blinked at us in surprise. "Who are you folks?"

"Zeke's parents sent us," Quimby said cheerfully.

The short man scowled. "You look like ruffians to me. What are you doing here?"

"We're here to talk to Lenora."

For such a small man, his temper was towering. His unlined, patrician face was terrible. "You're looking for information about Zeke. What are you? Bounty hunters?"

"Sometimes," I told him in a low voice.

He stared at me. "What sort of woman are you? What sort of woman dresses in men's clothes?"

Vaughn straightened. He loomed several inches over the angry little man. Lenora's father quelled slightly. His expression cleared. "We're just looking for the truth," Vaughn said. "We talked to Zeke's parents. They think he's innocent of what they're accusin' him of. We're lookin' to find out if it's true."

"Why? I thought you folks just wanted to make a buck."

"Not all of us. Some of us are in it for the excitement," Hazel told him, smiling brightly.

"Daddy?"

26

We turned toward the young woman framed in the doorway from the kitchen. She was very slight. Her hair was long and honey blonde. It was tucked beneath a wide sunbonnet. Her green apron was stained with dirt from the backyard. A garden trowel stuck out from a pocket of her apron. "Lennie," the man said in a gentle voice. "These folks are here about Zeke."

Lenora sighed. She looked sad, but she was a very pretty woman. I glanced sharply at Quimby. He looked unaffected by her. I wondered if it was the presence of her small but fierce daddy in the room with us. "Who are you?"

"They're bounty hunters," her father answered for us.

She frowned. "Why would you think I would talk to you?"

"Zeke's parents seem to think he's innocent," I answered.

"'Course they do," Lenora's father replied coldly. "They're his parents."

"You sayin' you don't?" Hazel asked pointedly.

Lenora glanced at her father sharply. "'Course I ain't. I ain't sayin' Lennie didn't make a mistake when she picked up and left her family to move to Boston with him, but Zeke's a good man and I don't think he done what they said he done. He ain't a murderer."

"Why don't you tell us a little about it?" Vaughn asked in a low voice. Lenora's dad glanced at him with a very small sneer.

Lenora glanced at us shrewdly. "I do not intend to assist mercenaries in finding and taking in my husband for a crime he didn't commit."

"We're interested in the truth. If your husband is innocent, maybe there's something we can do to help him out," I told her.

She eyed me suspiciously. "Why would you?"

"We ain't in it for the money, ma'am," Hazel answered. "I'm richer than half the railroad big bugs out here. We're in it for the excitement."

Lenora raised her eyebrows. "You would help him?"

"It wouldn't hurt to tell us about it. Maybe we can."

I met Vaughn's eyes. We weren't exactly in the business of helping folks, but that didn't mean we couldn't be for a few minutes. At least long enough to get the information we needed. Lenora looked at her father in supplication. He shrugged. "Talk to them if you like, Lennie. I ain't gonna stop you. I'll have Ruth bring some iced tea."

She nodded and sat primly beside Hazel on the settee. Her father didn't remain to hear her tale. He spun on his heel and strode out of the room. She looked at us with apprehension. I didn't blame her. "Do you know Zeke?"

"No. We just heard about his story a few days ago," I replied. "It sounded interesting."

She sighed. "That isn't exactly the word I would use."

Hazel laid a hand on her arm in an eerily comforting gesture. "Tell us about him, Lennie. What happened?"

Lenora leaned back against the thin, narrow sofa. "Zeke would never do those things they said he did. He's not that kind of man. They said he killed Silas Ratcliff because he was having an affair with his fiancé, Becky."

"It's not true?"

"Of course it isn't! He barely knew them. When Becky went missing a couple weeks ago, Silas asked Zeke to help him find her. He didn't have anything more to do with them. He had no reason to kill him. He wouldn't kill anybody."

We glanced at each other. "If he didn't do it, who did?"

Lenora shook her head. "I don't know, not for sure."

"What do you mean, 'not for sure'? You got some idea?" I asked keenly.

She looked at me. "You won't believe me. None of the Marshals or Pinkertons or lawmen believed me."

"We ain't lawmen. Give us a chance to form our own conclusions."

"I don't know everything. I didn't get a chance to hear the whole story, but Zeke liked to talk to me about his investigations sometimes."

She paused as Ruth entered the room with a tray of iced tea in tall, sparkling clean glasses. I was reminded for a brief, poignant moment of summer afternoons in Georgia. Ruth's tea wasn't as sweet as Vaughn's older sister Belle's, but it was all right with me.

Lenora sipped her tea and smiled wanly at us. "Becky worked for Sterling Rush."

Quimby's eyebrows traveled up into his golden hair, and Hazel looked excited. I'd heard the name before. Even on the frontier, we picked up a paper now and again. I didn't know much more than that he ran a company back east called Rush Scientific Advancements and Steam-Powered Innovations. It was a ridiculous name for a company. Folks just called it Rush AI.

Quimby, of course, knew all about him. "I heard about him. His company is responsible for half the weapons developments in the U.S. Folks say he's been selling to foreign countries these days, and he's suspected of bribes and payoffs of officials from the Department of Scientific Progress and Questionable Developments to keep faulty weapons on the market."

Hazel looked interested. "They have one of those?"

"You ought to be lucky you ain't ever heard of them," I told her, grinning. "They'd just have a ball with you."

She shot me a glare. "My weapons aren't faulty."

"But they are questionable," Vaughn put in.

I wasn't so much interested in east coast robber barons. "He sounds like a bad guy," I remarked impatiently. "But what's it got to do with anything?"

"Well, Zeke discovered that Becky was informing to the press about her boss."

"Informing about what?"

"Well, we don't really know. It had something to do with the rumors of payoffs and things, but there was nothing solid yet, and whoever she was informing to hasn't printed anything about it. Whatever it was, he and Silas suspected it was the reason she went missing."

"He thought Rush was responsible?"

"Well, him or someone who was working for him. Right before Silas was killed, Zeke told me he suspected there might be another Pink involved."

"A Pink who was working for Rush."

"Yeah. Or one of Rush's people. I don't think he wanted to tell me much. He thought it was safer I didn't know."

I frowned. "Why'd he tell you anything at all?"

She sighed. "I don't think he realized how high the stakes were until the end. Fact is, I would do anything to be with my husband right now and trying to clear his name, but I reckon he'd want me here where it's safe. Where Rush won't look for me if he gets it in his head to do the same to me as to Becky."

"You got any evidence of all this?" Quimby asked. His voice was gentle, but his expression was narrow.

Lenora shook her head. "No. Of course not. I only know what Zeke told me."

"Where do you think he is right now?"

Her eyes narrowed. "The Marshals already asked me that. I don't know where he is. My husband isn't a fool. He wouldn't come here. He wouldn't put his family in danger."

"You got any kids?" I asked.

She brushed a delicate white hand across her ivory brow. "No. He's afraid his life is too dangerous for kids. That's the sort of man he is. He doesn't want anyone hurt on his account. He's a good man. Not a murderer."

I eyed her shrewdly. "Well, if he ain't here, where do you think he might be?"

She met my gaze. She was silent a long moment. "If I know him, he's back in Boston investigating his frame up."

My posse glanced at each other. Boston was a long way away. It might as well be another world. "That's where you think he might be?"

"It's possible. He'd want to know why his life has been taken away from him. He'd want to know who hurt that poor girl and her fiancé. He isn't the sort of man to run away and hide."

"It must be dangerous for him in Boston right now with the Pinks and Marshals on his tail," Vaughn said.

Lenora took a hitching breath. "Yes, I suppose it is. There aren't many people he can rely on now. I discovered that myself; our friends are all Pinkertons or Marshals. They don't know him like I do. They don't believe he's innocent. I had no one in Boston to turn to."

"If he were going to lay low until the smoke settled, where'd he go?" Vaughn asked.

She stared at him silently for several moments. She considered the question. "Well...I suppose he might be in Oklahoma."

"Oklahoma," I repeated. My mouth turned up slightly. We could handle Oklahoma.

"Zeke's dream is to own a horse ranch. It's why we went east to begin with: to make enough money with his cases to come home and build our dream home. He's got an old childhood friend who moved out to Oklahoma and started his own ranch a few years ago. Eli's probably the only one Zeke can rely on right now."

"Eli?"

"Eli Grant. He's just outside Oklahoma City. He's a good man. He and Zeke grew up together. If Zeke needed a place to hide, Eli would help him." She looked between us with large, supplicating, honey-colored eyes. "You seem like decent people. You don't seem like the types to let an innocent man go to jail."

"We don't make a habit of it," Quimby replied with a charming, lop-sided smile. "We prefer bad guys, ourselves."

"They're a lot more fun," Hazel agreed.

"Can you help my husband?"

We blinked at each other in bemusement. I didn't rightly know what we could do for him, even if his wife and parents could be believed. Of course, it wasn't the first time we'd heard such sparkling recommendations for loved ones. In fact, they almost always claimed their loved ones were innocent. No matter how charming Quimby's smiles or how reassuring Vaughn's honeyed tones, we were bounty hunters, pure and simple. Angel Cooper was a bounty, not a charity.

"We'll do what we can," Quimby promised earnestly.

Hazel rose abruptly to her feet. She patted Lenora's arm. "We ought to be gettin' back to town," she said. I was impressed that she wasn't vibrating with excitement. Her eyes were smoldering. I wasn't sure such enthusiasm for a gunfight and inevitable death was strictly proper. All the same, I was pretty anxious to get back to town myself.

Lenora stood to see us out. "Thanks for your time, Mrs. Cooper," Vaughn said respectfully. She smiled a little warily, as though she wasn't sure how she should behave around the big black man.

"Thank you for listening to me. If you see my husband, tell him I'm thinking of him. Tell him I know it wasn't him who killed Silas."

I did not roll my eyes, but I felt a little like it. "We will," I promised.

We didn't speak to each other until we were on our way back to town. "What do you think, Tess?" Vaughn asked several moments later, slowing his horse, Asa, to trot beside Lady Jay.

Hazel and Quimby perked up, as though listening for my reply. I frowned. "'Bout what?"

"Come on, Tess. 'Bout Angel. You think there might be something to the frame up idea?"

I considered. "I don't know much about Rush AI or big business, but I know men like Rush don't care about small fries like Angel or Becky."

"That don't mean one of his men didn't do somethin'," Hazel said.

I shrugged. "Yeah. So, what? We're thinkin' our bounty's innocent now?"

"He could be. Sometimes they are. You know not everyone done what they said they done."

I lifted a shoulder. "It ain't for us to decide. It's for the courts. He might be innocent, but that don't mean his bounty ain't still good."

Vaughn gave me a disapproving look. "That ain't no way to talk, Tess. It matters if he's innocent. You care about that."

"Just because it's what his wife and parents think don't mean it's the way it is."

"Just because it's what the Pinks and the law thinks don't mean it's the way it is, either," Hazel added.

"Yeah, all right. But the evidence is pretty damning."

"Sure it is. But it ain't bein' caught red-handed," Quimby put in. "It could be a frame up, right enough. I heard a lot of things about Sterling Rush, and he's a bad guy."

"How do you know? You ain't met him."

He lifted his chin. "I met some folks down in Denver who were run out of town by him."

"Run out of town?"

"Sure. They say folks speak out against him--'bout how his products are faulty and dangerous and end up injurin' or killin' folks sometimes--wind up missin' or dead."

"Ain't no evidence of that. Just talkin'. Or the Marshals would have done somethin' about it."

"Yeah, maybe so, but that don't mean he ain't got them all in his pocket."

"Sounds like a heap of rubbish, is what it sounds like."

"That don't mean some of it ain't true," Vaughn said reasonably. "There might be something to it."

"It might be Rush's way of runnin' Angel out of town if he learned something incriminating."

"Why are you all so eager to believe he's innocent all of a sudden?"

"Ain't. Not really," Hazel replied. "But ain't many Pinks go bad. They do pick the best of the best. He might have been in the wrong place at the wrong time."

"Yeah, but Lenora said he found out another Pink might have been involved."

"She didn't know nothin'."

"I don't know, Tess. Something about all this doesn't sit right with me," Vaughn admitted. "I think we ought to try to find out what's really goin' on here."

I lifted my eyebrows. Our hiatus must have addled their brains or something. I'd never heard them talk like this before. "All right, you bunch of bleedin' hearts. When we catch him, we'll hear what he has to say. But I don't intend to give up a five hundred dollar bounty 'cause you three went soft. You better get it together before we meet him. If he's as good as everyone says, you'll need your wits."

Chapter Three

Black Eyed Susan's was as boisterous as when we'd first rode into town. The patrons had spilled out into the street and were gathering in small, noisy clusters around a dusty fountain in the town square a little ways up the main road. They were only talking about one thing, and that was Jimmy Steele.

"Looks like Jimmy hasn't changed his mind," Quimby remarked, glancing around incredulously at the townsfolk gathered excitedly along the main road.

"If there's one thing that never fails to bring folks out of their homes, it's bloodshed," I remarked.

The saloon was deafening with buzz over the shoot out. Some of the patrons seemed excited about the coming fight, regardless of the outcome, but others looked like mourners at a funeral. I supposed no one really believed Jimmy Steele stood a chance against big bad Owen Spencer.

We sidled up to the barkeeper. He nodded to us without any sign he'd noticed we'd been gone. "Another round?"

"You bet," I replied, slapping down a dollar. I snatched up one of the tumblers of whiskey. I didn't knock it back. I turned to peer around us at the patrons. "There seems to be a lot of excitement over this there shootout this evening."

"I reckon not much happens 'round here. It's probably the most excitement these folks have had in a long while," Quimby replied.

"It's a quiet town," the barkeeper put in sternly from behind us. "These are good folks. We don't go 'round shootin' at each other."

"Until today."

"Right."

A young, handsome dark-haired man burst into the saloon. The bar suddenly went quiet. I lifted an eyebrow. The man was dressed in scuffed leather calfskin chaps and a fringed jacket. His hat was in his hands. His expression was cold and determined, but his dark eyes looked wild and glazed. I didn't have to ask to know who he was. The men and women in the saloon patted him bracingly on the back and shoulders as he made his way to the bar.

The barkeeper didn't ask him what he wanted. He placed a shot of whiskey on the counter beside me. Jimmy Steele tossed it back without taking a breath. He winced and wiped his mouth. He slammed the glass down on the bar and nodded to the barkeeper.

I placed my hand over the empty glass. He looked at me as though realizing for the first time that I was there. "Whoa there, Jimmy," I said gently. "You don't want to lose your head so early in the game."

He looked at me blankly for several seconds. His dark eyes slid past me to my posse. His brow furrowed. "Who are you?"

"I'm Tess Mercury. This is my posse."

He nodded and offered his hand. "Jimmy Steele."

"This here is Lightning Hazel Harley, Vaughn Blair and Quimby Burton."

His mouth quivered. "You here for the fight?"

"No. We're bounty hunters. We were here for somethin' else. We just happened upon your business with Owen Spencer."

He lifted his chin. Quimby looked at him narrowly. "You fast?" he asked.

Jimmy's mouth tightened grimly. "Not as fast as Owen."

"Then why are you doin' it?" Hazel demanded with a frown.

Jimmy looked green around the gills. He was a strong man, in his early twenties. He looked as though he worked hard. There was an innocent, boyish quality to his handsome, rugged features. It would be a damn shame to see him shot dead in the street.

"It has to be done," he said firmly.

He was strong and handsome and earnest, but he was still a damn fool.

"You're just going to die?" I said.

"For my lady's honor, I will fight to the death, yes."

"That ain't gonna help her. It ain't gonna do any good."

He looked at me. His dark eyes glinted. "I can't just let him get away with it."

"You can testify in court against him."

"Marshal Beamer won't arrest him. He's in his pocket. He's more scared of him that anyone."

"He isn't the only Marshal. We know people. We can get them here. Someone will arrest him."

Jimmy shook his head vigorously. "By then, he'll have killed her."

I sighed. He was a frustrating young man. "Not if you take her away from here."

He squared his shoulders determinedly. "I have to do this. It's the way of things."

"It ain't the way of anything. What will your lady think? You think she'll be happy you're dead?"

"I have to do it. You're strangers. You don't understand anything."

I scowled at him. "We understand a whole lot more than you think," Hazel remarked. "And this is plumb foolish."

"You must be plannin' somethin' damn stupid if Lightning Hazel's the voice of reason," Vaughn told him.

"If you're set on goin' through with this, let me stand in for you," Quimby said abruptly.

We all turned to him in surprise. "What?" Jimmy asked.

"If Owen's a fast gun, you will lose, and in this case that means you'll die. I am the fastest gun you ever saw. I'll beat him. It ain't cowardly to have a stand in."

Jimmy scowled. "It's not fighting my own battle. You don't got nothing to do with any of this. It ain't right having you fight for me."

The kid wouldn't be convinced otherwise no matter how much we cajoled him or how many protests we offered. Yeah, he was a damn fool all right, and there wasn't nothing anyone could do about it. When the clock tower in the town square began to chime five in the evening, Jimmy Steele lifted his chin with a chilling resolve.

"There's still time to back out, Jimmy," I tried one more time.

He ignored me. He strode through the grim gauntlet out of the saloon. We followed him, streaming out into the street with the rest of the patrons. They formed two rows on either side of the main thoroughfare. They chattered to each other in hushed, excited voices. As Jimmy paused in the center of the street, some of the women sniffed loudly and dabbed at their eyes with handkerchiefs. I wondered if Clara Mills was among them. If she was, she didn't rush forward to beg Jimmy to stop. She didn't rush forward to say goodbye, either.

Jimmy was as hopped up as a Mexican jumping bean. His shoulders quivered as he stood motionless in the street, awaiting his opponent. His head snapped to the side as a tall man in a sleek, grey suit and bowler hat strode swiftly through the street from the large, elegant mansion on the edge of the main road. He was older than Jimmy by several years, and as handsome as a marble statue. His pale hair was long and curled down below his collar. His blue eyes were brilliant in the late evening sun. He looked more like an angel than a villain. I knew looks could be deceiving.

Owen Spencer paused several paces away from Jimmy. His hand hovered cautiously over his gun. The expression on his angelic features was gentle and sad. "You still have a chance, Jimmy. You can still back down."

Jimmy glared at him. "What you did to Clara was wrong. She deserves justice."

Owen sighed. "Jimmy, Clara isn't the girl you think she is. You do no service to her like this."

"I have to defend her honor!"

"Why isn't she here, Jimmy?"

Jimmy's face contorted. His hand twitched over his gun.

"I don't want to do this, Jimmy, but I will if you make me."

The younger man did not back down. He reached for his gun.

Owen was so fast, he fired a shot directly into Jimmy's chest before the young man's gun was half-way out of its holster. Jimmy staggered for a brief moment. Then he collapsed backward on the dirt ground. He didn't move. A large, crimson sunburst spread out across his chest. Around us, the crowd gasped and exclaimed. It was all over, just like that. I shook my head in disgust. A damn shame.

"Dumb kid," Hazel said angrily. "What'd we even hang around here for? To watch a good kid die?"

Quimby made a strange, surprised noise in the back of his throat. I looked up at him. He was not watching the short, balding doctor in round, frameless glasses lean over Jimmy, checking his vitals. Behind the doctor, a tall, thin man with sharp, angular features and steel-grey hair hovered with a gleaming, eager expression in his dark eyes. I reckoned he must be the town mortician. The sight was morbid, but Quimby was looking at the winner, Owen, who stood in the center of the street with a sad, pitying expression.

"What's up, Quim?" I asked.

"Come on," Hazel said, scowling. "Let's get out of this town."

"Hang on," Quimby said. "That's not Owen Spencer."

"What are you talkin' about?"

"That's Donnie Rio. He's wanted in El Paso for bank robbery."

I lifted my eyebrows and glanced back at Owen. He turned away from Jimmy and strode back toward the big house at the end of the street. There was no triumph in his step or in the hitch of his shoulders. He just looked disappointed. "Are you sure, Quimby?"

"He's done a lot worse than bank robbery here if what Jimmy says is true," Hazel said, glaring eagerly at Owen.

"Now hang on," I said. "I ain't sure it is."

"What are you talkin' about, Tess?"

I shook my head. "I don't know. It just seems like we might not know the whole story. Where is Clara, anyway?"

"I wouldn't want to watch my man die."

"We could take him in," Quimby said.

I frowned. "We're working another bounty."

"Well, yeah, but you and Vaughn can handle the Pink. Look what he did to that poor kid."

"I ain't so sure he did anything. He tried to stop the duel. If he hadn't shot Jimmy, Jimmy would have killed him. He didn't shoot him in the streets in cold blood or anything."

They looked at me incredulously. "You sayin' you'd rather hunt an innocent man than take in this devil?" Hazel asked.

I looked away. "No, I'm not sayin' that. I'm sayin' I ain't sure what sort of devil he is, and we've already come pretty far to catch Angel."

"We could split up. You and Vaughn get Angel, and Hazel and I can take Donnie Rio to El Paso."

Hazel looked at him in disgust. "I ain't goin' anywhere with you, Quimby."

He sighed. "Fine. I could take him in myself."

"What's the bounty on him?" Vaughn asked.

"A hundred."

"Come on, Quim. We've already got a job," I said. "Just send Sadie a telegram, tell her he's here. She can send one of the Marshals to sew him up."

He scowled petulantly at me. "What kind of woman doesn't want justice for their kind?"

"You don't know what you're talkin' about, Quimby. I ain't seen a damn sign anything's happened here but some fool kid who can't shoot challenging the town big bug and losin'. I ain't stoppin' my whole life to avenge a damn idiot."

Quimby scowled. "She's right, Quimby," Vaughn put in, and the matter was settled.

"I don't suppose I could just shoot him?" Quimby asked.

"Not unless you want a price on your head. Lord knows, it's amazing you don't already have one," I replied.

Hazel tugged on my arm. "Can we get out of here please? This town ain't feelin' so friendly anymore."

I glanced around at the crowd, who were slowly dispersing now that the duel had ended. Most of them were moving back towards Black Eyed Susan's. "Suppose we ought to." I glanced at Vaughn as we turned as one toward our horses. "So what do you reckon? Should we head to Oklahoma, see if Angel's gone to see his old friend Eli?"

Vaughn shrugged. "It don't seem like we got any better ideas."

Quimby's sullen expression brightened. "You know what's on the way to Oklahoma?"

We all turned to look at him. "Oh, here we go," Hazel said. Her lips quivered as though she were suppressing a smile.

"Well," said Vaughn in a rumbling voice. "It is on the way."

"We might be able to learn somethin' about Angel or Rush."

"We'll learn somethin', anyway," Hazel added.

I sighed. "All right, all right. We can stop in Colorado Springs. Just for a night. We ain't stayin' for a week like last time."

They all grinned at me. "Thanks, Tess."

* * *

The lights of Esther Star's Governor's Mansion twinkled between the thick, lush green trees surrounding the three story, French-style white house. The winding drive through the trees to the house was smooth and well traveled. It opened into a wide roundabout with a sparkling stone fountain in the center, which spurted water into a crystal clear pool at its base. Around the fountain, a procession of carriages waited to drop an endless stream of passengers at the front door, where a tall, burly man in a tight-fitting black suit waited to let them in.

We led our horses to the drive. Two valets approached us, dipping at the waist in low, respectful bows. Vaughn lifted his chin slightly. He liked Esther's place. At the Governor's Mansion, everyone was treated the same until they gave the management a reason for them not to be. Vaughn was well liked here. He handed off Asa's reigns to the taller of the valets. The well-built man did not even blink at the enormous dappled horse.

"Miss Star will see you in the foyer," the doorman told us as we reached the front door. He smiled at Hazel as he opened the door and bowed us in. She paused a moment to murmur to him in a low, flirtatious voice. I rolled my eyes.

Miss Esther Star had an uncanny knack for offering exactly what her guests might want. I wondered if there would be a hot tin bath and a shot of whiskey waiting for me in my room. If I knew Esther, there would be. There might even be a stack of old newspapers by the bed and a penny dreadful or two.

Quimby and Vaughn wouldn't have any trouble finding something they wanted at the Governor's Mansion. The vestibule glittered with gold and brass trim, and expensive, tasteful art decorated every wall. A crystal chandelier hung from the cathedral ceiling, casting soft, gentle light over the evening's guests, who were already filling the enormous, richly festooned room. Ester worked hard to maintain a beautiful home, but the room itself was hardly the attraction.

The vestibule was already teeming with the day's guests. Women in elaborate, lush gowns greeted them with wide, welcoming smiles. They looked like jewels sparkling against the gold and brass of the room. They led the guests up the flights of stairs winding up each side of the room to the guest rooms on the second and third floors. We waited in the entryway. None of the women approached us, though a few of them eyed us in interest. Esther must have told them we were coming.

A tall, voluptuous woman appeared at the top of the stairs. Her long, thick, chestnut hair was twisted into a complex braid around the crown of her head, and her emerald green gown slightly shone in the light bouncing from the glittering chandelier. She peered down at us over the gold banister. Her beautiful, ivory pale features lit up in a gracious smile. "Well, Tess Mercury, I do declare."

I laughed. "Esther Star. How's tricks?"

"Now, Tess, don't insult the guests." She descended the stairs in a cloud of floating green satin. She hugged me happily.

I'd met Esther years ago when Vaughn and I had first joined the bounty hunting life. She'd been working a saloon as one of the girls, and I'd rescued her from one overeager wrangler who didn't understand the difference between a girl and a whore. He'd turned out to be a pig thief from Arkansas. Vaughn and I had made a few bucks, and Esther and me had been friends ever since. When she'd come up in the world as the Madam of the Governor's Mansion, which she'd gained in a very questionable inheritance from an old, dying widower, she'd returned the favor and helped us out whenever she could.

She turned away from me to smile widely at Vaughn, who tipped his hat to her politely. Esther was a little uncomfortable around Vaughn, but most women were. His size alone would scare most women, but there was an expression in his eyes sometimes that reminded people where he really came from. He'd lived a rough life, and he'd been hurt many times. Even after he'd been freed, the scars of slavery hadn't faded. He was a good man, and he wouldn't hurt another man--'less he deserved it, of course--but there were a lot of people thought there might be a time he might decide to turn on us and take revenge for the treatment he'd received at the white man's hands most of his life. I reckoned there might be someday.

Quimby stepped forward and swept his Stetson from his head. He smiled at Esther. I saw her expression change instantly. Her large, dark, almond-shaped eyes softened, and she stepped toward him to kiss him soundly on the mouth in greeting. "Quimby Burton," she drawled, wrapping her arms around his neck.

He smiled. "Good to see you, Es."

She fluttered her hand across his high, sculpted cheekbone. "I was wondering when you'd come back to me. I missed you."

Every damn time. We couldn't take Quimby anywhere.

Esther seemed to realize we were watching them with varying expressions of disgust. She smiled unashamedly and stepped out of the circle of Quimby's arms. "Always happy to see you folks, but to what do I owe the pleasure of this visit? Are you on a hunt?"

"You know it," I replied. "We're looking for the crooked Pink wanted for murder."

She lifted elegantly arched eyebrows. "Angel Cooper?"

"You know him?"

"I know of him."

"What have you heard about him?"

"People are talking about him. Seems a lot of folks think he might not be guilty."

I glanced at my posse. "Yeah? We heard something like that, too."

She lifted an arm in a gracious gesture. "Why don't we step into the parlor where we can talk about it a little more privately? I don't exactly like my guests to know I'm in league with folks like you."

I laughed. "You sure know how to flatter, Es."

She chuckled. "I reserve the unabashed praise for my paying guests."

There were a few ladies and slender young men in black suits lounging together in the enormous, elegant parlor, but there weren't any of the usual lawmen, politicians, solicitors, robber barons or other rich big bugs who typically hung around the Governor's Mansion. Esther strode to a wooden bar in the corner of the room and set down five glasses. She poured two inches of a dark, amber liquid into each of them from a plain, unlabeled bottle. She handed them around and raised her glass. Without giving a toast, she sipped the liquid.

It was rich and sharp and went down like hot, liquid gold. If there was one thing I loved about the Governor's Mansion, it was the whiskey. "Angel's never come here?" I asked, bringing the conversation back to the point. It was easy to get sidetracked at Esther's place.

She shook her head. "He's been around town once or twice working a case, but he never made it here."

"I thought everyone made it here eventually."

"Not everyone. There's a certain kind of man don't come to places like this, no matter how famous and popular they are. Last I heard of him around here, he was working a bank robbery ring in Denver. The papers said he infiltrated the gang, got to their inner circle and eventually took them all down one by one."

"On his own?" Hazel asked, lifting an eyebrow.

Esther inclined her head. "So I hear."

"Who says he ain't guilty?"

"Some of the Marshals and lawmen around town come in here now and again, and they're all talking about it. It isn't usual for a Pinkerton to go bad."

Quimby nodded. "We thought the same thing, but the evidence is pretty strong."

"They seem to think it's possible it was planted in order to frame him. It isn't exactly hard evidence." Esther considered. "I've seen a lot of men, and a man who avoids a place like this probably wouldn't go to bed with a random secretary. A man like that tends to be loyal to his woman."

"Yeah, but you never met him," I protested. "You don't know what he'd do. And even if he wasn't cheatin' on his wife with the secretary, that don't mean he didn't do it."

She lifted her bare, ivory shoulders in a delicate shrug. Her dangling diamond earrings swayed like small pendulums and sparkled in the sunlight filtering in through the thin sheers covering the wide panoramic window behind the bar. "No, perhaps it doesn't. It merely proves the caliber of man he is. It's nothing to me whether he murdered the young man or not. You're the one who asked what I knew about him."

I frowned. "I wanted facts, not wild assumptions."

Esther laughed. "Why don't you all stay the night? I'm throwing a very special party this evening."

Hazel grinned. "I love parties."

"I do know how much you enjoy a good shindig, Hazel. I do ask that you keep your usual antics to a minimum this evening, however. We're expecting a very special guest."

I lifted my eyebrows. "What guest?"

"Congressman Josephus Caine from Boston."

I exchanged a meaningful glance with my posse. "Boston?"

Esther inclined her head. "He is meeting with one of our Congressman from Colorado, Charles Lockley. Charlie thinks he might enjoy the atmosphere. We're putting on a marvelous show."

"Pretty ironic, huh, a Congressman from Boston showing up here while we're searching for a bounty from Boston?"

"I doubt it is related, Tess," Esther replied reasonably. "Caine is presenting a bill to Congress for which he requires the support of his party. He's been meeting with Congressmen all over the country for the past several weeks."

I didn't buy it. "Somethin' about this seems a little too convenient."

Hazel glanced at me skeptically. "What could this have to do with Angel?"

I shook my head. "I don't know. Maybe nothing, but my gut says it's something."

Hazel shrugged. She looked at Esther. "Mayhap one of your girls can find out somethin' for us."

Esther inclined her head gracefully. "Of course. If there is information regarding your query to be found, I am sure one of my girls can extract it quite easily."

"Thanks, Es."

She appraised us with dark, narrow eyes. "If you ladies are going to be at my gala, I expect you will present a respectable appearance."

I sighed in vexation. "Come on, Esther."

She shook her head firmly. "I'm sorry, Tess, but this is the Governor's Mansion. We maintain a particular standard of decorum. Dirty chaps and a scuffed John B. is not acceptable attire, especially for a lady."

I huffed sulkily. "Fine."

Esther smiled and stepped away from the bar. She inclined her head to Quimby and Vaughn. "If you'll excuse us, gentleman, the ladies and I have work to do." She winked at Quimby. "We'll have plenty of time to catch up later, Quimby."

He winked at her. "I'll wait for you in your room."

Every damn time.

Chapter Four

I smoothed my hands self-consciously over the ruffled blue skirt of the silky satin gown. The fabric was rich and glossy beneath my freshly scrubbed fingers. I almost didn't recognize my reflection in the tall, full-length mirror. Esther's girls had worked magic on me. My long, black hair was pulled back from my face in an intricate braided bun. Long, curled stray strands cascaded over my bare neck and shoulders and around my temples. The gown's low-cut décolletage was fringed in black lace that matched my elbow-length gloves. The sapphire blue satin was the exact shade of my eyes.

It had been a long time since I'd seen myself like this. I felt a small, traitorous shiver of pleasure. I stomped mercilessly on it. I preferred buckskin and dungarees to satin and lace.

"Sometimes I forget you were once a lady, Tess," Esther said, peering at me with a satisfied expression.

"Yeah, well, I ain't no lady now."

She chuckled. "There is no shame in enjoying being a woman now and again. Perhaps you'll find it much easier to learn what you need to know like this than with fists and death rays."

I snorted. "Yeah, mayhap, but I do not want to hear what Quimby and Vaughn are going to have to say about this."

"I am sure they will be just beside themselves."

"That's really what I'm afraid of," I admitted quietly, but Esther wasn't paying attention. That was probably best.

"Ah, Es, can't I just wear my own dress?" Hazel complained, stomping into the room. "This one just don't suit me."

Esther rolled her eyes. "Hazel, you will act like a lady in my home."

"Yeah, but this dress is as bad as wearing a burlap sack."

It was, in fact, a very pretty scarlet dress with a lacy black bodice that showed off her callipygian figure. It didn't look like a burlap sack at all. It had a full skirt and a high neck that displayed her long, slender neck and shoulders. Her curly blonde hair tumbled down her back. She looked more respectable than I'd ever seen her.

"It's very nice, Hazel. Stop complaining."

She seemed to notice me in the same instant. Her dark eyes widened in surprise. "Is that you, Tess?"

"Aw, come on. You've seen me dress like a girl before. Don't make a fuss about it."

"How come Tess looks like that, and I look like a school teacher?"

"Hazel, what sort of school teacher wears a dress like that?" I demanded.

"One with exceedingly exquisite taste, I'm sure," Esther replied with a toss of her chestnut head. "You will wear the dress, Hazel. You both look lovely. You'll make two fine additions to the party."

I narrowed my eyes at her. "Your guests will be able to tell we aren't two of your girls, right?"

Esther lifted her shoulders. "Now, how would I know what my guests will think?"

"Es..."

"You want information. I am certain you'll have no trouble obtaining it." She lifted her arm in a sweeping gesture. "Shall we head downstairs? I hear the party beginning without us."

I sighed and glanced at Hazel. She wrinkled her nose in irritation, but she nodded and threaded her arm through mine. We followed Esther through the halls of the third floor. We passed several closed doors, behind which we could hear the low, husky murmurs of men and the giggles of Esther's girls. Esther didn't seem to notice. She descended the stairs with graceful dignity. Quimby was waiting at the foot of the stairs with Vaughn.

When the boys saw us, they lifted their eyebrows in surprise. Quimby's blue eyes sparkled a little, and his mouth turned up at the corners. I knew he wanted to make some remark, but he held out his hand to Esther without commenting on our transformation. "You ladies look very nice," he said with a short bow.

Esther laughed and took his hand. "Is that all you have to say to us, after I slaved away to make your ruffian women presentable?"

"We ain't their women," I argued. Vaughn smiled at me. He looked very smart and comfortable in the trim black suit and black bowler hat. I grinned back at him. "You look real nice, Vaughn."

"You, too, Tess."

46

"What about me?" Hazel asked in a hurt voice.

We looked at her with identical grins. "You've never looked so sweet and innocent, Hazel," Quimby remarked with a note of awe in his voice.

She didn't take this as a compliment. She scowled at him. She took one of Vaughn's arms and turned toward the ballroom where the guests and the women were gathering. I took Vaughn's other arm, and we followed Quimby and Esther into the party.

The ballroom was handsome with tall, gold trimmed archways and pillars. The high windows were stained glass. Above us, a chandelier sparkled and tinkled as it swayed gently back and forth. The party was already in full swing. A band struck up a spirited melody on one side of the room, and Esther's guests and ladies danced together on the wide, polished dance floor. The ladies and their admirers were already crammed into dark crannies where tables with silk coverings and padded benches lined the walls.

Vaughn was not the only black man in the room. Several other men and women in fancy clothes danced together or with white men and women. Vaughn, however, was the largest. The guests eyed him warily as we entered. His expression didn't change. He was used to this sort of reception by now.

"Is the Congressman from Boston here yet?" I asked, glancing around the room.

Esther's eyes swept the room. She shook her head. "Not yet. I am sure he will arrive in due course." She extracted her hand from Quimby's arm and smiled up at him. "I'd better mingle a bit, greet my guests. You'll behave yourselves, won't you?"

"Just point us toward the bar," I replied.

Esther rolled her eyes, but she nodded toward the wide, polished stone bar along the west wall. We moved toward in it in a single motion. She laughed and glided away. The crowd swallowed her up immediately. My posse and I walked toward the bar, where a handsome, slender young man in a pinstriped suit and top hat greeted us.

I ordered whiskey, and he looked at me with a skeptical, disapproving expression. I sighed. "How about a white wine?"

He smiled as though he were on firmer ground. I suppose a lady doesn't order a shot of whiskey straight up, not at the Governor's Mansion, anyway. The white wine was crisp and refreshing. I didn't like it. "Why are you so interested in the Congressman?" Hazel asked me, sipping her own glass of wine. She didn't seem to mind the tartness of the beverage.

I shrugged. "I dunno. I just am."

"You think it has something to do with Angel?"

"No, not really. Not exactly. But I think it has something to do with something, and I want to know what it is."

They looked at me like I was speaking a foreign language. I sighed and turned my attention to the party. A young, pretty Indian girl approached us. Quimby grinned his charming bedroom grin, but she only had eyes for Vaughn. She stepped up to him. He looked down at her in surprise as she offered her hand. "Would you care to dance with me, sir?"

Vaughn looked around at us. I gave him a shooing gesture. "Go on, then. Someone of us might as well have a good time."

The Indian girl led him away to the dance floor. I watched after him with a small smile. The moment he was gone, a short, plump man with thinning, mousy brown hair approached me. He dipped a short bow and offered his hand. "May I have the honor of this dance?"

I frowned. "No thanks."

He blinked. A crease appeared between his brows. "No? I beg your pardon?"

"I ain't one of the girls."

This did not seem to appease him. He looked highly offended. "Esther is going to ream you for that," Hazel told me absently. She seemed to be craning her neck to catch a glimpse of something across the room. "You see Hank anywhere?"

"He's probably still at the door. The party's just starting," Quimby told her. "You should go see."

Hazel looked at him shrewdly. She glanced over her shoulder at me, but she didn't say anything. She disappeared into the crowd. I could see another man approaching me from out of the throng. This one was young and lanky with big buckteeth. I gave him a sharp look and turned away abruptly. Quimby chuckled. I glared at him.

He winked at me. "You aren't being very nice, Tess. Esther would be ashamed of you. These men are just admiring you. You clean up real nice."

I smiled reluctantly. "Thanks, Quim."

He held out his hand to me. I stared at it. "Dance?"

"I don't dance."

"Come on, now. I bet you do. You did grow up a rich lady on a southern plantation. I bet your mama gave you lessons on the social arts every day."

"I didn't have no mama. She died when I was little. My daddy raised me on his own. He taught me how to hunt and shoot, not dance and swoon like a girl."

Quimby laughed. "You miss your daddy?"

I shrugged. "Sometimes. We don't see eye on most things, though. If he had his own way, Vaughn would still be in chains, and I would be married off to another of his rich buddies' sons."

Quimby's blue eyes were suddenly serious. "You don't talk about him much."

I shrugged uncomfortably under his intent gaze. "There ain't much else to say."

"I don't mean your daddy." My brow drew together, but he ignored it. "I mean your husband."

I looked away into the crowd. "I ain't got a husband no more. He's dead."

"It ain't healthy to pretend he didn't exist."

I scowled. "I don't pretend he didn't exist. I just don't go 'round talkin' about him with you."

"You still miss him?"

I sighed. "Why you askin' me about Jace? It don't got nothin' to do with anything."

He shrugged, but his drawn brow belied the casual gesture. "I just thought maybe..." His expression changed so abruptly, I was startled when he turned to me with a grin. "Nothing."

I narrowed my eyes at him. "I know what you're about, Quimby Burton. Don't you try to sweet talk me into your bed. I ain't goin'."

He laughed. "I wouldn't dream of it, Tess. Besides, I don't think Esther would appreciate the competition tonight."

I snorted. My gaze sought Esther. He was right about that. She flitted gracefully from group to group of men and women, flicking her fan coyly as she laughed at their jokes and flirted with the rich gentleman. Her dark eyes, however, drifted every few moments to Quimby. "I reckon she's taken more than a shine to you," I remarked.

He grinned and lifted his hands. "What can I say?"

"How do you do that?" I demanded suspiciously.

"You can't tell? My charm is irresistible to the ladies."

I rolled my eyes. I looked around for Hazel, but she had already found Hank. They were dancing together on the floor. Vaughn and the Indian girl had disappeared into one of the crannies. "You've got a big fat head, Quimby."

"Nah. I just got a good idea of the way the world works."

Esther glided over to us. She fluttered her fan across her lips and slipped her arm into Quimby's. "Here comes the Congressman, Tess."

I lifted my eyebrows and followed the direction of her gaze. The man she indicated appeared to be in his mid-forties. He was tall and robust, dressed in a sleek grey suit with pin stripes that looked like they were spun from solid gold. His hair was thick, salt and pepper, and brushed back from his ruddy features. "Well, he's a right fat cat, ain't he?"

Esther laughed. "Don't let the other guests hear you talk like that."

Congressman Josephus Caine met another man near the dance floor. His companion was tall, thin and wiry. His features were sharp and rodent-like. His clothes weren't as nice, but he held himself with a sort of quiet dignity that I liked. Somehow, he inspired confidence. "Is that your guy?"

"Congressman Charles Lockley, yes. Well. There you are. If you'll excuse me, I have to greet my newest guests."

She moved toward them, but I followed her. "If you don't mind, I'd like to listen in."

Esther smiled. "Suit yourself. Just try to remain inconspicuous, if that's even possible."

"I'll have you know, I can be very discreet when I need to be."

She chuckled. I followed her to the Congressmen, to whom she curtseyed gracefully. Lockley introduced her to Caine with a smile. Caine grinned hugely. His teeth were very large and white. They were all a single size and shape, like little porcelain bricks. He bent over Esther's hand and kissed it. She giggled and fluttered her eyelashes as though enjoying the attention. I cringed slightly in her stead.

"Ah, Miss Star," he greeted in a booming voice. "It is a great pleasure to meet you at last. You and your establishment are very enthusiastically lauded all across the country. My colleagues urged me most emphatically to visit."

She smiled and flicked her fan. "I do try to show my guests the most comfortable and enjoyable of times, Mr. Caine."

"I can see that. And please. You may call me Josephus."

"I thank you, sir. Is there anything in particular I can offer you gentleman?"

"Not just now, Essie," Charles Lockley said in a low, soothing sort of voice. "Thank you. We have some business to discuss."

Esther smiled at him. "Shall I send a couple of my ladies to your table?"

Lockley grinned. "Yes, thank you."

Caine frowned slightly. "No. We're discussing business."

She tapped her fan gently against his arm. "Now, Josephus, I assure you, my ladies are very discreet."

He smiled reluctantly at her and inclined his head. "All right."

Esther bowed to him and turned away. I met her halfway. She recognized the look in my eyes immediately. She sighed. "All right, Tess, but don't get yourself in trouble."

"I think I know how to keep my mouth shut and look pretty."

She didn't look convinced. "Do you really?"

"All right, it ain't exactly my strong suit, but I think I can manage."

Esther frowned. "If you mess this up, it will be a great detriment to my reputation and my business."

"I won't mess it up."

She considered me a long moment. "I'll send Constance with you. Just follow her lead."

"I think I can do that."

She looked at me skeptically, but she led me to a young, beautiful Chinese woman with long, braided black hair and dark eyes. She murmured in the Chinese girl's ear. Constance glanced at me with a slightly annoyed expression, but she inclined her head. She stepped forward and took my hand to lead me toward the Congressmen, who sat in a small, shadowed table in the corner of the ballroom on the opposite side of the dance floor. She paused by their table and smiled.

"Good evening gentleman," she greeted in a thick Chinese accent. I suspected she was putting it on. It didn't sound much like the Chinese accents I'd heard from the railway workers I'd run across. The men didn't seem to notice. "May we join you?"

Caine hesitated, but Lockley grinned widely. "Of course." He offered his hand to me. I felt Constance nudge me firmly. I steeled my resolve and took Lockley's hand, allowing him to draw me down beside him on the bench seat across from Caine. Constance lowered herself gracefully beside Caine. She laid a hand on his thigh and moved it slowly up and down his leg as he spoke.

I glanced at Lockley. He was smiling at me. I returned his gaze and laid a clumsy hand on his knee. He seemed satisfied. He leaned back in his seat and looked at Caine. "I hear you'll be presenting your bill in the House this session. I assume that's why you wanted to see me."

Caine smiled. "You've heard about it, then."

"I have. The clauses are a bit stiff."

"They are necessary to regulate the industry. As you know, there are a lot of dangerous products out there on the market."

"Yes, and many of them are put out by Rush AI."

I perked up slightly at this. So it did have something to do with something, anyway. Then I remembered I wasn't supposed to be listening. I smiled vacantly and sipped my wine.

Caine frowned. "Rush AI has been vetted by the Department of Scientific Progress and Questionable Developments."

"Yes, I heard about that, too. I heard many things about that."

Caine's expression was slightly dangerous. "You would do well to remember who is financing this little pleasure jaunt."

"Indeed, I have not forgotten who is paying your bills," Lockley replied smoothly.

The Congressman from Boston's eyes narrowed. "You want to be careful, Charles."

Charles sighed. "I am sorry, Cephus. I did not mean to imply I am not behind your bill."

Caine relaxed. "It is an important regulation in this era of innovation and rapidly advancing scientific discovery. We must control the companies who create and make available dangerous products."

"I'm glad we see eye to eye, Cephus."

"I can drink to that." They leaned across the table and clinked glasses. I wondered for a moment why Caine had bothered to even come all this way for such a conversation. It seemed to me they could have corresponded much more easily over telegraph.

Caine reached down toward his feet and hefted a large, black leather case onto the table. He pushed it across the table toward Lockley. Ah. That. Lockley lifted his eyebrows. He did not open the case.

"A gift from our mutual friend," Caine said in a sly voice. He smiled.

Lockley's mouth twisted into a smirk. He seized the handle and looked at me. He drew a finger across my cheek. "If you'll excuse me a moment, young lady, I think I need to visit the john."

I smiled back at him. When I turned back to Constance and Caine, they seemed too wrapped up in each other to notice me. "Well," I said to myself. "This is awkward."

I slid discreetly out of the booth and met Quimby by the bar. He frowned. "You were a little chummy with that Congressman, weren't you?"

I looked at him incredulously. "You're complaining to me about that?"

For a moment, he looked annoyed. Then he chuckled. "Yeah, I suppose I see your point. You learn anything interesting?"

"Interesting, yes, but nothin' that really helps us any."

"Caine came a long way to have a ten minute meeting with Lockley."

"That's not all he came for. Ten minutes and a big suitcase full of money."

Quimby lifted his eyebrows. "A payoff?"

"Yeah, I think so. They was talkin' about some bill in Congress about regulating scientific advancement and tech companies."

He nodded thoughtfully. "I heard about that. It just puts regulations on companies so their products and R&D is safer. Seems like a no-brainer to me."

I considered. "Yeah, it does, but the question is, why is Rush so interested in getting it passed?"

"Rush, huh? That is a bit of a coincidence."

"I told you."

"But I don't see how one has much to do with the other. Rush has his hands in a lot of pots."

"Yeah, but why would he want more regulations put on his company? 'Specially if his products are faulty. Seems counterintuitive."

"Not if he's paying off the regulations committees."

Realization struck. "Yeah. I guess that's right."

He held up his hands, glancing cagily around. "I don't want anything to do with this. It's got nothin' to do with us. What the robber barons do in the east ain't got nothin' to do with us."

I waved my hand irritably. "I know, but somehow it feels like it does have somethin' to do with us."

"I don't know why. I don't feel a damn thing but anxious to turn the other way."

I rolled my eyes. "I've never known you to be a coward, Quim."

"It ain't cowardly. A gun fight is one thing, Tess, but I don't mess with business."

"I wonder if Angel did. Assuming it was a frame up, that is."

Quimby looked at me incredulously. "You on his side now?"

I shrugged. "I ain't on anyone's side. I'm curious, is all. I want to find him, and I want to find out what he knows about all this. It could be nothing; it could be something."

"I thought this was about five hundred dollars."

"It was about five hundred dollars. Now it's about finding out what's really going on."

"I didn't think you cared."

"Neither did I." I glanced up at Congressman Lockley, who was approaching us with a tight expression on his narrow features.

Before I had a chance to realize what was happening, he seized my arm above the elbow and drew me up to his side. "Now that business has been conducted, I'm ready for some attention," he said gruffly in my ear.

I blinked in surprise. I hadn't really expected the whole pretending to be a whore thing would end up biting me in the butt, but I reckon I might have thought it through a little better. "I think there's been some kind of mistake--"

"What mistake?"

"I'm not--" I hesitated. If Esther found out I revealed to the Congressman the truth about me, I didn't think we'd be friends anymore. I looked around for her to come to my rescue and clear up the misunderstanding, but I noticed her several yards away in a group of men. If she saw my predicament, she wasn't coming forward to bail me out.

I felt Quimby's hand on my other arm, big and warm and reassuring. He drew me toward him, away from Lockley. "This lady's already spoken for," he told Lockley in a bright, amiable voice.

Lockley's eyes narrowed. "Yes. By me. Do you know who I am, boy?"

"Do you know who I am?" Quimby replied in a low, dangerous voice.

Lockley stepped toward us, but Quimby moved so fast, the barrel of his gun butted into the Congressman's belly before Lockley realized it had even come out. He blinked in surprise. He lifted his hands in the air. I sighed.

Esther was beside us in a flash. Her dark eyes were blazing. "What is going on here?"

Lockley looked at her angrily. "What sort of people are you bringing in here, Es? I thought this was a respectable establishment. I didn't think you allowed ruffians and gunslingers in here."

Esther glared at me, though I was pretty sure this was all Quimby's fault. She stepped forward to thread her arm through Lockley's. "It's just a misunderstanding, Charlie," she purred, leading him away. "I'm so sorry. I'll make it up to you. I promise."

I frowned at Quimby. "You always got to resort to violence."

"I was helpin' you out. You might be a little more grateful."

"I could've pulled out my own gun, if I wanted it to escalate."

Esther returned in a huff. She scowled at me. "Tess, Quimby, what the hell are you doing? Are you trying to ruin me?"

Quimby looked innocently at her. "What? I was only trying to let him know he was barking up the wrong tree with Tess."

She scowled at me. I sighed. "Sorry, Esther. It won't happen again."

Her expression softened almost immediately. She wrapped an arm around Quimby's waist. "I can't stay mad at you." She laughed and kissed his cheek. "I forgive you, Quimby. But the next time you come into my place, leave the guns in your room."

He looked shocked. "Now, Es, you don't make a man leave his guns. That ain't no way to be."

She sighed. "Then at least try not to draw them on Congressmen, won't you?"

"All right, all right." He smiled.

I might as well have been invisible. She kissed him on the mouth and glided away without even glancing back at me. I turned a sour expression on Quimby. "I don't get what it is with you and women."

He chuckled. "That's because you don't know what you're missing." He winked at me and moved closer. "You let me know any time you want to find out."

I took a step back and curled my lip in disgust. "I am not that kind of lady."

"Tess, every lady is that kind of lady. She just don't know it yet."

* * *

Breakfast the next morning was a languid, extravagant affair. The ladies and their lingering guests took their first meal in their rooms, but my posse and I ate in the dining room with Esther. She was wearing a long, flowing red silk dressing gown and slippers. She was practically glowing. She sipped her coffee languorously and smiled smugly around at us. I rolled my eyes and nibbled the crisp, salty bacon on the plate in front of me. It was almost worth watching Esther and Quimby making morning after mooneyes at each other just for the food. It was damn good.

"I always enjoy your visits," she told us all. Her hand slipped under the table. I saw Quimby start and smirk. "But why don't you come by more often when you aren't on a hunt?"

"We're always on a hunt, Essie, you know that," Quimby replied.

My posse and I grinned at each other. That was the truth.

"Well, I hope you enjoyed your time here, anyway," she said. "It was certainly interesting for us all, but I don't think the Congressman appreciated your personal attention, Quim."

"Yeah, well, he ought not to go grabbin' ladies," he replied sullenly.

"Josephus was delighted, however. He's never been to Colorado. He doesn't really know the ways of the west. I think he would have liked it if you'd pulled your gun on him."

We chuckled. "Easterners," I said with a slight sneer. "They got no idea what it's like over here."

"It's a different world here." Esther smiled. She pushed aside her half-eaten breakfast and rose. "Well, I reckon you'd better get a move on if you're going to make it to Oklahoma to find your crooked Pink." She leaned down and kissed Quimby soundly on the mouth. "Good to see you as always, Tess. Vaughn. Hazel."

With a flick of her fingers, she glided from the room. I lifted my eyebrows and glanced at Quimby. "That sounded like a dismissal," I remarked, frowning at him. "You do something to my friend?"

He leaned back in his chair grinned. "You bet I did."

I narrowed my eyes. "Maybe she ain't so keen on you pulling a gun in her place," Hazel offered absently. She scooped a forkful of scrambled eggs into her mouth.

I looked at Quimby. "I think it might be something else gettin' her petticoats in a bunch," I said. "What'd you do, Quim?"

"Don't you worry about it. She'll have forgotten all about it by the next time we get here."

I scowled. "What'd you do, make bedroom eyes at one of her girls?"

"Nah. Nothing like that." He lifted a shoulder. "I think she just wishes things were different, is all."

"I reckon there are a lot of girls wish things were different with you."

"Yeah, you know that's right. But I can't change who I am, can I? I'm footloose and fancy free, and I ain't settlin' down for no woman."

Hazel and I rolled our eyes. Vaughn sipped his coffee impassively. When he spoke, his voice startled us all. "You won't be sayin' that when you meet the right woman, Quimby."

We stared at him. He lifted his shoulders. Quimby rose abruptly from his seat. "I reckon we ought to head out, like Esther said. We want to make it to Oklahoma before Angel gets wind we're on the hunt for him."

Oklahoma was a pretty fair distance from Colorado Springs. The weather was beautiful this time of year. The mountains in the distance were still white with snow, but the flat land was warm and breezy and green. We preferred to ride horseback across the frontier, but when it came to a hunt, we needed time on our side. We'd need to catch a train to make the distance in time. I hated switching horses, but weren't many trains as allowed you to bring them along. There was one in Amarillo, though, and I reckoned we might make it that far in a day or two if we rode hard and slept on the range a night or two.

We rode into a small, sleepy town not far from Amarillo the day after we left Colorado Springs. Night was approaching, and our horses were weary and hungry. A small, hand-lettered sign on the edge of a small thoroughfare read Muskrat, Texas. Population 150. It would do for a night. Any town with a population over six or seven usually had a saloon.

They did. It was early in the evening, but there was already a girl crooning on a piano inside the Cyclone Alley Saloon. It didn't look like a very large inn, but the stairs round the back suggested there were some rooms for let. We led our horses to the hitching post in the small corral behind the stairs and filled some buckets of water from a pump on the side of the three story wooden building for them to drink. I fed Lady Jay some oats from a bag. I brushed long, stray strands of hair from my forehead and glanced around at the others.

"I reckon we should stop for the night," Hazel said.

We exchanged a look. "I reckon we should spend some time in the saloon," Quimby added.

I smiled. "I could use a drink and some dancing."

Vaughn lifted his shoulders. "It's been a long couple days. I wouldn't mind a drink."

"Hey!"

We all spun around in a single motion with our guns drawn. A man with shortly cropped hair dressed in a long, brown duster stood in the alleyway between the saloon and the shop next door. I couldn't make out his face, but his glasses gleamed in the late evening sun. He drew his gun in a flash and pointed it at us. Hazel let out a battle cry and fired. Her particle blast whizzed through the air and struck the wooden wall beside the man's head. He dove to the side and fired back.

We ducked for cover behind the stairs, water barrels and crates behind the saloon and fired back at him. Bullets splintered the fence around our horses, which whinnied in fright and danced around the corral. I cursed and popped my head over the barrel behind which I was crouching for cover. "Damn. The horses."

"Why are you shooting at me?" the man shouted, poking his head cautiously around the corner.

"You shot at us first!" Hazel shouted back.

"No, I didn't! I didn't even pull my gun until you did!"

My posse rose slightly from their crouched positions behind the rubble out back of the saloon. We looked at each other, nonplussed. "All right, then, what are you doing sneakin' up on us like that in the dead of night?" Hazel demanded.

He paused. His voice sounded incredulous when he replied, "It's not even dark."

I rose to my feet to get a better look at the man framed in the alleyway. "Yeah. All right. Who are you?"

"I'm Zeke Cooper. I heard you've been looking for me."

Chapter Five

We stared at him in stunned silence for a long moment. I was surprised I hadn't recognized him sooner. Even from the distance between us, his even features and long patrician nose were unmistakable. He didn't look much like a murderer. He looked irritated. He mopped his shortly cropped hair with a neckerchief and frowned at us.

"You know who we are?" I called out.

"Yeah, I know who you are. I'm a Pinkerton. I make it my business to know which folks are out there hunting bounties out from under the noses of honest people."

We narrowed our eyes at him. "You want us to start shooting again?" Hazel asked dangerously.

Angel Cooper sighed. "No."

"Can we get out of the alley and talk about this?" I asked.

"You mind not shooting at me this time?"

"Yeah, all right. We'll call a truce for now."

"You try anything, and Quimby Burton will shoot you dead," Hazel promised. "He's the fastest gun in the west."

Angel nodded. He didn't look very afraid, though. "Yeah, I heard that."

Quimby perked up. "You heard they call me Bonny Burton?"

"No. I haven't heard that."

Quimby sighed in disappointment. "Well, it'll catch on."

"I'm coming in."

He stepped into the yard behind the saloon with his hands up. He looked slightly thinner and more ragged than his WANTED poster would have had us believe, but I reckoned that was to be expected. He was on the run, after all. He was pale and drawn, but he didn't look as though he was afraid of us at all. We're a scary bunch. It must've been the shock.

His pale, translucent blue eyes looked resolute and intelligent behind the round, rimless glasses. "You turnin' yourself in?" I demanded.

He snorted very slightly. "No. I haven't done anything. I'm asking for your help."

We blinked at him in surprise. "We got off on the wrong foot, I reckon," Quimby said. "But we ain't never had a bounty hunt us down before. We don't know the protocol." He offered his hand to Angel to shake. The Pinkerton stared at it for a moment. Then he took it and pumped it vigorously up and down.

I frowned at him as I shook his hand in greeting. "I'm a little disappointed. I would have liked to have caught you."

At this, Angel chuckled. "You wouldn't have. You really think I would have been hiding out in Oklahoma? I was framed for murder. I'm not hiding out until I find out by whom."

Vaughn crossed his thick arms over his broad chest and looked down at Angel. The Pink was almost a head shorter. "We heard a lot of recommendations for you. We're prepared to listen to your story."

"Yeah, but if we don't believe it," I told him sternly, "we're taking you in."

Hazel lifted her eyebrows. "Are you prepared to take that risk?"

Angel shrugged. "I already have. I reckon I might as well see it through to the end."

"Should we talk about this over a drink?" Hazel suggested cheerfully.

"I think it's best I keep my head down," Angel replied. His voice was a low, husky rumble. It was oddly like a caress. He wasn't a handsome man, but Angel Cooper was eerily charismatic. He seemed to stand out against the barren, dusty town like a flash of light in the darkness. "Why don't you folks go inside and get a room. I'll meet you back here."

Hazel lifted her eyebrows. "I think I'll stick with you, if it's all the same, Angel."

He frowned. "That isn't my name. It's just a ridiculous nickname the Pinkertons gave me. The name's Ezekiel. Call me Zeke."

"Whatever you're called, I ain't lettin' you out of my sight."

"You think I would come out in the open and set this all up just to take off when you turn your back?"

"No. I don't reckon you would," I said, eyeing him thoughtfully. "All the same, I think Hazel should stick with you. She'll keep you in line in case you get a wild hair."

Zeke shrugged. "Yeah, all right." He glanced warily at Hazel. "Just keep your hands to yourself, missy. I'm a happily married man."

"Don't flatter yourself, Pink. I ain't into lawmen."

I rolled my eyes. There was no sense in hanging around listening to them bicker. I turned and strode toward the road and the entrance to Cyclone Alley Saloon. Quimby followed me. Vaughn didn't. I suspected he thought it would be easier for me and Quimby to do business this far south. I doubted it was because he actually wanted to hang around listening to Zeke and Hazel getting better acquainted.

Cyclone Alley was not a boisterous saloon. There were as many saloon girls as patrons this early in the evening. They all looked up from their glasses as we entered. No one but the saloon girls paid us much attention. A pretty blonde one in a green dress sidled slowly toward us. Quimby flashed her his charming smile. She fluttered her eyelashes. I caught his arm and steered him toward the publican before she had a chance to reach us.

The publican looked at us dubiously as we approached him. He was an old man in a yellowing white, button up shirt. He did not set down the soiled rag with which he was drying greasy pint glasses. "Drink?"

"Nah. We're looking for a couple rooms for the night."

"A couple?"

I glanced at Quimby. He lifted an eyebrow. "That's right. Two rooms."

He stared at us for a few seconds. Then he turned and set down his glass to hand us two keys on wooden plaques. "Three dollars."

Quimby did not move to pay him. He looked at me expectantly. I rolled my eyes and dipped a hand into the rucksack slung over my shoulder. "Yeah, yeah." I slapped the banknotes on the counter. "Thanks."

When we spun around, the pretty blonde saloon girl was nearby. She smiled brilliantly at Quimby. Her teeth were beautiful, pearly white. She'd apparently been listening. Quimby glanced sidelong at me. "I don't suppose you could handle this without me for a little while?"

"Sure, Quim," I said cheerfully, and he looked at me in surprise. "That is, if you want to be left behind. I hear the Pinks are trained at shootin'. We don't need your fast gun so much with the Pink around."

Quimby stared at me with a wounded expression. Then he sighed sullenly. "All right, all right. I'm comin'."

I turned around to speak once more to the publican. "Send up dinner for five to room Three," I said, slapping another stack of bills on the counter. He blinked at me in surprise. I glanced at Quimby, then back at him. "Don't send one of the pretty girls, right? It will save us all a lot of trouble."

He looked as though this was something he understood. The corner of his mouth turned up in a half-smile. He nodded. "Yes, ma'am. Rooms are around back."

I snorted. "Yeah. We'd figured that one out already. Thanks." I caught Quimby's arm and dragged him toward the exit before the blonde could ensnare him. Hazel, Vaughn, and Zeke were waiting in the yard where we left them. When we reached them, Hazel's eyes twinkled wickedly. Zeke scowled at us. I glanced at Vaughn, but he was as impassive as ever. I didn't ask what they'd been doing. I tilted my head at them and preceded them up the stairs to one of the rooms.

Two twin beds filled most of the space in the small room. The walls were wood and the single window was covered with a faded blue curtain that matched the threadbare coverlets on the narrow beds. There was no private bath. I opened the door into the interior hall. There was one washroom to accommodate the five guest rooms. I reckoned it was better than nothing. I turned back to my posse and our prisoner. I gestured them to sit. When we were perched as comfortably around the cramped room as we could be, we all looked at Zeke.

"Well, Pink," I said haughtily from beside Hazel on one of the beds. "Since you came to us, we'll give you the chance to tell your story."

"Rather than trussing you up and taking you to the nearest Marshal duty station," Hazel added.

Sprawled in a small, rickety wooden chair in the corner, Zeke snorted. "That's mighty big of you."

"How'd you know where to find us?" Quimby demanded, leaning against the headboard on the other bed. Vaughn stood in the opposite corner from Zeke, eyeing him warily.

"I heard you were asking around about me in Wyoming."

"You were there?"

"I was laying low. I was trying to get a message to Lennie, but it was too dangerous. The Marshals are still watching her."

"We didn't see any Marshals," I remarked.

"You didn't see me, either."

"So, how'd you get here?"

"I followed you here."

We blinked at him in surprise. "All the way from Wyoming?"

"That's right."

"But why?"

"There's not much else to do when you're on the run but keep on running."

"Why us?" Hazel asked, frowning at him. She looked nonplussed by the news the Pink had tracked us across two states. I, too, was feeling a bit sheepish that I hadn't noticed his tail.

"You have a reputation."

We glanced proudly at each other. "Yeah we do," Hazel said smugly.

"I thought maybe you could help me."

"I don't think there's anything in our reputation about us helping people," I remarked.

"No," he agreed. "But they do say you do good work and you don't mess with innocent people." He looked around at us with a disdainful expression. "Of course there was nothing in your reputation about you being completely oblivious to a two states long tail."

Now we looked around at each other sheepishly. "Well, I reckon a reputation ain't everything," I replied reluctantly.

"I'm innocent. I did not kill Silas Ratcliff. I was framed."

I lifted a shoulder. "What do you want us to do about it?"

"I want you to help me prove it."

I exchanged a glance with my posse. "Us?"

"I can't very well hire the Pinks, can I? And the lawmen are required to take me in to face the law. You aren't lawmen or Pinks, and you won't be in any trouble if you don't bring me in." He sighed, and his expression was sullen. "I don't have anyone else to ask or believe me, I would."

I frowned. "That ain't really what we do."

He looked between us all. "I will pay you the price of my bounty to help me instead of taking me in."

We considered this. "Seems like it would be less work to just take you in for the same amount of pay," Quimby remarked thoughtfully.

"Quim," I scolded. I glanced at Zeke. "Sounds reasonable enough. It's worth a listen, anyway. You go on and tell us your story and we'll decide what to do about you."

Zeke nodded and reached into the rucksack slung over his shoulder. He extracted an unlabelled bottle of amber liquid. Vaughn lifted an eyebrow. "If you'd have brought that out sooner, you might have received a much more enthusiastic response," he remarked.

Zeke's mouth turned up slightly at the corners, but he didn't reply. He handed around the whiskey, and we filled the tin cups from our saddlebags. We sipped. In the same moment, we all winced. The whiskey might have been made of pure fire. It burned straight down my gullet to my belly. "So let's hear it," I ordered.

He settled back in his chair for a long tale. "It started before I got involved. I'm not even a major player. I just got mixed up in it all. It was bigger than I expected. Bigger than a young girl going missing and her fiancé being murdered."

"Sterling Rush?" I guessed.

He inclined his head. "You know about him?"

"A little. Not much. Your wife mentioned he might have had something to do with your frame up and I think I saw a Congressman from Boston bribe someone for him."

Zeke's eyebrows shot up. "Are you sure?"

"I may be a bounty hunter, but I'm not dumb. I know a pay off when I see one."

"What Congressman?"

"Josephus Caine."

He nodded. "Yeah. Mayhap you did. I suspected he was in with Rush."

"Does it got anything to do with Silas Ratcliff?"

"You don't understand. It isn't Silas it has anything to do with. He was just an innocent kid. He didn't have anything to do with any of this. He was only killed to frame me up."

We glanced at each other. I inclined my head for him to continue.

"Lennie and I met Silas and Rebecca at a party in Boston honoring one of Rush's charities. Something about the families of folks lost in the pursuit of scientific advancement. Becky was a secretary for Rush AI. She worked closely with Rush himself and his closest people. A few months ago, Becky went missing. There was no evidence of where she'd gone, and there was no sign of her anywhere. The police and the Marshals don't seem to think there's a problem, so Silas came to me to help find her."

"And you didn't."

"No. Wherever she is, I don't think she's coming back."

"You think she's dead?"

"I'm sure of it, but I don't think they'll ever find a body."

"Why?"

He sighed. "She told Silas she was talking to a member of the press about Rush and the bad business practices at Rush AI. She didn't tell him what she was feeding the reporter. She didn't want to get him into any trouble or put him in danger, I guess."

"Did she tell him who she was talking to?"

"No. Just that she was informing on Rush."

"And that's what got her done up?" Hazel asked. Her eyes were glittering. I hadn't seen her so keen on anything that didn't explode in a long time.

"Silas and I suspected so. I didn't find out anything about that, though. There were just the usual rumors about the faulty death rays and the payoffs to government agency officials. No one had any proof of anything. Some of the papers printed stories about his latest weapons malfunctioning and blowing off the R&D guys' hands."

Hazel's eyes lit up. "Did that really happen?"

He shrugged. "I don't know. No one really knows. No one will confirm it."

"Well, what about the R&D guys? It should be easy enough to tell whether or not their hands have been blown off."

"Well...you know those R&D guys. It's hard to tell what was done to them and what they did to themselves."

"They should have hired Hazel," I remarked proudly. "Her particle guns never blow up unless you want them to."

Zeke lifted an eyebrow, but he ignored this. "Whatever Rebecca was telling the press, there wasn't any evidence of it in her apartment. Someone might have scrubbed it before I got there, or she was passing it to someone else."

"Did you find anything?"

"One thing. There was a telegram in the grate. It had been mostly burnt up, but I was able to trace it. It came over the telegraph in her apartments, and the operator still had the information."

I lifted my eyebrows. "What did it say?"

"It was a note from someone named Horace Greeley."

"Who's that?"

"He's a journalist. He founded the *New York Tribune*."

"What was he sending her telegrams for? Was he the one she was informing to?"

Zeke rolled his eyes. "Of course he isn't. He's long retired. I suspect it is the code name the reporter she informs to was using."

"Okay. What was in the note, then?"

"It was a message to meet him at a particular address. When I checked it out, it turned out to be an empty warehouse in the industrial district."

"So what's the significance? Is the reporter involved?"

"I don't think so. It's not what the note said that was important. It's where it came from."

"Well? Where did it come from?"

His mouth tightened grimly. "It was sent from the local Pinkerton headquarters."

We all blinked at him in surprise. "Is there anyone other than the Pinks who can access the machine?" Quimby asked, frowning.

"No. Not in that particular office. It's monitored by a security guard day and night."

"So there really is a crooked Pink."

"Yeah. It just isn't me."

I leaned forward in interest. "Have you found out who it is yet?"

He scowled and shook his head. "If I had, I wouldn't be here asking for your help. I would be in Boston digging up what I need to expose him and clear my name."

"Right, right. Don't get tetchy."

"I asked around a little about who was at HQ the night Becky went missing, but I didn't want anyone to figure out I was onto them."

"Well, obviously they did."

"Oh, thanks, Tess. I hadn't put that together myself."

"There's no need for sarcasm. We're all here for the same thing."

He frowned. "I don't think that's strictly true, but let's go with for it the sake of argument."

"So what happened to Silas?"

"Like I said, someone must have figured out I was looking into the telegram that night. When I went to meet Silas the evening of his death, to update him on the case, I found his body there. He'd been murdered."

"Did you call the police?"

He shook his head. "I knew what was happening. I left, and I didn't come back."

"What have you been doin'?"

"I still have a few friends who believe I'm innocent. I've been able to move around from town to town. I've stayed on the range a few nights, under the stars."

"I mean about the case. I know what it's like to travel around the frontier."

He frowned. "A friend of mine is a dispatcher in the Pinkerton office. He's looking into the telegram."

"Does he know why?"

"Nah. He's just getting the dispatch logs of who was on assignment that night and where they were, if any of them were in the office around nine o'clock that night to send the telegram."

"It's not much," Vaughn remarked.

"It's the best I got right now."

"You heard from your friend?"

"No. I've been out here. I don't want to endanger him by trying to contact him right now. I tried lurking around Rush for a while to see if I could find out anything, but I reckon he isn't the one doing the dirty work."

"Sounds like it's another Pink."

"Maybe. I won't know until I figure out who sent the telegram. It's the only lead."

"So what do you want us to do?"

"Help prove me innocent."

"We covered that bit real good," I replied. "How?"

"Find out who actually killed Silas and lured Becky out to that warehouse the night she disappeared."

I rolled my eyes. "I feel like this conversation is goin' round in circles."

"First I want to find out who Becky was talkin' to."

"Horace Greeley?" Hazel put in.

Zeke nodded. "Well, whoever Horace Greeley really is."

"What do you think that will accomplish?" I asked.

"It might give us a clue what she knew, which will point us in the right direction. If this has something to do with what she found out while informing on him, we should know what it is."

"All right. So how do we do that?"

"Becky wasn't the only one who talked to that reporter. There were some people with the Department of Scientific Progress and Questionable Developments that spoke out about the faulty guns first. When they started talking, some of them disappeared. The ones who didn't talk left town to get away from it."

"You know where they are?"

"A few of them, yeah. All we need to do is get them to tell us the name of the reporter."

I glanced around at my posse. I shrugged. It sounded good enough to me. Now that we had Zeke, we didn't have much else to do with ourselves. "Yeah, okay. Guys?"

"Sure," Quimby drawled.

"I'm in," Hazel added.

Vaughn lifted a shoulder. "I reckon there ain't much else to be doin'."

"What do we do after we find out who the reporter is?" Quimby asked, a furrow in his brow.

"We head back to Boston and talk to him."

"It's not much of a plan."

"You got a better one?"

Quimby shrugged. "I ain't a Pink. This is your show. You're the boss now, right?"

"Yeah, and I am a Pink. I follow the strongest leads I've got all the way to the end."

"So you're hoping between the reporter and your dispatcher friend, you'll be able to figure out who killed Silas and Becky and framed you for it."

"That's the size of it, yeah. And maybe we'll get enough evidence against Rush to put him away."

I lifted my eyebrows. "You're planning to go after the big guy?"

"Well, yeah. If the one who framed me is working for him, he deserves to face justice just as well."

"And he's flooding the market with faulty weapons," Hazel added disgustedly. "When there are perfectly good weapons that function the way they're supposed to."

Zeke looked at us. "So are you guys going to help me or not?"

I turned to look at my posse. We exchanged a long look. Quimby looked skeptical. "We could always just go back to Cheyenne and pick up Donnie Rio. I don't know if all this is worth five hundred dollars."

"Come on, Quim," I scolded. "It ain't about the money. We aren't mercenaries."

"What? Yeah, we are."

"Well, yeah, but we only capture bad guys. We don't mess with good people."

"If all this is true," Vaughn said smoothly, "someone else is going to find and pick up Angel for his bounty. They might kill him in the process or he might go to prison for a crime he didn't commit, and the real bad guys will get away. No one else is going to try to uncover what really happened to those people."

"Yeah, but Sterling Rush?" Quimby said. "He's the biggest robber baron in the U.S. He's not someone to mess with. We might as well take on the entire Confederate Army."

"Well, they lost," I said reasonably. "That's something, anyway."

"This ain't what we do," Quimby complained. "We hunt bounties. We aren't champions of justice or whatever it is we're doing here."

"Don't you get tired of taking down bank robbers in a shower of bullets and turning them in for money?" I demanded, frowning.

He looked at me incredulously. "No. I love doin' that."

I grinned. "Yeah, me too, but this sounds kind of important. We can go back to the shoot outs with outlaws after."

Quimby sighed. "'Sides," Hazel put in. "I reckon we're the best, and no one else would be stupid enough to help this guy. What have we got to lose?"

Zeke looked between us with a bland expression. "Is all this banter going to lead up to something, or should I just go?"

"Hey. You want our help, you'll be respectful of our methods," I told him sternly.

He rolled his eyes. "Should I take that as a yes?"

"All right, don't get twisted. We'll do it."

Hazel considered. "If someone tries to take him in along the way, Quimby, you can gunfight 'em. You'd like that."

I scoffed. "Come on. Ain't no one gonna argue with old Tess Mercury and her posse when they're escortin' a bounty cross country."

"Where's this informant we need to go see, anyway?" Quimby asked.

"Fortune City, New Mexico," Zeke replied wearily.

Hazel threw her hands up in the air above her head. "All right! I love that place! And that place loves me."

I frowned at her. "We ain't goin' there for a good time, Hazel. We're working right now."

"Aw, come on, Tess. When do you ever say no to a good time?"

My mouth turned up reluctantly into a smile. "Yeah, you know that's right."

Zeke sighed. "Well, unlike you people, at least I'll behave professionally."

Hazel scoffed. "You say that now, Pink, but have you ever been to Fortune City?"

"No."

"Well you just wait, then. You got no idea how unprofessional we can be."

Chapter Six

We stayed off the main roads and stuck to the frontier land on our way to Fortune City, New Mexico. The Pinkerton didn't seem to mind. He was a quiet, patient travel companion. Hazel on the other hand, was so hopped up she might have been a Mexican jumping bean. The hotter the weather became and the closer we drew to Fortune City, New Mexico, Hazel got wound tighter and tighter.

She was bouncing in her saddle upon her long-suffering steed, Tesla, the afternoon we drew towards the small, desert town. It was so blazing hot, a haze rose up from the ground and blurred the edges of the town ahead. I wiped at my forehead, but it was so bone dry, the sweat evaporated off my brow before it rolled into my eyes. I reached down to sip from the cantina on my belt. The water was as hot as a sulfur spring.

No one accosted us as we rode toward town. The Indians in these parts were used to the white folk and travelers coming through here, and they didn't seem to mind too much or it was just too damn hot for them to come out of their hidey-holes this late in the sweltering afternoon. I hated the desert, but Hazel was as happy as a savage with a new scalp.

In the center of Fortune City was a huge, bronze statue of a black bear. From its angry, toothy maw water shot serenely into a small pool at its clawed feet. I couldn't even see the bear, affectionately referred to as Old Dusty, despite its frequent buffing and polishing by the local townsfolk. They were sure proud of that bear. Old Dusty was surrounded with noisy, excited people spread out on blankets on the stone roundabout around the fountain or settling in rickety wooden chairs they'd brought from home or the saloons and restaurants nearby.

"What is going on?" Zeke asked with a wary expression. I reckoned he wasn't exactly keen to be thrust in the apex of a large, teeming crowd of laughing, shrieking and singing folks who might recognize him as a very, very wanted man, even this far southwest.

Hazel gasped in excitement, pointing toward a large, hand-lettered banner strung from one side of the storefronts on the main thoroughfare to the other. *10th Annual Silver Festival Fortune City, New Mexico*. I lifted my eyebrows and looked around at my posse. Hazel was beside herself with glee. "Fortune City's made most of its money on silver mining," she explained. "Every year, the miners take a couple days off with their families and celebrate in the center of town." She clapped her hands together. "Oh, boy, I forgot about this. Three years ago at the festival, there was this huge fireworks display in the town square right over Old Dusty. Well, the city didn't exactly know about it until it happened, and it took me forever to sneak in all those incendiaries and sparklers..."

"So you mean, you put on a fireworks display."

"You think I have time to do it again this year? I still have some materials buried out in the desert on the edge of town--"

"No, Hazel," I told her firmly. "We're on the job. Just 'cause the festival is going on don't mean we get to run wild. We still got to do what we came here to do."

Hazel looked deflated for a split second. Then she perked up again. "I can work with that."

"Why is it so hot here?" Zeke asked, swiping a hand across the top of his head. His scalp was turning pink beneath the closely cropped pale hair on his head, and his glasses were foggy. He drew them off to wipe them with his dusty kerchief. It didn't help much.

"It's the desert. You ought to get yourself a hat."

He frowned. "Vaughn doesn't have a hat."

Vaughn smiled. "I don't turn pink."

Zeke eyed him a moment, then shrugged. "You know a place to get a hat, Lightning?"

"I prefer to win mine in battle."

I rolled my eyes. "Hazel, we are going to attempt to avoid a bar brawl today if that's at all possible."

"Fine. Black Bear General Store a little ways down the road."

"What's the deal with black bears?"

"Folks around here are a little superstitious. They think they can ward them off by payin' them respect."

"That's ridiculous. It's uncivilized nonsense."

Hazel frowned at him. "Yeah, well, don't tell folks 'round here that. They'll rear up their uncivilized heads and beat you down in the street."

Zeke blinked at this, as though he weren't sure whether or not she was joking. I wasn't so sure myself. Lightning Hazel Harley was as unpredictable as Wyoming weather. As though to illustrate this point, she darted away from us and capered into the crowd surrounding Old Dusty.

I turned back to Zeke, Vaughn and Quimby. Quimby wasn't there. I didn't see him in the crowd, but I could guess he had found the prettiest young girl and was chatting her up. I sighed in frustration. "Well, I reckon the three of us can question this guy right enough. What's his name?"

Quimby appeared beside me so quickly, the loose hairs on the back of my neck stirred. "Patrick Granger," he announced. "I hear he's a mine inspector."

"They have those?" Hazel hadn't stopped dancing, but at least she was dancing nearby. A crowd of tiny children at her feet mimicked her steps, kicking their heels up and pumping their arms at their sides.

"Is it going to be like this all day?" Zeke asked resignedly.

I lifted my shoulders. "Yeah, probably."

"'Course they have those," Quimby answered Hazel. "They got to make sure conditions are reasonable, don't they?"

"I don't know. I ain't never heard of such a thing in the west."

"Yeah, well, it's a new era of enlightenment and scientific advancement, Hazel," I told her sternly. "That means folks got to be more civilized and care about safe working conditions."

"Weird. I always just do it right the first time."

"Not all folks are like you, Hazel. And you don't always do it right. Remember that time you nearly lost your finger when that incendiary went off early--"

"Why you always got to bring that up, Tess?"

"Can we actually get to work on the case?" Zeke demanded. "Are you folks always this unprofessional?" We all looked at him in the same moment. He took a step back and held up his hands. "Shucks, I didn't mean anything."

"We ain't professionals," Vaughn told him.

"Wouldn't be any fun if we were," Quimby added.

"We might actually have to put work first," I put in thoughtfully. "So, are we headed to the mine, then, or should we hit the saloon first?"

"Saloon," Hazel replied happily. "Wouldn't do any good to go to the mine. Ain't no one there. No one works during the Silver Festival. Wouldn't be no point in celebrating if none of the silver miners were around, would there?"

"All right, so how do we find Patrick Granger?" Zeke asked doubtfully.

She grinned. "You leave that to me. Keep your head down, Angel. I've got this one."

We followed her through the flood of people lingering on the wooden boardwalk outside the shop fronts of the main thoroughfare. She greeted a few of them like old friends, but she didn't pause to speak to any of them for long. She made directly for the Tarnished Band Saloon at the end of the road. It was packed and noisy, and the patrons were drinking, singing and dancing along with the music from duel piano players on the center stage.

Saloon girls milled around in the crowd, laughing, flirting and dancing with the men to the music. They were all finely dressed, very pretty and dripping with silver baubles. Quimby looked like a kid in a candy store. I didn't try to stop him from darting into the crowd. Hazel held her head high and strode inside.

A chorus of "Lightning Hazel!" greeted her entry, and the crowd swallowed her up. I rolled my eyes. "Two down," I remarked. "Either of you two next?"

"I think I'll stick with you," Zeke replied, glancing cagily around for lawmen. If there were any, they didn't seem to notice us. Even Vaughn didn't get more than a few glances and gasps in the jubilant crowd.

We ordered a round of beer at the bar and found one of the few empty tables. The crowd jostled us a bit, but it was better than trying to have a conversation near the poker game in the corner, which looked tense and dangerous. The players eyed each other so coldly and suspiciously, I was sure someone was about the draw and start shooting everyone in the room. I hoped Quimby stuck with the girls. I wasn't in the mood to break up a bar brawl today.

Zeke looked warily around. His translucent eyes were alert, and he held his shoulders rigidly. I suspected he wasn't in much danger here. Folks seemed much more interested in having a good time than hunting bounties, even if they did recognize him. I saw a man in the corner of the room with a U.S. Marshal badge taking shots of tequila out of a saloon girl's shoe. I doubted he'd give us much trouble.

A crowd of dirt-encrusted wranglers lifted a giggling Hazel up onto the bar. I shook my head in exasperation and sipped my warm beer. It wasn't bad, but it was a little flat. I didn't mind so much. I glanced around the room with interest.

"I think there might be some kind of misunderstanding here," Zeke said sullenly. "How are you people considered the best bounty hunters in the west?"

76

I lifted my eyebrows. "Who says that?"

He ignored this. "You people are complete amateurs."

I frowned. "We might be amateurs by your way of thinking, but we get the job done. We got skills you never even seen before."

Zeke glanced around for the other two members of our posse. Hazel whooped and hollered as she danced across the top of the bar, kicking glasses onto the floor. The patrons around her laughed and crowed raucously. Quimby was ensconced in a corner with a pretty, dark-haired saloon girl. She was perched on his lap. I couldn't tell what they were doing, but I doubted it was talking. I didn't strain myself to find out. "Right," Zeke muttered.

Vaughn's mouth turned up slightly at the corners. "It's underestimating us that gets most arrogant people caught," he remarked quietly.

Zeke glanced at him sharply. He sipped his drink silently for a moment. "I guess I can see that."

"Anyway, they'll have already learned where your snitch is."

He didn't look as though he believed this. He rose abruptly from his seat and started toward Hazel with an irritable expression. I glanced at Vaughn. He flicked his fingers toward Zeke. I hopped up to follow the Pink through the crowd. He paused in front of Hazel with a scowl. She didn't notice him for several moments. She shrieked with laughter at one of her own jokes in the center of a crowd.

Zeke pushed through them to reach her. The cowboys didn't seem to mind. They stepped aside to allow him to pass. He frowned at her. "Hazel!"

"Hooooooooeeee! I love the Silver Festival!" she shouted, holding her empty glass in the air. Around her, the cowboys whooped.

"Hazel! You learn anything?"

She didn't even glance at him. "Barkeep! *Uno mas*! Another tequila!"

Zeke sighed in frustration and turned away with a scowl. I glanced up at Hazel and snorted with laughter. "Amateurs," Zeke muttered.

Hazel wiggled her hips in a funny little caper. "Patrick Granger's been courting a saloon girl the past couple weeks. Name's May," she said to Zeke's back as though there had been no pause. "He's trying to take her out of the life."

Zeke spun around. "That isn't very respectable."

"Saloon girls ain't what you think," I told him. "You ought to be more respectful, city boy, or you'll find yourself in trouble."

He glanced cagily around. A couple of the cowboys frowned at him as though he'd said something mortally offensive. He held up his hands. "Sorry, sorry. I didn't mean anything."

"Well?" I asked Hazel.

"Granger's girl ain't here yet, but she's comin' in later. He comes in whenever she's workin'. We don't even gotta go find him. He'll come right to us."

I smirked at Zeke. "How's that for bein' amateurs."

His mouth quivered as though he were suppressing a smile. "When's the girl coming in?"

"'Bout six," Hazel told him. "Means we got about three hours. I know what I'm doing with that time. I reckon you ought to try to have a little fun yourself."

Zeke sighed, but he followed me back to Vaughn at the table. Vaughn had three empty glasses in front of him, and he was sipping on another. Zeke looked surprised that he'd managed to get through so many in such a short amount of time. I wasn't. I'd seen him put away more than that and shoot a fly off a wall fifteen feet away. 'Course I'd been matching him drink for drink. My recollection of the night was a little hazy.

The music in the Tarnished Band was good, and the beer was hearty. I was enjoying the Silver Festival. I sang along to some of the popular songs I knew. Vaughn smiled and drank steadily. Even Zeke seemed to loosen up a bit after the first couple drinks. He even made some polite conversation, and we swapped thrilling stories about our most exciting cases. His was a train robber and his wife in Arkansas, who had knocked off six trains and killed eight people before he'd finally caught up to them in Montana. They'd gone down in a blaze of gunfire. Vaughn's and mine involved a madam who was poisoning her rich clientele, several whores and a very well-placed explosive that had brought twenty dead bodies floating up to the surface of a small pond out back of the brothel. It had been pretty horrific, but we laughed all the same as Vaughn imitated the cat-soaked-with-water look on the madam's face when she'd realized she'd been caught up.

A young, pretty oriental saloon girl glided up to our table. She smiled at Vaughn and dropped down into the seat beside him. She laid a hand on his knee. I lifted my eyebrows. Zeke smirked. "I reckon you ought to sit somewhere else," Vaughn told the young girl gently.

She looked slightly hurt. "But I like it here."

"I think it's best for all of us if you sit somewhere else. Right now, you're sittin' with a table of outlaws."

The saloon girl lifted her eyebrows and looked around at us in interest. "What you done?"

Zeke smirked. He tossed back the contents of his glass. "Murder."

She blinked. "Oh." She smiled, but the expression wavered slightly. She rose unsteadily to her feet. "Well. Enjoy the festival, folks."

She was gone in a flash. I barked with laughter. "I reckon you aren't so bad to have around, Pink."

"Don't get used to it. I'm getting this over with, and I am going home to Boston. I'm not sure I'm ready to be back in the Wild West. It's changed since I left Wyoming."

"Yeah. We saw a nice kid get shot in the street in Cheyenne."

He frowned. "What kid?"

"Jimmy Steele. Nice but dumb."

Zeke thought about this. "I think I remember him from back when I was courting Lennie. He was just a pup then. He's dead?"

"Yeah."

"Who did it?"

"Big bug named Owen Spencer. Jimmy challenged him, and Owen was faster. That ain't his real name, though. Owen's really a bank robber from Texas called Donnie Rio." I took a sip of my beer and glanced at Vaughn. "When we get done haulin' you in, we're goin' after him next."

Zeke thought about this. He nodded. "If you help me clear my name, I'll help you. I liked Jimmy. He was dumb, but he was a sweet kid. He was real nice to Lennie. He used to help her carry her sundries from Howell's General Store every Tuesday morning."

Vaughn and I grinned at each other. "We don't need help bringin' in some bank robber," I told him. "'Sides, we' like divvyin' the bounty four ways. I reckon one more hand split might be too much."

He rolled his eyes. "I wouldn't do it for the money. I'd do it for Jimmy."

I shrugged. "Well, I reckon if we clear your name, you can do whatever you want. You'll have to go back there to get your little wife, anyway. She seems like a good little woman. She's loyal to you."

He stared somberly into his drink. "I reckon I did her a disservice, marrying her."

Vaughn lifted his eyebrows. "Why do you say that, Angel?"

He sighed. "Look at the trouble I'm in."

"Yeah, but that ain't your fault. That's on whoever set you up in Boston. You were just doin' your job."

"I chose a dangerous job. Even if my name is cleared, she'll probably end up a widow someday."

"Well, you could always retire when you're a free man," I suggested.

He seemed to consider this. "Yeah. I s'pose."

"And it sounds like the local Marshal 'round Cheyenne needs to grow a pair. They might need some new blood."

Zeke waved his hand. "Nah. It's not really my thing. I'm not interested in keeping law and order. I prefer to investigate things my own way."

Vaughn and I smiled. "Yeah, we can feel that."

He looked between us. "So how'd you two start running together?"

I grinned at Vaughn. We heard that question all the time. Vaughn never liked talking about it, but he didn't seem to mind when I told the story. He didn't pay attention to it, though. His coal black gaze wandered around the saloon. "We grew up together," I explained. "My daddy owns a plantation in Georgia. I reckon you know what that meant for Vaughn."

Zeke inclined his head, but his eyes slid to Vaughn with an awkward expression I'd seen before.

"The war ended, and all the slaves were freed, but my daddy didn't want to give his up. So, Vaughn and I took off."

The Pinkerton frowned slightly. "That doesn't seem like a thing for a respectable lady to do."

"You sure got a lot to say about what is and ain't respectable, but I reckon you ain't got any right to say it where I'm concerned."

He looked slightly ashamed, but he lifted his chin. "I bet your daddy didn't like you running off with a slave."

"I reckon he didn't. We ain't spoken in five years."

He lifted a shoulder. "I'm not surprised. Even in this enlightened era, it wouldn't be the first time a bi-racial couple --"

Vaughn leaned forward abruptly, and I held up my hands. "Now you just hold up one minute," I said. "It ain't like that! There ain't nothin' wrong with Vaughn, no matter what color his skin is, but we ain't a couple. Right, Vaughn?"

"The very idea is thoroughly revolting," he agreed.

"Thanks a lot, Vaughn!"

He chuckled. Zeke's pale cheeks colored slightly. He looked between us as though he was unsure what to say. I leaned back in my chair and sipped my beer. "How--uh--how did you become bounty hunters, then?"

I smiled. "Out on the road, you meet a lot of people. Some of them are bad people and some of them don't seem to understand the South lost the war. We had a few scuffles. We lost some; we won some. One night we got into a brawl with a posse of guys who turned out to be wanted for horse theft in the next county." I smiled at Vaughn. I knew he remembered the brawl as well as I did. We hadn't won that one, but we'd gone back for our revenge. "We trussed them up and dropped them off at the local Marshal duty station."

"We got our bounty and moved on," Vaughn added.

"We ran into some more outlaws here and there, and it seemed like a pretty interesting way to make some money. Later on, we met Quimby at a saloon in Amarillo. He was sharping cards at a poker game, like he does. He got into a fight with some wranglers from Fort Worth. He has a fast gun. Fastest I ever seen. He was traveling around with one of those Wild West rodeo shows, standing on the back of a horse and jumping through lassoes and shootin' apples off girls' heads."

Zeke snorted with laughter.

"Yeah. I know. He can still do some amazing tricks, boy, but he was tired of the circus life. He wanted out. Me and Vaughn talked to him about hunting bounties, and he thought it sounded like a good way to make a living. We've been running with him ever since. Turns out he knows a lot of the country from his traveling days and has some friends in the Marshals."

"And he seems to know a whole lot about outlaws," Vaughn added. "He's got an uncanny ability to memorize WANTED posters. We catch half our bounties by chance when he recognizes someone in a saloon out on the road."

"Lightning Hazel, well..." I grinned and gestured around. "Would you believe we found her in this here city in a saloon across the street? About three years ago, it was. A loan shark out of Chicago named Rudy the Roll Ricone hired us to find her and bring her to him. He was claimin' she was his wife who ran off on him, but what he was really after were her weapons and inventions. Quimby recognized him and knew he had a bounty on his head, so we got together with Hazel to lay a trap for him out back of a saloon in Kansas."

Vaughn and I exchanged a grin. I tilted my chin at him, and he continued the story, "We had her trussed up in the back of the Dirty Dandy. When he came back to get her, she jumped up and knocked him out with a cattle prod."

"We brought him in, cashed in his bounty, and that's how Hazel joined the posse."

Zeke narrowed his eyes at us. They glittered. "You sure that's all true? You aren't pulling my leg?"

"I don't pull legs," I told him sternly. "Ask Vaughn. He ain't ever told a lie in his life."

Vaughn snorted. "It's all true."

"It sounds a bit farfetched."

"It's the wild west. Everything's farfetched here."

Zeke laughed. "Yeah, all right. I reckon it doesn't matter how you came to do what you do, so long as you do it well."

I grinned. Then I sat up straight in my seat as Vaughn said in an aggravated voice, "Ah, hell."

"What's up, Vaughn?"

"Quimby." He jerked his chin toward the corner of the room where I'd seen the rough-looking men around the poker table. I didn't even have to follow his gaze. I could guess what he was seeing. I sighed.

"What is it?" Zeke asked.

"Quimby found himself a game."

"So?"

I rose abruptly to my feet. "He's a bit of a problem gambler."

"You said he was a card sharp."

"Yeah. That's a bit of the problem. He gets himself in trouble."

82

Zeke drew a watch from the pocket of his dusty white button-up shirt. "We haven't got time for a bar brawl right now. It's six o'clock. Granger should be here any time."

"You know which one he is?"

"No. I'm assuming your friends will point him out to me."

"We are useful." I glanced over at the poker table and sighed. "You boys stay here. I'll deal with Quimby."

He was kicked lazily back in a rickety wooden chair. His hat was tipped precariously back from his handsome features, and a stray lock of blonde hair fell over his forehead. When he rolled his brilliant blue eyes up to me and gave me a crooked smile, I felt a little jolt. It was irritation. "Quimby, what the hell?"

He dropped the front legs of the chair firmly on the floor and gave me an innocent look. He lifted his hands to indicate the other players around us, who looked up from their cards with various expressions of interest, irritation and impatience. "I'm just playin' some poker, Tess." He grinned at the pretty dark-haired saloon girl, who appeared at his side with two shots of whiskey. She sat down in his lap and handed him one of the glasses.

I looked at her then back at Quimby incredulously. "Nah, you ain't. We have work to do, Quim. We ain't got time for you to play poker."

"Shucks, Tess, there's always time for poker."

A toothless cowboy in a huge-brimmed hat grinned at me. "Why don't you sit down, little lady? We got room for one more. Join the game."

I glanced at him in disapproval. "No thanks. I got things to do, and so do you, Quimby."

He rolled his eyes and draped an arm around the saloon girl's shoulders. "You can't talk to the city boy on your own? You don't need me."

I scowled. "Quimby..." I said warningly.

He sighed. "Aw, come on, Tess."

I leaned down to talk near his ear. "Quimby, I ain't pulling you out if you get in over your head this time. We're gettin' what we need, and we're walkin' right out that door. You'll have to catch up with us."

He looked up at me with a hurt expression. "You'd leave me behind, Tess?"

"You know I would. Just like that time in Arizona."

His full, sensual mouth pushed out in a pout. "I spent the night in jail until that saloon girl Jane finally bailed me out. It was the worst night of my life."

I lifted an eyebrow and straightened up. "So? You comin' with me or are you gonna have to catch up to us two states over again?"

He sighed deeply and tossed down his cards. "Fine." He nudged the dark-haired girl gently. "Maybe later, honey. I got to work." She looked disappointed, but she rose and flounced away into the crowd. Quimby brushed himself off and looked at me with a smirk. "You sure you ain't just jealous of Betsy?"

I scoffed. "I ain't jealous of your women."

"You sure about that?"

"I'm pretty damn sure."

He leaned closer to me. I could smell the whiskey on his breath. "You keep tellin' yourself that, Tess, but I know you think about it sometimes."

I crossed my arms over my chest. "No, I don't."

He chuckled. "You should. I do."

"Come on," I said disgustedly. I spun away from him. "Let's find out which one of these girls is Granger's intended."

Hazel was sitting on the bench beside one of the piano players, crooning My Wild Irish Rose in a wavering alto. She was actually pretty good, and the folks around her sang along and swayed to the melody. Quimby and I paused and waited for the song to end. When it did, she held up her hands. The audience cheered.

"They love me here!" she said, bounding up to us.

"I can see that," I replied. "But we got things to do. Which one of the girls is ours?"

"Oh. That one." She lifted her hand to indicate a tall, voluptuous woman in an emerald green, low cut, bustled dress with long, curly red hair under a hat with a lacy veil that covered one of her stunning green eyes. Her lips and cheeks were ruby red. She was talking to a young man dressed in a white button-up shirt and baggy grey trousers with black suspenders and a tweed cap. She reached over and laid a hand on his arm, covering a coy smile with a black-feathered fan.

"That Granger?" I asked in interest.

Hazel shook her head. "Nah. They said he's a short feller with black hair down

84

to his shoulders. That guy's too tall, and he's ginger."

"A man with black hair down to his shoulders?" I demanded. I scoffed. "That might describe half the men here."

"No, Granger's a city boy. He stands out. Wears suits and things like a dandy. It should be easy enough to spot him. Can I go play some more now?"

Quimby scowled petulantly. "No, Hazel. Tess made me stop playing poker when I was about to win the pot."

Hazel hopped down off the stage and pouted up at me. "Tess, you ain't no fun when you're on the job."

"The job is fun," I argued.

"Yeah, 'cause we get to dance and drink and play poker while we're doing it. No other reason."

I rolled my eyes, but Hazel and I turned to watch the door while Quimby kept an eye on our saloon girl. It wasn't long before a short young man with black, shoulder-length hair wearing a black bowler hat and brown pin-stripe suit walked into the bar. He swept the hat off his head and fingered it anxiously as he craned his neck to look around. I tilted my chin toward him. As he walked toward the bar, his posture grew rigid with anger. He strode swiftly toward May and the young man in the tweed hat.

The black-haired man seized May's arm, drawing her away from the other man. The man in the tweed hat surged to his feet with a scowl. The men squared off against each other. I glanced interestedly at May. She looked irritated, but she stepped between the two men, pressing her palms to their chests to push them gently away from each other. She said something to the man in the tweed hat. He sat back down in his stool, scowling. May drew Granger aside.

She leaned close to him, speaking earnestly. He reared back, looking surprised and anxious. She laid a hand on his shoulder. He shook his head vehemently, but he finally sighed. May looked around. When she caught sight of us, she lifted her hand and pointed. I raised my eyebrows.

"What's that all about?" I asked.

Hazel smirked. "I figured he'd listen to May. She's suggestin' he have a word with us. I didn't think he'd appreciate us ambushing him and springing questions about the guy who chased him out of Boston all the way to the other end of the country."

I considered this. "Nice work, Hazel."

"Can I go play now?"

"No."

Patrick Granger approached us with narrow, beady hazel eyes. He wasn't wearing glasses on his long, hawk-like nose, but he looked as though he should have been. He looked like a regular bean counter. "May said you wanted to speak with me," he said in a fussy sort of voice. He lifted his chin. "I'm Patrick Granger."

"We'd sussed that. I'm Hazel Harley," she told him, sticking out her hand to shake. "This is Quimby Burton and Tess Mercury."

We nodded to him. He looked at me skeptically. "Tess Mercury? Is that a real name?"

I looked at him sharply. "So far as you need to know."

He shrugged. He glanced pleadingly over his shoulder at May, who hovered just within earshot. She smiled at him and flicked her hand in a dismissive gesture. "Go on, Pat, honey. Talk to the folks. Lightning Hazel is a good friend of mine from years back."

Patrick sighed. She stepped forward and kissed his cheek. She patted it gently and slipped away. He watched after her. Poor guy. May was a sweet girl, and she was fond of Patrick Granger, but he was barking up the wrong tree. I tilted my head at him. "Why don't we head over to the table where we won't be disturbed."

He nodded and followed us back to Zeke and Vaughn. Granger barely blinked at the big black man. I reckoned he was a Yankee boy born and raised. He didn't seem to recognize Zeke. He looked around at us warily. "You wanted to talk to me?"

I nodded. "I know this ain't what you expected, Patrick, but we want to talk to you about Rush AI."

He started. "I don't know anything about that." He rose halfway out of his chair.

Quimby began to rise beside him, but I laid a hand on Granger's arm. "None of us work for Rush," I told him earnestly. "We're lookin' to take him down. You might be able to help us."

He looked between us warily.

"You want your life back?" Zeke asked, leaning forward. "So do I."

Granger stared at him. After several tense moments, he sat back down. He frowned. "I have a life here now. What if someone finds me?"

"No one's going to find you," Zeke told him firmly. "We just need to ask you a few questions."

Granger sighed deeply. He looked around as though ensuring he knew the patrons around us. Finally, he leaned forward. His shoulders hunched, but he looked resigned. "All right, go ahead. I'll answer."

"You worked for the Department of Scientific Progress and Questionable Developments?"

Granger nodded stiffly. "Yes. I was in charge of inspecting the R&D labs at Rush AI. I was attached to the new hand held directed energy weapon project."

"And it didn't pass inspection?" I asked, leaning forward in interest.

"It shouldn't have passed. The weapons are faulty. They explode unpredictably on discharge. They've taken off a few of the R&D guys' hands."

"They've taken off their hands?"

"Well, they won't admit that's what happened. They have—replacements."

We all looked at each other. "Replacements? What do you mean?"

He grimaced. "Mechanical and clockwork replacements of various shapes and sizes and...unique abilities."

"And somehow no one's noticed?"

"It sounds neat," Hazel put in.

"It's not neat," Granger told her. "It's horrible. They claim the replacements were voluntary. No one would confirm anything. After the inspection, one of Rush's guys showed up at the Department office with a briefcase of money. He suggested we return a positive inspection result."

"You did."

He lifted a shoulder. "I didn't feel right about it. I knew the weapons were faulty, and I knew they shouldn't be out on the market. I wasn't the only one in the department who felt that way. We refused to doctor the results."

"What happened then?"

"Our supervisor was under Rush's thumb. The ones who dissented were asked to leave the department."

"You were fired."

"Yeah. I was fired. I didn't want to work for a department that was rendered useless and ineffectual by corporations who can buy results."

"Good for you, Pat," Hazel told him bracingly.

"What happened to the others who dissented?" Zeke asked. "They disappeared?"

Granger nodded. "Yeah."

"Dead?" I asked.

He shook his head. "I don't know. Not for sure. Maybe. Maybe they took off like me."

"Were any of you talking to the reporter?"

Granger blinked in surprise. "You know about that?"

"Not everything. Did you talk to him?"

"No, not me. He was asking questions, but most of us didn't want to get involved any more than we already were."

"Who did?"

"Winston Smyth. He was one of my colleagues. He must have talked about the faulty weapons. I saw it in the paper a few days later. After that, I never saw or heard from Winston again. Then the rest of us decided to take off, too. It was safer."

"Do you know who he was talking to? The reporter?"

He considered. "Sort of. I never talked to him, but I saw the story in the *Boston Daily*. I don't remember his last name, but his first name was Jason."

I snapped my mouth shut with an audible click. I met Vaughn's eyes then looked away.

"Jason at the *Boston Daily*," Zeke said, nodded thoughtfully. "Okay. That'll do. There probably isn't more than one. If there is, it shouldn't be too hard to figure out which one Smyth was talking to."

We all looked at each other. The conclusion of our business in Fortune City was a bit of a letdown. I felt like I'd been cheated.

"Is that all?" Granger asked, frowning.

"You know anything else that might help us take down Rush?"

He looked grim. "I know you'd have a better chance getting this guy elected president." He jerked his thumb at Vaughn. "You're better off not wasting your time."

"I think we'll decide how we prefer to waste our own time," I told him.

He shrugged. "Suit yourself. Good luck."

Hazel grinned at him. "Well. Thanks a lot, Pat." She laid a hand on his arm. "You go on and get that girl. She's a tease, but she's worth the trouble."

Granger smiled a tiny smile. His cheeks flushed pink. "Yeah. All right." He rose and inclined his head to us.

When he was gone, I turned to Zeke. "Well? What now, boss?"

He leaned back in his chair and sighed. He didn't say anything for a moment. Finally he said, "I guess we head to Boston."

My posse and I looked at each other.

Zeke scrutinized us narrowly. "You're going to need some new clothes."

"Oh, come on now," I complained.

"It's a different world out there, Tess."

I sighed. My posse looked back at me in alarm. "I don't think we much like the sound of that."

Chapter Seven

The nearest airship port this side of the Mississippi was in St. Louis. It was about a ten days' ride from Fortune City, give or take, and we didn't have that kind of time. We'd have to catch a train eventually. Zeke didn't seem to want to. I didn't know if he was attached to his horse, California Cal, or if he just didn't want to show his most-wanted face on a crowded car with no other escape than a death-defying leap from a racing train.

The road was flat, and we made good time toward Amarillo where we could catch our train. We reached a small, nondescript town on the border of Texas and New Mexico. The sun had begun to dip below the endless, flat horizon at our backs. The heat hadn't abated, despite the darkening sky. Even Zeke didn't protest as we hitched our horses in the yard behind the Spongy Boot Saloon for the night.

There wasn't any music in the Spongy Boot, but Hazel didn't seem much in the mood for dancing. We hunkered down in a shadowy corner table and sipped our beers without saying much to each other. We were tuckered out, and there wasn't much to say to folks with whom you've been riding day and night the last few days. Even Quimby was putting less effort than usual into chatting up a pretty, tearful girl by the bar, who turned out to be a disappointed mail-order bride. I suspected his heart wasn't in it, even though he was a sucker for a girl in tears.

"This ain't any fun," Hazel complained, slunk low in her chair with her arms crossed sullenly over her chest.

"Not every town can be Fortune City," I replied.

"There'll be plenty of wild nights when we ain't saddled with the Pink," Vaughn told her calmly. Zeke barely looked offended. He must've been getting used to my posse by now. "We ain't drawin' unnecessary attention to ourselves tonight."

Zeke glanced warily around the room. "I think we're drawing enough attention to ourselves just sitting here," he remarked in a low voice.

He was right. There weren't many patrons in the quiet saloon, but most of them were eyeing us cagily. Expressions of disgust and anger crossed a few of the faces. I wasn't surprised. This far South, the war might not have even happened.

I'd felt this big bad vibe before, on nights when the war had just ended, and we'd been run out of a few towns to spend the night out on the range, licking our wounds.

I glanced at Vaughn. There was no expression on his face, but his coal black eyes were alert. His huge hand hovered slightly over his hip where he kept his holster. I leaned back in my chair and glanced around us from under the brim of my Stetson. I tucked my thumbs into my belt above my gun. The quiet was loaded and tense.

The poker game in the corner seemed paused as the players glanced covertly over the tops of their cards at us as though they sensed the sudden electricity in the air. I wasn't worried about them; they were just wranglers and cowboys fresh from a ride. It was the group of mean-looking men that had just walked in that worried me. They took a table on the other side of the saloon.

They weren't like any men I'd seen. One of them, a short stocky man with disheveled, dirty blonde hair wore a brass patch over one eye with a short, stubby spyglass attached to it like an eye extension. As he glanced our way, the spyglass obtruded as though it were focusing on us. Beside him was a man wearing scratched and tarnished goggles on his head and up into his wild, wavy black hair as though he'd just pushed them from his eyes. These two uncanny characters sat with a burly man with a gleaming brass hook instead of a left hand that moved in jerky circles. Even from the distance between our tables, I could hear the hook tick with each movement as though it were operated by tiny clockwork gears.

The three men's clothes were tattered. They looked rode hard and put away wet. They looked like they hadn't seen a tin bath in about a month or more. They also looked anxious and keyed up like they were anticipating a fight. There wasn't much question about with whom they were planning to fight. They didn't take their eyes off us.

They seemed to be waiting for the order from the last man with them. He was a large, dark, ruddy skinned man in a long, black, military-style jacket and a wide brimmed, silver banded hat and bandana over his long, curly dark hair. He looked like a Spaniard, but he might have been an Indian or a Mexican. He had a thin, curling moustache, and he looked as clean as a whistle beside his filthy companions. He leaned back in his chair with his black, silver-toed boots on the table and chewed the end of a cigar. He stared at us without blinking. I shuddered slightly under his gaze. One of his thickly-lashed eyes was sparkling, clear blue. The other was milky white.

He was a young man, and his face might have been handsome once, but the skin on the left side of his face was puckered and shiny, as though he'd walked through a fire. The corner of his mouth turned down in a gruesome snarl. He looked like he might be hard enough to take on Vaughn, but he didn't stand or try to approach us. He still made me very, very nervous. It was time to get out of there. There was no point pushing our luck with these ruffians, not when we had a very long road ahead of us.

I glanced at Vaughn. "You see them."

"'Course I see 'em. Can't miss 'em."

"I don't like them."

"No, I can't say as I do, either."

Zeke's face was perfectly impassive, but his voice was tense. "I reckon we ought to turn in."

"Yeah. I think you might be right, Angel." I kept my gaze on the big Spaniard. "Hazel? Get Quimby. Do it quick."

She didn't hesitate, but her swagger looked perfectly natural. I watched her catch Quimby's shoulder and murmur something in his ear. He didn't turn around to look at the sinister hombres, but his shoulders tensed slightly. He leaned toward the blushing mail-order bride. He said something in her ear. She giggled and nodded.

Quimby swung off the barstool and spun toward our table. He met my gaze. There was no expression on his face, but I recognized the cool, alert look in his brilliant blue eyes. He was ready for a fight. We all were. I could feel the tension at our table. These boys had neat toys, but they were no match for Tess Mercury and her posse. My lips twisted up slightly in a tiny, smug little smile. Bring it on, boys.

We stood in a single motion as Quimby reached us. We didn't speak to each other. We didn't have to. The man with the ticking hook for a hand half rose from his seat, but the big Spaniard held up his hand in the air as if to stop him. The hook-handed man sat back down. I tilted my head to my posse, and we started for the door.

Night had already fallen over the rough Texas town. The saloon was well lit, but the string of glowing lanterns that illuminated the main road faded out back of the saloon, where stairs wound up to our rooms. I wondered briefly why we kept staying at places like this. We would have been a hell of a lot better off walking through the saloon to our rooms. At least there we were covered.

The hombres from the bar came out shooting. My posse and me dove for cover behind the barrels and kegs out back of the saloon, cursing. I had expected it, but I had thought there might have been some spirited shouting or fist-a-cuffs before the actual shooting began. I supposed these guys must be professionals.

"What the hell? Who are these guys?" I growled. I peeked out from behind a stack of boxes and fired back.

"Bounty hunters," Quimby called back. "It's Che Chucho and his posse."

I cursed. "What the hell are they doin' comin' after us?"

"Why do you think? They're probably after Angel!"

"Ain't no one gone up against us for a bounty in years." As the gun smoke began to settle, I leaned around the boxes and called to Chucho and his boys. "What are you shootin' at us for, Chucho?"

"It's the fastest way to kill you!" the man with the spyglass for an eye called back. To illustrate the point, he emptied his barrel into the saloon yard behind us.

I waited until he'd emptied his six-shooter. "What are you tryin' to kill us for?"

"You're worth $100 apiece dead or alive," Chucho replied. His voice was low and sharp. "I reckon it'll be easier to take you in dead."

I paused and peered out at my posse. They lifted their heads from behind barrels, boxes and from under the stairs. They looked as dumbfounded as I felt. "I think you got us mistaken for someone else," I said.

"I don't think so. I know who you are. Ain't no other woman runnin' around with a freed slave, a trick shooter, a mad scientist and a crooked Pink!"

"I think he knows who we are, Tess," Vaughn said.

I scowled. "What the hell is he talkin' about, a price on our head? We ain't done nothin'!"

Zeke looked grimly back at me from under the stairs. He held a large, serious-looking six-shooter. "I think I know. Someone must have seen us together. They know I'm running around with you."

"You think Rush got all the way out west?" Hazel demanded.

"His Congressman got to Colorado, and you aren't exactly discreet."

I sighed. "This is just a hell of a thing."

Chucho and his posse didn't seem interested in our conversation. A shower of bullets sent us diving back undercover. We fired back without much enthusiasm. "We ain't goin' with you, Chucho," I called.

"It don't matter. We don't much care whether we take you dead or alive."

I looked around at my posse. "So what now?"

Hazel scowled. "Aw, hell. I've had about enough of this. Everybody get down."

She dipped into the rucksack on her hip and drew out a small, smooth brass ball. There was a ring sticking out of the top of it. Hazel seized the pin with her teeth and yanked it out. Quimby dove toward me and flattened himself on the dirt beside me. Zeke looked confused. Vaughn lifted a huge hand and pushed Zeke's head down to the ground.

Hazel tossed the brass ball toward Chucho and his men. For a moment it spun rapidly like a top, emitting loud, whizzing and popping noises. Chucho and his boys stared at it in confusion for several moments.

"Come on," Hazel said. "Shoot at it, you big dummies."

They did. They always shoot at it. For a moment, the bullets seemed to have no effect on the brass grenade. Then it exploded in a shower of sparks. Black smoke billowed from its tiny belly, filling the air around us. It stank horribly. My eyes watered. I could hear Chucho and his men shouting in the black cloud.

"Tess, come on!" Quimby yanked me to my feet and dragged me out of the haze toward our horses hitched in the yard several feet away. They were pawing listlessly at the dirt as though they sensed our predicament and were anxious to be out on the quiet frontier.

We didn't wait to make sure Chucho and his boys had stayed down. We hopped on our horses and spurred them toward the road right out of town. If they wanted to follow us, we'd have a good head start. The road was barren and flat. We rode hard for several hours until our horses started to slow and Hazel's glowing, toxic blue globe faded to a pale smolder.

I was cold, hungry, tired and irritated when Vaughn finally said, "We ought to stop for the night."

"I don't know, Vaughn," I said. "Chucho and his posse could still be behind us."

"They'll have a hell of a time tracking us. They don't know where we're headed. I'll stay up and keep watch."

94

"We can take turns," Zeke said grimly from out of the darkness.

"Yeah, all right."

Lady Jay seemed all too eager to stop. I poured her a saucer of water and fed her some oats. I patted her chestnut flank affectionately. She didn't seem to be feeling too friendly toward me. She snorted and tossed her head back and forth before turning her back on me. I smiled. I didn't blame her. I hadn't been treating her quite as sweetly as I should have been.

Zeke gathered some kindle from the ground around us, but Hazel snorted with laughter. She made a pit from the dirt and rocks and tossed a small, flat, shiny black disk in the center. Zeke looked at her incredulously. "What the hell is that?"

"Incendiary device."

He didn't look like he thought this was such a great thing. "I can start a fire."

"Yeah, and it will burn out in a couple hours, if it lights at all. You let me take care of the fire. It's what I do."

Zeke still looked doubtful, but he gestured as though welcoming her to try.

She smirked at him. The small, flat disk suddenly ignited. Zeke started. She threw out a hand to push him back away from the sudden blaze. The fire burned in a perfect, crackling ring. I sighed in contentment as I dropped Lady Jay's blankets on the loose dirt nearby the flame. I didn't mind camping out on the range, not when I had a nice, warm fire to curl up next to.

"You want to share my blanket, Tess?" Quimby asked. His eyes glittered at me over the fire. He held up one side of the blanket to offer the empty space to me.

I rolled my eyes. "No"

"Quimby, you watch yourself or you'll be sharing my blanket," Vaughn told him in a low, serene voice.

Quimby's brow knitted together, and his lips pushed out in a pout. "Fine."

"So what now?" Hazel asked from under a huge quilt. I could barely see the top of her curly blonde head.

I settled comfortably back in my blankets. "Sounds like we're wanted," I remarked.

"Amarillo is not far from here," Quimby said grimly. "We ought to ride until we get there and hop the first train we can."

"We might have to leave the horses," Zeke said.

I sighed. I glanced at Lady Jay. She didn't seem to notice that we were talking about her. "If we do, we can catch a passenger train in the next town. We won't have to wait for the cargo cars in Amarillo."

Vaughn sighed, but he didn't protest.

"We should split up," Quimby suggested hesitantly.

We were silent for a moment as we considered this.

"I don't like it," Vaughn finally said.

"No, I don't much like it either," I replied. "But I think Quimby might be right. We need to get to the airship port in St. Louis as soon as we can."

"The quicker we get this settled, the quicker we can get back to our normal, happy-go-lucky lives," Hazel added.

Zeke sighed. "I'm sorry I got you folks into this."

I scoffed. "No, you ain't."

He was quiet a moment. "I'm paying you more than I ought to, considering how unprofessional you all are most of the time."

I snorted. "It don't matter. We'll figure it out. We always do."

"Get some sleep," Vaughn ordered in his honeyed voice. "We got a hard ride in the mornin'."

"I want to see one of those WANTED posters," Hazel put in abruptly.

"What posters?" I demanded.

"Well, I reckon we got ourselves some. Chucho picked one up somewhere."

"I hope they got my good side," Quimby said. He chuckled. "Who am I kidding? Every side of old Bonny Burton's good."

I snorted. "Quimby, no one calls you that."

* * *

We didn't split up when we rode into the next town. We stood out like a dude in a rodeo, but I thought we all felt safer together. I know I did. I reckoned Vaughn and me traveling together was a big red sign, but I hadn't been separated from him since we were kids. I wasn't ready to start now. I suspected he felt the same way. He and Asa stuck close by Lady Jay and me as we paused on the edge of Sunspot, Texas.

I looked around at my posse. "Well? How we goin' to do this?"

Quimby grinned, tipping back his hat to look at me. "I reckon you and me ought to go into town together, Tess."

I rolled my eyes. "Forget it, Quimby. I ain't goin' 'anywhere with you. I know what you got goin' through your head."

Quimby's grin transformed into a leer, but Vaughn looked like he was considering this. "Actually, Tess, I reckon Quimby's right. Hunters will be lookin' for two women, two white men and a big Negro. They won't recognize you and Quimby on your own."

I scowled. "I reckon it won't be hard to spot me. You don't see many ladies lookin' like me."

My posse eyed me skeptically. Quimby's grin widened, and Hazel's face lit up. "I think I can take care of that," she said with an ominous twinkle in her eye.

Five minutes later, I was struggling into one of Hazel's dresses behind some boxes in the yard out back of the local general store. An old, owl-faced woman with wild, curly grey hair under a threadbare bonnet watched us from a rocking chair on the back porch behind the store. Her glasses looked like they'd been made from the bottoms of a couple whiskey bottles. She looked interested, but she didn't look much like she knew which way was up and who should or shouldn't be changing out of chaps and a buckskin vest into a ruffled blue dress out back of a general store.

"Hazel, I don't know about this," I said, frowning.

She giggled. I felt her boot in my back as she tugged more tightly on the laces of the corset around my waist. I gasped and flailed my arms around. "Hold still, Tess."

"I don't need to go in looking like a five dollar whore!" I growled. The old woman stretched her thin lips into an amused smile.

"It never hurts."

"Yeah, it does. We're trying not to draw attention to ourselves."

"It's called distraction. No one would expect Tess Mercury to waltz into town dressed like...like--"

"Like Lightning Hazel Harley?"

She laughed. "Yeah."

"I'm thinkin' maybe this is a bit more for your own personal enjoyment than an honest attempt at dressing me up like a decent lady."

She sighed. "I was hopin' it would take you longer to catch on to that."

"Tess! Hazel! What the hell are you two doin'?" Quimby demanded, rounding the corner into the yard. When he saw the old woman, he paused in alarm. She turned her vacant, loony smile on him, and he relaxed, tipping his hat to her. "Ma'am."

"We're done," Hazel said in disappointment. She appraised me narrowly. "The dress is a little small, but you'll do all right."

Hazel was a full six inches shorter than me and much curvier. The blue checked skirt of the dress she'd leant me was too short, and the bodice was too low. The ankles of my booties hung out. I could tell by the vacant leer on Quimby's face that my décolletage was downright indecent. Well, it was still more respectable than a woman in dirty chaps and a weathered John B.

Quimby didn't say anything as we strode out from the yard to meet Zeke and Vaughn on the outskirts of town. Zeke's eyebrows shot up, but he didn't say anything. Vaughn took one look at Quimby and scowled in disapproval. I rummaged in my saddlebag and wrapped a fringy shawl around my shoulders, despite the high heat of the day. "All right, we've put enough work into this. Let's get this over with, Quimby."

I turned away from my posse to stride toward the wooden boardwalk outside the shops on the main thoroughfare. Quimby caught up to me and wrapped an arm around my shoulders. I tried to shrug him off, but he tightened his hold. He smiled. "Now, we got to make it look believable, Tess. If you stomp on my foot, these good folks might think we're hiding something."

"Bring me a poster!" Hazel called after us. I didn't turn around. My cheeks blazed scarlet with irritation and embarrassment.

"Yeah, yeah."

"Where to, darlin'?" Quimby asked with a very mischievous grin.

I curled my lip. "Let's just head to the post office and see what this is all about."

"Anything you wish, my love."

"Knock it off, Quimby. I ain't really your girl."

"You know that's right. No one would believe it. You are a little past your prime these days--"

"Past my prime? Past my prime!" I shrieked. I dug my elbow into his ribs. "Why you son of a--

He hissed with pain and dropped his arm from around my shoulders to massage the bruise.

"Aw. Come on, Tess, have a heart. I was only jokin'. You know I think you're--"

"Quimby."

My muscles tensed suddenly. Beside me, Quimby's steps slowed slightly, and I knew he saw what I was seeing. A tall, well-built young man in brown trousers and a tanned leather vest strode toward us. His hawk-like features were drawn in concentration beneath a mud-spattered white hat. A silver badge gleamed on his breast. U.S. Marshal.

"Just take a breath and smile, Tess."

Quimby tipped his hat to the Marshal as he passed. I inclined my head demurely. The Marshal's concentrated expression cleared, and his eyes narrowed at us. He paused beside us, and we slowed to face him. My heart thumped in my chest. Quimby caught my hand and squeezed it in an oddly reassuring gesture.

"You folks new in town?" the Marshal asked. He didn't sound suspicious. He just sounded curious. My muscles uncoiled slightly

"Just passin' through on the way to Amarillo," Quimby replied so casually, I almost believed he wasn't nervous at all. He had a hell of a poker face.

The Marshal tilted his head back to look at us. "Yeah? What for? You visitin' someone there?"

I glanced up at Quimby. He smiled. "We're catchin' a train to Denver. We're on our way to meet our families and get married."

The Marshal smiled. "Ah. Congratulations. You're a lucky man."

I tried to look demure and grateful for the compliment. Past my prime, indeed.

"Thanks, Marshal."

"You folks have a nice day. Good luck to you."

When he strode away without a backward glance, I relaxed against Quimby's side. He chuckled. "Come on, Tess. You've seen me sweet-talk my way out of tighter situations than that. You didn't trust me this time?"

I rolled my eyes and stepped away from him. "I've seen you talk your way out of bein' shot my some cheatin' woman's husband, but we ain't never been wanted by the feds before. I don't reckon I'd really like to test the limits of how smooth you can talk."

"There is no limit to how smooth I can talk."

He must not have been as confident as he seemed. He steered me toward the post office with a lively step. No one paid us any attention along the main road, aside from a few women who fluttered their lashes at Quimby. I felt indignant about this. What was I, invisible? We might not be a real couple, but they didn't know that. Women are shameless when it comes to a handsome face.

Quimby noticed my ire. He smirked. "Jealous, Tess?"

"Jealous of what?"

He wrapped an arm around my waist and drew me up to his side. "I think you know. You look like you're trying to light those ladies on fire with your brains."

I considered this. "I don't think you can do that."

"Yeah, but you aren't sure, so you better be careful who you turn that evil eye on." He caught my chin between his thumb and forefinger and turned my face away from him.

I laughed and pushed him away. "All right, all right. I ain't jealous, but what kind of lady bats her eyelashes at another woman's man when she's right there beside him?"

He looked surprised. "I was under the impression they all did."

I snorted in disgust. "Let's just get this over with."

The post office was bustling with customers, but none of them spared us a glance. Quimby and I sidled over to the WANTED wall. There weren't many of them, but there were some torn edges of paper still tacked up, as though someone had ripped the pages off the wall. We glanced at each other. There was a bounty hunter in town, or there had been.

"You see it?" Quimby asked, frowning. He glanced tensely behind us.

"No..." And then I did. I barked with laughter.

The customers around us glanced at me in surprise and disapproval. I covered my mouth. Quimby saw it a second later. He scowled. "It doesn't even have our names on it!" he hissed.

"Shh! Dang, Quimby, are you trying to get us hemmed up?"

"Sorry." He sounded sullen. He reached forward and yanked the poster off the wall to get a closer look.

WANTED

Dead or Alive

Tess Mercury and posse

$100 a head

Known to be traveling with the wanted killer Ezekiel "Angel" Cooper

He made a strange, tortured noise through his nose. I snorted with laughter. The rendering on the poster did not flatter. His features were uneven and gaping, and his hair was wiry and wild. He was grinning through huge buckteeth. Hazel had a gap-toothed smile and a hairy mole on her cheek. Vaughn looked mean and dangerous with a scar down one side of his face that I was pretty sure hadn't been there the last time I'd looked at him. I looked rough and haggard with tangled, wild hair and a feral twist on my lips.

"I guess now we know why the Marshal and the good folks of Sunspot haven't recognized us," I remarked cheerfully.

Quimby did not seem relieved. His feelings were hurt. "They think I look like this?"

I laughed. "Just be thankful we ain't likely to be recognized any time soon."

"I do not have buck teeth!"

He continued to complain as I dragged him out of the post office, tucking the poster into my rucksack. I didn't care about his pride. I was happy to browse the shelves at the general store without anyone sparing me more than a glance or two. I didn't even mind when a couple young wranglers on their way to the ranch smiled and winked at me over a stack of canned beans. In fact, I smiled back.

Quimby slipped up beside me and scowled at the young men. "We ought to get back to the others, you reckon?"

I rolled my eyes. "Sure, Quim."

Our posse was waiting on tenterhooks when we strolled casually out of town. Hazel met us halfway. "Did you get it?"

Quimby scowled, but I laughed and extracted the poster from my rucksack. "Got this, too." I held up the loaded rucksack. "Some jerky for you, Vaughn. Hazel, the sweetbread, 'cause I know you like it. I wasn't sure what sort of thing you'd like, Angel, so I just brought you a tin of sardines and some crackers."

Zeke adjusted his round glasses on his nose and frowned. "You had time to shop? While we're wanted by the feds?"

Hazel cackled and handed him the poster. "I reckon this is why."

Zeke laughed. He was pretty nice-looking when he smiled. "I see your point."

Vaughn chuckled low in his throat, but Quimby grunted unhappily. Hazel glanced up at him. "You actually upset, Quimby?" she asked, grinning hugely.

"You ought to be pleased no one's going to recognize you," Zeke told him, but his mouth quivered as though he was suppressing a smile.

"They didn't even say our names!" he complained. He seized the poster from Vaughn and tossed it angrily to the ground. "I look like the Hunchback of Notre Dame!"

We laughed, and he glared around at us. "Come on, Quimby," I said. My voice shook with the effort of maintaining a straight face. "I think this is all right. Put your ego aside and appreciate the lucky break."

Zeke frowned thoughtfully. "Che Chucho and his crew at the saloon recognized you. All together, we're pretty hard to miss."

I considered this, and some of my good cheer faded. "Yeah. He's right. A lot of bounty hunters have met us on the road. They know who we are right enough."

Hazel scoffed. "Most of the bounty hunters we met on the road know better than to mess with us. It's the Marshals we need to worry about. They aren't dumb. They'll put two and two together, they see us traveling around."

I sighed and looked grimly around at my posse. "Let's just ditch the horses and catch the next train to St. Louis. We've been riding out on the range for days, and I could use a good night's sleep."

Vaughn ran a hand absently over Asa's dark mane. He sighed deeply. I knew he didn't want to leave his horse, but I knew he'd do it when the time came. Vaughn had never had possessions growing up, and I knew it hurt him to lose the ones that meant something to him. There'd be other horses, though, and Vaughn would get over Asa.

I patted his shoulder gently. "Let's find Asa a good home and get the next train east. We got a job to do."

He smiled slightly. He nodded. "When we get back home, you're buyin' me a new horse. I'm callin' it Asa."

He'd said that before. He always meant it.

Chapter Eight

We caught a train at a little station near Sunspot a few hours later. Quimby and Hazel sold the horses to a young ranch owner who was buying supplies at the local general store while I purchased five tickets. Zeke and Vaughn laid low on the platform. Folks waiting for their trains eyed them warily, but no one bothered us.

"Right," Hazel said grimly as we gathered together on the platform. "I'll board with Zeke."

"What?" he exclaimed indignantly.

We ignored him. "Tess and Quimby will go together."

"Hazel!" I protested. "That ain't appropriate."

"What's the matter, Tess? You afraid of what you might be tempted to do all alone with Bonny Burton in a private—"

"Quimby, you watch your dirty mouth," Vaughn ordered, nudging him just enough to send him skittering a few feet away. Quimby snapped his mouth shut. Vaughn's shoulders slumped almost imperceptibly. "I reckon I'll be on my own then."

I frowned. "Why can't Vaughn and I board together? We've been boarding together forever."

He shook his head, even though his big dark eyes looked a little sad. "Nah, Tess. Even without the others, you and me running around together would draw too much attention, even going northward. I'm better off on my own for all our sakes."

"Yeah, but what if you get into trouble?"

He scoffed. "I can take care of myself. Somethin' happens, I reckon I got one of Hazel's gadgets tucked away somewhere."

I laughed. "Yeah, all right. I know you're a big boy now. You don't need old Tess lookin' after you."

He rolled his eyes, but he glanced sharply at Quimby. "You take care, Quimby. You act like a gentleman now, you hear?"

Quimby chuckled. "Come on now, Vaughn. You know me. I'm always a

104

gentleman."

"You mean you know Tess can kick your ass," Hazel put in.

"You know that's right, Quimby, so you keep your paws to yourself," I told him.

He scoffed. "Yeah, yeah. Whatever you say."

Our train rolled into the station. Zeke and Hazel boarded first. They were already bickering like an old, unhappily married couple. It would be a long few days for them. It would be worse for Vaughn, though. He looked a little melancholy. I wrapped my arms around his neck in a quick hug. He looked surprised, but he patted my back awkwardly. "Thanks, Tess. I reckon it'll be nice have a little peace and quiet, away from Quim and Hazel."

"I'm still here. I can hear you."

We ignored Quimby. "You got those books I gave you?"

"Yeah. Mark Twain and Jules Verne. I reckon I might enjoy a little light reading. You make sure Quimby behaves himself. If he don't, I'll help you bury his body when we get to St. Louis."

"Seriously. Still here."

I laughed. "Thanks, Vaughn. You're the best pal a girl could have. See you tomorrow."

He inclined his head and boarded the train. I glanced at Quimby. He was grinning. I sighed. "Let's just get on with it."

"This is going to be the best trip ever."

"You better behave yourself, Quimby. I have had a rough week. I do not intend to deal with a wily man. I will put you down on your face."

He laughed and wrapped an arm around my shoulders to guide me onto the train. "Sure you will, Tess. Don't worry. I'll be a perfect gentleman. That is, if that's what you want. I reckon after a few hours alone with me, you'll be singin' a different tune."

"Don't flatter yourself. You ain't sweet talkin' me into your bed."

"Don't flatter yourself, Tess. I ain't tryin'."

I snorted with laughter as we ducked into a small, closed compartment. There were two scuffed leather benches that slid together to form a double-sized bed. A dark shade covered the small, square window. There wasn't much else in the compartment. I sighed. It was going to be a long trip.

He grinned at me. "Looks like I won't even have to."

"You watch your mouth or I'll kick you out into the third-class car."

He looked appalled. "You wouldn't."

"Try me."

"Last time I stayed in a third-class car, I think I got the pox."

"You didn't get the damn pox."

"You don't know. I might have had 'em."

"If you did, they didn't look like any pox I ever saw. I'm pretty sure what you got was bit up by fleas."

He considered this. "Yeah. That man who sat next to me did look like he might have been hosting a small community in his beard."

I rolled my eyes and hoisted my saddlebag into the luggage racks above our benches. Outside, I heard the conductor shouting the last boarding call. I dropped gracelessly into the bench and peered out the window. Quimby took the seat across from me. He didn't say anything, even when the train whistled and began to chug slowly out of the station.

I rested my head against the cool glass window. There wasn't much but prairie and small, lonely towns to see outside. I sighed softly in contentment. Camping on the range was nice. I enjoyed the stars overhead and the quiet hum of wildlife, but I was bone weary from the rough living. Even the thinly padded leather seats were a nice change. I closed my eyes, and my head lolled.

When I opened my eyes again, Quimby was kicked back on the bench across from me with his hat over his face. His feet were propped up on the seat beside me. I glanced at him. His arms were tucked tightly around his lean torso. There was the faintest smile on his full, sensual mouth. I watched him sleep for a few minutes. He really was a handsome man when he wasn't smirking or flannel-mouthing.

"I know you're thinking how good-lookin' I am."

And just like that, he was back to be an arrogant pain in the ass.

He tipped his head back and pushed his hat from his face with the tip of his first two fingers. He grinned at me. I felt a slight tinge in my lower belly. I curled my lip. "I was thinkin' no such thing."

His brilliant blue eyes twinkled as though he didn't believe a word of this. "This is a stroke of prodigious luck, ain't it?"

I blinked. Sometimes I was sure Quimby wasn't quite what he seemed. I narrowed my eyes. "What do you mean?"

He smirked. Other times, I was sure he was exactly as he seemed. "Here we are, alone at last. You can't pretend you aren't a little excited about it."

I scowled. "Quimby, if you try anything, I have my gun under this skirt. I will shoot you dead."

His eyes crinkled at the corners as he smiled at me. "You wouldn't shoot me, Tess."

"Try me, Quimby."

He chuckled. "Ah, put your claws away, darlin'. I ain't gonna try anything unless you ask me to. I just want to talk."

"You want to talk?"

"I talk."

"You flannel-mouth."

"Aw, Tess, you know I ain't all sweet talk and flirting."

"Could have fooled me."

"I ain't fooled you at all."

I frowned and looked away from him. "Fine. You want to talk, go right ahead. I ain't stoppin' you."

He lifted an eyebrow. "You think Angel did it? You think he killed that girl and her fiancé?"

I shook my head without hesitation. "No. I think he's all right. He's not bad in a crisis, either."

Quimby nodded thoughtfully. "You reckon he'll still be alive after spendin' the night with Hazel?"

I laughed. "Well, ain't no one able to know for sure 'til morning. They might end up killin' each other by the end of it, but I reckon they'll come to an understanding."

"How about us?"

"Quimby, why you always got to talk in riddles?"

"'Cause you're only pretendin' not to understand me."

I sighed. "Fine. You want to hash this out? I reckon you'd be happier just to leave it alone."

"I reckon I wouldn't. You're the one avoiding the issue."

"I think I've made myself perfectly clear in that regard."

"You think I don't know what you're about, Tess? Why you're fightin' it so hard?"

"'Cause I ain't interested in competing with every saloon girl and five dollar whore in the west!"

He waved his hand dismissively. "You know it ain't really like that. I like to have my fun, but it don't go too far."

I looked at him incredulously. "What about Esther Star?"

He grinned wolfishly. "Esther...well, she's a special case."

I snorted in disgust. "You see what I mean, Quimby?"

His expression was suddenly serious. "It would all be over, Tess. You know that."

I glanced away. "I ain't interested in findin' out."

"Those other women, they ain't really the reason, are they?"

My eyes snapped warily to him. "What do you mean?"

"I think you know what I mean. You don't talk about it much, but I know you still think about him."

I narrowed my eyes. "Don't start on this, Quimby."

"Why? You don't ever talk about it. Maybe now's the time."

"It ain't the time."

"What better time is there? You never told me the truth about Jace. I want to know."

"Why you so interested in him all the sudden?"

"You know why I'm interested. Stop pretendin' to be thick. You gonna tell me, or am I gonna resort to every trick I know to flannel-mouth you into my bed?"

I glared at him. "It wouldn't work."

108

He moved so suddenly, I didn't have a chance to take a breath. His face was inches from mine. His blue eyes glittered. "You sure about that?" he asked. I felt his warm breath against my lips. I leaned away, but he came with me. He drew a finger down the side of my cheek. A curl of heat shot from the top of my head to my toes and back up again to pool in my belly.

I shoved feebly at his chest, but I didn't turn away from him. I exhaled shakily. "Quim..." He leaned back so abruptly, I rocked slightly in my seat. I huffed in irritation. "That ain't appropriate behavior, Quimby."

He grinned. "You should feel lucky I let it go when I did."

"I ain't interested in being another one of your scarlet ladies."

"So you keep sayin'. You gonna tell me about Jace or not?"

I sighed. "There ain't much to tell."

"I don't believe that. You and Vaughn runnin' around together ain't exactly normal southern plantation girl behavior."

"Well, I ain't exactly a normal southern plantation girl."

"Yeah, I think I got that sussed." When I didn't reply, he gave me a dangerous, glittering look. I drew back in my seat as if to escape him, but the compartment was small. It seemed a lot smaller now.

I huffed. "All right, Quimby. If I tell you about Jace, will you leave it alone? I don't want to hear about it anymore."

He considered this with a slight furrow in his brow. "I ain't promisin' anything."

"Then I ain't sayin' anything."

He lifted an eyebrow. "We play it my way, then." He moved as though he intended to come at me again.

I put up a hand to stop him and gave him my coldest glare. "What happened with Jace was nine years ago. It don't even matter now."

"The hell it doesn't."

I scowled at him. "What do you know about it, Quim? You never been in love with anyone in your life."

He laughed. "I've been in love lots of times."

"Yeah, about once a night." I rolled my eyes, but my mouth quivered slightly as he winked at me. "I'm done talking about this."

"You ain't said a thing. Anyway, we're just havin' a laugh. Why's everything got to be so serious with you all the time?"

"It ain't!"

"Yeah, it is. Anytime anyone tries to get close to you for a second, you turn into a porcupine."

"Now that just ain't true at all."

"You gonna tell me what happened or not?"

"It ain't no big secret."

"Then why ain't you ever told me about it?"

"It never came up."

"It's comin' up now."

"Fine. I met Jace when I was eighteen. We were the same age, and we both grew up in Savannah. Our daddies knew each other. Jace's daddy was a newspaperman from the Old States. He'd been running the local rag for a few years, and he attended a lot of parties at the plantation. Anyway, our daddies thought Jace and I ought to get married. Preferably but not necessarily to each other. They thought we'd get along real well." I sighed and crossed my arms over my chest. I frowned out the window. "I didn't want to get married. I thought I was too young. I was popular in town, and I liked the attention."

Quimby scoffed. "You?"

"Yeah, well, I was young once. I haven't always been so serious."

"You would have made quite a debutante."

"You're damn right I did. I don't think Jace was really interested in me at first, but eventually we got to know each other, and we fell in love."

He made a strange noise out of this nose.

I scowled out him. "If you're going to be a jerk, Quimby, I ain't tellin' you the rest."

"I ain't bein' nothin'. I was just sniffin'."

"Whatever. You be polite, or I ain't sharin'."

He snorted slightly and waved a hand. "I'll be a perfect listener. You can put it off as long as you want, but I got time. I'll wait."

"Right. Well, we got married, like our daddies wanted. We had a house in the city, close to our fathers. It was nice. I got to visit Vaughn most days."

"What did Jace think about Vaughn?"

"Jace didn't really understand; he was an only child, and his daddy didn't own any slaves. He didn't have any siblings and didn't know what it was like to have a brother--well, someone like a brother, anyway. He didn't try to stop me visiting him. He knew better." I looked out the window away from him. "He didn't believe in ownin' slaves. When the war came, he took the Union's side. He and his daddy argued with my daddy about it. Jace wanted to go North and fight. I tried to stop him goin', but I couldn't tell him anything when he set his mind to somethin' We fought about it for a few weeks. He wouldn't change his mind, so I left him and moved back in with my daddy. Jace went North to join the fight."

"What happened to him?"

"You know what happened to him. I never spoke to him again after I left our house. He died in Virginia in the battle of Hatcher's Run. I received a telegram a few days after it happened. That was it. That was the end of Jace. The war ended soon after, and you know the rest."

"That why you're still carryin' a torch for him after all these years? You fell out, and you left him and never got to say goodbye?"

I rounded on him with a scowl, but there was genuine compassion on his face. I lifted my eyebrows. "You can't just forget somethin' like that, Quim. Just 'cause we fell out don't mean we didn't still love each other. Even when I left him, I knew he still loved me. I thought we'd reconcile when he came home. But he never did." I took a deep breath. It wasn't something I enjoyed remembering, but I could talk about it these days without getting all emotional.

He frowned slightly. "Yeah, but you can move on."

I lifted my chin. "I have moved on."

"I don't think that's strictly true."

"What do you know about it?"

He sighed. "I know a lot about it actually. And I know a lot about you. We've been runnin' together for four years. I know a lot." I rose abruptly to my feet. He caught my arm. "Where you goin'?" he demanded.

I shook him off. "Goin' to see what Hazel and Angel are doin'. I'm not really sure we can trust them alone."

He scowled at me for a moment, then his expression smoothed and it was like

111

he'd never been serious at all. He perked up. "You think they're up to no good?"

"I reckon our definitions of no good differ slightly."

He chuckled. "I don't know that they do."

"I think I ought to make sure they ain't killed each other yet. Between the two of them, they sure got a lot of weapons."

* * *

Quimby didn't ask any more uncomfortable questions the rest of the way to St. Louis. I reckoned he wished he hadn't done to begin with. I didn't mind. He was actually pleasant company when he wasn't insinuating things and pushing my buttons. I might have even enjoyed spending time with him, if I didn't know what a flannel-mouthed charlatan he could be. I was almost disappointed when the train rolled to a stop in the station in St. Louis.

We waited on the platform with our rucksacks, watching for the others. When Vaughn disembarked with his rucksack slung over his shoulder, I started toward him. Quimby caught my arm. "Tess, where are you going?"

"Leave me alone, Quimby."

"I thought we was layin' low."

I sighed. I knew he was right, but right now I felt like being near my best friend, whose big, solid presence was like a soothing balm. Vaughn was like a big child in many ways, and I knew I was the one thing in his life that had made living it bearable growing up. Nevertheless, I felt like he was the one who had raised me half the time. He'd been forced to grow up so fast and experienced so much hardship I'd never experienced, I felt like he knew more about this life than I ever would.

He caught my eye, and something in his rigid posture seemed to relax. I smiled. He smiled back, and I felt all right again.

We weren't planning to meet up with the others until we reached Boston. I didn't want to stay separated that long, but Angel was sure we'd be better off. I had to admit he probably knew a little more about it that we did. We were the best and toughest bounty hunters in the west, but he was a professional. And, though none of us would admit it to his face, he probably had a bit more sense. We didn't argue. Quimby and I waited for Vaughn to leave the station first. We followed at a distance.

St. Louis was a different world than the west. A faint haze of smoke hung in the air from the chimneys of factories in the industrial districts. The streets teemed with crowds of people bustling to and from their jobs at the factories, from schools or their daily business. It was hard to keep our eyes on Vaughn's broad back. He wasn't the only large black man in the city. In fact, there were an impressive number of black men, women and children moving among the diverse population. No one even paid much attention to Vaughn.

I wondered briefly if he ever thought about moving to a city like this, where he would be free to join others like him and stay put in one place for more than a week or so. Maybe he would pick up the piano or some other instrument and learn to play ragtime. Maybe he could even go to college and become a scholar or invent some really helpful gadget. Things weren't perfect; there were still people--lots of people--who thought folks should be treated differently for the color of their skin, despite what they were worth on the inside. I reckoned he would have a hard road his whole life, but St. Louis had been sympathetic to the Union. There would be a place for Vaughn here.

I wasn't sure I could say the same for me. I liked the frontier. I liked the wilderness and the lawlessness. I liked taking matters into my own hands and being in control of my own destiny. Maybe it was growing up with a closed-minded, overbearing bigot for a father. I liked my freedom. What would I do in a city like St. Louis? I didn't think I was cut out for factory or seamstress work. Folks didn't look so kindly on ladies in men's clothes round here, and they had sheriffs and Marshals and policemen who took care of the criminals on the streets.

Maybe Quimby could teach me to card sharp. I could play cards on the riverboats along the Mississippi with the rich big bugs from town and fleece them for everything they were worth. I smirked slightly at this and glanced over at Quimby. Nah. It wasn't worth inflating his big fat head over. 'Sides, I didn't think it would be a good idea, getting Quimby on one of those boats. I reckoned he'd be thrown overboard in a matter of minutes.

"I reckon I'll be happy to get back to the quiet life," Quimby told me in a low voice. We pushed through a thick crowd leaving the factories and beer breweries. They looked soot-stained and weary. Quimby caught my hand to keep me close to his side. For once, I didn't pull away. I squeezed it tight and pressed up against him. I didn't fancy getting caught up in the throng and carried away.

"Quiet life? You mean hunting outlaws and having shoot outs out back behind saloons with insane clockwork bounty hunters?"

"I reckon it's better than factory work."

I didn't reply. I didn't really feel like admitting I'd been having the same thoughts. Quimby wasn't so bad. Sometimes, he was a lot more like a kindred soul than I wanted to admit. "Yeah. I reckon I'll be happy to get home once we get this job over with."

"You ever think about settlin' down somewhere? Takin' all the money we have stashed and buyin' a ranch or a homestead or somethin'?"

I laughed. "Can you image us runnin' a ranch? You've got some experience with that sort of thing, and I did once work that dude ranch for a week. We wouldn't be so bad. Hazel, though, would probably replace all the horses' and cows' legs with pegs or copper plate them or build an army of clockwork wranglers to tend them. Vaughn would probably be a good foreman."

He looked at me incredulously. "You reckon we'll still be together when we settle down?"

I considered this for a moment. "I hadn't ever really thought about it. I reckon we haven't been apart for three years. It never occurred to me we would be."

"Is that what you want?"

"What do you mean?"

"You want it to be like this forever? The four of us?"

"Why not? It works, don't it?"

"It's kind of nice havin' a new member of the posse. It wouldn't be so bad to get some new blood. I'm thinking an Indian or a Mexican."

"You serious?"

"Why not? I reckon we'd be a force to be reckoned with if we was bilingual."

"I speak Spanish," I said.

"Not very well."

"I know some French, too."

"You know Southern socialite French. That ain't the same."

"I don't think that's a real language," I argued.

"It's a lot like Cajun French only way more pretentious."

"I'm pretty sure you just made that up right now."

"The Pink ain't bad. You think he'd join the posse permanently?"

"You don't want Angel in the posse."

"He keeps Hazel in line. She ain't acted up much since he came."

"I don't think that has much to do with Angel. I think she just ran out of incendiary devices after we went up against Che Chucho. We've been too busy for her to whip up any more."

He considered. "I think you might actually be right about that. Well, all the same. He ain't so bad."

"I like him okay. He's got some sense."

"Too bad he's innocent. If he wasn't, we could probably talk him into joinin' up."

"I reckon havin' a murderer on the team would negatively impact our credibility."

"We ain't got any credibility," Quimby replied. "People are afraid of us."

"In that case, havin' a murderer on the team would probably help."

The airship port was crowded as we approached it. There was a long line waiting at the ticket counter, but Quimby and I didn't pick back up the thread of our conversation as we queued up with the other passengers. I could see Vaughn ahead of us. No one jostled or bothered him, and I thought I saw a slight expression of contentment on his face. Vaughn would like it here. Maybe Quimby was right. Would my posse have to break up one day? I reckoned now wasn't the time to think about it.

I'd traveled by airship before, but I preferred trains. They seemed slightly less like defying God and the laws of nature. Nevertheless, they were quicker, and what we needed right now was to make time. I sat beside Quimby on a comfortable padded bench, facing away from the dome windows. I didn't feel much like peering down at the ground below; it reminded me exactly how far we would fall if the whole thing went crashing down. Quimby didn't seem to mind the heights. There was a small smile on his handsome face as he watched the clouds drift serenely by.

Zeke and Hazel had boarded a little while after us. They sat several seats away. They didn't acknowledge us. Their heads were bent together, and they seemed to be talking pretty earnestly. They might have been arguing, or they might have actually discovered some common ground. Either way, neither of them looked grievously injured or as though they'd sustained severe burns.

Vaughn was leaned back in his bench with his head buried in one of the novels I'd bought him at the general store in Sunspot. He'd learned to read when we were kids, when he'd been too little to pull the plow or work the tobacco fields. He'd been a house slave then, and he'd been able to sit in on some of my lessons with the sweet English governess my father had hired to mind me when her husband had passed away and left her alone in a strange country. She hadn't seemed to mind that Vaughn was meant to be polishing silver or cleaning floors, not learning reading and arithmetic. Since then, he'd loved to read, and I bought him a book every time we stopped in a civilized town.

The trip was long, but it was pleasant. I dozed a little, and Quimby told me tales of his days in the rodeo and sharping cards on a riverboat in Shreveport with some French buccaneers. I wasn't sure how much of what he told me was true, but I didn't mind. He was a talented storyteller, and I liked a little flash and pizzazz in a story. He sure knew how to keep up the drama, old Quimby Burton.

I should have known it was all too good not to come crashing down.

When the airship alighted with a gentle jerk in Boston, I felt a little thrill of excitement. I'd never been to the Old States, and I'd heard a lot of folks talk about how sophisticated they were, but I didn't care about that. I hadn't seen the ocean in almost a decade, and I couldn't wait to see that dark expanse of blue water again. It reminded me how big the world really was. Well, the barren Arizona desert did that, too, but in that case it reminded me how thirsty I was going to be in about an hour or so and how damn hot buckskin really was.

I gripped Quimby's hand almost unconsciously. He looked at me in surprise, but something in my expression must have silenced him. He smiled at me. I smiled back. I felt like we'd outrun a mob. I reckoned there wouldn't be any bounty hunters searching for old Tess Mercury and her posse in Boston. They ain't ever even heard of us here.

I was wrong about that.

The airship port was right on Boston Harbor. I could see the stretch of Massachusetts Bay in the distance. If I hadn't been looking past them, I might have seen the three large, thickly muscled men in grey suits stride up to Quimby and me. They blocked our path and flashed huge, sparkling silver badges.

"Tess Mercury? Quimby Burton? U.S. Marshals. You are under arrest."

Chapter Nine

Aw hell.

Quimby dropped my hand. I felt his muscles tense, and he crouched low as though preparing for a fight. We'd been in a lot of fights, but I reckoned the Marshals would not go down like a drunken, half-blind old sharp shooter in a saloon. I gripped Quimby's arm tightly. He didn't relax, but he seemed to understand. He didn't spring at the Marshals, anyway. Nearby, I saw two more of the lawmen approaching Vaughn. He met my gaze quickly before glancing away. He didn't put up a fight.

Seconds later, I realized why.

"Where's the other one?" a tall, grey-haired Marshal with deep wrinkles in a still handsome face barked.

I saw Zeke and Hazel slipping away through the crowd like the devil was on their heels. A few other Marshals were looking anxiously around for them. They seemed tense. I reckoned someone had told them about Hazel. She could bring down a crowd or whip them up into a riot in no time.

She did no such thing. She was gone. I cast a sidelong glance at Quimby. By the twinkle in his blue eyes, I knew he'd seen them, too. I didn't smile, but I felt a whole lot better about the cuffs clicking around our wrists and the covered wagon waiting to transport us to the local jail outside the gates of the airship port.

"Where's Lighting Hazel?" the steely-haired Marshal demanded.

I lifted my chin. "I don't know who you're talkin' about."

He narrowed his eyes at me. "She's in your posse, Mercury. You know. You don't run around without your posse. Where is she?"

"I don't know nothin' about no Lightning Hazel."

"You think you're cute, but you ain't."

"She's a little cute," Quimby put in, smiling serenely at the Marshals.

I rolled my eyes. "You boys goin' to take us in or just talk about it?"

"Fine," the steely-haired Marshal said. He caught my arm and shoved me toward the covered wagon. Beside me, the other Marshals guided Quimby and

Vaughn to join me. We didn't talk to each other as we sat peering at each other in the back of the wagon between three of the bigger lawmen. We didn't need to. We'd all been in this place before, and we could take care of ourselves, 'specially when the charges against us were trumped up and Hazel Harley was loose on the streets with nothing in mind but our escape.

We'd be just fine.

The men in the cage whooped and hollered at me as the Marshals led us through the holding cell corridor, but I ignored them. Behind me, Vaughn and Quimby glared at the wily prisoners as they were shoved inside the cage with them. The prisoners shut their mouths pretty quick. Even without their guns, my boys were pretty tough. No Old States drunks were going to get the drop on them, no sir.

The women's cell was almost empty. There were three women inside. They were haggard looking, as though they needed a good meal and a couple of hot tin baths. They lounged around the concrete room with sour expressions, as though they were beginning to integrate into a part of the scenery. They looked at me in interest as the Marshal shoved me inside with them.

When the Marshals were gone, my three cellmates rose to greet me. They looked all right, for jailbirds. I lifted my chin. "I'm Tess. What are you all in for?"

A short, thin woman with crooked features grinned at me. Several of her teeth were missing. "I'm Clara. Rita here and I are in for...well, for entertainin' men in ways that makes folks uncomfortable around here."

I laughed. The tall, sturdy woman with proud, angled features lifted her chin and gazed at me as though daring me to talk back to her. I didn't intend to. There was no sense starting a brawl in a tiny cell with three other women, even if I was pretty sure I would come out of it all right. "Elaine Moore. I was arrested for poisoning my husband," she told me in a gentle, cultured voice I found peculiarly soothing despite the words.

"Yeah? You do it?"

"We all did it," Rita replied. She was a plump woman with curly brown hair. Her low cut green bodice was stained with jail grime and what might have been cheap red wine. She might have been pretty a long time ago, but her thick makeup was streaked across her cheeks and she looked like she'd been living rough.

"What about you?" Clara demanded with narrowed eyes. "What'd you do?"

I lifted my shoulders. "No idea. I think I was set up," I admitted. When they looked at me mistrustfully, I grinned sheepishly at them. "Well, I done a lot. I suppose it don't much matter what they got me for, huh?"

The girls seemed to like this. They snickered. "You aren't from around here, huh?" Rita asked.

I shook my head. "Nah. Georgia. But I've been livin' out west."

They lifted their eyebrows. I didn't mention I'd been hunting bounties on the frontier. I doubted it would lead to much camaraderie among my fellow jailbirds. "You come in with the handsome one and the slave?" Clara said. Her cheeks pinked slightly.

"He's a freed slave. He ain't a slave anymore. You know about them?"

"We saw you from the street as you came in," Elaine explained. She tilted her head to indicate the tiny, dirt-smudged window above one of the rickety cots against the grimy stone wall. I didn't bother to climb up and peer out. I knew what the street looked like.

"Were they set up, too?" Clara's crooked mouth quivered a little into a knowing smile.

I laughed. "Yeah, I reckon they were. Same charges as me. I reckon we'll be out of here soon enough, when we sort it all out."

They glanced between each other in amusement. "Well, good luck with that, Tess," Rita said. Her yellow eyes glittered.

I lifted my eyebrows. "Why? How long you been here?"

Elaine sighed and dropped dramatically onto a cot. "Ages. I've lost track."

I looked at Rita and Clara. "You, too?"

They nodded. I frowned. "Days?"

"Maybe more."

"That ain't right. Ain't you gone to trial or faced a judge or anything?"

"No. Not yet, anyway," Elaine replied.

"I think they about forgot us back here," Clara added.

"You ought to tell somebody. I don't know all that much about the law, but I reckon they ain't allowed to do that," I said.

"You got a lot of heart, Tess, but you ain't got much sense. Who are we gonna tell?" Rita asked. "We haven't got a way to speak to anyone but the Marshals."

"They don't listen?"

"'Course not. They're too busy running around after folks like you."

I lifted an eyebrow. "What do you mean, folks like me?"

"I heard them talkin'. Said you all were wanted by the top brass."

"Top brass? Who's that?"

"We don't know. Just someone who we've heard them mention. Must be the supervisors or something."

"Hm. You seen any of the people they said were wanted by the top brass, 'side from us?"

"Yeah," Clara replied. "There was a guy they brought in. They brought him into the holding cell, and someone came and got him a couple hours later. We don't know where they took him. Maybe they let him go. Maybe they took him somewhere else."

I frowned. "I don't much like the sound of that." I sat down on one of the thin, flea-bitten cots along the wall. "You all know anything about Sterling Rush?"

They looked at me in complete surprise. "Sterling Rush? The businessman?" Clara asked.

"Yeah. Him."

"What's he got to do with anything?"

Maybe a lot more than they thought. I shrugged. "Nothing. I was just wonderin' if you know who he is, is all."

"Sure. Everyone knows who he is. He's the richest man in Boston. Probably New England."

"You know what he does?"

Clara and Rita shrugged. "He owns some sort of technology company."

Elaine rolled her eyes and tossed her head. "Rush AI. They are a technology firm. I hear they have been moving into weapons production. Don't you ladybirds ever read newspapers?"

"I don't know what that means," Rita said, scowling, "but I suspect it isn't nice, Elaine."

"It sounds nice," Clara offered.

"You hear anything else about Rush?" I asked Elaine. She seemed to be the

120

only one of the jailbirds with any damn sense.

"Just the usual things. The papers seem to think the good folks of Boston appreciate hearing where he spends his evenings and with whom."

"That passes as news these days?"

"I suppose there are some people who are interested in such things. Celebrity seems to attract more attention these days than issues of the day or significant social paradigm shifts that affect the state of the nation."

I looked at Elaine incredulously. "What did you say you were in for, Elaine?"

Her lips quivered slightly. "Murdering my husband."

"And why'd you do that?"

"He was an abusive, ignorant lay-about."

"Then why did you marry him to begin with?"

"He was very handsome once."

I laughed. "Elaine. How come you got caught?"

She sighed. The other two didn't seem all that interested in this conversation; I reckoned they'd heard it all before. If they'd been in there together for days on end, they probably knew a lot about each other by now. "I purchased the arsenic from the local apothecary. I should have known she would tell the police. She always did want Richard for her own."

I lifted an eyebrow. "I reckon that was a little irresponsible."

"Yes, I suppose it was." She considered. "A behavioral doctor might suggest I wanted to get caught."

"I don't believe any of that behavioral trash." I'd seen enough men and women running from the law. None of them wanted to get caught. "No wants to get caught or they'd just turn themselves in."

She smiled. "Well, perhaps I might have been more discreet. I did go to the pub after I laced his soup with arsenic and buy everyone a round of drinks in celebration."

I laughed. "I like you Elaine, even though I reckon you might be a little crazy."

She lifted a shoulder. "Yes, I might be. Most women who murder their husbands with poison are a little crazy."

"Not as crazy as the ones who bash them over the heads with things."

"You're rather crass, aren't you, Tess?"

I snorted. "Yeah, I might be a little. So what have you read about Sterling Rush?"

"Mostly human interest pieces. He contributes to many charities and foundations in town and around the state. He is influential in Washington. He takes many trips there."

"To spend time with Congressman Caine?"

Elaine narrowed her eyes, but I reckoned she didn't really care what I had to do with any of it. She probably just enjoyed someone new to talk to. "You know a bit more about what's going on in Boston than you let on, don't you, Tess?"

I shrugged. "I just hear things."

"You heard about the rumors in the papers about the Department of Scientific Progress and Questionable Developments and the faulty weapons?"

"Maybe a bit. What have you heard about it?"

"Just what I've read. One of the journalists at the Daily had a confidential source, who admitted there might have been a payoff, but Rush had the whole thing swept under the rug. He's got friends all over."

"Like in the top brass?"

Her eyebrows travelled up into her hairline. "You catch on pretty quick, Tess."

"Yeah, I do. Anything I might be missing?"

Elaine shook her head. "How would I know that? I just read the papers; hear things in the wind. I don't really know anything."

"How come you're so interested in all this?" Clara asked, narrowing her eyes at me. "You just got to town, right?"

"Sure. I just been hearin' things, is all."

"Well, perhaps you ought to pretend you haven't heard them," Elaine told me in a low voice. "It's safer if you do."

I lifted my eyebrows. "Safer for who?"

"For everyone."

"So you do know more about it."

122

She shook her head. "Not much. Like I said, just things I've heard."

"Like?"

"Like some people who talk about him disappear. People who tell the truth go missing. No one's ever proved anything."

"I hear he owns the Marshals and the local law."

Elaine glanced around. "Who are you really?"

"I reckon you're all better off not knowin'."

"You think he's the one who set you up?"

"If he was, would you really want to know about it?"

"No."

"Besides, I ain't got nothin' to do with him. I ain't ever even seen him before. He sure don't know who I am."

"You better hope that's true," Elaine said.

"A lot of ladies pass through here asking about Rush," Rita said out of nowhere. Her expression was a little glazed, as though she'd been trying to follow the conversation and failed miserably.

I looked at her in surprise. "Do they?"

"Sure. He's single you know. A lot of ladies like you come around throwing themselves at him."

"Ladies like me?" I demanded, outraged.

"Ladies who want a leg up in life."

"What makes you think I want that?"

Rita smiled. "You look like the kind of lady who could use a man, Tess. You've got looks. If I had your looks, I would bring in more than a few bucks a week. But you look like you got some problems only a man can solve."

I snorted in disgust. "That's crazy. I don't need no man."

"It's ladies like you think you don't that do the most," Clara told me knowingly.

I rolled my eyes. "Assuming a lady did need a man, why would she choose a man who people suspect is responsible for disappearances and government payoffs?"

Rita and Clara snorted with laughter. "What do we care about stuff like that? He's rich, single and good-looking."

"That's just plumb crazy."

"Well, most ladies want that sort of man. You saying you don't?" Clara said.

"I'm sayin' I ain't here to consider how eligible he might be."

"You ought to. You cleaned up a bit, you might stand a chance."

I glanced at Elaine as though she might have some sense to contribute to the conversation, but she didn't seem to be paying any attention anymore. Her head was cocked to the side as though she was listening to something. I frowned and listened. There was someone coming—a few someone's, actually, by the sound of the sharp, heavy footsteps on the concrete outside our cell. I shot to my feet.

Hazel's curly blonde hair preceded her. She poked her head around the corner and grinned at me through the bars. "Hey, Tess!"

"What's goin' on?" I demanded.

"I'm gettin' you out of here!"

"Yeah? They're droppin' the charges?"

"Nah. But we pay a couple fines, and we're back on the streets. "

One of the young, angular Marshals from the airship port stepped past her to unlock the doors. My three cellmates moved as though driven by a single, senseless consciousness toward him. "Just her," he barked at them. "You get back, you harpies!"

They made a collective hissing noise at him. They'd completely transformed. They'd only been in here a few days? Dang. I slipped cautiously past them and out into the corridor with Hazel. I took a deep breath. The air was still fetid and stifling, but it smelled a little sweeter now that I wasn't behind the bars with the harpies.

"When are we getting out of here?" Clara demanded, leaning against the bars with desperation in her expression.

The Marshal glared at her. "It ain't for me to say."

"I want to speak with my lawyer," Elaine added.

"You'll have your chance."

"When?"

"It ain't for me to say."

"The lawyers aren't coming," Rita sighed.

I turned back to them. "I'll tell someone about this, girls," I promised them, ignoring the sharp look from the Marshal.

"Thanks, Tess, but I don't think it will do much good," Elaine replied with a small smile.

"It was nice meeting you. Thanks for the company."

"Bye, Tess."

I was relieved to be clear of them. I would keep my word, but I reckoned those three might be better behind bars and off the streets. They didn't seem quite right in the pertinent places. The Marshal looked like he would be happy to see the back of us, too. He guided us swiftly through the halls. The men in the holding cell at the end of the corridor didn't whoop or holler. They all looked away as though the sight of us might blind them. I smiled. I was pretty sure Vaughn had something to do with that.

He and Quimby weren't in the cage anymore, though. They were waiting in the lobby for Hazel and me. When I emerged, they both looked a little relieved as though they expected I might not come out in one piece. I reckon there are a lot of rumors about what women get up to when they're locked away in a cell together for a few hours, but they're mostly disgusting fantasies thought up by imaginative men.

"So who have we got to thank for this?" I asked suspiciously. "I don't reckon they just let Hazel waltz in here waving cash, and our friend certainly didn't pull any strings."

"That does usually work," Hazel said thoughtfully. "But this time we got ourselves a new friend."

"What are you talkin' about?

Vaughn stepped aside to reveal a tall man in a black suit. The man tipped his hat to the lady at the reception desk. "That's it then?"

"Yes, sir. You have a nice day. "

He tucked his wallet into an inside pocket of his jacket as he turned to face us. When he did, my stomach sank right into my knees. He looked exactly the same as the last time I'd seen him. His dark hair fell in slight waves around his high, sculpted cheekbones. His eyes were a clear, startling green. There was something different in their expression now. He'd seen war and death and pain since the last time I'd seen him. His eyes were alert, intelligent and so alive, they seemed to reflect every moment of the ten years we'd been apart. His mouth dropped open in surprise as he caught my gaze.

"Tess?"

My posse looked between us in surprise. "You two know each other?" Quimby demanded.

I looked at Vaughn. "Did you know about this?"

He looked at me incredulously. "You think I know about this?"

"How did you not see him?"

"He just turned around."

"Is someone gonna explain what's going on here?" Hazel demanded. "You know this guy?"

"Yeah," the man in the suit answered for me. "I'm Jason Holt."

I sighed and looked grimly at my posse. "He's my husband."

Chapter Ten

"Your husband?" Quimby repeated. He looked as though the earth had just moved out from under him.

I ignored him. I looked at Jace. "I thought you were dead."

"Well, I'm not."

"Yeah, I can see that."

Jace strode toward me so suddenly, I took a step back, and Vaughn tensed beside me. He didn't try to stop Jace, though. "What happened to you?" Jace asked in a low voice.

I opened my mouth then snapped it shut. My cheeks flushed slightly. I frowned at him. "I got a life now, Jace. It don't got nothing to do with you."

His high, smooth brow furrowed. "You don't get to decide what does and doesn't have something to do with me. I'm still your husband."

"Yeah? Well, where you been all these years, then?"

He lifted his eyebrows. "I've been here. In Boston."

"You—really?"

"Sure. My father came here during the war. I came after. You're the one who disappeared, not me."

I stared at him for several moments. There was something different about him, sure enough. He looked at me as though he didn't know who I was or what he was looking at. He looked at me as though he didn't know if he wanted to. I wished I'd taken more care with my appearance that day. At least I wasn't wearing chaps and a John B. "All right. Yeah, I disappeared, but I thought you were dead. They told me you were dead."

"Nathan didn't tell me."

"Yeah, there's a lot my daddy didn't tell you, I reckon. I ain't talked to him in five years."

Jace frowned. "Hey," the Marshal said, scowling. "This is nice and everything, but do you mind taking it out of my station? I got a jail to run here. This is not the place for this."

Jace and I glanced at each other. Hazel caught my arm. Her touch was unexpectedly gentle. "Come on. We got a place we can talk this over."

I wasn't so sure I wanted to talk anything over at all. I felt like Hazel had dropped one of her little brass grenades in my brain and scrambled it all up. Jace looked like he felt about the same way, but there was a steely, determined glint in his green eyes that I had seen before. He wasn't going to let this go, not any time soon. I was in for a world of explanations and awkward moments.

He followed Hazel and me outside. He didn't wait to see if Vaughn and Quimby followed. They did, and I was thankful they both seemed too surprised to make any sly comments about my situation. I reckoned they might be thinking them up now. It had sprung on us without much warning or chance to deliver any witty one-liners.

Jace hailed a carriage on the street. He knew where we were going. He called out to the carriage driver to stop in front of a small, quaint colonial hotel near the Bay. There weren't any bellhops or valets to tend to us, but it was a much finer establishment than any of us were used to. There was a lobby rather than a rowdy saloon, and there weren't any whores wandering around waiting to be invited up to the rooms.

Not to mention, it was clean. I had almost forgotten what it was like to be really clean after spending five years in the dust and dirt of the frontier. The stairs and corridors of the freshly painted, gilded walls and rich, royal blue carpets under our feet sparkled from the constant attention. I felt shabby and soiled in comparison, as though I might track in the grime from the range. Confronting the realization my dead husband was actually alive could wait until after a long, hot bath. I reckoned I'd earned it.

It would have to wait. We were silent as we climbed a winding staircase with a glittering gold banister toward the third floor. Hazel paused in front of room 315 and jammed a skeleton key into the lock. I hadn't stayed in such a nice room since I'd left my daddy's plantation. It had a low ceiling from which hung a small crystal chandelier. Two twin beds filled the center of the room. They each had rich gold and blue coverings and little night tables with pitchers of water, glasses and an oil lantern for late night reading. The art on the walls was tasteful and serene, depicting landscapes and still lives in muted tones. I didn't care about any of that. It had its own washroom.

Zeke sprawled morosely in a chair in the corner of the room. When the door banged open, he shot up to meet us. He glanced between us for a moment. Then he frowned. "What is it? What's happened?"

"Things just got real interesting," Hazel said in a low voice. She dropped down on the edge of one of the beds. "You got that whiskey we brought from Fortune City?"

"Yeah. Sure."

"I reckon now's a good time to bring that out."

Zeke didn't ask any questions. He seemed to know when to keep his mouth shut. He rummaged in his rucksack and drew out the bottle of homemade whiskey one of Hazel's friends had brewed up for the Silver Festival. He poured us each a nip in our tin cups. He handed Jace one of the sparkling clear glasses from the nightstand beside Hazel's bed.

We didn't make a toast or drink to anything. We all tossed back the contents of our glasses. The silence was awkward and tense. I avoided Jace's gaze, but I felt his eyes on me like a lead weight in my stomach. The whiskey burned like wildfire down my gullet. I held out my mug to Zeke for another shot. He blinked at me in surprise, but he poured it.

Finally, I glanced at Jace. I couldn't read the expression in his eyes, but they were electric. I was relieved that, for the moment, there were more important matters to be hashing out than our marriage. He glanced away from me to peer at the others. "All right, so is someone going to explain to me what's going on? Why I'm helping a bunch of fugitives?"

He seemed remarkably calm, under the circumstances, but, then, he wasn't ever one to get riled up unless it came to me. I reckoned it was only a matter of time before the dam broke.

"'Cause you're married to one," Hazel replied with a tiny frown on her brows.

Zeke lifted an eyebrow. "What?"

"Yeah. It turns out Jace is Tess' long lost husband."

Zeke blinked and looked between us. I felt my cheeks heat. "Is this going to be a problem?" he asked.

"No," Jace and I replied together. I met his eyes for a split second before glancing back at Zeke.

"Right. Well, glossing over that ridiculous coincidence, I suppose you know who I am, Jace?"

"Hazel explained a little. I know who you are, Angel."

"Zeke." He sighed. "Well, I reckon I ought to tell you I'm innocent."

Jace sat heavily on one of the small, polished desk chairs beside Zeke. I was impressed he kept his cool. He didn't even scoff. "Okay. I'm listening."

"I was the Pinkerton Silas Ratcliff hired to look into Rebecca Palmer's disappearance," Zeke began. I could sense we were settling in for a long story. We'd heard most of it before. I leaned back on the headboard beside Hazel. Her muscles were tense, and I thought maybe she pulled away a little when I leaned against her. Maybe it was just my imagination; she relaxed against my arm.

"Yeah, I know." Jace's even, patrician features constricted into a pained expression. He looked sad.

"She was informing on Rush to you, is that right?" Zeke frowned at him.

Jace sighed deeply. "Yes. It's my fault she disappeared. I never wanted that to happen. If I'd known that would happen, I wouldn't have approached her." He looked genuinely aggrieved. I felt dreadful bad for him, but I didn't reach over to comfort him.

"Well, it's too late for that now," Quimby said darkly. I looked at him in surprise. He was scowling at Jace. "One person is dead now and the other is missing because you wanted a story."

We all looked at him in surprise. "Hey!" I said, scowling at Quimby. "It ain't his fault this happened. He didn't do it."

"You're defending him?" Quimby demanded. His blue eyes flashed angrily.

"Yeah. You're attackin' him for no reason."

"Not no reason," Quimby muttered, but Vaughn glanced at him sharply.

"We ain't gonna point fingers here," Vaughn said. "That's not what we're here to do."

"Jace, what did Becky tell you about Rush?"

He hesitated. He didn't meet my eyes.

I narrowed my eyes. "Whatever it is, she's missing now. She must have told you something. What was it?"

He sighed. "Yeah. She told me something."

Zeke sat forward. "What was it?"

"I was talking to a couple of the officials from the Department of Scientific Progress and Questionable Developments. They told me about the defects in the handheld directed energy weapons Rush AI has been developing for the last few years. According to them, Rush had the negative results of the inspection hushed up. My informants had all been fired when they threatened to go public with the results. Some of them went to the Marshals about it, but it didn't do any good. They didn't have anything they could arrest Rush for, and even if they did, most of the Marshals in town are in Rush's pocket."

"So they talked to you instead," Zeke said.

"Yes."

"Okay."

"What's wrong with the guns?" Hazel asked keenly.

Jace frowned. "What's wrong with them is that they blow off people's hands. I've seen a few of Rush's R&D guys."

"Yeah, we heard about their replacements," I told him. "They as horrible as they sound?"

He nodded grimly. "Worse."

"I reckon I wouldn't mind having a hook for a hand for a little while," Hazel said. Her dark eyes were gleaming. I had come to associate that look with trouble.

"Now, Hazel, you wouldn't be able to play the piano," I reminded her.

She considered this for a long moment. "Maybe only for a couple days, then."

"Just don't go shootin' off your hand anytime soon," I told her sternly.

"Just don't go firing one of Rush's guns," Jace suggested gravely.

"Did you try to talk to any of the R&D guys?" Vaughn asked.

Jace glanced at him. "Of course I did. They were the first ones I went to. I reckoned they would be eager to out Rush, but they all insist the replacements were part of a voluntary lab experiment."

"They volunteered to have their hands cut off and replaced with mechanical ones?"

"Some people would," I remarked.

"Anyway, it didn't get me anywhere."

"We talked to Patrick Granger, one of the government guys who was run out of town," Zeke told him. "He said some of the people who talked to you disappeared, too."

Jace sighed. "Yeah. They did. A few of them went missing. I never heard from them again."

"And you still approached Becky?"

"Well, I don't know what happened to the department guys," Jace said defensively. "They might have just moved away like Granger."

"All right, all right, everyone just leave Jace alone," I ordered. "This ain't his fault."

"You're just sayin' that 'cause he's your husband," Hazel said darkly.

"No, I ain't."

"She's right," Zeke put in, and I glanced at him gratefully. "This isn't Jace's fault."

"Thanks, Zeke," Jace said, but his expression was pinched. I suspected he was feeling guilty all the same. "Once I lost my source, I went looking for another. Becky seemed like a nice girl. She worked closely with Rush. I met with her one day during her lunch hour."

"Met with her?" I asked suspiciously.

"I approached her. I talked to her, felt out her position toward Rush. I told her if she ever felt uncomfortable with her employer to talk to me. I didn't pressure her to do anything."

"But she did?"

"Yes. She did. She had been hearing talk around the office about the faulty guns. She thought Rush was covering something up."

"So what did she tell you?" Zeke repeated. Jace's eyes slid away. Zeke frowned. "It must be big. What is it?"

Jace looked slightly ashamed. "I'm not sure what it is, to tell you the truth," he answered finally.

"What do you mean?"

He sighed. "I've been trying to decipher it. The night before she disappeared, she stayed late in the office. She was looking for some positive proof we could print and use to expose Rush once and for all; some kind of document or ledger proving Rush was paying off the Department, amongst other people."

"Okay. But what'd she find?" Zeke persisted. His expression never changed; he looked as serene as ever, but his translucent eyes glinted behind his round glasses.

"No documents."

"Rush isn't that stupid or careless. He wouldn't keep evidence of his crimes around for an innocent secretary to find."

Jace ignored this. "Becky pulled a couple messages from the telegraph in his office."

"What messages?"

I watched Jace in interest. He drew a crumpled piece of paper from the pocket of his jacket. It looked as though he'd spent many hours studying the tight, even scrawl. He handed the paper to Zeke. For a moment, the Pink stared at them.

"Well?" Hazel demanded. "What do they say?"

Zeke sighed deeply. "The first one is: EWNY506."

"EWN--what? What the hell?"

"The second is: DBVA525." Zeke looked at her archly. "You got any ideas, Hazel?"

She scowled. "I reckon that don't mean a thing. It's nonsense."

"It ain't nonsense," I put in. "If it were nonsense, why would someone bother to send it in the first place? It somethin' to somebody."

"I just don't know what it is," Jace said regretfully. "When she brought it to me, she told me Rush had caught her snooping around the office after hours. She told him she'd been looking for some reports she needed to correct. Rush must not have believed her. She was scared." He sighed and pushed his dark, wavy hair back from his smooth forehead. I felt a peculiar swooping in the pit of my belly. I ignored it. "I should have warned her or taken her away somewhere right then. If I had any idea what would happen..."

"It's no one's fault but Rush's," Zeke said firmly.

"Yes, well, she was a sweet girl."

"And Silas was a good kid, but I'm not blaming myself for his death because he was killed to frame me up."

"Is that why he was killed?" Jace said, frowning.

"I think so. He didn't know anything about Becky informing to you. He knew she was talking to someone, but she didn't tell him anything. She must have thought it was too dangerous."

"Okay," I said, sipping on my whiskey as though I thought it might help all this make a little more sense. "We got Becky informin' to Jace and we got Silas who hired Zeke to find out what happened to her when she went missin'."

"And they're both dead," Hazel put in, frowning.

"We aren't sure Becky's dead, but it's pretty likely," Zeke said.

"Let's assume for the sake of the case that she is. So who killed them?"

We looked at her incredulously. "Hazel, if we knew that, we wouldn't be here, would we?" Zeke said in a remarkably gentle voice.

"Right, so let's get on with findin' out who it was," she said impatiently.

I smiled slightly. "Sometimes you got to talk before you shoot, Hazel. It ain't all bar brawls and shoot outs. The rest of it's important, too." I glanced at Jace. "I saw Congressman Caine at the Governor's Mansion in Colorado Springs."

His brow furrowed deeply. "What were you doing in a brothel in Colorado?"

"What do you know about it?" Quimby asked sharply.

Jace scoffed. "Everyone knows about it."

"We were diggin' up information about Angel. But I reckon we learned more than that," I told him. "Caine was meetin' with Congressman Lockley from Colorado. I think I saw Caine pay Lockley off for his vote on a new bill Rush is pushing for in Congress."

He lifted his eyebrows in surprise. "Do you have any proof of this, Tess?"

I shook my head. "No. Nothing but what I saw and heard."

He considered this. "That means Rush is trying to push through the bill."

"What's it say?"

"Caine's proposed a law that requires all research and development companies to be vetted by the Department of Scientific Progress and Questionable Developments."

I thought about this. "So, Rush is trying to buy up the agency and put everyone else out of business?"

"Sounds about right."

"And he's got the Congressman traveling around the country, payin' folks off to vote for it."

"I sure wish you had some evidence of that," Jace said. His eyes glittered.

134

I frowned. "Hey, I ain't one of your informants, Jace. I don't work for you. Right now we work for Angel. We ain't interested in pay offs and legislature. We're interested in who framed him up."

Jace frowned at me, but he nodded. "Right. Sorry."

"Can we focus on who's responsible for all this? If it ain't Rush directly, he must have someone else doing his dirty work."

"Yes," Zeke put in calmly. "The Pinkerton."

Jace looked at him in surprise. "A Pinkerton?"

Zeke looked at Jace. "I think that's why I was framed up. I got too close to figuring out who was really responsible for all this. Becky received a telegram the night she disappeared. It was from you."

Jace blinked in shock. "What? I didn't send her a telegram."

Zeke inclined his head. "I figured that out already."

"It was from me? Are you sure?"

"It was from Horace Greeley."

Jace stiffened. "That was our code name for each other. But I didn't send any telegram. What did it say?"

"It was a message to meet Horace Greely at a particular address at 11pm. The address turned out to be an empty warehouse in the industrial district," Zeke explained.

"She knew Rush had caught her snoopin' on him, and she still went to an abandoned warehouse?" I put in.

"I reckon she didn't know it was a set up," Zeke told her. "Anyway, she obviously trusted Jace or she wouldn't have gone. She wasn't stupid."

"So how did you come to the conclusion that a Pink is involved?" Jace asked. "Why didn't you simply think it was me?"

"I found the telegram in her fireplace. I searched her apartment after Silas hired me. The message had been totally destroyed, but I figured it must have come to the apartment office. I checked the messages that night on the telegraph and from where they'd been sent. It didn't come from you or the *Daily* office. It came from the telegraph at the Pinkertons duty station."

I considered this and turned to Jace. "Where did Rush send those messages Becky pulled off his telegraph?" I asked him.

He shook his head. "She didn't get a chance to find out. She barely got the messages jotted down before Rush walked in on her."

"Damn."

"Indeed, I believe they would be infinitely simpler to decipher if we knew to whom they were directed. At least we could place them in context."

"Zeke, any idea who would send a message to Becky using Jace's code name to lure her out and kill her?" Hazel asked impatiently. I wasn't sure what was eating her, but she was unusually short-tempered. She didn't usually mind the buildup.

He shook his head. "I've already told you I have not. It could have been anyone in the office. "

"Other than the Pinkertons, who uses the office?" Jace asked.

"No one. I didn't know whom I could trust. I've got a friend who's a dispatcher there. He's a good guy. I was able to meet with him right before I went on the run. He's trying to dig up who was on the duty roster that night and who might have been lurking around the office. We might be able to eliminate suspects and determine who had access to the telegraph that night."

"Have you talked to him?"

Zeke looked at him blandly. "Of course I haven't. I've been in hiding. I can't exactly walk into Pink headquarters and start asking questions, can I?"

I snorted. Jace frowned at me. "I reckon not," he said.

"It sounds like your boy is the closest thing we have to a lead right now," I said. "So how are we going to find out what he's got?"

"Someone has to meet with him."

"I'll do it," Jace said immediately.

"No," Zeke replied. "Not you. If you start meeting with my contacts in the Pinks, they'll know something is going on. You'll have to steer clear of him."

"Made quite a name for yourself, haven't you, Jace?" I said. He looked at me sharply.

"Me? What about you, Tess Mercury?" I bristled a little, but it wasn't the time for this conversation. Jace turned back to Zeke. "I understand your position, but I have a contact in the Pinkertons. He might be able to help."

Zeke frowned. "Who is it?"

"Lafayette Jackson."

The Pinkerton nodded thoughtfully. "I know Lafe. He's a good man and a good investigator. All the same, we can't be sure who to trust in there. Anyone could be involved; they're all good men and good investigators."

Jace considered this. He looked a little put out. Maybe he was feeling a little irritated that Zeke didn't seem to trust his judgment of his friend. Maybe he was just still feeling guilty over Becky. All right. He was probably put out with me most of all. "I could talk to him; see if I can get a feeling of what he knows about all this, if anything."

"Why?" Hazel demanded. "You heard Zeke. What good will it do if you can't even trust him?"

"I trust him," Jace told her, frowning a little.

"It could be too dangerous," I added, feeling a little guilty about it.

He glanced at me as though I'd just stabbed him in the back. "But it could dredge up some leads."

Zeke sighed. "All right, but be careful what you say. He may be your friend, but he's still a Pinkerton. He's obligated to track me down and bring me in if he gets wind of where I am."

Jace nodded. We all turned to stare at him for several long moments. Finally, he glanced back at us warily. "What?"

"Can we trust you not to go to the authorities?" Vaughn asked in his honeyed voice. It was what we were all thinking.

Jace looked offended. "I'm not a bounty hunter. I'm a journalist, and if all this is true, this could be the story that makes my career. I intend to see what you all come up with. I won't tell anyone about Angel."

Now all their eyes turned to me, as though they were looking for confirmation. I nodded. "We can trust Jace."

"How do you know?" Hazel asked sullenly. "You haven't even seen him in ten years."

I met Jace's eyes. "Yeah, well, some things don't change. Besides, like he said, he wouldn't get his story if he turned Angel in now. We're working for the same thing."

"For different reasons," Vaughn reminded me in a low voice.

"It doesn't matter. Zeke, I'll go talk to your contact and see if he's come up with anything."

Zeke considered this for several moments. Finally, he nodded. "All right. I reckon he'll talk to you."

"This is all we got to go on right now?" Hazel demanded.

"Yeah, pretty much. If Rush ordered these killings and has a Pinkerton on his payroll, they aren't going to make it easy to uncover what they're up to. We have to be careful about how we go about investigating. Even if you're all cleared of the charges, you stick out like sore thumbs over here."

"We stuck out like sore thumbs in the west, too," I remarked a little proudly. "I reckon we're unusual no matter where we are."

Jace scowled. "I wish I'd known my wife is Tess Mercury. I might have paid a little more attention to the rumors and tall tales."

"I reckon they're only partially exaggerated," I told him.

"Are you planning on explaining to me how this all came about?" he demanded.

"Yeah. Another time, maybe. Not now."

He sighed. "Okay. But how'd you all get involved in this in the first place? You're bounty hunters, not investigators."

"This is a side project," Hazel told him. "We were bored and we tried hunting for Zeke."

"And you decided to clear his name when you found him, rather than turn him in for the bounty?"

Zeke stiffened. "They didn't find me. I'm a Pinkerton. A good one. They wouldn't have found me if they'd had all the time in the world. I found them."

"Excuse me," I put in indignantly. "We're the best damn bounty hunters in the west. We would have found you. We ain't never failed. We weren't goin' to start with you."

Zeke snorted. "You keep on telling yourselves that."

Hazel stuck her tongue out at him and turned back to Jace. "Anyway, he asked us to help prove him innocent."

"All right," Jace said. "And now you want me to help you do it."

"We don't want nothin' from you," Quimby barked.

"Quimby," I growled.

Jace glanced shrewdly between Quimby and me. I wasn't sure what conclusion he reached, but I didn't think I'd like it. "You sure wanted something from me when I was paying your jail fines," he said smoothly.

"Thanks for that, Jace," I said. "What do we owe you?" He waved his hand dismissively. "All right, then. We've all got a common goal. Let's not fight, all right? We ain't got time."

Quimby slunk low in his chair, but he nodded sullenly. Jace inclined his head. Then he pulled a small gold watch from the lapel pocket of his jacket and glanced down at it. He shot abruptly to his feet. "I have to head back to the office. I have a deadline."

I almost sagged with relief. It was hard enough discovering my dead husband was alive. It was worse trying to make polite, meaningful conversation in the middle of a crowd.

He glanced at me sharply as though he sensed my feelings. "We aren't done here, Tess."

I sighed. "I know."

He lifted a hand to the others and turned toward the door. He turned back. "I'll be back tomorrow."

"All right."

"Leave the code Becky pulled off the telegraph," Zeke ordered absently. "We might be able to come up with something."

Jace frowned. "I think if there was something to figure out, I would have by now."

"I don't think so," Zeke replied matter-of-factly. "It obviously means something, or Rush wouldn't have bothered to send it at all. If you haven't figured it out, maybe you could use a new perspective."

Jace sighed, but he nodded. "All right." He stepped toward Zeke, but the Pink wasn't paying attention to him anymore. I rose and reached for the folded sheet of paper. Jace's fingers brushed mine as I took it from him. My stomach did a little flip, but I held his gaze impassively.

"Thanks, Jace."

He stepped away. "Nice meeting you all."

"Yeah right," Hazel said.

When he was gone, they all turned to look at me expectantly. I bristled. "What?"

They all looked away. "Nothin'," Quimby replied meekly.

"It's late," I said, scowling at them. "I just spent the last few hours in jail and then cooped up with you guys in this tiny room. I'm tired, and I'm dirty. I want a bath and a good night's sleep. Anyone got a problem with that?"

I glared around at them with my hands on my hips. "Nah," Zeke replied, sighing.

"Good. Now get out."

They didn't argue. The boys got up and left Hazel and me alone. I didn't know what their sleeping arrangement was, and I didn't care. I soaked in the porcelain tub for what felt like hours, and when I came out of the bathroom in a soft, cotton nightgown, I felt like a new woman. I almost felt ready to think about what had happened today.

Hazel was lying on top of the counterpane on the bed right where I left her. She stared up at the ceiling. There wasn't any expression on her face, but I sensed she was upset about something. "You takin' a bath, Hazel?" I asked cautiously.

"Nah."

I climbed into the bed next to hers and pulled the covers up to my chin. I sighed in contentment. "I could get used to New England," I said. "The beds are real nice."

Hazel turned to face me. "Are you thinkin' about stayin' then?"

I blinked at her in surprise. "What?"

"Well, I mean. Jace..."

"I ain't stayin' here. We have a life."

"Yeah, but..." She scowled and glanced away.

I lifted my eyebrows. "What's the matter, Hazel?"

"I thought you was a widow. Like me. I thought Jace was dead."

"So did I. If I'd known he was alive, I would never have run off with Vaughn and become Tess Mercury. We wouldn't have even met at all."

"I know." She sounded troubled. "And now we found out he's alive."

"Ah. Hazel, I ain't runnin' back to Jace."

She narrowed her eyes at me. "How come you didn't know he was alive?" she demanded in an accusatory voice.

"What?"

"You told me he died in the war."

"Yeah. I thought he did."

"How come you didn't check? How come you didn't look for him?"

"I got a telegram from the Union telling me he was missing and presumed dead in the Battle of Hatcher's Run. When the war ended, I never heard from him again. I never heard anything about him coming home to me or being alive. I was sure he was dead. It never occurred to me to look for him."

Hazel frowned at me. "Maybe he's been lookin' for you all this time."

"Maybe he has. I reckon it don't matter now, not after all this time." I stared at her. "Hazel, why are you so upset?"

She sighed deeply. "I thought you was like me."

"I am like you."

"No, you ain't. You're married. You got a man."

"Yeah, but I don't want him."

She lifted a shrewd eyebrow at me. "You don't want him?"

I sighed. "I ain't seen Jace in almost ten years. We were kids back then. I don't even know him."

"You ought to get to know him, Tess."

"What?"

"I thought you was like me, but you ain't. That don't mean you ain't still my friend. I been runnin' around with you for three years. I know you're still carryin' a torch for that man."

"I ain't carryin' no torch for nobody."

She rolled her eyes. "Yeah, right. Look, I seen what's goin' on with you and Quimby."

"There ain't nothin' goin' on between me and Quimby!"

"I know that, Tess. And ain't no woman in their right mind says no to Bonny Quimby Burton."

I laughed out loud. Her mouth quivered, and she grinned. "Hazel, you better never let him hear you say that."

"Oh, I wouldn't. Believe me."

"I ain't interested in bein' another one of Quimby's conquests."

"I don't think you would be. I think it would be different."

"It don't matter, anyway."

"So, what are you going to do then?"

I shook my head. "I ain't going to do anything."

She frowned at me. "You got to do something. You're married now. You can't pretend you ain't."

"I've always been married, apparently. It hasn't made a bit of difference."

"Yeah, but now you know about it. You got to do something."

"Why?"

"'Cause you can't just keep runnin' around the frontier hunting bounties while your husband is here in Boston. It's ain't right."

"I don't see why not." When she gave me an incredulous look, I sighed. "Look, Hazel, I don't know what I'm gonna do. For all I know, Jace has another wife by now."

"He can't have. He didn't think you were dead."

"Yeah, well, he never went after me, did he?"

"And how was he supposed to find you? You ain't been in one place longer than a week or two since I met you."

I shrugged. "If Jace wants a divorce, I'll give him one." Somehow, saying turned my insides to ice. "We weren't married that long, anyway."

"You been married ten years."

"Yeah, but we were only together a few months."

"What happened?"

"The war happened. He wanted to fight for the North, and I didn't want him to fight at all. He didn't listen to me. He joined the Union, and I went home to my daddy. I ain't seen him since."

Hazel sighed. "You better ask him what he wants."

"I reckon I don't care what he wants. He ain't a part of my life anymore. I ain't stoppin' what we've been doin' just 'cause he's alive. I like our life."

"I don't think it's gonna be that easy."

"I'll make it that easy. Don't worry, Hazel. I ain't leavin' you guys anytime soon."

She smiled a little. "We'll see." She leaned over and turned down the oil lamp between our beds. "Night, Tess."

"Night, Hazel." I sighed and leaned back on the spongy feather pillows. They felt as soft as sleeping on a cloud. Still, I stared up at the ceiling, and I didn't sleep for hours.

Chapter Eleven

The following morning, I felt weary and tense. I hadn't slept well the night before, and to make matters worse, the reason I hadn't was on his way here. When I thought of Jace, it felt as though a swarm of angry insects were trying to flutter out of my belly through my throat. I paced up and down the small hotel room as swiftly as the tight sapphire blue dress Hazel had forced me in to would allow me to move. The bustle flopped up and down against my behind as I walked. I felt ridiculous, but Hazel insisted I was as flash and fashionable as Tess Mercury was capable of being.

I hadn't always felt so out of place in fashionable society--fashionable society in this case being Jace, I reckoned. When we'd first met, I'd been a regular social butterfly. I was rich and clever and pretty back then, and I'd been well liked in the best circles in Savannah. I'd had a lot of suitors, but I'd never much been interested in getting married and making a home for my husband. My father and I fought constantly about it, but marriage didn't really suit my personality, not like hunting outlaws through the frontier.

Jace had changed that in a heartbeat. He was smart and charming and interesting. He could talk for hours about nothing and make it seem exciting. I hadn't even minded so much that my father liked him or that his father wanted him to marry me for my father's money. None of that mattered. Jace and I had loved each other. I'd never forgiven myself for our last words to each other or the time we spent estranged from each other while he'd fought in the war. I hadn't even written him letters. When I'd heard he was dead, I think Tess Holt just shriveled up and died. Running off with Vaughn had seemed like the only thing that made any sense at the time.

Hazel hadn't been wrong. I'd never stopped loving Jace. But that had been the Jace before the fighting and the war and the estrangement. He wasn't the same person now any more than Tess Mercury was the same woman Tess Holt had been. Things were different now. Those two people who'd loved each other were just kids who'd lost track of themselves long ago.

When Jace walked through the door, though, I felt the same jolt of excitement I always felt when I saw him, even after we'd been married. He still had the same intense green eyes that had attracted me all those years ago. His wavy dark hair was slightly longer, and his patrician features were slightly sharper, as though he'd lost a little of his youthful softness. He didn't look older so much as he looked as though he'd grown up a bit. I felt suddenly ashamed. I wished I'd had Hazel fix my hair or put some make up on my face. I'd been living hard the last five years. I wasn't the young, soft, tender girl I'd once been. I was a tough, sharp-tongued, cynical woman now, and I looked it.

He stared at me in silence for a long moment. He didn't say anything, and I couldn't read his thoughts in his flashing eyes. I didn't know him at all anymore. I felt tense and awkward. Hazel didn't say anything, but I could feel her watching us from the desk where she'd been writing some sort of formula out in a leather-bound journal while I'd dwelled on my lost youth.

Jace glanced at Hazel. "Hazel, may I speak to Tess alone, please?"

Hazel sighed dramatically, but she rose to her feet. "Yeah. All right. I'll get us some breakfast and some coffee, Tess."

I nodded, but I didn't tear my eyes from Jace as she slipped out of the room. It was too early, and I was far too sober for the conversation I sensed was coming. Jace stared at me for a long time. I tried to hold his gaze, but I glanced away.

"You look so different," he said finally.

My cheeks flushed. "I know. I'm not the girl you married anymore, am I?"

He stepped toward me and caught my chin between his thumb and forefinger. The sudden contact surprised me, and I leaned back, away from him. He looked a little hurt, but he stepped away from me.

"What happened to you, Jace? They told me you were dead."

He nodded. "I was injured very badly in the war. I was shot in the stomach during the Battle of Hatcher's Run. I thought I was going to die right there in the trenches. Most people do die from a wound like that." He didn't break our stare. "I thought of you. I wished we hadn't fought. I thought if I could just get back to you, everything would be okay again. I didn't mean any of those things I said, Tess."

I looked away from him. I didn't know what to say to this. I reckon I wasn't really ready to admit that I hadn't meant what I'd said, either.

He looked a little disappointed. He didn't try to touch me again or anything, but he kept on. "Then I passed out. When I woke up, I was in a tiny little house. An old nurse, Sally Massie, had found me there on the battlefield barely alive. She nursed my wound and brought me back to life. It was months before I could go anywhere, and when I did, the war was over. I went back to your father's plantation, and he told me you ran off with Vaughn." He said this in a strange, cold tone of voice.

I glanced at him sharply. "You know I didn't *run* off with Vaughn, right? Not like that."

He blinked. "What?"

"My daddy didn't want to let Vaughn and his family go after the war, so we left him. He knew he couldn't keep them there, but he tried, right enough. Vaughn and I got his mom and sisters out, and then we took off on our own." I met his gaze squarely now. "I thought you were dead, and I didn't want to stay in Savannah with my father anymore. He was angry and hateful, and he said all sorts of hurtful things about me and you and everyone else in the world. He couldn't accept that the South lost. It was all he talked about. So, I took all the money I'd squirreled away and ran off with Vaughn."

He lifted an eyebrow. "How did you become a bounty hunter, then?" His Savannah accent had seemed almost gone the night before, but now I heard it again, just barely: the slow, gentle drawl. It was nice. I hadn't thought of it in years, but I'd missed it.

I shrugged. "It was sort of simple enough. Even after the war, people don't take kindly to Vaughn, especially running around with a white woman. We got into a few scuffles. We usually came out on top. After one fight, we learned our opponents were wanted in the next county. When we met them again, it came to blows. We knew we could make a penny off 'em this time, so when we beat them, we trussed them up and took them in." I smiled slightly. "We realized it was a hell of a good way to make money."

He frowned. He didn't seem to like my narrative. I wondered if it was the cussing. "There are more respectable ways to make money."

I lifted my chin defiantly. "I don't care what you think about my profession. You don't have a say in my life anymore."

He stepped toward me with a scowl. "I am still your husband!"

"Jace, you're only my husband in name. Tess Holt don't exist no more. I'm Tess Mercury. I got friends and a life and a job I like."

"Tess, I looked for you."

"Not too hard though, huh?"

"You think I didn't look hard? Do you have any idea how hard it is to find you? I sent the Pinkertons and everyone, and they didn't find a single sign of you."

"Truth to tell, I'm a mite proud of that. I wasn't even tryin' to evade them."

"Tess, you can't just--"

There was a loud, insistent rapping on the door. I glanced at Jace. He looked irritated, but it wasn't the sort of rap you could pretend you didn't hear. I strode forward to pull open the door. It was Vaughn, Quimby, Hazel and Zeke. They all looked between Jace and me. Hazel was juggling a stack of bread and pastries from the lobby. Vaughn lifted his eyebrows, and Quimby frowned, but Zeke didn't seem to care one bit. He re-adjusted his glasses on his nose and strode into the room.

"What are you two doin' in here?" Quimby demanded.

Jace barely glanced at him. "I'm talking to my wife, not that it's any of your concern, Burton."

Quimby stiffened. I sighed. "All right, boys," I said. "None of that."

Zeke's impassive expression didn't change. "We got work to do here. You can hash out all your personal problems when we've sorted out this business with Sterling Rush."

Leave it to the Pink to get me out of trouble. "All right, so where are we?" I asked cheerfully. "Have you guys figured anything out about that code Jace got from Becky?"

They all frowned as though it was giving them some trouble. I reckoned I wouldn't have done any better. "Not yet, but we're working on it," Zeke replied. "If anyone can sort it out, it's me."

"I like your confidence, Zeke," Hazel told him, chewing on a scone. I wasn't feeling very hungry myself.

Zeke didn't reply to this. "So what now?" Jace asked. There was a crease between his eyes, but he didn't look as though he intended to insist on continuing our conversation, at least at the moment.

"We talk to Zeke's dispatcher friend. He might have a lead on who's doing the dirty work for Rush," I replied decisively.

"It's probably the only way we're ever going to figure out what that dirty work is and get some evidence it's Rush running the dirty show," Hazel added.

"So how do we contact this guy?" Quimby asked. He seized one of Hazel's pastries and shoved it into his mouth. I snorted slightly in laughter. He looked over at me with a grin. Jace snorted in disgust. We ignored him.

Zeke considered Quimby's question. Finally he said, "He takes lunch the same time everyday at a small cafe in Quincy Market. It's where I met with him before I went on the run. He's probably expecting to be approached there again. He won't talk to you unless he believes your working with me."

"So write him a note or somethin'," I ordered impatiently.

"A note?"

"Yeah. Why not? It's as good a thing as any. What else are you going to do; have us wear roses on our lapels?"

"Okay. A note, then."

"I don't like this," Jace said. "I should go with you, Tess. What if something happens?"

My posse and I grinned around at each other.

"If something happens to Tess, I doubt a big city dude will be as good by her side as me," Quimby told him proudly.

Jace's eyes narrowed. "Yeah? Why's that?"

I didn't realize Quimby had brought his guns to our little rendezvous, but they were out in a flash. Jace reared backward in alarm. I scowled at Quimby and cuffed him roughly on the arm. "What the hell, Quim?"

He shrugged and holstered his pistols. "I'm just pointin' out I'm the fastest gun in the west."

I rolled my eyes. "Right, well, he didn't need a demonstration."

"Everyone just calm down now. It's not the time to be comparing the size of our guns," Zeke said.

"By the look of it," Quimby said, smirking, "he ain't even got a gun."

"You'd be surprised by what I've got, Burton," Jace told him in a low, angry voice.

"All right, boys," Hazel piped in. "We've got a job to do. Let's not get distracted. While Tess and Quimby go talk to that contact of yours, Zeke, what are the rest of us going to do?"

Zeke's face looked determined. "Work on the telegram Becky brought Jace. We need to crack this code, or we'll never be able to prove Rush is the mastermind."

She looked extremely put out by this. "But it might not even be anything."

"It got a sweet young girl and her fiancé killed. It's something," I said. "You don't just send out messages like that to no one for no reason."

"I don't like being on cipher duty," she complained.

"It can't all be sparks and explosions, Hazel. Sometimes you got to do the tedious work to get to the fun bits."

"We need more information." Zeke was staring at the crumbled piece of paper. "We don't have all the information that we need to solve the cipher."

Jace sighed. "I've been over everything I know about Rush, and I couldn't find the connections."

"Then you ain't got all the information," I offered fairly. "Good thing we got Zeke here."

Jace didn't seem offended. He looked around at us. "What about me? What do I do?" We all looked back at him silently. He lifted a shoulder. "What?"

"You ain't exactly an investigator, Jace," I replied.

He frowned. "Me? I'm an investigative reporter. I've blown more lids off things than you have. I'm as good as a bounty hunter, anyway. You don't investigate anything; you just round up the outlaws afterward. At least I earn an honest living."

"Hey, what we do is honest!" Hazel growled.

Jace scoffed. I frowned at him. "It's honest enough, and we don't rightly care what you think about what we do, Jace."

He snapped his mouth shut. He looked a little hurt. "Let's not argue," Zeke put in as though he were refereeing a bunch of volatile children. "Look, Jace, you got anything that might help me solve this cipher?"

"Well, I have some ideas, sure."

"Okay. We can all look at it together."

Jace scowled. He glanced for a moment at Vaughn. I thought he looked a little wary. Vaughn didn't seem to notice. He was as calm and impassive as ever. I wondered if they'd ever even spoken to each other before. I didn't think they had. Vaughn had been my friend growing up, but he'd known his place when he'd been a slave. He hadn't taken liberties with anyone but me. I reckoned Jace didn't know what to think about Vaughn and me.

"I need to stop by my house," Zeke said thoughtfully. "I have some notes on the case I wasn't able to bring them with me when I went on the run. I'd like to take a look at them again."

"You house?" Hazel demanded. "Are you crazy?"

He shrugged. "It's already been searched by the Marshals. They probably aren't staking it out anymore."

Hazel seemed genuinely concerned for his well being. "It ain't worth the risk, Zeke. What did you learn that could possibly help? You didn't solve the case then."

He frowned at her. "I have a list of Rush's contacts, people who might have had something to do with him and Becky and her disappearance."

"Yeah, but what does that have to do with this?"

He exhaled heavily from his nose. "It might be a person."

"What? What might be a person?" I demanded.

He held out the cipher. I examined it with narrow eyes and passed it to Hazel. Jace, though, looked as though he'd been struck by lightning. "I never thought of that. It might be someone's initials."

"Yeah, but who has four initials?" Hazel asked.

"Maybe they aren't all initials for people," I offered.

"I should get my notes, too," Jace said.

"All right. You two can compare notes while Quimby and I do some talking." When Jace looked up at me sharply, I rolled my eyes. "With Zeke's contact." I eyed Jace for a moment then turned to Zeke. "Maybe Jace should go to your place, Zeke. It's probably best you stay here. You're the most wanted man in Boston right now. It's not as safe to be running willy-nilly around here as on the frontier."

He frowned and opened his mouth to retort, but Hazel cut him off. "Actually, she's right about that, Zeke. It's safer not to be out in the open. I know you hate hidin', but there ain't much choice here. If the Marshals get you before we figure this out, it's all over for you."

I glanced at Vaughn. His face was blank, but his dark eyes were as surprised at this as I felt. We hadn't realized Hazel and Zeke had grown so fond of each other. I shrugged and looked at Jace. "That all right with you, Jace?"

He nodded. "Sure. I'm not meeting Lafe until tomorrow. I'm free today."

Zeke scowled. "You talked to Lafe?"

"Sure. I'm a man of my word."

"Well, what did you tell him?"

"Just that I wanted to ask about Becky. And you."

"What?" we all demanded, turning to him in surprise.

"I thought we were trying to keep this under wraps," Hazel said, scowling.

Jace lifted his eyebrows. "I'm not an idiot. He knows I was working with Becky, and I told him I'm doing a story on how a Pink goes bad. I told him I just wanted some background information on you to see if there was anything in your history that indicated you might turn on your client."

We considered this. "That's not too bad, actually," Zeke said.

Jace shrugged. "It's not strictly a lie. I might do a story like that if it turns out you're actually guilty. I might as well take the opportunity to get a head start on my research."

I smiled slightly at this. Jace hadn't changed. "I was kind of thinking the same thing," I said. "Well, if he's guilty we've already got him hemmed up, anyway."

Zeke frowned. "It is a little unsettling that none of you mind much that I might be guilty. Are you all just thinking of how you'll profit if we fail to prove me innocent?"

We all shrugged. "We all have our jobs to do," Vaughn told him unapologetically. "You're just lucky we're working with you right now, not against you."

Zeke sighed. "Yeah. That's true enough. Jace, you be careful what you say to Lafe."

He nodded. "I'll be careful. I can be very smooth when I need to be."

"Not smooth enough to keep your informants from being caught," Quimby muttered.

"That ain't necessary, Quim," I said. "We'd better get ready to meet Zeke's boy. Hopefully we can learn something from him that will help. At least we might learn what questions we need to start asking."

"Well, I hope it gets us something," Hazel complained. "'Cause we got nothin' right now."

"No," Vaughn argued. "Not nothing. We've got quite a bit. We know this cipher is what got Becky killed, and we know it was a Pink who did it. That's a lot."

"Yeah. So close, yet so far away." I looked at Zeke. "You'd better think about what you'll tell your boy in that note to get him to talk to us." I paused. "What's his name?"

* * *

Quincy Market was bustling during the busy lunch hour. It was a clear, sunny day, and the outdoor vendors shouted to the passing shoppers to try their fare or examine their wares. My heels clicked on the cobblestone street as we strode through the market square. Quimby looked more debonair than I'd ever seen him. He was wearing a blue suit that made his eyes look like the night sky. He looked irritated, though. I had other things on my mind than Quimby's eyes or his temper.

Apparently, he had things on his mind, too.

"So what are you gonna do?" he demanded.

"What?"

"About Jace. What are you going to do?"

I sighed. "Man, I don't know. Why are you people so interested in me and Jace?"

He looked at me incredulously. "You're our leader."

"I ain't nobody's leader."

"'Course you are."

"I always thought of Vaughn as the leader."

He snorted. "Nah. He just talks when he needs to. We all do what you say."

"I'm not sure how I feel about that."

"Everything's different now," he said grimly.

"Why's it got to be different?"

"No matter what's going on, Tess, you and Jace are still married. You have to deal with it eventually. It's not fair to him if you want to run around all over the frontier and leave him here." He glanced at me. "You should divorce him so he can get a new wife."

This gave me a little jolt. I looked at him in surprise. "It's none of your business, Quimby," I snapped.

He scowled. "You always say that. Why isn't it my business?"

"It don't got nothing to do with you, Quim."

"You got something to do with me, Tess."

"I don't want to talk about it no more. I don't know what I'm going to do, and all you people asking me about it ain't helping me figure it out."

He sighed. "All right."

"I know it ain't going to be so simple. I know we can't just go back to our normal lives now, knowing each other is alive. We're still stuck with each other. We have to sort it out." I shrugged. "This isn't the time to be worrying about it. We got other things to do. We have to prove Angel innocent so he can get on with his life."

"You really think he's innocent?"

I glanced at him in surprise. "Don't you?"

He shrugged. "I don't know. I've seen some people bluff real well. I reckon it don't matter much to me whether he's innocent or not. I make my money either way."

"You don't even care?"

"Do you?"

"Sure, I care. If what he says is true, and Rush is responsible for all this, all these deaths and the people who were run out of town, someone should stop him."

"Why's it got to be us?"

I shrugged. "I don't think it does. I think maybe it has to be Jace and Angel."

"Then why do we have to help them?"

I frowned at him. "Because, Quimby, it's the right thing to do."

"Since when did you care about that?"

"I always cared about that. Besides, why not? What else have we got going?"

"We could go back for Donnie Rio."

"Oh, when are you going to give up on that? I told you, when we've sorted this out, we'll get Donnie Rio. He ain't goin' anywhere, and he ain't gettin' away with what he did."

He looked at me shrewdly. "Yeah, but since when did something like this get in the way of you stoppin' a man like that?"

I frowned. "I don't know. It just did. It seems important. It seems like we could let someone else take Donnie Rio. We got to be here."

Quimby scowled, but he didn't say anything.

"You want to go, Quimby? You want to go take care of Donnie Rio?"

"No! That ain't what I'm sayin'. I don't want to go hunt Donnie Rio on my own. I need you all."

"Then what's your problem?"

"I ain't got a problem."

"You got a problem."

"I just don't think any of this is our business. We're in over our heads. Politics, robber barons, muckrakers, government conspiracies--well, it just ain't our sort of thing, is it? We're rough and tumble organic, simple cowboys and Indians types."

I lifted an eyebrow. "Are you scared of Rush?"

"I ain't scared of nobody so long as my gun is faster. We just ain't cut out for this."

"How do you know? We ain't never done it before."

"That's exactly my point."

I nudged him. "How can you know what you're capable of until you give it a try, Quim?"

He frowned. "I just don't think this is a good idea. These ain't our kind of people. This ain't our kind of town."

"Well, it is right now. Get a hold of yourself, Quimby. I reckon things are going to get a lot worse before this is all over." I sighed. "We might even need your fast gun."

He glanced at me. "Why?"

"Whoever is behind this probably isn't going to just turn themselves in when we figure it out. We're going to have a good fight on our hands."

He smirked. "Whoever they are, they won't be much of a match for us."

154

"I think they might be."

He stopped walking when we reach the large outdoor cafe where Zeke's contact would be waiting. The tables were filled with businessmen and women eating together or alone on their lunch hours. Zeke's friend was a man in his mid-thirties. He was a simple, good-natured-looking fellow, but I reckoned he was shrewder than he looked, or he wouldn't be Zeke's only hope. "Is that our guy?" Quimby asked.

"Yeah."

"How can you be sure? He looks a little soft."

"He looks the way he's supposed to." He looked at me doubtfully, but I lifted my chin and strode toward our contact. He was eating a sandwich alone at a table beneath a canopy. When I stopped beside his table, he looked up at me in surprise. I smiled and twirled my parasol. "Are you Jesse O'Brien?"

He looked startled, but there was no suspicion in his expression. "Yes. Who are you?"

"I'm Tess Mercury."

He blinked. "You're...really?"

"You heard of me?"

"I'm a Pinkerton. I have heard of you." He narrowed his dark eyes slightly. "What do you want with me?"

I smiled and took the seat across from him at the table. Quimby hovered behind me, but I didn't think we'd need his gun today. Jesse O'Brien seemed like a sweet guy. "Angel Cooper sent us."

Jesse sat straight up in surprise. "Angel? Seriously?"

"Yeah."

"Are you hunting him or something?"

"We already found him. Well." I smiled. "He found us. We're working with him."

He frowned. "How can I trust you?"

"Why would I tell you that if it wasn't true?"

"I don't know. Maybe you think I know where he is."

"I don't think that. I already know where he is. I don't need you to tell me. He

155

says he was framed."

"Yes. I know. He came to me before he disappeared for good."

"You believe him?"

"Yeah, I do. I've known him a long time. Five years. He wouldn't kill that boy. He was trying to help him."

"Well, I believe him, too, and we're trying to help him find out who framed him for this."

Jesse inclined his head. "Okay."

He looked like he didn't quite believe me. I rolled my eyes and handed him a folded piece of paper. Zeke had scribbled only two words: Peggy Erickson. I didn't know what it meant, but it must have meant something to Jesse. His expression changed instantly, and he relaxed.

"That's good enough for me. So what's he sent you for?"

"The information he asked you for. Do you know who sent the telegram on the night Rebecca Palmer disappeared?"

Jesse sighed. "No. I don't know that yet. I got a list of who was out in the field. I know who didn't send it."

"That's a start. You don't know who was around the office?"

"We have a door guard who keeps a record of who comes in and out."

"Okay, so we need to see who was in the office."

He nodded. "I'm still trying to get the information without anyone figuring out I'm looking into it. It's delicate. I don't want anyone to know I'm helping Angel. He's the most wanted man in the city right now. We've got all hands on deck searching the countryside for him. If word gets out, I could get fired or worse. I've got a wife. I don't want to get her mixed up in any of this."

"I understand."

"There are as many people coming and going in the office. I have to find a way to get a hold of the doorman's notes. I can't exactly just ask for them."

I considered. "You think you could try a little harder? I reckon it's important."

"I think I can figure something out."

"Okay. Just be careful, all right? We got enough problems without having to

156

worry about you, too."

"Sure."

"You know what a Pink named Lafe Jackson was doing that night?"

He thought about this. "Yeah. He was still in New York on an assignment."

"You sure about that?"

"Yeah, pretty sure. Why? You think he's involved?"

"No. I just wanted to be sure he was safe. We've got a mutual friend. You got that list?"

"No, not here. I'm not carrying it around with me."

"Right."

"I can get it. Meet me back here at five o'clock?"

I nodded. "Sure. Thanks, Jesse."

He smiled a little. "It was real nice meeting you, Tess Mercury. I've heard a lot about you. You're not what I expected."

"Is that a compliment or an insult?"

"It's a compliment. You seem like quite a lady. You're not what I expected at all."

Quimby stepped forward, as though he was taking exception to this. I tilted my head back to look at him. "It's okay," I told Jesse. "He's with me. This is Quimby Burton."

Jesse raised his eyebrows. "Ah, yeah. The rodeo clown."

"Rodeo clown!?" Quimby barked indignantly. "I'm a trick shooter."

"Uh, huh. My mistake." Jesse's eyes twinkled, and his mouth turned up slightly at the corners. He glanced at me. "I'll see you at five, Tess."

He nodded at Quimby, and I took that as my cue to leave. I stood and caught Quimby's arm to lead him away. "What is it with you and the men in Boston, Quimby? They don't seem to like you at all."

He tossed his head, sending his golden curls swinging. "It ain't my fault I'm so handsome."

I rolled my eyes. "Yeah, but it's your fault you're such a jerk."

Chapter Twelve

I whipped off the blue-feathered hat as Quimby and I strode back into the hotel room and tossed it on the bed beside Jace. He looked up at me in surprise. I lifted my chin and ignored him.

"Did you see Jesse?" Zeke asked, rising to his feet.

"Yes."

"He talked to you?"

"He seemed keen enough to talk to Tess," Quimby piped in.

"What does he have?"

"He has a list of the jobs he dispatched that night and who was out in the field."

"Where is it?"

I rolled my eyes, even though I'd asked Jesse the same thing. "He wasn't carrying it around with him, was he? I'm meeting him at five to get the information."

"What about who was in the office? All that list will tell us is who didn't send it."

"That's still more than you have now. Jesse's trying to get the information. It's delicate with the other Pinks around. He doesn't want to get caught. He still wants to help though. He'll do his best." I glanced at Jace. "He thinks your guy Lafe was in New York that night."

He lifted his eyebrows. "You asked?"

"Well, I thought it was better to be safe than sorry."

He smiled. "Are you worried about me, Tess?"

I pressed my lips together in a tight line. "I just don't want to risk this whole operation on blind faith." He rolled his eyes. Hazel scowled at me from her place on her bed. I ignored them both. "So what have you guys got?"

There were papers scattered over every surface in the room. I picked one up, but it was just a list of times and places. I didn't know the significance of them. I tossed the paper down again. "Some contact names, surveillance notes, interviews," Zeke said.

"Anything that might have something to do with Jace's cipher?"

"Some of it, maybe." He gestured over his shoulder where there were papers covered in tight, black scrawl tacked to the walls. "We aren't sure yet."

I rose to peer at the ciphers tacked up beside the notes. "Who could he have been contacting? Where did the telegram go?"

"Becky wasn't able to find that out before she was caught," Jace told me.

I sighed. "It might have been helpful."

"Yeah, but if we figure out what it means, we might be able to figure out who it was sent to," Hazel put in.

I stared at the ciphers: EWNY506; DBVA525.

I tilted my head to the side, as though the new angle would illuminate the code. I didn't turn to face my posse. "Do these initials mean anything?"

"Of course they mean something," Zeke replied. "We just don't know what yet. They don't seem to correspond to any of Rush's contacts or the people on our lists."

I shook my head. It wouldn't do any good for me to study the ciphers. I was a woman of action, not words. "I don't know enough about Rush or his operation to know what this could mean." I spun to face them. "I want to meet him."

"What?" Quimby demanded.

"I want to see him, talk to him, see what he's like."

They looked at me incredulously. "You plan to just walk up and introduce yourself?" Zeke asked dubiously.

I shrugged. "Sure. Why not?"

"Well, how do you expect to do that?"

"I don't know. I'll find a way."

Jace stood and looked around at us with a grin. "I think I have an idea."

We turned to look at him. "What idea?" Zeke asked warily.

"There is an expo this weekend at the Omni featuring the latest technological advancements from Rush AI and his competitors."

"An expo?" Hazel asked. Her face was lit up suddenly, as though someone had flipped a switch.

"They will be exhibiting the newest advancements in technology and weaponry."

"I want to go to that, Tess." Her voice was tight with excitement.

I considered. "Rush will be there?"

"Of course. He's one of the presenters, and he'll be talking to the public about his latest inventions. He'll be accessible."

I met Jace's eyes for a moment and grinned. He grinned back at me, and I almost felt like we were friends again. I looked away. "All right. We'll go see what we're up against."

"He always loves to see my face," he said with a little too much gleeful mischief.

"Don't shake him up too bad," I warned. "We don't want to tip him off."

"I promise. I can't do anything worse than I already have." He shrugged. "Anyway, he would never guess I was working with the lot of you."

Zeke considered, leaning back in his chair to eye us thoughtfully. "That might not be a bad idea."

"Maybe we can check him out, see who's hanging around him. If he's got a Pink lurking around, maybe we'll find a connection with the names Jesse's digging up."

Everyone nodded. Vaughn frowned thoughtfully. "It's not much of a plan."

"Vaughn's right; we got nothin'," Quimby put in.

"Will everyone just quit bein' so negative?" I scolded. "We ain't never failed before. I don't intend to start now. We just need to figure out which Pink is the crooked one."

"When we do, what are we plannin' to do about it?" Hazel asked.

We all looked around at each other. "Well, I assume when we do find him there'll be some evidence we can use to give the lawmen," I replied.

"What if there isn't?"

I rolled my eyes. "Can we just get to the end before we start worrying about what problems might arise when we do? Damn, you folks are pessimistic lately."

* * *

"Tess, you are not going with me."

"Why?"

"Because this isn't that sort of thing. This is not some social visit."

I frowned at Jace. "You think I want to make new friends? I just want to make sure you don't say something stupid and blow our cover."

He scowled at me. Zeke and my posse looked away, pretending not to listen to the argument. I appreciated the effort, even though I knew their little ears were as sharp as needles.

"I'm not going to blow our cover," Jace replied indignantly. "I have been doing this a long time. I know Lafe, and he knows me. I'm not going to say something to get Zeke caught."

"What's the point of talkin' to this guy? It's dangerous."

"It might dredge up a lead. It's more than anything else we've done so far. We need all the help we can get."

"Tess is right, Jace," Zeke said with a tiny frown between his eyes. "How can he help?"

"Maybe he knows something."

"He wasn't even in town when the telegram was sent," I said. "What would he know about it?"

"He might know something about Rush," Jace argued. "He might know who does work for him. On and off the books."

I opened my mouth to retort then shut it with a snap. "Actually, that's not bad," Zeke said. "He might know something we can use. It's worth a shot." He sighed. "We really do need all the help we can get. All right. Go on, then."

I looked at Jace expectantly. He scowled. "No, Tess."

"Why not?"

"This is business."

"Yeah, it is. And it's my business as much as yours."

He sighed. "All right. Fine. You can come."

Hazel huffed. "How come Tess gets to talk everyone, and I get stuck in this hotel room with these stinky fugitives?"

"'Cause you got no self control, Hazel," Vaughn told her in a perfectly matter-of-fact voice.

Hazel looked pleased by this. "He's right, Hazel," I said. "You cannot be trusted to act within the confines of common sense."

"Hey, I found Jace and got you all out of jail, didn't I?"

Zeke rolled his eyes. "Actually, that was my idea."

"Don't underestimate Hazel," I warned him. "She can get the job done when it gets down to the brass tacks."

She cuffed me on the arm. "Aw, thanks, Tess." She looked around at the others defiantly. "You boys don't know nothin'."

I stepped forward and took Jace's arm. He stiffened. I drew back from him. "Shall we go, Jace?" I smiled brightly at him, but I felt my cheeks heat.

He lifted his chin, but he glanced at Zeke. Zeke waved his hand dismissively. "We'll keep on these notes and see if anything crops up."

"Sounds boring," I remarked cheerfully.

"Yeah," Hazel sighed. "It will be."

"We might drink some whiskey, too," Quimby added.

Hazel perked up. "Sounds marginally less boring."

"But infinitely less productive," Zeke sighed. "Can we refrain from taking body shots until we've found something else, please?"

He rose abruptly and strode toward me. He gave me an ominous frown. "Be careful what you say to Lafe. He's a decent man, and he has an alibi, but he's still a Pinkerton. If he gets any inkling you're with me, he'll follow you and he won't stop until he finds me."

I smirked. "We'll make sure we aren't followed before we come back. I'm good at that." I jerked my head at Jace.

He glanced sidelong at me the moment the door slammed in the hallway. "Why do you really want to come with me?"

"I'm going crazy inside that hotel room."

"That's not very charitable of you, Tess."

I shrugged. "No. Probably not. I'm not going to start feeling guilty about it, though." I glanced at him as we strode through the hotel toward the row of carriages waiting in a semi-circular queue outside the glass and brass doors.

Jace hailed a carriage and offered his hand to me. I stared at it a moment in indecision. Then I seized it and allowed him to assist me into the cab. "Union Street, please."

It was a small carriage, and the quarters were close. His after-shave smelled like wood smoke. It was the same after-shave he'd always worn. I turned my head away from him. "Do you really think Lafe will help us?" I asked tightly.

I felt him shift as he turned to look at me. "He might. Truth to tell, Tess, I've got no idea where to go from here. I've been trying to crack those codes for a month, and I've got nothing. We need more information and I don't know how else to get it." I turned back to him in time to catch his scowl. "I might not even be looking in the right place."

"You think this might not have anything to do with Rush?"

"What?" He sounded as though he thought I'd lost my mind.

"Well, I mean, we know Becky was lured out by a Pink pretending to be you the night she disappeared, but what if it's got nothing to do with Rush at all?"

He was silent a moment, as though he didn't know what to say to this. "How could it not? What other reason did someone have to lure her out?"

"I don't know. I didn't know Becky. All we've got on Rush are those cryptic messages. They might not even be criminal at all. They might not have anything to do with it."

"But--then--" He frowned at me. "Then why did she go missing right after he caught her snooping?"

"Coincidence?"

"Come on, Tess. I heard you're good at what you do."

I rolled my eyes. "I am good because I don't focus my attention on a single thing, even if it isn't panning out. I'm willing to be open to suggestions and change my thinking when it's appropriate."

He frowned at me, but he thought this over for a few moments. "All right. If you can offer an alternative explanation that makes any sense, I am willing to explore it."

I shrugged. "I don't have one. Not yet. I need more information. I was hoping maybe your boy would give it to us."

"So it's not just about being out of the room with the stinky fugitives."

"Only one of them is a fugitive, and I reckon he's the cleanest."

"You always could convolute a conversation, Tess." I snorted. "If you don't have an alternative explanation, why are you arguing with me?"

"I am merely presenting an idea."

"Well, it isn't helpful."

I laughed. "Sure it is. You need to be willing to consider that someone else is responsible for her disappearance." I lifted my eyebrows. "Maybe she isn't dead at all."

He blinked. "What do you mean she isn't dead?"

"No one ever proved anything like that."

This seemed to trip him up. He frowned. "But Silas is dead."

"Yeah, and Becky probably is, too. I'm simply saying we don't know anything for sure."

"You must admit it's unlikely she's just gone off. If she'd just gone off, why would anyone need to frame Angel for getting too close to figuring out what happened to her?"

I nodded thoughtfully. "Yeah. Or maybe it's some other reason."

"Maybe he wasn't framed at all. Maybe he's guilty. Maybe he was the one that called Becky out in the middle of the night."

I waved my hand. "Don't get excited. He didn't have anything to do with it."

"So we know nothing."

"No. We know a Pink is involved. That's what we know." I glanced at him. "And we're about to meet with one."

The carriage drew to a gentle stop. Jace hopped out and offered his hand to me. My heels clicked on the cobblestone street. I wobbled slightly. Jace caught me around the waist to steady me. I didn't glance up into his eyes. I muttered a 'thanks' and straightened up. "This way," Jace said in a low voice.

He tucked my hand into his elbow and led me toward a small, quiet tea shop. I glanced at him doubtfully. "A tea shop? This is where we're meeting your friend?"

"We like our tea here. Besides, it's quiet and most of the people who know us don't hang around places like this."

"I would have preferred a whiskey bar," I muttered. "We have meetings like this in saloons, not tea shops."

"It's ten o'clock in the morning."

"I don't understand what you're getting at."

"That's not very ladylike."

"Yeah, yeah. So you keep saying."

He didn't seem anxious at all. In fact, he seemed perfectly at his ease as he strode inside the small shop. A bell tinkled over the door as we entered. I curled my lip. The place was draped in garish paisley brocade and small lace doilies. Jace looked huge compared to the small white-topped tables and petite chairs carefully arranged around them. Most of the patrons were young women in their finest day dresses or old ladies reminiscing about their youth.

There was one man there. He was tall and gangling, sprawled on a stool at the counter. He was older than Jace and I by about ten years, but he still looked in fine health. He had even features, pale, shortly-cropped hair and dark eyes. His suit was as nondescript as he was. He didn't look much like a Pink. None of the Pinks really did. There was really no way to tell what they were supposed to look like. They usually had the sort of faces you would forget the moment you looked away.

Despite this, Lafayette Jackson looked good-natured. He rose when he saw us approaching him. He was smiling, and there were lines around his eyes and his mouth. I reckoned he smiled a lot. In fact, I wondered if he ever stopped smiling. It probably unnerved his opponents. It unnerved me a bit. He lifted his eyebrows as he caught sight of me beside Jace. "Jason? I was under the impression you wanted to talk. I didn't realize this was a social call."

I bristled a bit, but I plastered a smile to my face. Jace glanced at me pointedly. I lifted my chin. "I didn't have a choice. When Tess insists on something, it's hard to tell her no."

Lafe eyed me in interest. He offered his hand. I shook it. "It's nice to meet you, Tess. Lafe Jackson. Are you another reporter?"

"No, actually. Tess is my wife."

I enjoyed the shock on his face. "Wife? Jace, I've known you for three years. I had no idea you were married."

"Turns out I am." He looked at me. "Tess and I have been...estranged."

Lafe inclined his head delicately. "I see."

I considered. Estranged. I reckoned I sort of liked that.

Lafe gestured toward a small corner table. "Why don't we sit down?"

Jace pulled out my chair for me. I stiffened a little, but I didn't argue about this. I reckoned I could let him play the doting husband for a couple hours. At least we didn't have to talk to each other.

Lafe glanced between us with that easy smile, and I found myself warming up to him. "So, Jace, what outlandish rumor or innuendo are you hoping to substantiate today?" Jace chuckled. Lafe offered us both a tiny, delicate cup of tea from a flowered teapot. I'd have rather had whiskey, but I accepted a cup.

"Have you ever done any work for Sterling Rush?"

Lafe laughed. "Oh, Jace. You're still on that? Hasn't anyone else done anything? Are you still looking into the Palmer girl's disappearance?"

I looked at Jace in exasperation. So much for being delicate. "I'm going to continue looking into it until I find something."

Lafe leaned back in his chair with an indulgent smile. "Yeah, I've done some work for Rush."

"Like what?"

"Come on, Jace, you know I can't tell you that. We don't talk about our clients." He lifted a shrewd eyebrow. "I never killed anyone for him, though, if that's what you're getting at."

"It isn't. I was just wondering if you've worked for him before."

"Yeah. Some security work; some private inquiries. The usual menu."

"Are you the only one who's ever worked for him?"

"Hell, no." He cleared his throat. "Pardon me, Mrs. Holt. That was crude."

I barked with laughter. "You go on. I'm not delicate."

"Lots of Pinks work for Rush. He has many varying needs."

"You got any names?" Jace asked.

"Are you planning to question them all about what they've done for him?"

"I was thinking about it." Jace smiled.

Lafe's smile widened into a grin. "Well, good luck with that. I'll give you their names, but they won't talk with you."

"How can you be sure about that? I can be very persuasive."

"I don't doubt you can. You go ahead and give it a shot." Lafe drew a small notepad and pencil from his jacket pocket and dashed off a list of names. He handed it to Jace. "These guys have worked for him a few times, off the top of my head. If I come up with anymore, I'll send you a note."

"I appreciate that."

"They won't talk to you."

"So you said."

"Our policy is not to talk about our clients and the work we do for them."

Jace shrugged. "That doesn't mean I won't still try."

Lafe chuckled. "So you heading to the expo at the Omni this weekend?"

"Of course."

"Will you be on the job or just harassing Rush?"

Jace laughed. "Maybe a little of both."

"I suppose it won't be breaking my code to tell you I'll be there, too."

"Yeah?"

"I'm on security detail with a few of the other Pinks."

I leaned forward in interest. "Is that sort of thing usual?"

"Yeah, sometimes, sure. It's a big showing; an exhibition of the latest in weapons technology and national defense. There will be a lot of Marshals, local police and private security to make sure no one gets any ideas."

"It's quite a big deal, then."

Lafe nodded and eyed me in interest. "Where are you from, Mrs. Holt?"

I lifted my chin. "Savannah, Georgia, same as Jace."

"I see. And where have you been all this time?"

Jace and I exchanged a glance. He was a smoother talker than me. "She never left. Tess' father and I had a falling out during the war." His mouth tightened slightly. "We were on opposite sides."

For a moment, he narrowed his eyes. "Yes. The war tore many families apart." He sighed. "Well. I'm glad you two have reconciled." He glanced between us, but he didn't say anything else about it. I appreciated that. "So have you heard anything new about Angel Cooper?"

I nearly choked on my tea.

"What do you mean?" Jace demanded. His ears turned slightly pink in alarm. I doubted Lafe noticed.

He rolled his eyes. "I thought it was him you came to talk with me about. I don't know too much about him, truth to tell. I never had the pleasure of partnering with him. He had his own way of doing things. He was a good man, and a good Pink, though. He was good to his wife. Beyond that, I don't know much. Why he turned—well, I don't know. You can't ever tell with things like that. Sometimes you just don't know a man. Anyway, it's you who seems to have an uncanny line to the underworld. I was just wondering if you heard of any leads I should follow up on. I thought maybe, for once, you had information for me instead of the other way around."

"Nah. Sorry to disappoint you. My only real line to the underworld is you, Lafe. You got anything for me?"

Lafe snorted. "I heard he was running around with a posse of bounty hunters out west."

Jace laughed. "Yeah? Is that confirmed?"

"Some witnesses saw them together in New Mexico. I heard they were traveling together in St. Louis. A couple suspects were picked up at the airship port here in Boston, but they turned out to be the wrong folks, I guess. Angel wasn't with them. The trail went cold after that."

"Any idea where he could be now?" Jace asked. I was impressed by how cool he sounded.

"Who knows? I heard he might have a friend in Oklahoma, but nothing's panned out."

"Are the Marshals checking out his friend?"

"Sure. I think so. I haven't heard back from anyone yet. They don't always tell us what they've got going on. We hear it through the cracks in the walls most times."

"What about you guys?" I asked. "Aren't your people out there looking for him?"

"Sure we are, but those of us who've worked with him don't want to get involved. It's a conflict of interest. You know what I mean?"

"I understand. But what do you think?"

He blinked. "What do you mean?"

"Do you think he did it?"

Lafe frowned. He looked as though he hadn't really thought about this. "I don't know."

"Really? You know him, don't you?"

"Sure, but...working with a man and knowing him aren't necessarily the same thing. I guess you never really know anybody. It took everyone by surprise." He looked at Jace with a stern expression. "Some folks even think maybe he had something to do with Becky's disappearance. It's a fine coincidence, anyway."

Jace nodded. "It crossed my mind, too. I reckon you'd have to be a fool for it not to have, but I haven't found anything to substantiate that. You?"

Lafe waved his hand dismissively. "Nah. What I think is, if you really want to figure out what happened to your friend Becky, you ought to stop looking into Rush."

We looked at him in surprise. "What?" Jace glanced at me as though I were the cause of this remark.

"It seems to me that if you want to find out what happened to her, you go looking into her. It's the way we do it, anyway."

"Her?"

"Yeah, her. Her life, her friends, what she might have done to get herself killed. That is, if she has been killed."

Jace scowled. "I think I already know the answer to that."

"Yeah, you think you do, but have you even considered any other possibilities?"

"No." He sounded a bit sullen.

"Haven't the Marshals and the local police looked into it?" I asked.

"Sure, but not closely. A secretary disappearing isn't unheard of. She isn't reported dead; she's just missing. The only person who even missed her was Sterling Rush." He glanced at Jace pointedly. "You know he's the one who reported it."

I lifted my eyebrows and glanced at Jace. "He did?"

"He said he saw her the night before she went missing. She was working late in the office. The next day, she didn't come in to work. In fact..." He looked at Jace sharply. "You were the last one to see her, Jace, weren't you?"

"Yeah, but I'm pretty sure I didn't do it."

Lafe laughed. "I'm glad you have confidence in yourself, at least."

Jace have him a suspicious look. "Are you just trying to put me off of Rush?"

"Well, you are my friend, and I don't like to see you make a fool of yourself. I'm just suggesting there might be other explanations for what happened. She might have run off with someone, for all anyone knows."

"She was engaged."

"Yes, and her fiancé was murdered a couple weeks later, wasn't he?"

"Sure he was."

I stared at Lafe thoughtfully. "So you think all this might be a lover's quarrel?"

"Well, I'm not saying I think so, but it could be. The most common motives for murder are love, money and revenge."

"He might be right, Jace."

Jace looked at me as though I'd stuck a knife in his back, but I didn't mind. I glanced at Lafe. "So what about Angel Cooper? What do you think he's got to do with all this, if it's got to do with a lover's spat?"

"Well, some folks do believe he had something going on with Becky."

"Do you?"

Lafe chuckled wryly. "Nah. Truth to tell, I think he was in the wrong place at the wrong time. Maybe he saw something he shouldn't have seen."

I exchanged a look with Jace, but we didn't say anything to this. Lafe drew a watch from his breast pocket and glanced down at it. He rose. "Well, it's been fun, Jace. I always enjoy our little chats. Nice meeting you, Tess. I've got another meeting to be getting to." He winked. "If you decide you want to look into Becky and want a little help, let me know. I always enjoy a good creeping around people's houses." He dropped a black bowler hat on his head and tipped it at us. "Just wait until after the expo, though, okay? It's going to be murder. See you there."

With that, he inclined his head to us and spun around. His stride was long and confident. I watched after him thoughtfully. When I turned back to Jace, he looked annoyed. "You see? I like him. He talks sense."

* * *

Zeke looked up at us when we strode into the hotel room. His expression was impassive, but there was a slight tightness around his mouth. I reckoned it had been a long few hours for him stuck in that hotel room with my posse.

"Did you actually learn anything?" he asked, "or has all this been a waste of everyone's time?"

"Actually, yeah, we learned a thing or two."

"Don't sound so surprised, Tess," Jace scolded, crossing his arms over his chest. "I did say it wouldn't be a waste of time."

"Yeah, yeah."

"So what did he say?" Hazel asked impatiently.

I rolled my eyes. "Well, he knows more about Jace than I reckoned."

Zeke frowned. "What do you mean?"

"Apparently, he knows all about Jace's investigations into Becky Palmer's disappearance."

It didn't look like Zeke liked this. "Did he suspect you had an ulterior motive for speaking to him?"

"Nah. We were cool. Actually, he suggested he reckons you might be innocent. That you were in the wrong place at the wrong time. Or you just seen somethin' you shouldn't have seen."

Zeke leaned back in his chair and sighed. "That's a little comforting."

"Anyway, he reckons maybe we're looking in the wrong place."

"What do you mean?"

"Well, maybe what happened to Becky and Silas and the frame up has nothing to do with Rush at all."

They stared at me incredulously. "But what about the code? She was caught with this code and went missing right afterward," Hazel protested.

"Lafe reckons that might just be coincidence."

"He knows about the code?" Zeke demanded.

"No. Not strictly speaking. I never told him what information she'd dug up for me," Jace replied.

"Yeah, so he don't have all the information," Hazel said.

"Well, what evidence do we have that Rush is actually involved in what happened to Becky and Silas?" I asked.

They considered this. "Well, if we had something solid, we wouldn't be doin' this," Hazel said, but there was some doubt in her voice now.

"Nothing indicates Rush?" Quimby asked.

"Not strictly speaking," Jace replied grudgingly. "It's circumstantial."

"It's just a conspiracy theory," I added.

"Just because it's circumstantial doesn't mean it's not true," Zeke said in a perfectly calm voice, though I saw some doubt in his translucent eyes.

"Rush is guilty of the government pay-offs and having the results doctored. We know that," Jace said firmly.

"Yeah, we know that. It's not murder, though," I replied. "Lafe reckons maybe Becky ran off with another man. And that she might have been indirectly responsible for Silas' death."

"What about the frame up?" Zeke growled. His face didn't change, but I could tell he was angry now.

I soldiered on. "Maybe that's coincidence. I reckon there are other people in the world who wear glasses like yours that might have gotten smashed in the scuffle, and since the war, you're not the only one with a Colt .45."

He sighed deeply, but he didn't say anything. His chin dropped to his chest. He looked as though he were thinking hard about this. He stayed that way for several minutes. The rest of us kept quiet. Zeke rose to his feet so quickly, I took a step back and bumped against Jace behind me. Jace raised a hand to my waist to steady me.

"I knew them. I knew that girl. She wouldn't do that to Silas. She didn't run off. Someone lured her away."

I sighed. "Okay, okay. I won't argue about that."

"And we know it was a Pink who lured her away," Hazel added. "What we don't know is whether or not that person was working for Rush. That's what we got to prove."

"Or disprove."

"It's worth looking into the alternative, anyway," Vaughn said in his melodic voice, and we all looked at him. "We ain't in the habit of leavin' a lead unexplored because we've already formed the conclusion. Go with the evidence; don't make the evidence fit your conclusion."

"Yeah, yeah, all right," Jace said.

"I've already looked into Becky," Zeke said. "I searched her house. I didn't find anything that suggested she left of her own free will. Everything was still there. There was even a suitcase in her closet. I looked everywhere she could have been. I interviewed everyone who knew her."

"Rush?" I lifted my eyebrows.

"No, not him. It's dreadful difficult to get a meeting with him, even if he was the one who reported her missing."

"No signs of a body, either, I take it?" Hazel asked shrewdly.

"No. 'Course not."

"Okay. So, maybe we should take a look at the house like Lafe suggested," I said. "It can't hurt. Maybe we'll see something you missed."

Zeke narrowed his eyes, but he didn't argue. "Sure, why not? We haven't got much else going on. I'll go take another look."

"No," Jace argued. "It's too dangerous. The feds are still looking for you."

Zeke scowled. "I hate not being able to work."

"I know, but it's the way it is until we can clear you. We still haven't cracked the code. It's the only thing that connects Rush to this right now."

"But it might not have anything to do with Becky," Hazel piped in.

"That doesn't mean we should stop working that lead, either," Vaughn told her calmly. "We work them all. There's enough of us to get the job done."

"Lafe offered to help us search the house when the expo is over," I said. I sat beside Hazel on the bed and removed my floppy blue-feathered hat.

For a moment, Zeke looked like he was going to argue. Then he nodded thoughtfully. "That might not be a bad idea. He'll know what to look for, if there's anything new to find."

"And we don't know?" I demanded.

"No. You don't. You're amateur bounty hunters. You aren't trained like we are."

I decided not to argue. It was true, but I reckoned it didn't matter; we still got the job done. "Fine. If you say so."

"It can't hurt to have him around, anyway," Jace said.

"What?" Hazel demanded. "We're trusting a Pink now?"

I shrugged. "He seems all right. Besides, we ain't really trusting him, anyway. He doesn't know what we're really up to. He might be able to help, and he doesn't really believe Zeke did it."

"That doesn't mean I want him knowing you're working with me, Tess."

"'Course not. What sort of fool do you think I am?"

He lifted his shoulders. "I'm not sure of the sort yet."

I snorted. "We got good enough reason for looking into Becky's disappearance without needing to mention you at all."

Hazel rose up onto her knees and looked at me with barely contained excitement. "So...what now, Tess?"

"The expo this weekend, I reckon. Then we'll look at Becky a little bit closer."

She looked at me with large, glittering dark eyes. "Can I go, Tess? Can I?"

"I don't see why not. We' ain't wanted by the law anymore. It's safe enough."

She spun around to look at Quimby. "You want to go look at some guns, Quim?"

His face lit up. "Do I?"

I shook my head. Zeke glanced sourly at Vaughn. "I suppose you want to go to the show, too?"

Vaughn shrugged. "Nah. I'm not interested in technology. I'm more interested in old fashioned fist-a-cuffs." Zeke chuckled. "It's all right considering another lead in Becky's case, but I still think we can get Rush on something. The two murders might not be related to him at all, but I still think this code means something. I want to keep trying to figure it out."

"How can you stand being cooped up in here, Vaughn?" Hazel asked.

He smiled. "I don't mind a little actual quiet time. There are no bar brawls in here."

"We came close that time Quimby and me wanted the same scone."

"Lucky for me, you two will be Tess' problem."

I sighed. "That ain't very charitable of you, Vaughn."

"I ain't the charitable type."

"Yeah, all right. You keep Zeke in line, then. If he starts to go stir crazy, you know what to do."

He nodded. "I'll give him a shot of whiskey and punch his lights out if he gets too uppity."

Zeke's laugh was slightly awkward. I reckoned he wasn't sure whether or not to take Vaughn seriously. If Vaughn did get it in his head to knock him out, there wouldn't be much he could do about it. "You think you can handle a few more days on the lam, Zeke?" My voice was cheerful.

He sighed. "I suspect you all don't care much whether or not I'm enjoying myself."

"Don't start feelin' sorry for yourself. We care right enough. There just ain't much else to be doin' right now."

"And we want to take a look at the guns," Hazel added.

"Do I really have a choice about this?"

"Sure. You crack the code and expose Rush as a murderer or at the very least a criminal."

Zeke curled his lip. "I don't like not doing anything."

"We're all doing the best we can. Vaughn can keep an eye out for telegrams. We're waiting for the rest of the information from Jesse."

Jace drew the list Lafe had given him from a pocket inside his jacket. "Here's the list of Pinkertons who do work for Rush. We can compare it to the duty roster from the night Becky disappeared. You have about a hundred names to go through. It might help narrow down the possible suspects, at least."

Zeke snatched the paper from him. "Right. Well. You all have fun at your expo."

Chapter Thirteen

9TH ANNUAL BOSTON EXHIBITION OF TECHNOLOGY

MODERN MARVELS! ASTONISHING BREAKTHROUGHS!

SEE THE LATEST IN INDUSTRIAL EVOLUTION AND SCIENTIFIC DISCOVERY!

The words glittered upon the clear glass banner above our heads. The lobby of the Arc Lighter Hotel and Symposium Center was already jam packed with businessmen, exhibitors, speakers, presenters, guests and men and women in lab coats emblazoned with small company logos or garish name tags. They moved in and out of the various exhibit halls and gathered to speak in excited voices in the enormous, gilded lobby.

I looked around us in awe. The domed, clear-glass ceiling was several stories high and trimmed with gold. This early in the day, the windows above were frosted, but the hotel's brochures boasted a clear view of the glittering night sky. Crystal chandeliers swayed gently several stories above the sand-colored marble floor, and two large, wide staircases with polished wood banisters spanned the east and west walls. The ivory walls and gold-filigreed pillars were plastered with posters and flyers from the expo's exhibitors and vendors.

Jace seemed to know many of the richly dressed guests. He avoided introducing Hazel, Quimby and me when he could. I was relieved I'd bought a new dress for the occasion and allowed Hazel to style my long, black hair. I reckoned even a big city boy like Jace would have a hard time finding something to complain about. I might not be a trophy wife, but I had been beautiful once, and I reckoned I could still hold my own in a room full of debutantes if I really wanted to. I didn't, so I was happy Jace didn't seem all that interested in lingering in conversation with his acquaintances.

I paused in front of a large, brightly colored illustration of a large pistol with a thick, padded grip and a bulbous blue glass barrel trimmed in shining brass. RUSH SCIENTIFIC ADVANCEMENTS AND STEAM-POWERED INNOVATIONS presents the FIRST MASS-PRODUCED HAND-HELD AUTOMATIC SELF-CHARGING PERFECTLY CONTAINED DIRECTED ENERGY BURST WEAPON. SEE THE LATEST IN INNOVATIVE DEFENSIVE WARFARE! NOW ON EXHIBIT IN THE CELLULOID BALLROOM. I spun toward Hazel. She ought to see the competition. I reckoned she'd enjoy the design, anyway. Even I could see why the flimsy things blew off people's hands.

She wasn't paying attention to me. Her face was luminous. She gripped Quimby's arm. "Quim! Guns! Now! Come on!"

He chuckled and allowed her to drag him toward one of the exhibition rooms. They were gone before I had a chance to remind them what we were here to do. I reckoned they couldn't get into too much trouble. I didn't expect the exhibitors were foolish enough to leave their toys out where Hazel and Quimby could reach them. If they were...well, I reckoned that was someone else's problem.

I spun toward Jace. He was directly behind me. "Those are the faulty guns?" His voice was perfectly even, but there was a strange intensity to his gaze I wasn't sure I liked. This was not the time to discuss our peculiar situation.

"So it would seem. I reckon Hazel would have liked to have a look at it. The glass is too thin to contain the intensity of the beam, and the energy generator is too close to the grip. It's no wonder they're blowing up unpredictably."

He blinked at me in surprise. "Do you know about directed energy weapons?"

"I've seen Hazel build a few of them. I've seen her built a lot of things that don't make a lot of sense to me, but sometimes she feels like explaining. Sometimes I even listen."

He chuckled. "Well. I wouldn't have ever reckoned you as a woman of science."

"I'm not. I'm just fond of the convenience." I glanced around at the crowd. "So who are all these other guys? Rush's competition?"

"Some of them. A lot of them are defense and weapons manufacturers from all over the world. Others produce more mundane and less destructive innovations. I reckon there are a lot of inventions on display that won't come to the public for decades or more. It's really just an exhibition of who has the bigger ideas and the most money to spend on them."

I laughed. "If Rush gets that law passed in Congress, though, he'll put them all out of business."

"That's the general idea, I expect."

"Can't he just play in the sandbox with the other kids? There's room for everyone."

"When one has power and money, it seems like all they want is more power and money."

"I just don't get that."

"Most of us normal people don't."

I smiled. "Any word on what's going on with that bill?"

"Just lobbying. Mostly on behalf of Rush; sometimes on behalf of others. Congressman Caine is back in Boston for the time being. I reckon we'll see him here somewhere. He's usually right at Rush's elbow."

"What do the other companies think of the bill?"

"Most of the bigger companies don't want it. The vetting process is stringent, and it will cost a lot of money for them to get up to specifications."

"Not Rush, though."

"He doesn't need to get up to spec. He'll pass inspection regardless."

"Is he even trying to pretend to be meeting standards?"

"Oh, sure. He puts on a good face. You'll see. It's impressive. You would almost believe he is a real person with a conscience."

I laughed. It felt natural to tuck my hand into his elbow and allow him to conduct me through the hotel and symposium center. The ballrooms and exhibit halls were filled to bursting with goggling guests admiring interesting and unlikely inventions: an army of tiny brass mechanical men that marched in time and fired bullets from their child-like fingertips; binoculars that fit over the eyes and enhanced the wearers vision; cannons that fit over the arms and replaced the hand-held guns; and brass boots with rockets on the soles that propelled the wearer several feet into the air but did not appear to have a strategy for returning safely to the ground again.

Jason knew many of the guests, and they greeted him cheerfully. He was popular. He'd always been popular in the social circles of Savannah. He was smart and clever and witty. He could even be charming. I suspected he could even out flannel-mouth Quimby if he wanted to. I reckoned I might enjoy watching him try, anyway.

I plastered a smile on my face and nodded and curtseyed when it was required of me, but otherwise I remained silent by his side as he nattered with various guests and exhibitors. They all seemed interested in me, but none of them seemed to think it was unusual when he'd explained our circumstances. We weren't the only couple or family to be torn apart by the bitter war. 'Course, he left out the wild west bounty hunter bit, but I reckoned folks ought to be a bit more skeptical of our arrangement. Mayhap they were, and they were just putting on a smile. Yeah, that was probably it.

He caught me staring at him and lifted his eyebrows. "What's that look for?"

"Is this what you do?"

"What are you talking about?"

"This. Mixing with the upper class, going to parties, smarming around."

He blinked at me incredulously for several seconds. "This used to be your life too, Tess."

I considered. "Yeah. You're right. It wasn't by choice, though."

He frowned. "Yes, I can see what sorts of things you get up to when it is your choice."

"I know I live rough, and I ain't much of a lady anymore. But I like my life, Jace. I wouldn't change anything."

"Nothing?" His voice was low, and the injured expression on his face was unsettling.

I looked away. "No. Nothing. My posse and me have a good thing going. We live like we like."

"This is what you want? To run around on the frontier, living wild and rough, scuffling with low lives and outlaws?"

"Don't forget gun fighting. We have a lot of gunfights."

"Tess."

I sighed. "Well, it's what I've been doing for five years. It's what we're used to."

He turned and strode away from me. I followed him as he darted into one of the exhibit halls. I wasn't sure if he was trying to escape or make me follow him. All the same, I caught up to him at the front of the small, less crowded exhibition hall. There in the center of the stage was a large, gleaming brass horse. Its joints connected with clockwork gears, and its eyeballs were glittering black jewels. The long, flowing black mane looked as sleek as obsidian. It rippled as though it were blowing in a slight breeze. I reached out to run my fingers gently along the horse's hair. It felt smooth and solid to the touch like polished glass.

I stepped up to the stage to get a closer look at the beautiful automaton. A short, robust man with thick, shock white hair appeared by my side as though I'd tripped a silent alarm somewhere. His rosy round face was smooth despite his advanced age. He was smiling. He looked like the sort of man who was always smiling, though his translucent blue eyes looked tired and anxious.

He stuck out his hand for me to shake. His grip was hearty and keen, and I thought he seemed like a nice enough guy. "Barnaby Hubble, CEO of Hubble Modernization and Technology," he said. "I see you've noticed my beauty, Gertrude."

I smiled and glanced at the shining horse. "Yes. It's very impressive."

Hubble smiled and smoothed an affectionate hand along Gertrude's flank. "I've been working on her for seven years. She's finally ready." His pale eyes glittered almost manically. "She's just the first. There are more like her. Hundreds, eventually thousands more."

Jace tilted his head to the side to admire the horse. "What is her purpose?"

Hubble chuckled heartily. "Isn't it obvious? Gertie here will replace a traditional horse. She can run faster, she never tires, and she doesn't require food and water. That, and her ride is as smooth as a common meat horse. Smoother."

"Well, how about that," I murmured. I reckoned my posse and me could use horses like these. We could even store them somewhere when we needed to catch a lift somewhere instead of selling them off and feeling like we were losing our companions.

"But are they practical?" Jace asked.

I opened my mouth to disdain his narrow eye for the future, but Hubble didn't seem to mind. He chuckled. "Who are you, son?"

Jace smiled. "Jason Holt."

Hubble's eyes lit up. "Ah. The reporter for the *Boston Daily*. I've heard of you." He nudged Jace gently. "You do ask the tough questions, then." He looked at me. "And you, miss?"

"I'm Tess Holt."

"Indeed? His sister? Cousin, perhaps?"

I smiled, but Jace didn't seem to like this friendly jostling. "Wife," he said sharply.

"Ah. A shame." Hubble grinned. "Well, Gertie and her sisters still have a few hitches. They aren't quite ready for mass production yet. They cost too much to manufacture, and their efficacy is outweighed by their cost." He sighed good-naturedly. "Anyone who can afford her doesn't need her." His laughter was infectious. "Still, in a few years, we'll have sorted out all the kinks."

"I hope you do," I told him sincerely. "I would love to ride one of those."

He chuckled. "You do a lot of riding, Mrs. Holt?"

"You can call me Tess. I sure do."

"Around here?"

I glanced quickly at Jace, but he didn't offer any assistance. "Back home."

"And where are you from?"

"We're from Georgia," Jace answered for me. "Savannah."

"Ah. I see. A Southern belle and her gentleman." He grinned and gestured grandly toward Gertrude. "So, Tess, how about a ride? You want to give Gertie a go?"

"Do I?" I exclaimed. Jace opened his mouth with a scowl, but I held up my hand to stop any protest he might have voiced. "You shut your mouth, Jace. Don't ruin this for me."

Jace snorted. Then he smiled. "I would never dream of refusing you anything, my dear."

I smirked. "You've gotten smarter since we first got married, then."

Hubble grinned. He offered his hand to me to assist me into Gertrude's gleaming bronze saddle. I reached for it, but Jace stepped in suddenly and gripped my waist in his hands as though he intended to lift me into the saddle. I rolled my eyes and shrugged him off. I'd never needed help mounting a horse before. I gripped the horn and swung myself expertly onto Gertie's sturdy metal back. She didn't feel as cold on my backside as I'd expected.

Hubble laughed as I arranged my voluminous skirt around me. "I see you have some experience."

I tossed my head. "How do I work her?"

"The same as a real horse." He handed me the thick, brown leather reigns.

I snapped them. Gertrude advanced several steps. Hubble was right; she was as smooth and responsive as an organic horse. Hubble didn't seem to be worried about what I might influence his little beauty to do. He and Jace watched indulgently as I prodded Gertrude down from the low stage and nudged her into a gentle trot. The brass horse was noisy. Her metal hooves clacked against the marble floor, and her clockwork joints spun and whirred with each motion. It was sort of nice.

The exhibit hall was long and narrow, and I leaned down over Gertie's neck as I nudged her into a canter. My carefully curled hair blew back from my face with the increased speed. I laughed in exhilaration and turned her sharply around to pelt toward Jace and Hubble. They were smiling.

I grinned at them as I yanked Gertie to a halt at the stage. I swung out of the saddle and offered the horse's reigns back to her master. He smiled. "Perhaps you would be willing to ride old Gertie for the demonstration this weekend, Tess? You are a fine rider. My aunt isn't the rider she once was, not since the wooden leg."

I laughed, but Jace frowned. "If you want a rider," I replied, "you want Quimby."

Hubble lifted his eyebrows. "Oh?"

"A friend of mine. Quimby Burton. He's an old wild west show trick rider."

His face illuminated with interest. "Indeed? Is he around?"

"Sure he is. He's around here somewhere. He's easily distracted by shiny things that fire directed energy beams, but he loves to show off. If I find him, I'll send him your way."

"Great!"

"While we have you here, Mr. Hubble--"

"Barnaby, please, young man. We're friends now, aren't we?"

Jace inclined his head. "Then you won't mind sharing your thoughts on the new bill proposed in Congress this session regarding stricter standards and practices for research and development firms?"

Hubble sighed. "I didn't think you were here just to introduce me to your charming wife." He considered for a long moment, as though he were practicing his response in his head a few times. "Most of the business owners in my industry are opposed to the new bill. Under the new law, inspection standards will be stringent and difficult. It will cost a lot of firms a lot of money to comply with the proposed specs. It will put many of the smaller companies out of business." He lifted a shoulder. "If the law passes, Hubble MT is prepared to meet the new specs and standards. We will do what we have to do."

Jace nodded. I saw his emerald eyes narrow shrewdly. His voice was perfectly blasé when he asked, "And what do you think of your major competitor, Sterling

Rush? He is putting pressure on Congress to pass the law. Any thoughts on why he would want this while all the rest of you oppose it?"

Hubble smiled. "Ah, young man. I know all about your campaign against Sterling. I'm not getting involved in any of that. I am not privy to any of Sterling's motivations for the things he does. I can only assume he has his reasons."

"You bet he does," Jason replied darkly.

"Well. You are charming, Mr. Holt. Everyone says so."

The voice from behind us was smooth like liquid gold. We all turned to the new arrival to our party in surprise. He was a tall, well-built man in his early forties with thick, wavy salt and pepper hair combed back from a tall, tanned forehead. His features were lined but they were handsome still, and his dark eyes were large and intelligent. He was smiling. His teeth were brilliant white against his full mouth and tanned skin. His charcoal suit looked very expensive.

I didn't know who he was. Jace and Barnaby did.

Jace stiffened and lifted his chin. His green eyes flashed in that keen, intense way I remembered. He smiled. I suddenly realized who the man in the expensive suit was. "Mr. Rush. How nice to see you," Jace greeted brightly. "I've come to admire your competition."

Sterling Rush smiled back, and his dark, almond shaped eyes crinkled at the corners. He inclined his head politely to Hubble. "A clockwork horse is no competition for Rush AI's newest line of handheld directed energy weapons."

Hubble's own smile remained fixed, but his pale eyes narrowed. "That's what you're showcasing, then, Sterling?"

"Indeed."

"You've worked out the design flaws, then?" Jace asked cheerfully.

Rush chuckled. He turned his gaze to Gertrude. "This is remarkable, Barnaby. What do you call it?"

"Gertrude."

He laughed heartily. "Of course. Lovely. Is it ready for mass production?"

"Ah. Not just yet. We're a couple years out. You and your handheld death ray?"

"We prefer directed energy burst weapon. You've seen the flyers?"

"Indeed, I hear you weapons boys do. I must have missed them."

"I like death ray," I piped in merrily. "It's very succinct and to the point."

Rush turned toward me. He caught my hand in his and bent to kiss my knuckles in the elbow-length black gloves. "And who is this lovely, laconic woman?"

I laughed. Jace moved closer to my side, but his expression was impassive. "This is my wife, Tess."

I was a little proud of Jace. It looked as though he'd caught Rush out. I doubted it was easy. Rush recovered himself quickly. He lifted an eyebrow. "Your wife? Is that so?"

"Indeed."

"We've not had the pleasure, Mrs. Holt."

"No, indeed we have not." I smiled at him.

"And how is it I was not aware such a creature existed?" He looked reproachfully at Jace. "Have you been keeping her a secret, Jason?"

"Something like that," he replied.

Rush gestured us toward the door. "Come. Allow me to show you the Celluloid Ballroom. My exhibit hall."

I stepped forward. "I would be delighted, Mr. Rush."

He grinned. "No, Mrs. Holt, I am the one who is delighted. Barnaby?"

Hubble nodded, but his smile quivered unhappily at the corners. He trailed a few steps behind us as we allowed Rush to lead us toward the Celluloid Ballroom. Rush strode confidently beside me. On my other side, Jace's hand clenched around my elbow.

"And what is it you do, Mrs. Holt? Keep your husband's house? Back his outrageous accusations and bolster his spirits?"

I laughed. "No. Not so much of that, Mr. Rush."

"Don't tell me you're a journalist, as well? I have seen many women with very impressive resumes."

"No. I'm not a journalist, either."

"So what, then, my dear?"

"I am sure you wouldn't be interested."

"I assure you, I am extremely interested in you, Mrs. Holt."

I lifted my eyebrows and glanced at Jace. His jaw was slightly rigid, but he looked as though this conversation were of little interest to him. His arm slid around my waist to draw me closer against his side. "My wife is...an investigator of sorts, Mr. Rush."

"Is that so?" He looked at me in surprise. "A Pinkerton?"

"No. I'm not a Pinkerton."

"I thought not. I do know most of the Pinkertons in Boston."

"Do you?" Jace asked. "Are there any in particular that you recommend for entrusting your more delicate business?"

I glared sidelong at him. Rush laughed. "Such pointed and insinuating questions you ask, Jason, but this time I confess I have no idea to what you might be referring. Your wife is ever so mysterious. Why don't you tell me more about your business, Mrs. Holt? Or may I call you Tess?"

I shrugged. "It's all the same to me."

"I would prefer that you don't," Jace put in.

Rush laughed. "It is truly astonishing that you are married to such a man, Tess. You seem so much more amenable."

I chuckled. "Oh, Mr. Rush, you really don't know me very well at all. I assure you, Jace has always been the sweeter tempered half of our marriage."

"Ah. Here we are, then."

Rush gestured grandly toward the huge, wide-open double doors of the Celluloid Ballroom. Inside, guests and Rush AI employees tested and demonstrated an impressive collection of steam-powered gadgets and oddities, engines, miniature models of flying machines and steam cars, weapons and other curious-looking objects that probably possessed extraordinarily dramatic and singularly gratuitous uses.

Rush AI did appear to be the center of attention. Gertrude and her master had been a sideshow in comparison. The room was as large as the lobby with the same glass and gold domed ceiling. It sparkled in the rays of the late afternoon sun shining down through the roof and glinting off the impressive spectacle of brass and gold and copper.

Rush looked upon his collection with pride. "What do you think of my little endeavor, Barnaby?"

Hubble rolled his eyes almost imperceptibly. "Very impressive as always,

Sterling."

"Thank you. Perhaps one of my mechanical soldiers can hitch a ride on your clockwork horse."

I laughed. Rush gestured us toward a display on the west side of the room. The brass mechanical soldier to which he had referred was nothing more than a hollow suit into which a man might climb and wear as very cumbersome brass armor. The arms terminated in enormous, heavy cannons. The dinner-plate shaped feet might have been equipped with propulsion technology, but I doubted they could support the weight of the armor as well as the rider. The helmet was a large, globular head with goggled eyes and ear trumpets.

Hubble eyed them so impassively, I couldn't ascertain the direction of his thoughts. "I don't believe Gertie is equipped to support such a thing, Sterling," he said in a neutral voice. "What exactly are they?"

Rush seemed almost offended by this question. "A mechanical suit, which a man might wear, of course."

I lifted my eyebrows. "Why would he want to?"

He laughed and glanced slyly at Jace. "Oh, I do like her, Jason."

Jace smirked. "She can be sassy when she wants to be."

"Sometimes when I don't intend to be," I added. "Where are the death rays, then, Mr. Rush?"

He laughed and held up his hands. "Oh, no. I'm saving the very best for last. And please, call me Sterling."

I didn't. "Are they better than the mechanical suits?"

"Oh, yes." He winked at Hubble. "Don't you think so, Barnaby?"

Hubble lifted a shoulder defensively. "I'm not in the weapons business, Sterling, you know that. I have no way to judge which weapon is better."

Rush laughed. "Don't you both like my friend Barnaby? He is always a riot. I would be delighted if you would join me here tonight, Tess. There is a party in my honor."

"In your honor, Sterling?" Hubble asked. "I understood it was to be a party in honor of the exhibitors."

"Ah, semantics. Are there any more exhibitors who matter?"

I glanced at Jace, but we managed to keep perfectly even expressions. "I think a party might be just the thing, Mr. Rush."

He grinned. "Ah, you might as well bring your charming husband along. I'm sure he wouldn't want to miss out on the fun and the opportunity to ask more inappropriately insinuating questions."

I laughed. Jace lifted his chin and smiled disarmingly at Rush. "I wouldn't miss it for the world."

Chapter Fourteen

I hadn't been so gussied up since my wedding day. I didn't know where Hazel was keeping these gowns, but I was a little glad she'd thought ahead. The Celluloid Ballroom of the Arc Lighter Hotel and Symposium Center sparkled. Rush AI's latest innovations lined the walls like lonely women waiting for dance partners. The guests strutted like peacocks in their finest gowns and tuxedos.

Quimby grinned around at the women in the latest fashions with their dates. None of them were as handsome as Quimby. He knew it. He always did. "Nice party, Jace."

"It's not my party. Tell Rush about it." Jace glared around at the party as though it had nastily insulted him.

I smiled. "Jace is a little put out about Sterling right now."

They all looked around at me in surprise. "He's Sterling now?" Quimby demanded. "Since when?"

"He's actually quite charming."

Jace scowled. "That is what everyone thinks until he orders your murder."

I laughed. "He seems to like you, Jace."

"He rather seems to like you."

Hazel and Quimby exchanged a meaningful glance. "Anything to drink at this party?" Hazel asked.

Jace tilted his head toward the large bar on the east wall of the room. A crowd of glittering, chattering guests surrounded the bartender. Hazel pushed through without regarding the outraged exclamations of the plumed ladies and their escorts. I snorted with laughter. Jace looked a little scandalized, but when we reached the bar, he perked right up.

"Whiskey," Hazel said, slapping her hand on the bar.

The barkeeper was a young man in a black suit with long, dark hair pulled back into a sleek queue. He looked at Hazel a little uncertainly. I doubted he was actually a bartender, but he did improve the luster of the room. He poured Hazel her drink and passed it to her. I opened my mouth to order, but Jace was already ordering white wine. I sighed in disappointment.

"For you, miss?" the barkeeper asked me.

I grimaced. "White wine."

Hazel and Quimby looked around at me in shock. Hazel snorted into her glass. I avoided their gazes and sipped the bone-dry liquid. Jace smiled at me over the top of his own glass, so I suppressed my grimace.

"So what's on the agenda this evening?" Quimby asked, glancing around as he sipped his beer.

"Agenda?"

"We didn't come here for a good time, did we? I thought we had stopped having good times."

I laughed. "We ain't never stopped havin' good times, Quim. We just have to be responsible with them."

"We keep an eye out for any Pinkertons who are here working for Rush or anyone to whom he pays particular attention in case something comes up," Jace said.

"Sounds boring," Hazel complained. She looked around sullenly. Her face suddenly illuminated. "Those death rays over there look pretty interesting." She drifted toward the large glass cases in the center of the room, around which couples were already dancing to the spirited orchestra on the large stage at the far end of the room.

I lifted my eyebrows at Quimby and Jace. "You want to see what all the fuss is about?" I asked. "What everyone's dying over?"

"'Course I do." Quimby didn't glance over his shoulder to ensure Jace and me were following him.

The First Mass-Produced Hand-Held Automatic Self-Charging Perfectly Contained Directed Energy Burst Weapons looked exactly the same in reality as they had in their artistic renderings. The bulbous blue glass barrels sparkled like diamonds in the light from the crystal chandeliers. Their grips were carefully engraved in brass and copper and padded with thick brown leather.

Quimby eyed them narrowly. He lifted an eyebrow. "The components are all in the wrong places. No wonder they're blowing off people's hands."

"I know!" I exclaimed. "Hazel?"

Her dark eyes were big and bright. "Oh. Pretty."

"Hazel, you have dozens of these things and they all work better," I reminded her.

"They're not this pretty. Look at the shiny gold rivets and copper triggers and blue sparkling glass--"

"Hazel, don't touch the glass--"

A bell chimed loudly around us. "See what you done?"

Two men in sleek, nondescript black suits with discreet badges on their belts materialized out of the crowd as though they had been waiting for the signal. One of them was Lafayette Jackson. When he caught sight of Jace and me, his stern expression transformed. He laughed heartily. "Ah, I should have suspected it would be you here setting off the alarms, Jace."

Jace laughed and offered his hand to shake. I grinned. "Hazel, Quimby, this is Lafe Jackson. He's a Pink."

Lafe turned his good-natured censure on Hazel. Her cheeks turned slightly pink, and she smiled sheepishly. "You're the one who touched the case?"

She clasped her hands behind her back. "Yes."

"Don't. They're for display, not for play."

She fluttered her eyelashes.

"I wouldn't touch one, Hazel," Jace warned. "It might blow your hand off."

Lafe smirked. "I assume you are here to disparage Mr. Rush and his latest innovations. Are you gatecrashing? Am I going to have to throw you out?"

I grinned. "Quite the contrary. We were personally invited by Sterling himself."

Lafe lifted an eyebrow. "Sterling?"

Jace shrugged and rolled his eyes.

"You're on first name terms now?"

"No. Just he and Tess," Jace replied.

Lafe laughed. "Well, isn't that just precious." He inclined his head. "Well. You all have a nice time" He turned and strode smartly away. I could still hear him laughing.

"I like him," Hazel said.

"I just bet you do," Quimby replied slyly.

"Ah, there you are. Lafe said I might find you here." Sterling Rush stepped up behind us with a wide, brilliant white grin. "I see you've noticed my latest invention."

"Hazel is quite the admirer," I told him, smiling.

"You like guns, Hazel?" He turned his large, cheerful dark eyes toward Hazel.

"I like death rays," she replied eagerly.

He smiled indulgently. "Do you know anything about them?"

"Do I? What sort of power source are you using? I prefer electro-static myself. If you get the generator just right, you can time the blast so it doesn't take as long for the beam to recharge before you can discharge it again, but it's really the biggest problem in the overall application of the design. I find the easiest way to ensure you have enough firepower to get the job done is to just keep a bunch of death rays around so by the time you get to the last one, the first one is charged again."

She didn't even take a breath. I snorted with laughter. Jace stared at her in unconcealed shock. Quimby wasn't even paying attention.

Rush looked at her blankly. "Young lady, I do not actually design the weapons myself. I have a team who does that."

Hazel glanced keenly around the room. "And where are they?"

Rush lifted an eyebrow. "Ah. Some of them are around here somewhere. I could introduce you, perhaps. If you'd like."

"Would I?"

"Perhaps another time, Hazel," Jace put in. "I am sure Mr. Rush is otherwise obligated this evening, basking in the lights of the flashbulbs and the beams of his admirers."

Rush laughed. "You flatter me, Jason."

"Oh, no, certainly not."

"So you've seen my collection. What do you think?"

"Shiny," Hazel cooed.

"Very impressive, Sterling, but what will you do with them?" I asked, smiling up at him.

"Ah, my dear, and here I thought you had an eye for the future."

"I regret to disappoint you."

"Oh, no. I am not disappointed. Quite the contrary. I am delighted to share my vision. My new directed energy weapons will be the end of war."

I glanced around at my companions. They looked as dumbfounded as I felt.

"How so, Sterling?"

"Well, with the might of my energy pistols, what nation will wish to war with the United States? We will possess the superior firepower."

"You believe other nations will be too afraid to oppose us?"

"Indeed. He who has the bigger guns makes the rules. Or bigger beams, in this case."

"Ah, but without war, what will you do? What will come of your business?" Jace asked. "Are you sure you want it all to end?"

"Oh, I assure you, Jason, Rush AI will never be without ideas."

Hazel's expression was unusually thoughtful. "I'm not sure your plan is practical, Mr. Rush."

He looked around at her in surprise. "Oh?"

"I carry around an arsenal and people try to scuffle with me continuously. I'm not sure superior firepower will be enough to quell an angry spirit."

We stared at her in silence for a several seconds. Hazel could be insightful when she wanted to be. Eerily so. I never could get used to it. Our gazes swiveled back to Rush.

His smile looked slightly fixed. "Well. I am sure one of us is right. Time will tell which one, and if it is you, I will tip my hat to you, young lady."

She beamed. "Yeah. Thanks. I'll be sure to hold out for that."

Rush looked slightly relieved as the band struck up a lively tune. A crowd of pairs exclaimed excitedly and moved as one toward the dance floor. "Ah. I see that is my cue to join the dancing. If you would all excuse me, I am off to find a willing partner." He bowed politely. "I do hope you two ladies will honor me with a dance this evening."

Hazel shrugged. "Yeah. Sure. Whatever."

I smiled and inclined my head to him. "If Jace doesn't mind."

Rush lifted his eyebrows, but Jace just smiled. "I reckon you can handle

Sterling, Tess."

"I'm sure I can."

Rush looked as though he wasn't sure whether he'd been insulted or not. "Well. See you soon, then." He dipped a short bow and spun on his heel to stride away.

Hazel glanced at me. "What is up with him?"

"I don't know."

"He's a dandy," Quimby put in.

I laughed. Hazel pushed her lip out in a pout. "I'm disappointed. I expected a genius, not a corporate windbag."

Jace snorted. "I reckon he's more than that."

"He gives me the creeps." Hazel lifted her eyebrows at me. "What about you, Tess?"

I thought about this. "No, not really." They all looked at me in surprise, but I shrugged. "He seems all right. A little smarmy, but which one of them ain't?"

"Are you tellin' me you like that guy?" Quimby demanded.

"I didn't say I liked him. I just said he seems all right. It don't mean nothin'. It don't mean he ain't still what Jace says he is."

Jace crossed his arms over his chest with a sullen expression. "He is."

"All right, Jace, I ain't sayin' he ain't."

He scowled. "I don't like him flirting with you."

"Flirting? I don't think he was flirting."

"He was flirting," Hazel put in.

"Oh, he's just trying to get under your skin, Jace. Don't let him."

He sighed. "Let's just get to work, all right?"

"Yeah. Sure. Where exactly do you think we'll find some?"

"I think I'll go look for clues in the bottom of a glass of whiskey," Hazel said.

"I think I'll go look for clues over there in that group of ladies."

I rolled my eyes as they darted off in opposite directions. Jace turned toward me. "Do they do that a lot?"

I snorted. "Yeah, pretty much all of the time."

"How do any of you people get any work done?"

I laughed. "We have our methods. Not everyone understands them."

"Methods. I see."

"I don't need your superciliousness, Jace."

This seemed to amuse him. "So, do you want to dance?"

I laughed incredulously. "You, dance? I seem to remember you hated to dance."

"Well, I've learned a few things. Some social pleasantries and such, you know."

I wasn't sure I liked this. "Have you had the opportunity to use them?"

He eyed me shrewdly. "Are you trying to ask me if there's another woman in my life, Tess?"

I didn't meet his gaze. "No."

"There isn't." I glanced up at him incredulously, but he just shrugged. "I'm a married man."

"We haven't seen each other in nine years."

"That doesn't make our marriage any less valid, Tess." He narrowed his eyes. "Have you got another man? Burton?"

I laughed. "Quimby? Lords, no. He's too busy chasing anything in a skirt."

"I didn't get that impression at all."

I rolled my eyes. "There isn't another man, Jace."

He shrugged. "You thought you were a widow. It wouldn't have been unjustified."

I looked away. "I don't want to talk about that. I'm not that kind of lady."

He smiled. "No. You never were."

We were silent a moment. I glanced around at the dancing, laughing and chattering crowd, but it didn't really offer any distraction or escape. "Tell me about your life, Jace. What have you been doing all these years?"

He shrugged. "After the war ended, I went to your father's plantation to get you back." I glanced at him sharply in surprise. "You were already gone. Nathan

194

didn't tell me where."

"He didn't know."

"Well, I had no home, no job and my wife was in the wind, but I had my education. You remember before the war, Father moved here to Boston to work for the Globe. Then he started his own paper and took me along with him."

"Everett runs the Daily?"

"He did. He's retired now. He sold it to some conglomerate and made a killing."

"They kept you on?"

"Are you kidding? I'm the star attraction."

"I'm not surprised. You always did like to stir up trouble."

"I don't stir up trouble, Tess. I point out the wrongs in the world and try to right them."

He sounded so perfectly sincere, I was silent a moment. Then I smiled. "You do, don't you?"

"I try to, anyway." I couldn't hold his earnest gaze. "It's all I've been doing the whole time. I've just been here. I sent people to find you. No one could. I gave up trying to find you, but that doesn't mean I didn't know you were out there somewhere. I didn't forget."

I sighed. "I'm sorry about that, Jace. I didn't realize anyone was looking for me." I glanced at him. "For what it's worth, I really did believe you were dead. If I had known you weren't, I would have waited for you."

There was sadness in his eyes, and I felt real bad about that. "So what now?"

I shook my head. "I don't know. I ain't cut out for this city life." I looked up at him sadly. "And you ain't cut out for the frontier."

"Maybe you're right about that, Tess. That doesn't mean we can't try to work it out."

"I need some time to think about it, Jace. Don't you?"

"No. Not really."

I frowned. "We don't know each other anymore."

"I'm the same as I've always been."

I turned my face away from him in shame. "I'm not the same woman. I don't think I could ever be that woman again." He looked a little hurt about this. "I'm sorry, Jace."

"What does that mean?"

"It just means I'm sorry the Tess you married is gone."

"I don't think that's true. You've been through a lot of things, seen a lot, done a lot that you never dreamed of when we were kids, but that doesn't mean you aren't the same woman."

"It does, Jace."

"I won't believe that."

I frowned. "I am who I am. I ain't goin' to change that for no man. I like my life. I don't want no one comin' in and messin' it up and tryin' to make me be someone I ain't anymore."

He lifted his hands in surprise. "Tess--"

"I hope I'm not interrupting anything important."

We turned towards Rush in a single motion. Jace looked irritated, but I was a little relieved by the interruption. I suspected Rush knew exactly what he'd done, and I wondered if he intended to rescue me from the awkward conversation or if he just really enjoyed brassing Jace off. It was probably a little of both.

Jace opened his mouth to reply, and I doubted it was going to be polite. I smiled a little stiffly. "No, not at all, Sterling."

Jace scowled at me, but he didn't argue.

Rush offered me his hand. "Would you care to dance, then, Mrs. Holt?" He smiled brilliantly at Jace. "That is, if you don't mind, Jason."

Jace inclined his head gracefully. "No. Of course not. It is of course Tess' privilege."

I smiled at him and took Rush's hand. He led me into the flock of plumed couples dancing to the complicated melody. Some of the couples were stiff and awkward, and others spun around the pairs with skillful grace. We were among the ones who were managing not to look as though we were utterly uncomfortable in each other's company. Rush was a good dancer. He guided me into a nimble waltz. All I needed to do was avoid stepping on his feet.

He smiled down at me. "Things seem a little tense between you and your husband, Tess."

I lifted my eyebrows. "I don't think that's polite conversation."

He didn't look at all abashed. His smile didn't waver. "I do apologize if I was out of line."

"You were."

"Forgive me."

"All right. Just this once."

"Truly, you are mystery, Mrs. Holt. How is it that five years have passed in which I have undergone the intense scrutiny of your dogged husband and I had no inkling of your existence?"

"Jace isn't exactly the type to share his personal business."

"I was under the impression he had no personal business. I saw him as nothing more than a newshound who continued to pursue his query late into the night without pause. I hadn't considered there might be someone to whom he might return home."

I laughed. "I have discovered, Sterling, that most people are more than they seem."

For the first time, his large, dark eyes narrowed, and I suspected there might be more to his flirtations than merely riling Jace. "And you? Are you who you claim to be?"

A chill ran down my spine. "So you suspect I am here under false pretenses for some other purpose?" I laughed, but I suddenly felt much less comfortable.

"The thought had crossed my mind."

"Ah, I suppose that's fair enough. I do know my husband has spoken out very publicly against you. That is why you really wanted to dance with me, wasn't it? To get me away from Jace and question me about what we're really up to?"

He laughed. It sounded sincere. "Perhaps. I suppose I was not as subtle as I believed."

"Oh, I'm sure you're very skilled at subtlety, Sterling. I am merely very perceptive, and I'm afraid the animosity between you and my husband is quite unconcealed."

"Yes, there is certainly no love lost between us. I have nothing against him personally, for I find him to be a very charming, clever and interesting man, but we do not see eye to eye professionally."

"I have nothing to do with your feud with Jace."

"All right. I apologize for the presumption, then." He smiled a charming, crooked smile. "Are we friends again?"

"Sure we are."

"Good." He was silent for a moment, and his gaze wandered over my head. I wondered if he even remembered I was with him.

Leaning against a gold-filigreed pillar on the edge of the dance floor, I noticed Lafe watching us with a small smirk. He met my gaze. I smiled at him, and he inclined his head. He tilted his head toward the center of the room. Hazel leaned over the glass case full of Rush's death rays. I rolled my eyes. Jace stood nearby her, but he didn't seem to care whether she tripped the alarm again. He was looking everywhere but Rush and me, but he still looked irritated.

Quimby was the only one who seemed to be having a good time. He leaned over a pretty girl in the corner of the room. She looked young and innocent and gullible. I suspected Quimby could get into a bar brawl even at a posh ball in New England. I hoped I wouldn't have to find out.

When I glanced back at Rush, he was eyeing me. There was no emotion or expression in his eyes, but I felt another chill. I tilted my head at him. He blinked, and he looked warm and friendly again. "So are you enjoying my party, Mrs. Holt?"

I smiled. "I thought it wasn't your party. I thought it was everyone's party."

"Ah, Mr. Hubble is a sweet man, but he does not know how to play with the big boys."

I laughed. "No?"

"His clockwork horse is ridiculous. Small time. The money is in defense. Now that the nation has stopped fighting itself, we're turning our attention to the tensions overseas. It's only a matter of time before someone looks to us as the next conquest."

I considered. "Do you really believe another nation would invade and attack us?"

"It's possible. With my technology and defense systems, they won't. It will never be a problem. Our shores will be safe."

I thought about this. I held his gaze. I wondered if he really believed that. "That's very noble, Mr. Rush."

"Perhaps some would say so. Others would call me a villain." His eyes drifted a moment over my shoulder. I suspected he was seeking out Jace in the crowd.

"There is nothing like a little healthy opposition to force a man to strive for nobility."

"Ah, that is a perspective I had never considered. How very insightful you are, Mrs. Holt."

A large, burly man appeared apologetically at Rush's elbow. He was big and strong and handsome in his nondescript black suit, but he didn't look like a smart fellow. He was wearing a badge on his belt like Lafe's. He gave me a big, goofy grin. "I'm sorry, sir," he said.

Rush paused. "Ah. Arthur. To what do I owe the interruption of a very pleasant dance?"

I didn't think he was in earnest. He didn't seem to mind that the Pink had interrupted our dance. I reckoned I didn't, either. Arthur looked extremely sheepish. "The Congressman needs to speak to you, Sir."

"Ah." Rush glanced at me. "I am sure you don't mind, Mrs. Holt?"

"Oh, no. Of course not. You do seem to have a lot of friends in high places, Mr. Rush."

"Oh, no, dear. I am the friend in high places. You would do well to remember it." He stepped away from me and bowed smartly. I inclined my head. He spun on his heel and strode away.

Jace was beside me in a heartbeat. I started. He was scowling. "I think Rush is a little too interested in you, Tess."

I laughed and stepped into his arms. He blinked in surprise, but he guided me into a dance. "No. It's not what you think. He suspects me."

He frowned. "Does he?"

"Well, he thinks I'm up to something, anyway. I don't guess he dreams I'm Tess Mercury."

"Of course he doesn't. You look like a respectable lady."

I frowned. "Those two things are not necessarily mutually exclusive. Well, most of the time."

"So, did he tell you anything interesting?"

"Nothing worth listening to."

"What did he say?"

I shrugged. "Just touting his noble intentions and ideas for global peace." He looked at me as though I were speaking gibberish. "Who was that guy who interrupted us? Have you seen him before?"

"No."

"Are you sure?"

"If I have, it's never been important. What did he say?"

"He just said the Congressman wanted to speak to Rush. I'm not entirely sure he didn't give him some signal to come over and break up our dance. It was getting a little awkward." Jace grinned as though he appreciated this. "Maybe Quimby knows. He knows a lot about who's who, even around here."

Jace looked as though he didn't quite believe this. "He's been here before?"

"No."

"Then how could he possibly know him?"

"I have wondered that myself many times." I paused and stepped out of his arms. I smiled at him and jerked my head.

Quimby was spinning a young girl around the dance floor in a graceful, lively step. She was very pretty, with long, honey blonde hair piled in an elegant bun on top of her head. She smiled up at Quimby with the same adoring, mesmerized expression I'd seen on the faces of dozens of girls before her. They were dancing closer than was considered strictly proper, and I suspected someone somewhere was feeling quite scandalized.

Jace looked mighty pleased about it, though. He was grinning. I paused behind Quimby and tapped him on the shoulder. He stopped dancing, and his shoulders straightened. He knew it was me without even turning around. "Now, Tess?"

"Quimby," I said warningly.

He sighed and stepped away from the blonde girl. "Sorry, sugar." He spun around to face me with a sullen expression. "Again, Tess?"

Jace lifted his eyebrows. "Does this happen often?"

"Only anytime Quimby's awake. Sometimes when he ain't. He's a regular hound dog."

Quimby smirked. "I'm a little proud of that, actually."

200

"You shouldn't be," I replied sternly.

"So, what do you want?"

I looked around for the handsome, burly man who'd interrupted my dance with Rush. He was standing silently nearby while Rush spoke to a circle of distinguished-looking gentleman. "See that guy? The big one with the goofy look on his face? You know who he is?"

Quimby squinted as though to get a better look at him. He looked back at me and shrugged. "He's a Pink."

Jace blinked in surprise. "You really do know who everyone is?"

Quimby gave him a patronizing look. "He's wearin' a badge, Holt."

I chuckled. Jace curled his lip. "So the answer is no," he guessed.

Quimby shrugged. "I don't know him. He ain't never done anything to put him on the Marshal's list of people of interest on one side of the law or the other."

"Quimby knows most of the wanted men and women in the country. Sometimes the Pinks and the Marshals," I explained to Jace.

"Whoever he is, I ain't never seen him before. Why not ask your Pink friend, Lafe?"

Jace looked at me. "You think it's safe?"

"Why not? He knows what we're about."

"I don't see why not," Quimby added. "You go on then. I got something to tend to." He didn't wait for a response. He turned back to the blonde woman, who was waiting only a few feet away. She smiled radiantly at him. She didn't seem to mind being shunted to the side.

I rolled my eyes and glanced back at Jace. He was watching Quimby in interest. I nudged him. "Come on. I want to know who that Pink is. Maybe Zeke or Jesse knows something about him."

Lafe stood motionlessly at the head of the ballroom near a display of glass globes mounted upon what looked like squat, square mechanical bodies with short arms. Pale, toxic-looking blue liquid filled the globes to varying levels on each body. I wasn't sure what the contraptions did, but I reckoned it was safer to avoid them.

There was a large podium in front of the blue-headed dinguses where the exhibitors presented the finer points of their inventions, whatever they were. The Pinkerton called Arthur was a few feet away from Rush and his companions, who gathered around the podium, speaking chummily and sipping drinks. I recognized the tall, ruddy-featured man with thick, salt and pepper hair, but I doubted Congressman Josephus Caine would recognize me. I hoped he wouldn't, anyway.

Rush and his cronies didn't seem to notice us at all; they were wrapped up in their own heated debates and smug conversations. Lafe noticed us, though. He strode forward to meet us half way. "Jace, Tess, what's up?"

I nodded toward Arthur. "You know who that guy is?"

"Of course I do. He's Artie Moran. A Pinkerton. One of my partners."

"Yeah?" I asked. "Does he do a lot of work for Sterling Rush?"

Lafe lifted an eyebrow. "Sure he does. He works his security detail all the time. He's real strong and reliable. What do you want to know about him for?"

"We don't really," Jace said. "We were just wondering who he is."

"You saw him talking to Rush and Congressman Caine and thought he might have something interesting to tell you?"

Jace smiled a little sheepishly. "Well...you know me."

"Yeah. I do. And I don't think Artie knows much about pay-offs and government cover-ups. He's a nice guy. A good Pink. He does what he's told, and he's real loyal. He's not much of an independent thinker, though."

I nodded thoughtfully. "I sensed that." I smiled at Lafe. "Well. Thanks, anyway, Lafe."

He inclined his head. "So, have you seen anything interesting since you've been here, Mrs. Holt?"

"Loads. Clockwork horses, death rays, mechanical men with no obvious purpose. All sorts of things."

He smiled. "That isn't exactly what I meant."

I knew that. I shrugged. Jace sighed morosely. "Nothing interesting," he said.

Lafe looked at him meaningfully. "Then perhaps you're rethinking what I said?"

"Yeah?"

"Maybe Rush hasn't got anything to do with your little investigation."

"He isn't exactly going to be flaunting the evidence here. He probably isn't even thinking about the sweet, innocent girl he had killed right now."

Lafe laughed. "Jace, that girl might not even be dead."

"So you've said." Lafe grinned. He was always grinning. I liked that about him. It was hard not to grin back. He really knew how to bring up the mood. "All right," Jace said grudgingly. "I'm willing to consider the possibility that something else is going on here."

The Pink's eyebrows shot up in surprise. "Really?"

"No. But I'm willing to humor you and my wife."

Lafe laughed. "I suppose that's something, anyway."

"You want to meet us at Becky's place tomorrow night?"

Lafe considered. "Sure. How about nine o'clock? I'll be off the clock. I don't mind doing a little work for fun off the books."

Jace nodded. "See you then, Lafe."

He opened his mouth to reply, but Hazel slammed into my side, propelling me a few steps forward. We all turned to her. Her arms were loaded with gears, wires and strange, twisted pieces of metal and spare parts. Her eyes gleamed keenly. I opened my mouth incredulously. "Hey, Tess, this place is great!"

I gripped her shoulders and led her out of Lafe's earshot. Jace trailed behind us with a curious expression. "Where did you get those, Hazel?"

"One of the exhibition rooms. They're just giving them away!"

"Giving them away?" I asked doubtfully.

"Well, nobody was watching them."

"Hazel, put them back!"

"Aw, Tess."

"No, Hazel. We ain't got room for more parts."

She pushed her lower lip out in a pout. "Fine, but don't blame me when your spyglass winds down in the middle of a hunt and you're seeing double and can't figure out which fur-covered fake Indian is the real bounty and you don't have the parts to fix it." She tossed her curly blonde head and stormed abruptly away.

Jace looked at me incredulously.

I tilted my head thoughtfully. "She has a point. I do hate when that happens."

Chapter Fifteen

Zeke leaned back in his chair and frowned. He looked as though he'd spent too many hours cooped up in the small hotel room with Vaughn. His eyes were red and tired, and he looked as though the slightest irritation might send him on a tear. "Are you sure this is a good idea?" he grumbled.

"You got any better ones?" Hazel replied sharply.

I sat down beside Vaughn in the catawampus circle of chairs. His huge, coal black gaze was calm and soothing. I hadn't realized my world had been spinning until I felt it stop. "Any ideas, Vaughn?" He always had the ideas.

He stared silently into my eyes for several long moments. I could practically see the thoughts whirling around in his black eyes. Out of the corner of my eye, I saw Jace open his mouth to speak, but Hazel gave him a sharp look. He snapped it shut again. No one else said anything. They watched Vaughn and me breathlessly, waiting for further instructions.

After a long moment, Vaughn sighed deeply. "I don't know about this, Tess. We're bounty hunters. Simple folk. A man shoots another man in the streets in cold blood, we hunt him down and put him behind bars. This--the city, politics, government pay-offs, lobbyists, Pinkertons--it ain't what we do."

I leaned my hand on my chin and sighed. "I know, Vaughn. But we're here now "

"I know it." He looked away from me and laid one huge hand on the crumpled cipher on the desk beside us. "I don't know what these codes mean, but I think they're important."

"You don't think it's useful to search Becky's place?"

"I don't know what you'll find that Ezekiel didn't. He seems like he knows what he's doing."

"Thanks, Vaughn," Zeke put in.

Vaughn ignored him. He looked at me. "But we don't have all the information we need to crack this cipher yet."

"So what do we need to crack it?"

"If I knew that, we would already be on our way to doing it."

204

"You want to come with us to search the house?"

"Nah. Even at night people notice a man like me creeping around a dead girl's house."

I chuckled. "Yeah. I reckon you're right about that." I peered at him silently for another few minutes. He didn't seem to have much else to offer. "Quimby, you got any ideas about these codes?"

Vaughn held the cipher up between two long, thick fingers. Quimby snatched it from him and examined it for several moments. Finally, he shook his head and handed them to me. "Nah."

"What would they mean if you wrote them?"

He considered this. "I don't use codes."

I turned to Hazel and handed her the cipher. "Hazel? What about you?"

She lifted a shoulder. "Probably somethin' crazy. A formula for irradiating lizard spit or somethin'."

The boys looked at her as though she'd grown a second head, but I laughed. "Yeah, thanks, Hazel."

"It's true."

I held the cipher out to Jace, but he didn't take it. He looked as though he never wanted to look at it again. "I've been over them a hundred times or more."

"Yeah, but you've been thinking of them through Rush's eyes. What about you? What would they mean to you?"

He took the paper from me and stared at it. "They don't make words."

"Maybe they do."

He nodded slowly. "They'd be initials."

"What for?"

He pointed. "NY. New York. It's what it means to me."

"Okay. So if that's New York, what are the initials that correspond to it on the second one?"

"VA. What's that?"

"Veteran Affairs," Hazel said keenly. "Visual aid. Value added. Vulnerable area!"

"What's that got to do with New York?" Quimby demanded.

"I don't know. What's New York got to do with New York?"

"That ain't helpful, Hazel," I said.

"It's a place," Jace said, "VA must be a place, too."

"Yeah, okay," Hazel said grudgingly. "I guess it makes more sense than vulnerable area."

"Virginia?" I offered.

"Or Vermont," Jace replied.

"There's no A in Vermont."

"Yeah, okay. So we have New York and Virginia. That's something," Hazel said cheerfully.

We all looked at Zeke. His eyes were narrowed thoughtfully. "Yeah. It is something." He held out his hand for the cipher. He frowned down at it. "Give me a bit more time. I think I can get there."

"Okay," I said. "Good luck. While you're on that, Jace and I will go with Lafe to search Becky's house."

"How are you getting in?" Hazel held up the shiny, prong-tipped metal wand. I didn't know where she'd been keeping it. It materialized out of nowhere. "This?"

Zeke and Jace eyed the wand in interest. Vaughn and Quimby leaned away from it. "What is that?" Zeke asked.

"Lock pick."

"What?"

"It can open any lock. Guaranteed."

"It really will," I assured him. "It's pretty ingenious. I think she constructed it out of dreams and radioactive waste."

He looked doubtful. He reached into his pocket and drew out a ring of keys. He tossed it toward me. "That's not necessary." I caught the keys deftly in one hand and looked at Jace with a grin. "Silas gave them to me."

Jace frowned. "It was Lafe's idea to search the place. He might wonder how we managed to get the keys when no one but a dead guy and his suspected murderer had a copy."

I considered this. "Yeah, that's a good thought."

Hazel tossed me the rod. The boys shielded their faces, but I caught it. "Reckon you need a backup plan."

* * *

Rebecca Palmer's apartment was in a quiet, quaint neighborhood in a nicer part of the city. Large, leafy trees overhung the street, but it was illuminated by a row of bright street torches. It looked respectable, and it looked safe. The building itself was a small brownstone, a few stories high. Balconies boasted carefully tended garden boxes, and at this early hour, lights burned behind curtains in most of the windows.

Jace and I glanced at each other, but we needn't have worried about calling attention to ourselves. There was no security guard inside the entrance of the building. The lobby was bright and quiet. There was a small, empty office on the left, and a narrow flight of stairs on the right. We strode toward the stairs and took them rapidly to the second floor. Becky's apartment was 2F.

Lafayette Jackson lounged against the doorframe with a grin. He didn't move when he saw us. "Well. Fancy meeting you two here."

I rolled my eyes. "You got a way in or what?"

He straightened and shrugged. "I'm a Pinkerton. I can find my way in anywhere."

"What are you planning to do, kick in the door?"

"I thought something a little more elegant was in order for the evening." He held up a key.

"Where did you get the key?" Jace asked, leaning over Lafe's shoulder as he unlocked the door.

"I've got friends in high places. I can get the things I need to."

There was an uneasy feeling in the pit of my belly, but I followed Jace and Lafe into the dark apartment. It was so tidy, it felt as though someone had come in and sterilized it. The furniture was neat, feminine and old-fashioned. It was arranged as though by someone who valued comfort over style. The squat, gnarled wood table in front of the settee was padded as though Becky had enjoyed putting up her feet after a long day at the office. Two bookshelves directly across from the sofa were stuffed with books arranged in careful alphabetic order. Rebecca Palmer had been meticulous. I reckoned she'd been a good secretary.

"So what are we looking for?" I asked, pausing to pick up the book on the end table beside the settee. *Great Expectations*. I hadn't read it. A pair of thin, gold-framed reading glasses, perfectly polished, was lying beside the book beneath a shaded oil lamp.

Lafe shrugged, spinning around in a circle as though to take in the whole room at once. "I don't know," he admitted. "Something."

"That's helpful, Lafe, thanks."

He laughed. "You guys go ahead and look in here. I'll take a look in the bedroom."

"I'm not sure that's strictly appropriate."

"It isn't as though she's in there," Jace said darkly.

I shrugged and moved toward the small, polished wood roll-top writing desk in the corner of the room. The loose sheets of sparkling white paper were stacked neatly in their tray. The inkwell was still full. The plumed pens were as clean as though Becky had never used them. The blotter was etched deeply, however, and I knew she spent a lot of time at this desk. I sat down in the slightly shaky chair while Jace pulled the books carefully from their places on the shelves as if he expected secrets to fall from between the pages. Actually, they might. People kept strange things in books.

Becky had kept her desk in very good order. Bills were filed neatly with notations regarding the times and amounts paid. She always paid them on time. There wasn't anything personal or interesting in the drawers. There weren't even any unfinished letters. If she had kept a personal diary, she had hidden it somewhere else. Her check register was religiously notated with every expense in a neat, feminine hand.

"Does this feel a little wrong?" Jace asked from across the room. "Violating a young woman's privacy?"

I looked up at him. "The young woman is dead. It isn't violating her privacy when we're looking for clues as to why."

He sighed, but he didn't say anything else. He strode toward a side table near the front door to rifle through an unopened stack of mail. He laid it down again in disappointment. "Anything?"

I frowned thoughtfully, peering down at the check register. Becky had made very good wages for a secretary, and she had been very careful with her money. She'd saved most of what she made, and her expenses had been consistent each and every week. There was no deviation in her habits, none at all.

"You weren't paying Becky for her information?"

Jace looked surprised at this. "No. Informants are typically not compensated."

"They why would she want to risk everything to give you information?"

"Are you suggesting I'm the one she ran off with?" he asked dryly.

I barked with laughter. "Of course not."

"She wanted to do the right thing. Some people are motivated by morals rather than money."

I didn't rise to this. We didn't have time for an argument right now. I leaned back in Becky's chair. "Do you think a young woman who was having an affair would spend a little money to gussy herself up a bit?"

He looked at me incredulously. "What are you talking about?"

"When I first met you, I went right out and bought new dresses and hats and shawls and had my hair done before every party. Becky gets her hair done once a month, never fail. She almost never buys new hats."

He didn't look as though this made any sense to him. "You bought new dresses?"

I ignored him. "I reckon I've never seen a woman who didn't at least try."

"She was engaged. Maybe she thought Silas loved her the way she was."

"Yeah. But a new man might not. Women always think they got to impress a man."

"Women are very foolish sometimes."

"And men ain't? What did you do when we first met?"

"I got a good shave every few days and wore cologne."

"You see?"

"That doesn't prove anything."

"Maybe not. It's just a thought. Besides, you're the one on the no-man side. I was offering you a point of agreement."

He opened his mouth to respond to this, but Lafe burst back into the room so abruptly, we looked at him in surprise. His pale eyes were wide and excited, and his smile stretched across his face.

"What's up?" Jace asked.

"Look what I found in her bedroom."

"Her bedroom?"

"Under the mattress. It was tucked into the box spring." Lafe held up a stack of papers tied with a red ribbon. "They're letters. Want to take a look?"

I rose and strode toward him. "Do we?" I held my hand out for them.

He untied the ribbon and split the stack between us. I opened the first in my stack and read through it.

Dearest Becky, I cannot pretend any longer. Each day without you is a misery. I think of you always. I watch you when you are alone and when you are with him. Why do you continue to pretend it is Silas you love? You know we are meant to be together forever. Stop living this lie. You know I will never allow you to marry him. Come away with me. We can leave this city behind and live a simpler life....I reckoned I'd seen enough. I skipped to the end; it was the important part, anyway. Yours, Art.

I looked up at Jace and Lafe. Their lips were curled in similar expressions of disgust. I reckoned their letters had been about the same as mine. I traded letters with Jace. "Love letter. You boys?"

"The same," Lafe replied.

"A weird love letter," Jace added.

"Is yours signed by Art, too?"

"Art. Yeah."

"Where have I heard that name?"

Lafe frowned thoughtfully. "We were just talking about Arthur Moran yesterday."

"Arthur Moran?" I asked blankly.

"The Pinkerton," Jace reminded me.

"That's a coincidence."

"Yeah. Quite a one."

"It's not an unusual name."

"No," Jace agreed. "Not really."

210

I frowned. I couldn't place the frisson of unease that shivered along my spine. My skin felt creepy and crawly. I glanced down at the letter in my hand. Men are freaky. Of course, women aren't much better a lot of the time. It wasn't like Becky had thrown the letters away. She'd tied them in ribbon and hidden them carefully away.

"I think we should get out of here," I announced. "I don't think there's much else to find but these."

Lafe handed his stack to me. I pushed them off to Jace. "Why don't you hold onto these," Lafe said.

"Don't you want to bring them to the authorities?" Jace demanded, holding them out to him.

Lafe lifted his hands. "The authorities aren't looking into this. Becky's just a girl who went missing. There's no one to miss her now that her fiancé is dead. You can do more good with them."

I frowned. "That's convenient."

"Yeah, well, that's the way it works, I'm afraid. There's no proof this girl didn't just run off with this Art fellow."

This explanation rang oddly insincere, but the letters were pretty suggestive. I sighed. Lafe stepped forward and laid a hand on Jace's shoulder in a strangely comforting gesture. His voice was low when he spoke.

"Maybe you can get your story or decide to forgive yourself for her disappearance, Jason."

Jace smiled slightly, and I realized my misgivings wouldn't be appreciated just now. "Thanks, Lafe," he said.

Lafe nodded. "I'm always happy to do a little charity work." He lifted his hand in a salute.

"You got any idea who this Art might be?" I asked.

He smiled. "I think I could come up with some ideas."

"All right. If you got the time. It wouldn't hurt to have a Pink looking into it for us."

"I have some other assignments, but I think I can come up with something. Why don't we compare notes in a couple days."

Jace nodded. "The usual time, usual place?"

Lafe grinned. "You bet. G'night, you two." He tossed something in the air, and Jace reached out to catch it. "Lock up on your way out."

"Night, Lafe."

When he was gone, I looked at Jace. "Does this seem right to you?"

He looked surprised. "What do you mean?"

"Well, it seems awfully convenient, finding these letters even after Zeke searched the place."

"Well, perhaps Zeke didn't know what he was looking for. He was working a different angle. He was working the same angle as me."

"Are you suddenly off Rush as the suspect?" I asked in surprise. "Are you thinking it might be this Art guy who did it?"

His green eyes were sad when they met mine. "It doesn't make Rush any less evil, Tess."

"But maybe it makes her disappearance a little less your fault?"

"Maybe."

I strode forward abruptly and gripped his hands in mine. "It wasn't your fault, Jace. Becky knew what she was getting into when she agreed to inform to you. You didn't force her. You didn't force anyone."

"That's easy for you to say, Tess."

"I know." I tugged on his hand. "Come on. It seems to me it's a little interesting that a Pink named Artie works for Rush, and someone named Art was sending Becky creepy love letters."

"I thought that was interesting myself."

"I don't believe in coincidences like that. Let's see what everyone else has to say about it."

* * *

My posse looked tired and fed up when Jace and I returned to the hotel room. I didn't blame them; this wasn't exactly our sort of scene. I was really missing long, quiet nights out on the range when life was simple and uncomplicated. "Y'all find anything else?" I asked, dropped onto the bed beside Hazel with the stack of letters in my hands.

"No," Zeke replied wearily. "But at least we're focusing the search on things relating to Rush in these places."

"It helpin'?"

"Not really, but it's easier to eliminate what isn't important."

"There's a lot to look at," Vaughn said. He looked tired, and I suspected he was at his wit's end with all this. He wasn't much of a complainer, but he didn't have to do what other people said anymore. I reckoned it wouldn't be long before he'd had enough of being cooped up with the Pink and wanted to stretch his legs a bit. "It's difficult to decide what's important and what to ignore."

"You find anything at Becky's?" Zeke asked.

"Just these." I held out the stack to him.

"Where?"

"Box springs."

His brow furrowed a bit, but he nodded. He untied the ribbon and handed the letters out to the others to read through. I didn't take one; I knew what was there.

"These are creepy," Hazel said brightly.

"You think Becky ran off with this guy?" Quimby asked.

"I wouldn't run off with him. I might be afraid he would love me so much, he would want to crawl inside me and wear my skin."

I snorted, but Jace looked horrified at the idea. "Yeah, but it's interesting," I told her.

She shrugged. "Art?" Quimby said. "Like Artie Moran, that Pink we saw at the expo?"

"He does work for Rush sometimes," I agreed. "Private security, according to Lafe."

Zeke frowned thoughtfully. "Yeah. I know Artie."

"What do you know about him?"

"He's a nice guy. Really nice. Sweet, really. Not too bright."

"But he's a Pinkerton."

"Sure. He's good at his job. He's good at following orders and loyally protecting the client. He's not sent out on investigations, though. He's not that kind of Pinkerton."

"You think he could have something to do with this?" Jace asked.

"I don't know. I doubt it. He doesn't seem like the kind of guy who would stalk and murder a young woman."

"What if he didn't murder her?" Quimby asked. "What if she went off with him?"

"I don't think that many ladies would go off with a creepy obsessed stalker type," I replied.

"What are you talking about?" Hazel demanded. "Of course they would."

"Hazel's right, Tess," Quimby added. "Women are insecure. They love when a man professes his love to them, even if it's creepy and obsessive."

I scowled at him. "Quimby, that ain't true, and I don't appreciate it. Just 'cause you're a hound dog don't mean all women are totally stupid."

"Still, you should never underestimate how desperate people are to be loved."

"Yeah, but Becky was already engaged to another man. She had plenty of love."

"Silas was a good man," Zeke agreed. "He loved her."

I waved my hand. "Enough of this. We'll just accept it as a possibility. We don't need more discussion about it. But if it is, why would Art lure her out with a note claiming to be from Jace? Why not just say it was him?"

"That's true," Hazel said. "That's a little weird. And why murder Silas?"

"Maybe she didn't return Art's feelings," Quimby offered. "So he lured her out, and when she got there, she refused him. He killed her and then killed Silas in revenge?"

"But why wait so long between the murders?" Jace asked, frowning.

"Yeah, okay, it doesn't exactly add up. Anyway, it's all speculation."

Vaughn cleared his throat. "It would be helpful if we discovered if Artie Moran was around the Pink headquarters when the telegram was sent. If not, that solves the issue of whether or not he's a reasonable suspect."

Zeke pushed around the stack of papers on the desk. He found Jesse's list and scanned it. He sighed. "Yeah. Artie was on the duty roster. He was in town. He might have been in the office."

I nodded. "I'll get a message to Jesse to find out for us if he can."

Vaughn looked at me with a frown. "It seems a little convenient, doesn't it, that you see this Artie Moran at the expo and discover these letters the next day."

I nodded. "I thought the same thing myself."

We all considered this. "I'm willing to accept a little convenience at this point," Zeke admitted.

I shrugged. "All right. If you are, we are. You're the client."

"It's worth looking into, anyway," Hazel put in. "Even if it did come out a little conveniently, it's worth following up on the lead. I, for one, could use a good stake out."

* * *

"Ouch!"

"Shh!"

"You stepped on my foot!"

"Shh!"

"Do you always need this many people to stake someone out?" Jace demanded.

"We're a team," I replied. "We work together."

"This seems a little ridiculous," Zeke added.

"You didn't have to come along," Hazel replied.

"Everyone just shut up," I ordered. "Here he comes."

We crouched low behind the dumpsters and empty crates in the alley outside Arthur Moran's apartment building. I recognized the tall, handsome, burly man striding toward us on the street. Artie was whistling cheerfully. He carried a small paper bag of groceries into the building. A few minutes later, a light flicked on in one of the windows above our heads.

Arthur Moran lived alone. We watched silently as he moved around the apartment, cooking himself dinner and sitting down alone on the settee to eat it. Hazel glanced at Jace. "Do you look that sad all alone, Jace?"

He glanced at her in surprise. "Hazel," I scolded. "Now is not the time."

"I'm not sad," Jace protested.

"Shut up," Zeke ordered.

Artie opened the window above our heads, but he didn't seem to realize we were below him. He peered out into the night for several moments. Hazel was right. He did look sad. He sat back down on the settee and picked up a book.

"What's he reading?" Hazel asked.

"Shh!"

"I don't know. I can't tell."

"It doesn't matter!"

Whatever it was, he read it for over an hour while we sat in the alley below and watched. Hazel was dozing against my side. The boys were silent. I knew Vaughn and Zeke were wide-awake, but I suspected Quimby had nodded off, as well. I sighed. "Come on. He ain't up to anything."

"You think someone who murdered two people and framed someone else for it would read so peacefully?" Jace asked.

Hazel snorted softly and jerked away. "You'd be surprised," she said. "I once saw a mass murderer play patty-cake with a kitten for three hours."

Even in the darkness around us, I saw him glance at her incredulously. I snorted. "Shh," Zeke ordered.

Artie placed the book face down on the table beside the settee and turned down the gas lamp. He rose to his feet and moved out of the sitting room into his bedroom. After several long, dark, silent moments, Quimby rose. "Can we get out of this alley? It smells."

I sighed. "Yeah, yeah. Okay. It doesn't look like we're going to learn much else tonight. Who wants morning duty?"

"Not me," Quimby replied. "I ain't slept in days with Vaughn and Angel rifling through those papers all damn night."

"Then get your own damn room," Vaughn replied.

"Why don't you get your own room?"

"Do you guys always act like this?"

We all turned to Jace. "Stay out of this, Jace," I ordered. "It ain't none of your business."

"I'll do it," Hazel put in. "You guys go on. I'll stay here and keep an eye on the most boring bounty ever."

"Are you sure we can leave her here?" Vaughn said. "Remember last time we left her alone without anything to do. We had to replace an entire schoolhouse."

"Don't exaggerate, Vaughn. It was only a few desks and things."

216

"And the roof. That cost us three bounties, Hazel, and we worked hard for those. Don't you level any buildings or upset any children."

"I don't upset children," Hazel replied with a toss of her head. "They love me because my face is sweet and my smile is jolly."

I rolled my eyes. "Let's go. Hazel's got this under control."

"But if you don't find anything on this guy by tomorrow, I'm giving him up."

"Fair enough, Hazel. Have a good stake out."

"Are you sure it's a good idea to leave her alone in that alley?" Jace asked.

"Hazel can take care of herself."

"That's not really what I'm worried about."

"What are you worried about?"

He considered. "The street and the surrounding area."

"That's a realistic concern," Vaughn told him.

I turned to him. "What do you think, Vaughn? You like this guy for this?"

"I've been locked in a hotel room for five days. I don't like anyone for it."

I sighed. "Sorry, Vaughn."

He shrugged. "It's the way it is sometimes."

"You got any ideas?"

"I'm waiting to see what happens. There's something we're missing."

"Yep. I know. Think we'll figure out what it is?"

"Yeah, we'll figure it out. We always do."

"Where do you think we'll find it?"

"I ain't sure yet. I think we've already found it. We just ain't looked at it the right way yet."

I glanced at him in interest. "What do you mean?"

"I think we already know what we need to know. We just haven't put it in the right perspective."

I considered this. I glanced over my shoulder. Jace and Quimby seemed not to be listening. They strode a few paces apart, as if they were avoiding each other. I glanced back up at Vaughn. "There seem to be a lot of coincidences these days, huh, Vaughn?"

"Yeah. More than there ought to be, I reckon."

* * *

Jesse O'Brien was expecting us this time. He looked up with a smile as Quimby and I joined him at the table outside the cafe in Quincy Market. "I found out what you wanted to know," he said immediately. He looked grim, but his eyes glittered in excitement.

I lifted my eyebrows. "Yeah?"

"Artie Moran was in the office that night."

"He was? Are you sure? He was supposed to be at a security gig at a corporate HQ downtown that night," Quimby put in.

"No. Well, he was, but he was off the clock when he came in."

"How do you know he came in?"

"Luke, the night watchman, saw him. He said he remembered it especially because he wasn't expecting him. He wasn't on the list. He always checks the list every night he's on duty so he knows who to expect. He likes to know who he's going to be dealing with; he doesn't get along with everyone."

"Okay. So he saw Artie."

"Yeah. He came in around nine o'clock. Two hours before he was scheduled to be on detail. Artie said he forgot some papers he needed for a job the next day. Luke said Artie was in the telegraph office for a few minutes. He thought it was unusual because he didn't know what papers Artie might have left, and he should have just gone right to his desk."

"But he didn't."

"No. Luke went to see what he was up to and caught him in the telegraph office. He said he didn't seem to be up to anything. He was as sweet as always."

"He seems sweet," I murmured thoughtfully.

"Real sweet. Not too bright, though. Luke just dismissed it. He assumed he was waiting on a telegram or had just taken a wrong turn. He didn't think there was anything suspicious about it."

"Did you ask him if anyone else was in the telegraph office that night?"

"Yeah, actually, I asked him, and he didn't see anyone else. It was quiet that night at HQ."

I exchanged a glance with Quimby. "It seems pretty sewn up to me," he said.

"Yeah. It does," I sighed. "And I don't really like it."

"What are you talking about?" Jesse asked.

I shook my head. "Jesse, we appreciate your help. I think we know now everything you could tell us." I smiled at him. "I think we can clear Angel now."

Jesse smiled. "I'm real glad to hear that. He's a good man, Angel. I'll be happy to see him back at work."

"You think they'll give him his job back after this?" Quimby asked in surprise.

"Why not? It's not his fault he's been falsely accused."

I leaned back thoughtfully in my chair. "What do you think of all this, Jesse?"

He shrugged. "I'm a dispatcher, not an investigator."

"Yeah, but you've been around long enough to know what's going on here. What do you think?"

Jesse considered. "I don't know. There must be something going on; Angel wants to know all this for some reason. He knows what he's doing. I guess it must be important."

I lifted my eyebrows. "He didn't tell you what?"

"No. He just said he wanted to know who used the telegraph that night because it would help clear him."

"You didn't even ask why?"

"No. I trust Angel. He's a friend. He helped me out of a tight spot once; I owe him, so I'm doing the same for him."

"That's why you're risking all this for him?" Quimby asked with narrowed eyes.

Jesse frowned. "Yeah. Otherwise I wouldn't be helping him and talking to you. I would have turned you in and had you followed to lead the authorities to him."

We stared at him.

He held up his hands. "I'm not doing anything of the kind. You people are sensitive." I smiled. Jesse lifted his eyebrows in interest. "So you think Artie might have something to do with this? You don't really think he is the one who framed him, do you?"

I eyed him. "You don't think he could be?"

"He's not that kind of guy."

"What kind of guy is he?"

"The lonely kind. Sweet. Stupid. He's a good bodyguard. He's loyal and relentless. He is popular with VIP's."

"He's not married."

"No, not that I know of."

"Does he have a girlfriend?"

Jesse shrugged. "How would I know? I'm not the kind of guy who shares stuff like that." He frowned. "I'm not really the kind of guy who cares about stuff like that."

I chuckled. "All right."

"I guess I don't know that much about him."

"Well, if you notice anything unusual, send us a note, will you?"

"Sure." Jesse sighed. "I don't like any of this."

"None of us do, but we're doing the best we can to clear Angel."

He nodded. "Thanks."

Quimby and I rose. I inclined my head to him. "Thanks, Jesse. We'll see you around."

Jesse smiled a little grimly, and I suspected he'd be much happier if he never saw us again. There was strain around his eyes and mouth. I felt a little sorry for him. He really didn't have anything to do with any of this. He shouldn't have to bear Zeke's burden, even if he didn't really even know what it was.

"I don't like any of this, either, Quimby," I said as we strode swiftly away from the Square toward our hotel.

"When did you become so suspicious?"

I laughed. "When am I not suspicious?"

"That's not what I mean. Why are you so distrustful of this new information?"

"I don't know. It just feels too easy. It feels like we're being led by the nose."

"To Artie?"

"Maybe. Maybe somewhere else we haven't ended up yet."

"Well, led by who, then?"

"I wish I knew. Then we'd know the answer to all of this. It seems like everything we've learned so far has just fallen into our lap."

"Well, what do you intend to do about it?"

"See what happens, like Vaughn says, I reckon." I scowled. "It feels like this Artie thing is just a distraction."

"Well, we could just talk to him and see what he has to say. We might find out something."

I nodded thoughtfully. "Vaughn thinks we're missing something."

"Sure we're missing something. So what do you say? Go see the crooked Pink?"

"Let's talk to the others and hear what they have to say about it."

Chapter Sixteen

"You just want to confront him?" Zeke demanded.

"Well, Jesse says he's the only one who could have sent the telegram," I replied. "He was the only one in the office that night. It sounds pretty conclusive. It was Artie who lured Becky out of the house with that note from Jace, and then she disappeared. Regardless of whether or not he was the one who wrote the letters, he sent the telegram. What more do you want?"

Zeke sighed. "Are you sure about this?"

"No, but I'm as sure as we'll be about anything. Right now, other than Rush, against whom we have absolutely no proof of misbehavior or murder, Artie is all we've got. We know Becky got a telegram that night from Pink headquarters. Artie sent a telegram from Pink headquarters. If we were the law, we'd have already dragged him in for questioning."

Hazel grinned. "He's a big dangerous guy, Tess."

Vaughn chuckled. "So am I. I think I can handle a Pink."

Zeke eyed him warily. "Maybe you can. All right, then."

"What are you thinking, Tess?" Jace asked.

I sighed and tucked my legs under me on the bed beside Hazel. I glanced at Vaughn then around at Hazel and Quimby. "The usual thing, then?"

Hazel nodded. "Yeah."

"What does that mean?" Jace asked.

"Usually an unexpected and inelegant ambush."

Jace frowned. "That sounds a little risky."

"It usually is, but it's the only way to get it done."

"It's also the most fun," Hazel added. "They're usually so surprised, they don't even have a chance to fight back."

"I agree we need to speak to Artie," Zeke said. "All the evidence currently points to him."

I gave him a shrewd look. "But all the evidence seems to be a little conveniently placed right when we need it?"

"Yeah."

"I've been thinkin' the same thing myself. What are the chances we just happen to see Artie on duty for Rush, find the letters supposedly signed by him, then discover he's the one who sent the telegram, all in a couple days' time?"

"It did all fall right into place."

"So what are you suggesting?" Quimby asked.

"I'm suggesting this is all well and good, but there is a bigger picture here. Even if he was the one who sent the telegram and wrote the letters, what does he got to do with Rush?"

"He works for him," Hazel offered. "It's probably not unrelated to Becky's disappearance. What if the letters and his courting her was all part of Rush's plan?"

I blinked. We all looked around at her. "You mean, what if he used it as a way to trick her in order to accomplish Rush's goals?" Jace asked.

"Sure. Why not? It wouldn't be the first time a man lied about bein' in love with a woman, would it?" For some reason, she gave Vaughn a nasty look. I looked at him curiously. He shrugged.

"It would be convenient for Rush, anyway," Zeke said thoughtfully.

"But it still seems a little too easy," I mused.

"I'm not arguing that something isn't right. It isn't."

"Obviously. But unless Jesse is lying, Artie sent the telegram. It's the most conclusive piece of evidence we've got so far."

"Sure enough," she agreed.

"So, let's talk to him and get the rest of the story. It seems like the only logical next step."

We all looked at Zeke keenly. "When are we going to do it?"

"What the hell else are we doing right now?" Vaughn said.

"Sitting here, twiddling our thumbs," Hazel replied. "Let's just go get him."

Zeke rose to his feet. "I'm comfortable with that."

"Now hold on a minute," Jace said. "What exactly are we planning to do?"

I grinned. "What we do best, Jace. Catch a bad guy."

"Are you in or not?" Quimby asked.

Jace glanced at me. He smiled. "Sounds a little fun, actually. I'm in."

"Me, too," Zeke put in.

"You probably shouldn't be out in the open again," Hazel told him, but there wasn't much force behind it.

"I've been holed up long enough. If this is our last ditch effort, I'm not missing out on it."

My posse grinned around at each other. "When do we do it?" Quimby asked.

"Tonight," I said decisively. "When he gets off duty. We'll meet him outside his apartment."

"Is it safe there?" Quimby asked.

"Where else? There's pretty good cover in the alley. It's not so good as the back of a saloon in a one horse town when the law is looking the other way and you already got the cage ready, but it's the best we got."

"Artie's a sweet guy," Zeke said thoughtfully. "He will probably come quietly."

"If he really is Rush's guy or he killed Becky for his own reasons, he probably ain't exactly what you think he is," Hazel told him.

His mouth quivered slightly as though he was going to smile. "Yeah. All right. Maybe you're right about that. So how exactly do we do it?"

"When he comes home, Hazel can lure him into the alley and we can jump on him, restrain him and force him to talk to us," I replied. "Quick and easy."

"That's it?" Jace asked doubtfully.

"Pretty much."

"How do you know he'll go with Hazel?"

"They always go with Hazel," Quimby said.

She grinned. "Yeah. They do. They always regret it, too."

I rose. "Well, all right then. What we waitin' for? Let's get a wiggle on."

* * *

It was a little warm in the alley outside Artie's apartment. I could feel Vaughn's hot breath on the back of my neck. Beside me, Jace was tense. His breathing was slightly shallow. "It's a little stuffy over here," I complained.

"Shh!"

On my other side, Hazel was practically vibrating with excitement. "Maybe we're going about this the wrong way," I added.

"Shh! This was your idea to begin with," Zeke replied sharply.

Nothing happened for a long time. My muscles felt coiled and cramped, but I had sat through worse for longer. I could wait.

"Is he even coming?" Hazel asked impatiently.

"Shh!"

"How do we know he's coming?"

"Jesse sent us his duty sheet," I replied. "He should be off duty now. He'll be home anytime."

"Seriously, are we discreet here because I am pretty sure anyone who peeks down here can see us?"

"Jace, will you shut up? You're not helping."

"This is never a problem outside a saloon in a one horse town."

"You got that right."

We all perked up. There were thick, heavy footsteps on the street outside. Hazel's head snapped up. "Showtime!" She darted out into the street.

We watched as she stepped right into Artie's path as he strode past the alley. She swooned. He looked alarmed and rushed forward to catch her. "Are you all right, miss?" he asked. He looked the way most men looked when confronted with a weepy woman: scared. They always went with Hazel.

"I was attacked in the alley," she told him in a convincingly wavering voice. "He took my purse. I think he's still in there."

Artie released Hazel and turned to race right into the alley. Hazel caught herself with a slight frown and followed him. Vaughn and Quimby were waiting for him. They stepped forward and caught both his arms to drag him further into the darkness. He gasped and struggled, but Vaughn and Quimby were stronger than he was.

"Who are you? What do you want?"

Zeke stepped into the meager light filtering in from the street torches out on the street. Artie's jaw dropped in surprise. "Angel? What are you doing here?"

"We're just here to talk, Artie," Zeke said in a remarkably gentle voice.

Artie looked confused, but he didn't struggle anymore. "Okay. Are you going to shoot me?"

"No. Not unless you make us," I replied.

Artie looked at me as though he wasn't sure what to think. I reckoned there weren't that many respectable ladies talking about shooting people in this part of the world. Hell, there weren't many respectable ladies talking about shooting people in any part of the world.

"We're just looking for answers," Zeke added.

"Okay."

"Do you know Rebecca Palmer?"

Artie looked completely dumbfounded. "No. I don't know anyone named that."

He sounded so sincere, I actually believed him. Of course, I'd met many good liars. Quimby could probably convince the president he was Queen Victoria if given half the chance. "Are you sure about that, Artie?" I asked.

"Yeah, I'm sure. I mean, I don't remember everyone I meet, I guess."

"You didn't write her any love letters?" Hazel demanded.

Artie turned around to look at her. He looked a little hurt. I felt a little bad for him. "Love letters?" he repeated stupidly.

We all glanced around at each other. "Rebecca Palmer's the girl who went missing a few weeks ago," Zeke told him sternly. "It was her fiancé they said I killed."

Artie looked at him in surprise. "Did you do something to her, too?"

"No! I didn't do anything to anyone!"

"Really?"

"Come on, Artie. You know me. I didn't do those things they said I did. I didn't kill anyone."

"Well, you know who did?"

We all stared at him.

"What?"

We all glanced at each other. "Does this guy seem like a crazy stalker murderer to you all?" Hazel asked doubtfully.

"What?" Artie opened his mouth in astonishment. "Are you talking about me? You think I'm a murderer?"

"Did you send love letters to Becky Palmer?" Hazel asked him again.

"I didn't send love letters to anyone." His mouth turned down in a grimace. "My wife died five years ago. I'm all alone."

We eyed each other a little uncomfortably. I felt bad for Artie. He was a sad guy. "I knew this seemed too easy," I complained. "This guy doesn't know anything."

"He knows something," Zeke argued. "He still sent the telegram."

"Telegram?" Artie asked.

"Yes. A telegram. Did you send a telegram to the Newbury Street flats on May 3rd?"

He looked confused for a moment. His eyes slid away. He was silent for several moments. We waited, and I sensed the others were feeling about as foolish about this as I was. Their expressions were grim.

Then Artie's face lit up. "Yes!"

We blinked at him in shock. "What? You did?" Zeke asked.

"Yes! I did."

"This is not going the way I expected," Jace remarked.

"You're aren't alone in that," I replied in a low voice.

But Artie looked excited. "I sent a telegram."

"What did it say?"

"It was asking a girl to meet someone somewhere."

We stared at him. "Do you remember anything else about it?" Zeke asked, frowning.

"Nope. That was all it said."

"Why did you send it?"

"He asked me to."

"Who did?"

"The guy on the note…Horace Greeley. That was his name."

We all turned toward Jace in surprise. "Horace Greeley asked you to send a telegram," Jace repeated.

"Sure."

Jace shook his head. "I'm Horace Greeley."

"Oh. Hi, Horace." Artie smiled. "I sent your telegram, just like you asked."

"But I didn't talk to you about a telegram."

"No. I didn't talk to you directly. I just got the duty sheet. I do what I'm told."

We all sighed. "Yeah. This is getting us nowhere, isn't it?" I said.

"Actually, no. It's getting us somewhere," Zeke replied grimly. "It's telling us something isn't right." He glanced at Artie. "Who gave you the order?"

Artie looked as though he were on much more comfortable footing. He opened his mouth to reply. He didn't get the chance. A shot rang out. We had no time to react. It struck Artie right between the eyes. He fell backward as though in slow motion. He never saw it coming.

We exclaimed in surprise. Jace barreled into me, and I realized he was attempting to shield me from a further attack. Nearby, Vaughn was covering Hazel. Zeke didn't duck for cover. He darted toward Artie. I thought it was a waste of time; he was gone. I felt sick to my stomach.

"Ah, hell," I muttered. I shoved Jace away and jumped to my feet. Vaughn and Hazel were on my heels. We darted around the alley, searching for the gunman.

"It came from above, y'all!" Quimby growled.

Hazel turned and raced up the fire escape toward the roof of Artie's building. I growled in frustration and turned toward the rickety metal stair, but Jace caught my arm. "No, Tess. If he's still there--"

"You want Hazel up there by herself?" I threw off his arm and raced up the ladder. I heard him behind me. "Don't follow me, Jace!"

He didn't listen. It didn't matter. When we reached Hazel on the flat stone rooftop, she was leaning over the other side, cussing angrily.

"He gone?" I asked, striding to peer down into the empty streets.

"Yeah. He went over the other side."

"You get a good look at him?"

"Nah. He was too quick. He knew we was comin' for him."

I huffed in indignation. "No idea who he was, huh?"

"Yeah. I got a pretty good idea."

Jace and I looked at her in surprise.

"The guy who actually framed up Zeke and killed that poor girl."

I glanced at Jace. "Damnit. I told you this was too easy."

* * *

The hotel room was extremely quiet. Zeke's shirt was stained with Artie Moran's blood, but he didn't seem to mind. He didn't bother to change it. There was no expression on his face. I knew I looked strained, but I didn't care. Hazel stared blankly at the floor. Quimby and Vaughn looked angry. Jace was tense beside me. I reached out and took his hand. He clenched his fingers around mine and sighed deeply.

"Okay," I said in a low voice. "So clearly Artie Moran was not our guy."

Zeke scowled, but he didn't say anything. "Hazel, you didn't see the guy at all?" Vaughn asked her.

"Nah. He was fast. He fired off the shot and high-tailed it."

"Damnit, I knew this was too good to be true," I cursed. "It couldn't possibly be this easy."

"Yeah, well, we knew that going in," Quimby replied, frowning.

"So now we know Artie was just a pawn."

"Yeah, but what about the letters?" Hazel demanded.

"Obviously he ain't the right Art," Quimby said. "He ain't the only Arthur in the world."

"Okay, so does that mean we have to hunt down every Arthur in Boston until we find the right one?" Hazel sniped.

"I am pretty sure now this is over our heads," Vaughn said grimly.

"I ain't going to take that lyin' down, Vaughn," I replied. "This ain't over our heads. We're going to sort this out."

Jace scowled. "This is not going as smoothly as I would have hoped."

"Yeah, we're all disappointed. And now we got a dead body in an alley that deserves a decent burial and a full-scale investigation into his death."

"So someone else was pulling Artie's strings," Hazel mused.

"Yeah. And they gave him a bogus duty sheet," Quimby said. He glanced narrowly at Jace. "Unless it was really you who asked him to send the telegram."

"Come on now. You don't really think that," I argued.

"No," Zeke said. "Jace got caught up in this just like I did."

"So who is behind it?" Vaughn said.

"Seriously, we've lost our only lead," Hazel complained. "We've got no more ideas."

"So what do we do?" Quimby asked.

They all turned as one to look at me. I grimaced. I didn't really want to admit I didn't have any ideas, either. I lifted my chin and huffed. "That's one lead down, then. We've still got the codes."

"They're not getting us anywhere," Zeke said sullenly.

"Not yet, anyway."

"I'm ready to go back west," Hazel said. "I don't care much for city life."

"I'm with you," Quimby replied eagerly. "I want to get back to what I know. I don't like this much at all."

Jace frowned, but Zeke sighed resignedly. "I'm with you guys this time. Maybe being on the run in the west is better than hanging around here and clearing my name. At least no one's getting shot in dark alleys in front of me."

We all stared at him incredulously.

"Well, at least no one I know." He considered. Then he grimaced, and I knew he was thinking of Jimmy Steele. "Nevermind."

"We are not yellow," I growled. "We are not going anywhere. We are going to finish this job." They all opened their mouths to protest, but I held up my hand. "Y'all want to go? You can go. I'm stayin' here." I glanced at Jace. He smiled at me.

Hazel scowled. "I ain't goin' if you ain't goin', Tess."

We both looked at Vaughn and Quimby. "Well?"

Vaughn chuckled. "We ain't ever run out on a bounty before. Just 'cause we

230

don't know who he is yet don't mean we ain't taking it as seriously as any other hunt."

"Okay, then. Now we just gotta figure out who we're actually hunting."

"It could be worse," Quimby said. "We could be back in Montana with that cross-dressing sharp shooter who punched Vaughn in the face." He curled his lip. "Vaughn didn't even fight back."

"I don't hit girls," Vaughn said.

"That wasn't a girl."

"It looked like a girl."

"He put his hand--"

"Hazel!" I scolded. "None of that. It was a bad time. This is better than that. Probably."

"All right. Can we please focus?" Zeke asked with a sigh. "Are you guys always like this?"

"Yeah, pretty much. It works for us. We get the job done."

"You don't seem to be doing so well just now."

"Yeah, well, what have you got to offer that's any better?"

Jace leaned his chin on his fist. He frowned thoughtfully. "What if there isn't an Art?"

We all looked at him. "What? What do you mean?"

"There isn't anymore," Hazel muttered. "He's shot dead in an alley."

"A little sensitivity here, Hazel."

"Sorry."

"That's not what I mean."

"Then what do you mean?" Zeke asked.

Vaughn picked up one of the love letters and frowned down at it. "I know what he means. What if these letters are faked?"

"Why would they be faked?" Hazel asked.

"Well, they're what directed us to look at Artie to begin with," Jace replied.

"No," I argued. "Seeing him with Rush at the expo was what started it all."

"Well, yes, but then we found the love letters from Art and learned he was the one who sent the telegram."

"Yeah. It seemed to fall into place too easily," Quimby muttered.

"The point is how," I said.

"Huh?"

"Well, how did it fall into place?"

"Lafe," Jace said with a look of realization on his face.

"Right. He's the one who suggested we look elsewhere. He is the one who found the letters."

"He didn't have anything to do with the telegram, though, did he?" Hazel said, frowning.

"We don't know that," Vaughn replied thoughtfully. "It might have been him who gave Artie the bogus duty sheet."

We all thought about this silently for a moment. "I'm relieved you didn't mention I was with you, then," Zeke said. "If Lafe's the one who is working for Rush, we're all in trouble."

"What do you mean?" I demanded.

"If he's the one who set all this up, got Artie to lure Becky out to kill her, then killed Silas to frame me for it, he's been manipulating everything the entire time. He's been deceiving everyone for a long time. Me, the two of you, everyone else around us."

I frowned. I didn't really want to consider it. "He seems like such a stand up guy."

"Yeah, they usually do," Hazel murmured. She frowned and looked around at us all. "I don't know this guy well, but Tess usually isn't wrong about people. Could it be another set up? We thought Artie was the one, too."

"None of this makes any sense," I complained.

"Yes, it does," Jace replied sharply. "It's as simple as it was in the beginning. Sterling Rush is behind all this. Becky found something that Rush didn't want anyone else to find. Lafe had Artie send her a telegram claiming to be me, and he killed her."

Zeke pounced on this. "I got close enough to determine it was a Pink who sent the telegram, and he murdered Silas to frame me up."

"Then he directed us to Artie when it we got closer?" I asked doubtfully. "He would have to have anticipated we'd figure it out."

"Maybe he did," Zeke replied. "If he's clever enough to have fooled us all, he's probably been planning everything for a long time. He's probably been manipulating all the pieces since before anyone knew anything was going to happen."

"That seems a little far-fetched."

"Maybe, but that doesn't make it any less true."

"Well, we don't know what's true or not."

"So this all comes down to politics," Quimby muttered. "See, this is why I hate the city."

"I think I'm going to side with you on that, Quim," I told him. "Here's the rub, though. Assuming, it's Lafe, how did he know you had discovered it was a Pink who sent the telegram?"

We all thought this over.

"He could have been watching the whole time," Hazel offered.

"Or he isn't working alone," Vaughn added. "We've been receiving our information from your guy Jesse. Maybe he's turning around and feeding the information back to Lafe."

I didn't like the sound of this. "If that's true," Jace said in a low voice. "Then Lafe knows we're all here. He knows every move we've made. No wonder he was there, waiting for Artie."

Zeke looked green.

"Why does it feel as though we've put ourselves in terrible trouble?" Hazel demanded, scowling at him.

"I told you we were in over our heads," Quimby growled.

"This is worse than the time we were mistaken for that gang of train robbers and caught in that shoot out in Deadwood," Hazel said.

"Well," I said, shrugging. "At least this time it's only Lafe and not a posse of crazy Marshals with incendiary devices and cannons for hands."

"I promise you," Zeke said grimly. "This is that bad. Lafe is one of the best Pinkertons there is. He's smart and devious and clever." He looked uneasy. He rose and paced toward the window. He pushed aside the curtain with one finger and peered out as though he were expecting to see Lafe peering back at him.

"I don't think he's down there watching us," I told him.

He turned to look at me. His translucent eyes looked a little wild. "He probably is. He's probably been there the entire time." He frowned around at us. "We should get out of here."

"What?" I demanded. I shot to my feet. "I thought we were seeing this to the end."

"It's not worth it."

"You would rather be on the run for the rest of your life than face up to one Pink?"

"Yeah. If it's this Pink."

"Oh, this is ridiculous. You put your big boy pants back on. We are not going on the run from this guy. If you ain't afraid of taking on Sterling Rush, you shouldn't be afraid of taking on Lafe Jackson."

Zeke sighed, but he sat back down in his chair. He looked a little calmer. Hazel shook her head at him. "Yellow," she said disappointedly.

He straightened. "I am not yellow. But I'm not stupid, either."

"Look, we have a chance to get something on Rush," Jace said, and I was a little proud that he hadn't fallen apart like a little girl at the news of Lafe's betrayal. "We're not going to back down and run away."

"Jace is right," I said. "What happened to Artie was awful, and if Lafe did it for Rush, we've got to do something about it."

"So what have we got? How are we going to do it?" Hazel asked in a businesslike way.

"We've got the codes. And they mean something," I said firmly.

"So what do they mean?" Quimby demanded. "I don't think talking more emphatically about them is going to help us understand them better."

"Well, if Lafe's his guy, then maybe they were addressed to him," I told them. "And if they were, then they obviously have something to do with him. Now we have Lafe, New York and Virginia."

"I don't like this kind of hunt," Hazel complained. "It's awful and boring in turns. One minute we're cooped up for days in a hotel room sorting through surveillance notes and the next we're watching some poor, sweet dumb kid get

234

shot in the head."

"Then let's focus and figure it out," Jace said.

"Wasn't Lafe in New York the night Becky disappeared?" Quimby asked. "If he was, how could he have done anything to her?"

"He was supposed to be in New York, anyway. And he might have gotten someone else to do the actual deed. It ain't hard to find a killer for hire," I replied.

"Maybe that someone was Jesse," Quimby offered.

"I thought you liked him."

"That don't mean he ain't a murderer. You liked Lafe. And Rush."

I shrugged. "Yeah."

"Damnit," Zeke cursed. "Is there anyone in Boston who isn't crooked?"

"What you should be asking is, is there anyone in Boston who we've blown our cover to who ain't crooked," Hazel put in.

"This is ridiculous," I said. "We've done a terrible job."

"It ain't done yet," Vaughn said grimly. "We might get another couple innocent people killed before it's over."

"Hey, now, Vaughn, I've never known you to be such a pessimist."

"All I hear right now is you lot feeling sorry for the mistakes you keep making," Jace scolded us. "Can we try to turn our attention to how we're going to fix it?"

"Sorry, Jace."

"If New York and Virginia really are the places in the codes, maybe they mean places Rush needs Lafe to go."

"Okay, for what?"

"No good, obviously."

"So we need to know when he was in those places. It's a start."

"I have a friend in the Marshals--"

"No, Jace," we all said at once.

"We've already involved enough people in this mess. The ones who ain't part of the conspiracy are getting killed. Let's leave everyone else out of it."

Jace sighed. "Right."

"Is there another way to discover where Lafe has been?"

"We could break into Pink HQ and get the duty roster," Hazel offered keenly.

We all turned to look at her incredulously. "I don't think that's the solution," Zeke said. "They have a night watchman as well as any number of highly trained security professionals on hand at all times. I don't think you're going to have much luck with that."

She scowled. "If I can't blow anything up or break in anywhere, what fun is there in any of this?"

"Not much," I replied grimly. "We left the area of fun a long time ago. Right around the time Artie was shot in the alley."

"For the record, I never thought this was any fun," Zeke said.

Vaughn held up the cipher. "Could these numbers be dates?"

"What?" We all turned to look at him.

"0506 and 0525. Maybe they're dates."

"The telegram was sent on May 5th. Becky went missing the next day."

"He could have been in Boston. It's not impossible."

"But what do these dates have to do with these places?"

"Well, that's the question, isn't it? How do we find out what happened in these places on these dates that might relate to Lafe and Rush?"

We all turned to look at Jace. He looked a little sheepish. "I've had these codes a few weeks. I should have come to that conclusion."

"How do you think we feel? We've been cooped up in here for ages. We've been looking at addresses and street numbers for days," Vaughn replied. "Anyway, we didn't know who they were sent to at the time."

This didn't seem to appease Jace. "I should have thought of it sooner. If I had, it might have saved some innocent lives."

"You don't know that, Jace. And you can't think of it that way," I told him firmly. He nodded and he squeezed my hand.

"How do we figure out what happened in those places on those dates?" Hazel asked.

"We could get a hold of some newspapers," Quimby said reasonably.

236

We all turned to look at Jace. "Newspapers?" I said. "You think you can handle that, Jace?"

Jace grinned. "Now, that is something I can do without involving any potentially crooked lawmen."

"Imagine that."

"All right," Zeke said. "Go on, then."

Jace jumped to his feet and strode toward the door without looking back. "Hey, Jace," I called, amused.

He looked over his shoulder with his hand still on the doorknob. "Yeah?"

"Be careful, okay? I think we're probably made. It might not be safe to be by yourself. Lafe might be out there somewhere."

Zeke considered this. "Should someone go with him?"

Quimby rose. "I'll go."

I didn't think this was such a great idea. "No, I don't think that's such a good idea. Vaughn? You want to go with him?"

Vaughn shrugged. "Why not? It's better than staying holed up in this hotel, and if anyone asks, I can just say I'm his wife's former slave. It won't seem weird at all."

Chapter Seventeen

The door flew open and banged against the wall as Jace and Vaughn burst in. I jumped. Quimby snapped out of a doze with his guns drawn. Vaughn rolled his eyes. Jace scowled. "Do you mind, Burton?"

Jace had far spent too much time with us. "You found something, I take it?" I demanded.

Jace strode into the room. He looked excited. "I did." He tossed a stack of newspapers on the bed between Hazel and me.

"Where did you get these?" Zeke asked, picking one up.

"I work in the newspaper business," Jace replied off-handedly. "Our editor has subscriptions to every major newspaper in every major city in New England."

"Really?"

"Of course. We need to see what our competition is doing. Besides, we're newspapermen. We need to stay informed. We don't get every story over the Associated Press."

"Well, that's a little convenient."

"Yeah, and it probably won't even get anyone killed."

"So, what did you find in them?" I demanded.

"Take a look."

I frowned at him, but we all took a paper. I scanned the headlines in New York from May 7. *Former government official found dead of gunshot wound in apartment...*I frowned. *Eliot Wallace of Boston...*I didn't keep reading. I didn't need to. "Eliot Wallace died in New York on May 6th."

"EW-NY-506," Zeke said. For the first time in a long time, he grinned. "Nice work, Jace."

"Darrel Burke fell down a flight of stairs on May 25th in Fairfax, Virginia," Quimby announced.

"Let me guess," I said dryly. "He used to work for the Department of Scientific Progress and Questionable Developments."

"Yeah."

I glanced at Jace. "You know them?"

"I never talked to them, but they were two of the department officials who spoke out publicly about the corruption in their department."

"So these codes are orders to kill?" Hazel said.

"Looks like it. We can't prove it, and we can't prove he sent them to Lafe, but it's a pretty big coincidence," Jace replied.

Zeke sighed thoughtfully. "It would be enough for a judge to grant a warrant for the history on his telegraph."

"It might be," Jace said darkly. "It depends on the judge, I suppose. Most of them aren't going to be willing to risk angering Rush."

"Anyway, it's enough for us," I said.

"Well, we know what the codes mean," Quimby said doubtfully. "How does that really help us? We still need to prove Lafe was in those places at those times. Not to mention that these deaths were his doing."

Zeke sighed. "What we really need is Jesse."

"Too bad he's in on it. Probably in on it," I remarked. "That doesn't mean we can't still do what we do."

"And what is that?"

"I thought we'd established that."

"Ambush him in a dark alley and get him shot?"

"We'd like to avoid the getting shot part."

"If he's passing information to Lafe regarding our movements, it might be too dangerous to approach him."

"Hello? If he's passing information, he knows we're here and that Zeke is in town trying to figure out who killed Becky."

"So we're already hanged is what you're saying?" Quimby asked.

"Pretty much. Actually, I'm surprised we're not already dead."

"Nice, Tess," Jace said.

"So, basically, we've got enough to get us killed, but not enough to get anything decisive on Lafe," Quimby offered.

"Yeah."

"So what do we do?" Zeke demanded.

"Can we revisit the leave the city and go back west discussion again?" Hazel asked.

"My attention span is seriously overtaxed right now," Quimby added.

"No! We already decided to finish this."

"Maybe they're right, Tess," Vaughn admitted. "What else have we got to go on?"

"Okay, I admit we're a little out of our depth here, but that doesn't mean we should just give up. We probably aren't going to get Lafe and we definitely aren't going to get Rush. But we might at least be able to prove Zeke is innocent. That is what we came here to do."

"How do we do it?" Hazel asked.

"I don't know."

She shrugged and stood up. "Well, let's go on then."

"Do what?" Zeke asked.

"Talk to Jesse. What have we got to lose at this point?"

"That's actually kind of true. Okay," I said, looking around at the men. "Who's in?"

"I'm in," Jace said immediately.

"Me, too," Zeke replied.

"And me," Vaughn added.

"Oh, all right," Quimby said with a sigh.

I looked at Jace. "It might get a little hairy, Jace. You don't have to come along."

"I'm not going to back out of this now that it's getting interesting. I'm not a coward. I can take care of myself."

"It wasn't interesting before?" Zeke put in.

Jace considered. "It's been slightly interesting and often horrifying, actually."

"Oh, don't treat him like a child, Tess," Hazel scolded. "He's handled himself just fine so far."

I sighed. "Fine"

"The part where the guy got shot in the head right in front of us? That was one of the horrifying parts," Jace added for clarity.

"It might happen again, Jace."

"I know. I'm willing to take that chance."

"It might be one of us this time."

"Then I'd rather be there than worry that it's you getting killed."

"Well," Zeke said. "I think that settles that. Off we go, then."

* * *

Jesse O'Brien's house was a small, brick two-story on a quiet, shady street in Parker Hill. A tidy white fence surrounded the neat, carefully tended lawn. It didn't look like the home of a conspirator, but I'd discovered over the years that outlaws and criminals rarely lived in the sorts of seedy, dirty and sinister looking homes one would expect. The ones goods, anyway. The good ones live in huge manor houses with armies of servants and rooms filled with ill-gotten gold.

A single light burned in a second floor window of the cottage behind a blue curtain. I couldn't see anyone moving around in the room. "Looks like someone's home," Hazel remarked.

"He's married," I said grimly.

"Damn. That makes things a little more difficult."

"I'll deal with the wife," I told them. "We ain't gonna hurt him. We just need answers."

"Well, we hope we don't have to hurt him," Zeke replied, frowning. "Maybe someone should get the wife out of there."

"So she can run off to the law?" Hazel demanded. "I'll take care of her."

"I'm not sure that's such a good idea," Jace said.

She rolled her eyes. "I know how to put someone out of the game without hurting them. Just leave it to me."

"She's right, Jace. All right, Hazel. You take care of the woman," I said. "Step lively, then, folks."

"What are we going to do?" Jace asked, catching my wrist abruptly. "Just break in?"

"We could just knock on the door," Zeke offered.

"You think he'll just let us in?" Vaughn asked.

"If he doesn't, at least our foot's in the door. Anyone got any better ideas?"

"No," Quimby chimed.

I agreed. "It's all just bad ideas and last ditch efforts."

"This is the worst posse ever."

"I think you will find that our recklessness and lack of attention to detail is what makes us effective in the field," I told Zeke tersely.

"I find that hard to believe."

"So does everyone else," Hazel added. "That's why we're dangerous."

"Let's just go knock on the door."

No one answered. There was no sound from inside the house. We glanced at each other in the meager light on the front porch. My posse and I turned to look at Zeke. "Okay, your way didn't work," Quimby said.

"Can we try our way now?" Hazel asked. She whipped the lock pick out from some hidden pocket of her dress. It sparked and hummed.

Jace rolled his eyes and stepped forward. He tried the door. It opened.

"Well, that was anti-climactic," I remarked in disappointment.

No one was listening. We stepped into the dark foyer. It was empty and quiet.

"You think it's lucky or ominous the door isn't locked?" Hazel asked, looking around with narrowed eyes.

The house was as neat and tidy inside as out. Mrs. O'Brien was a skilled, dedicated housekeeper. There wasn't a speck of dust in the sitting room, which was decorated in pale green and beige. There was art on the walls, as though the mistress had spent years painstakingly gathering the landscapes and still lives which would complement the exact shades of blue and green in the brocade settee.

She wasn't there to take credit for it, though. No one was in the house, despite the unlocked door and the burning light on the second story. I frowned and exchanged a nervous look with Jace. "It doesn't look like he's around," I remarked.

"Shh!" Hazel snapped. We all looked at her in surprise. She prowled the room with her nose in the air. She was sniffing the corners of the room. She paused and listened. She spun toward us suddenly with wide eyes.

"What's up, Hazel?" Quimby demanded.

"There's an explosive somewhere in here. I can smell it."

"What?"

"Well, come on!" Jace growled. "We have to get out of here."

"Yeah, I think that'd be a wise idea," Hazel replied. She didn't wait to ensure we'd followed her. She raced out the door past the small white fence and into the street.

We followed, but I paused a few houses down the street. "No, wait!" I called to them.

"What?" Jace demanded.

"I think we should stick around and see if anyone shows up to admire their handiwork."

He stared at me blankly.

"I'm with Tess," Quimby said. What's the point of escaping a bomb if you aren't going to wait around to figure out who set it? It's been my experience that if you go through the trouble of setting up a bomb, you come back to see it go off."

"He knows what he's talking about," Hazel put in. "I always like to see my bombs in action."

Zeke rolled his eyes. "I'm not sure why I'm working with you people."

"You're the one who hired us," Quimby reminded him. "And you ain't got anyone better."

"There ain't anyone better," I added.

"Fine. We'll wait."

We hunkered down beside a tall, thick fence surrounding Jesse's neighbor's dark, quiet cottage. We waited. Nothing happened.

"Any idea when this thing is supposed to go off?" Jace asked impatiently.

Hazel scowled at him. "No. I just smelled it and heard it. I didn't hunt it down to check the countdown."

"Could be hours," I said.

"It probably isn't hours. Someone sets a bomb, they want to target when it goes off. Jesse must be expecting us or someone else. He'll have set it for the most likely time for a drop in visit."

"Any idea when that might be?"

"I ain't a mind reader."

"You think it might be intended for someone else?" Zeke asked in surprise.

"Well," I put in. "Maybe Rush sent someone after Jesse, too."

"There's no way to know that."

"I'd like to know when the bomb is going to go off," Jace said again.

"It could be minutes," Hazel told him. "It could be--"

KABOOM!

"It could be right now."

The house exploded in a cloud of smoke and sparks. We ducked, and the heat from the fire rolled over us. Hazel leapt to her feet and raced out into the street. Folks were beginning to flood out into the street to see what had happened. We ignored them. They were all staring in shock at the smoldering remains of their neighbor's home.

"Aha!" Hazel shouted suddenly. She pelted down the street after a figure darting away through the shadows. He was tall and lithe. "Tess!"

"There!" I cried and spun to chase after them. The boys' feet pounded the pavement on my heels, but Hazel and I were smaller and faster.

Our quarry darted in and out of the houses through the dark neighborhood. We sprinted after him, but he was faster than us, and he knew the area better. We stumbled over fences and through undeveloped patches of wood.

I gasped for breath and shouted out at him. "Lafe!"

His step faltered a moment. He seemed surprised we knew his name, or at least surprised I would call to him. He half turned his head under a flickering street torch as though to check our progress behind him. We were close enough that I recognized his high cheekbones and even features. He pulled a gun and fired it over his shoulder. A particle beam cut through the air near Hazel's head and struck a fencepost.

Hazel cursed and darted the other way. Her own gun was already in her hand. She fired back, but Lafe ducked behind a fence and fired out at us without looking around the slats.

"Get down, Hazel!" I called and dove behind a tree trunk. Nearby, Hazel dropped to her belly to fire at Lafe.

"Damn, ladies!" Quimby complained, sliding on the grass at our feet to press his back against a neighboring fence. "You couldn't wait for me to start the shootout?"

"You're not fast enough, Quimby," Hazel replied, firing toward Lafe's hiding spot.

Jace rounded a corner and dove to the side as Lafe returned the fire. He cursed and pressed against the tree trunk beside me. "I should have asked for a gun," he complained.

"Get your own gun. We ain't your babysitters," Hazel replied sharply.

I popped out and fired at Lafe. "I reckon you should let us worry about the shootin', Jace. You never were good at it."

He scowled and leaned around me to peer into the shadows. A beam sliced past his head. I pushed him back against the tree. "I don't suppose he's using one of Rush's guns?" Hazel remarked.

"We're probably not that lucky."

Vaughn and Zeke caught up to us and crouched low near Quimby. They didn't try to fire their weapons. "It would be nice if his hand blew off," Vaughn remarked. "He ain't much of a shot anyway, though."

As though to illustrate this, a beam blew off the slat beside Quimby's head. He ducked.

"If he's actually in on Rush's cover-up," Jace said darkly, "he knows better than to use his guns."

"Do you guys always banter this much during a shoot out?" Zeke demanded irritably.

"What else is there to do?" I asked, poking my head out to fire.

Hazel lifted her head. "Okay, this isn't getting us anywhere. We know it's you, Lafe!"

Lafe didn't reply, but a bullet whizzed over her head. "Must've run out of firepower," Quimby said smugly. He popped off a shot around the splintered fencepost.

Hazel leapt suddenly to her feet. "Cover me!"

"Damnit, Hazel," I cursed, jumping up to follow her.

Jace grabbed my arm and pulled me back down beside him. "No, Tess!"

"Leave me alone, Jace. This ain't the first time she's done this. Hazel, you get back here."

She ignored me. She dodged to the side to avoid Lafe's aimless fire and ran right at him. I saw him rear back from the fence with a shocked expression. He didn't fire at her. He turned and fled.

"Get back here!" Hazel shouted at him. She chased him, but he was faster than she was. He disappeared over a fence and into the shadows.

I caught up to her. She bent over her knees, gasping for breath. "That son of a bitch," she complained.

"You're lucky he didn't shoot your face."

The boys caught up to us, panting. "Ah, hell, Hazel, you let him go?"

She turned a glare on him. "I didn't let him do anything! He got away. That bugger is fast."

"Ah, that's just dandy."

"You're sure it was Lafe?" Jace asked.

"Yeah," I replied. "I saw his face."

"Clear as day," Hazel added.

"What about Jesse?"

"I don't know. He wasn't here."

"Unless he was in the house," I said darkly.

"I didn't think anyone was in the house," Jace said grimly.

"We didn't exactly search it, did we? He might have been knocked out in there or something."

"Or he helped Lafe set the bomb and high-tailed it."

"Do you guys ever catch anyone?" Zeke demanded tersely. "Or is it always one big, destructive, murderous failure?"

"That is not very charitable of you, Zeke."

He scowled and kicked his foot angrily on the pavement. "You let him get away! He was the one! He was all we had to clear me! Now what the hell are we going to do?"

I sighed and glanced around at Jace and my posse. "Yeah...it might be time to get back to the west."

"You have got to be kidding me," Jace snarled. "You're giving up now?"

"Well, six eyewitnesses to a shoot out is not nothing, is it?" Hazel asked hopefully.

"It is when you consider we're the eyewitnesses," Zeke replied.

"Could this situation possibly get any worse?" Quimby demanded.

"Yeah, actually, it could," I replied. "We could have been in the building when it blew up."

* * *

The hotel room felt like a prison. We were all silent and sullen. We didn't meet each other's eyes. Things were clearly not going as well as we would have liked. I hated to admit failure, but I didn't think we were going to crack this case anytime soon. I was tired, I was frustrated, and I wasn't the only one. Around me, Jace, Zeke and my posse looked as though someone had kicked their dogs.

"Now what?" Quimby asked glumly.

"Our last lead is blown up," Hazel complained.

"No, it isn't," Jace said bracingly. "A house was blown up, but it wasn't our last lead. We know what happened. We know that Rush sent Lafe to kill the two men in New York and Virginia, and we know he sent him to kill Becky when she discovered the telegrams."

"Well, we don't know that for sure."

"We know it right enough."

"Okay, so we've solved it," I said, sighing. "And Rush and Lafe intended to kill all of us by setting a bomb at Jesse's house because we got close enough to suss it."

"Do you think Jesse was in on it?" Quimby asked me.

I shrugged. "I don't know. Maybe. The poor kid probably just got mixed up in it all."

"I hope his wife's all right," Hazel murmured. "You think she's all right?"

I sighed. "Yeah. I hope so."

"If Jesse is smart, he took her somewhere safe to keep her out of all this. He knew the risk he was taking getting involved in all this." Zeke sighed. "It doesn't make what happened any better, though. Even if she's still alive, she's lost everything."

"Boy, you've gotten pessimistic since all this began," I complained.

"Things are not going as I planned."

"Yeah, yeah. So how do we prove all this?" I asked the room at large. "How do we prove Zeke is innocent, Lafe is the killer and Rush is behind it all?"

"You think we could find Lafe, tie him up and beat a confession out of him?" Hazel asked hopefully.

"That seems pretty unlikely," Jace replied.

"Let's try a less ridiculous alternative," Vaughn said.

"Like Rush turning himself in?" I offered wryly. The others chuckled humorlessly.

"Nah. I think we're out of luck," Hazel said.

"Well, what links them to each other?" Vaughn said. "The cipher."

"The kill orders."

My posse and I looked around at each other. I could tell by the look in their eyes that they had arrived at the same conclusion as me at the same time. We grinned at each other. Zeke had been hanging around with us long enough to guess what we were thinking. "Oh, no," he said. "Don't even think about it."

"Why?" I demanded. "It's the only way to clear you, Zeke."

"Do you want your life back or do you just want to roll over and let them keep on goin' like this?" Hazel asked, scowling at him.

"We can leave," Quimby offered. "They might not even follow us."

"Lafe probably will," Zeke replied glumly.

"What are you all talking about?" Jace demanded.

I turned to him. "There's only one way to prove Zeke is innocent and Lafe is the one doing the killing for Rush."

"We won't get a judge to listen to us," Hazel added. "We're a bunch of bounty hunters and fugitives. They'll probably blame us for the bomb at Jesse's."

"Well, they'd blame you," Quimby said.

"Come on. I would have blown it up way better."

"Anyway, we have to prove where these kill orders were sent. We have to prove it was Lafe to whom Rush was sending them," I told Jace. "It would be enough for a full-scale investigation. Even Rush's Marshals will have a hard time keeping his hands clean if we have proof to show the big bugs in D.C."

"That's great, but how exactly do you plan to do it?" Jace asked. We all turned to look at him, and he finally got it. "Oh, no."

"My thoughts exactly," Zeke said.

"No way, Tess. We are not breaking into Rush AI. There are security guards everywhere. It's like trying to break into Pinkerton HQ. We'd never get in and out."

Hazel grinned. She whipped out one of her devices from the folds of her skirt and flicked the trigger. Lightning arced between two metal prongs. Jace reared back. "I think I can handle some security guards."

I stood to face them. "Anyone up for one more last ditch effort?"

My posse grinned. "Now this is a little more like what we do," Quimby said approvingly.

"I reckon we haven't got any other choice," Vaughn added, smiling.

"You know I'm up for it," Hazel put in.

We all looked at Jace and Zeke. They looked pretty grim. They exchanged a glance.

"I reckon I don't have much of a choice, do I?" Zeke asked. "You folks are obviously going to do it with or without me."

"Yeah. We are. And you ought to come along, on account of us doing it for you."

Zeke's mouth turned up slightly at the corners. We turned to Jace. He shrugged. "I reckon I'm in it now. Lafe already knows I'm working with you all. I might as well take it to the end."

I grinned at him. "Okay. Let's take it to the end."

Chapter Eighteen

Rush Scientific Advancements and Steam-Powered Innovations loomed over a courtyard of trees whose tall, overgrown branches barely concealed the bottom half of the dark, mirrored glass and steel building from the prying eyes of the surrounding streets. The grassy courtyard was not guarded. We stole along the cobblestone paths toward the building unobstructed. I caught distorted glimpses of our creeping figures in the mirrored glass of the outer walls between the trees.

In the center of the courtyard was a huge, bronze statue of what looked like a bird's body with a clear glass cylinder for a head. The wings and legs attached to the plump figure with gears and sprockets. Wires, tubes and gauges stuck out from the body. A solid, still cloud of fluffy bronze steam floated above the glass head. I didn't know what it was supposed to be, but the plaque at the base of the statue called it Rush Scientific Advancements and Steam-Powered Innovations' First Steam-Operated Government-Sanctioned Mechanical Anti-Contamination Vulture Apparatus.

Honestly, where did they come up with these names?

A guard stood as silent and watchful as a sentinel in a pavilion surrounding the tall, sparkling glass double doors at the entrance. He didn't notice us skulking stealthily through the courtyard. Hazel waved her hand at us. We paused, ducking behind the trees around the pavilion. Hazel crept around to the guard's right and darted forward so quickly, he never saw what hit him. She struck him with the pronged end of the wand before he noticed her approach. He didn't jerk or convulse. He slipped silently to the stone ground in a heap.

Two more guards stood beside the double glass doors. They didn't speak or look at each other. Hazel and Vaughn grinned at each other. They both strode forward. Hazel zapped the guard on the left with the wand, and Vaughn seized the other between the neck and shoulder and squeezed. The guards both dropped as silently as the first had done. Hazel grinned over her shoulder at us and drew her lock-pick gadget from the folds of her skirt. It really was an ingenious invention. The double doors sprung open.

The lobby was dark. It was constructed of the same mirrored glass inside, which reflected us back at ourselves until we disappeared into tiny points. I wondered if the labs and offices were like this. I reckoned it would be extremely distracting to work in this sparkling building. There weren't any guards around.

The front desk was silent.

We glanced tensely at each other. It felt a little too easy. We strode along the narrow corridors. The brass doors in the halls were closed. Carefully hand-lettered names indicated the offices' owners. None of them were Rush's.

"His office is upstairs," Jace whispered, as though he'd read my mind. "The lift is at the end of the hall."

I hadn't realized he'd been here before, but I reckoned I shouldn't be surprised. He was a news hound, after all. He probably hung around here pestering the workers all day. I smiled a little at this. In the mirrored wall, I smiled back at myself.

The lift was a clear glass box that shot up a glass tube from which we could peer down into the offices and R&D laboratories as we rose toward the top floor. Inventions in various stages of development scattered the black marble floors below. Hazel cooed and pressed her face against the glass to get a better look. I didn't pay attention to Rush AI's latest innovations. My nerves were ragged and tense. I peered at Jace. His handsome, patrician features were eerily calm, though I thought I could see some tightness around his green eyes and his sculpted mouth.

"All we need to do is get in and get the information off the telegraph," Zeke said in a tight voice. "Then we get out. Simple as that."

We stepped off the lift at the top floor. Jace led us through the corridor to the end of the hall. Our shoes made soft, dull clicks on the polished black marble floors. The last door in the hall was taller than the others. The words Sterling Rush were plated in copper at eye level. There were no guards, but the door was locked. We stepped back for Hazel. She wielded the lock pick and flicked the trigger. Blue light arced toward the lock. The door sprang open.

The office was larger than our hotel room. The walls were a soothing ivory, rather than the tense, distracting mirrored glass of the halls and lobby. It was decorated with miniatures of Rush AI's greatest inventions. A large, leather settee and two matching chairs filled the east side of the room several feet from the large, polished dark wood desk.

I paused to examine a landscape on the wall. It was painted in shining metallic. It was a city made of brass, gold, copper and glass. The sun glinted off the buildings. A man with metal wings soured above the tall, domed and pointed buildings through a brilliantly blue sky. Was this Rush's vision of the future? It was a little shiny for my tastes.

The tall, brown leather chair behind the polished oak desk spun suddenly, and a light flicked on to illuminate the other occupant of the room. We stared at him in shock. He smiled.

"I have to admit," Sterling Rush said. "I'm disappointed. I expected you'd try this much, much sooner. Did you all come for the telegraph? I hate to disappoint you. It had to be replaced yesterday. It was...faulty."

We stared at him. Jace was the first one to recover himself. "I knew you were behind all this all along."

He didn't sound angry or indignant. He just sounded disappointed. I wasn't sure why. Maybe he was hoping for more fanfare.

Rush smiled a charming, pleasant smile at us. "So, Tess Mercury and her famous posse. I expected more bells and whistles, though I am impressed by how you managed to get into my office so quickly. I was not expecting you to actually reach me for another ten minutes."

"You've been playing us this whole time. How long have you been onto us?" I demanded, crossing my arms over my chest.

He laughed. "I've known all along who you are. Let's say since you picked up Ezekiel here in Colorado." At our shocked silence, he added, "I have many friends in many places. Mostly low."

I frowned. "Then why all of this? Why let us get this far and this close?"

"I wanted to see what you are capable of. I've heard many stories. I must say: they were not wrong." His large, dark eyes twinkled. "Besides, it wouldn't have been any fun if I hadn't at least let you try. I allowed you to be released from jail. I've been keeping track of your progress." He leaned back in his chair and folded his hands on the top of his desk. "I must admit, I was a bit thrown off by you and Jason actually being married. I thought it was a ploy at first, but when I looked into it, I was most delighted to discover the coincidence."

I glanced at Jace. His expression was blank. "Yeah, well, that threw us all a little off."

"So you're the one who ordered Lafe to kill Rebecca Palmer and the men from the Department of Scientific Progress and Questionable Developments," Jace said, as if for clarity.

Rush laughed. "Now, do you honestly believe I would admit such a thing on the record?"

"And Jesse?" Zeke asked. His voice was even, but I'd been hanging around him long enough to recognize the delicate shade of green on his face.

Rush shook his head sadly. "Poor Jesse. He was a sweet kid."

"He's innocent, isn't he?" I asked in a low voice. "He's just another pawn in all this. Is he dead?"

He looked at me silently. He smiled.

"You won't get away with this," Jace told him firmly. "We'll tell the Marshals."

"Tell them what? More wild accusations? How will you prove any of this? There's no evidence." He rose and smiled around at all of us. "You've lost, Jason. It's over." He rounded the desk. We all took a step back as though expecting him to strike. He chuckled and perched on the edge of the desk. "I am not without a little charity and good will." He gestured at Zeke. "Ezekiel, I've given you your life back. No need to thank me. Just consider it a small token."

We all frowned at each other warily.

Rush drew a shining gold watch from his lapel pocket and flicked it open. "Well. This has been fun, but I'm afraid we're all out of time. The Marshals should be arriving in about ten minutes. I did say you were earlier than I had expected. I suggest you 'get a wiggle on' as you frontier people say." He smiled widely. "It has been a real pleasure meeting you, Tess. And the rest of you." He winked at Jace. "I am sure I will be seeing you around the city soon, Jason. It is always a treat." He flicked his hands at us in a shooing gesture. "All right, then. Go on."

We didn't need any further urging. We all turned and rushed from the building without looking back.

Back at the hotel, we all stared around at each other with shell-shocked expressions.

"I can't believe he knew about this the whole time," Hazel muttered, voicing what we were all thinking. "We were just playing his game all along, right into his hands."

"He had me fooled," I admitted reluctantly. He was a more formidable foe than any of us had expected.

"He sure did," Jace said glumly. "I can't believe he practically admitted to it all and we have no way of getting to him. No telegraph, no evidence."

"And no one would ever believe us," Quimby added.

"I can't believe he just gets away," I complained.

We all sighed.

Zeke lifted his eyebrows. "So, what do you all think he meant by giving me my life back?"

* * *

None of us looked up in eager excitement as Jace burst into the room early the next morning. We were tired and weary. None of us had even bothered to get dressed. Hazel hadn't even bothered to get out of bed. She sat up under the covers in her dressing gown. The boys were sulking in their chairs around the desk and beds. They weren't looking at any papers or notes. We chewed sullenly on the pastries and breads from the lobby and sipped bitter coffee.

My posse and I didn't take failure well. At least none of us had started drinking yet.

Jace looked around at us. He laughed. I looked up at him in surprise. "You all look like your mama just died."

I sighed. "We ain't never lost before. 'Least not on this scale. We just ain't sure how to deal with it yet."

"Zeke, I have some good news and some bad news."

We all perked up a little. He handed Zeke the morning's *Boston Daily*. Zeke scanned it for a few minutes, then he tossed it violently aside. "You have got to be kidding me."

I reached for the paper, but Hazel leapt out of bed and snatched it up. Jace nodded grimly. "What is it?" I demanded impatiently.

Zeke looked as though he wasn't sure whether or not he should smile. I reckoned it was more bad news than good. I looked at Hazel impatiently.

"Will someone please explain what is going on?" Vaughn asked calmly.

"Jesse O'Brien was found dead in a motel room this morning," Hazel explained grimly. "He left a note confessing to Becky's and Silas' murders."

I blinked in shock for several moments. Quimby lifted his eyebrows. "What?"

"What about the boys from the Department of Scientific Progress and Questionable Developments? Does it say he did it for Rush?"

"Come on," Jace said disdainfully.

"He only copped to Becky and Silas," Hazel explained. "Rush isn't mentioned at all."

"They printed the suicide note," Zeke said. "He said he had his own reasons for killing them."

Hazel held out the paper, and we all reached for it again. Vaughn's large, thick hands were the quickest. He leaned back in his chair to read through it. He peered over the top of the paper. "Has anyone else noticed the handwriting is the same as on those love letters?"

Now I stood and peered over his shoulder. I gestured for one of the letters. Jace handed one over and I held it up beside the *Daily*. I glanced grimly around at the others. "It's the same."

"Poor kid," Quimby muttered. "He had nothing to do with any of this, did he?"

"Probably not," Zeke replied. "Lafe's smart. He probably caught on to him sniffing around Pink HQ. Maybe he knew what I was doing all along. Rush's got people in every corner, just like he said." He dropped his head in his hands and sighed. "It's my fault that kid's dead."

"Hey, we can't blame ourselves for any of these deaths," I said sternly. "Rush has flies on every wall, and there's no evidence against either him or Lafe."

He frowned thoughtfully. "Why do you think Rush did that? Cleared me?"

"He gave you back your life," Hazel said. "Just like he said. Maybe he's trying to get you on his side."

"He's not a fool. He knows I'm not going to work for him."

I shrugged. "Maybe he's trying to prove he is more powerful than you. He can take your life away as quickly as he gave it back."

We were all silent for a long moment.

"So Lafe's just in the wind?" Vaughn said, frowning.

"Seems like it," Zeke replied.

"You think anyone cares how contrived this all sounds?" I asked.

"No. Probably not. Folks like things to be easily wrapped up like this. Two murders are sewn up and no one has to think about any of it ever again."

"Yeah, but what about Jesse's wife?" Hazel demanded, scowling. "She's the one who suffers. She's the one whose husband is dead, and she has to live believing he was a murderer."

"Do you think someone should talk to her?" I asked, frowning.

"Do you think that would make it better for her?" Jace asked, sitting down on the edge of my bed to look at me.

I shrugged. "Maybe. I think I would prefer not to think you were a murderer after you were dead."

Zeke dropped his chin to his chest for several long moments. Then he looked up at us. "I should be the one."

"Do you think it's safe?" Hazel asked.

"What is Rush going to do about it? He's already proven he's the one with all the power."

"She might decide to go to the Marshals."

He barked with humorless laughter. "It'd do no good. No one would believe her any more than they would believe us."

"Yeah," I sighed. "Rush and Lafe are pretty safe. I don't think they have any reason to stop us doing whatever we're going to do."

"So. What are we going to do?" Jace asked, looking around at us.

We all looked around at each other. "We could hunt Lafe," Hazel offered.

"He's got no bounty. Not yet," Quimby replied.

"Maybe not ever," I added.

"It's not much good if we aren't getting paid."

"Is that all you care about, Burton?" Jace demanded.

"For the most part, yeah."

"I'm still here." Jace frowned around at us. "I will get something on Rush and Lafe eventually. Maybe we'll work together again."

"We made an awful team," I told him glumly, though my lips turned up slightly at the corners. "All we did was get people killed and framed up."

"It's not a win, but we did finish the job," Hazel protested. "Zeke's free and clear. He can go back to Wyoming, get his wife and buy that ranch."

Zeke shook his head. "No. I know I promised to help you bring in Donnie Rio, but I need to be here. Maybe between Jace and I, we can get something on Rush some day."

Jace smiled. "It would be an honor to work with you again, Zeke." He glanced at me. "What are you going to do, Tess?"

Everyone looked at me. I wished he'd asked that in private. I grimaced awkwardly and sighed. "We promised to pick up Donnie Rio and bring him to justice. My posse and me have been in New England too long. It's not our home. We need to get back to what we're good at."

Jace looked crestfallen, but he recovered himself and lifted his chin.

I reached over and took his hand. It seemed to surprise him. "But I ain't ready to let this go." They all looked at me in surprise. "I ain't ready to let Rush and Lafe get away with what they're doing."

My posse didn't look as though this was news they wanted to hear. Jace smiled, though. Zeke's mouth twisted up crookedly. I grinned around at my posse, and eventually they grinned back at me a little reluctantly.

"Rush doesn't know who he's dealing with," Hazel announced.

"I wouldn't mind wiping that smug look off his face," Quimby added.

"I reckon we've had worse ideas," Vaughn put in.

I met Jace's glittering green eyes. He smiled.

"Do I still have to pay you?" Zeke asked. "I reckon this didn't turn out exactly as planned."

My posse and I turned and looked at him.

He held up his hands. "Okay. Okay. Five hundred dollars it is."

* * *

It was a clear, warm, sunny spring day. The white dirigible sparkled in the rays of the mid-morning sun on its launch pad as it waited for us to board the short flight to Chicago. Passengers were already marching up the ramp into the fat, globular cabin. Zeke smiled around him. I didn't know what he was feeling, but I suspected it was as light as air. I knew he was anxious to reclaim Lenora and bring her home. My posse seemed to have gotten over the sting of our first failure.

Jace walked silently beside me toward the ramp to board the airship. I paused and turned to face him. My posse slipped tactfully away to let us talk. I appreciated that. I suspected it was going to be slightly embarrassing.

"When will you be back?" he asked.

"I don't know. We're just picking up Donnie Rio. It shouldn't take too long. We know where he is, and all we have to do is bring him back down to Texas."

"I suspect it isn't going to be as straightforward as you make it sound."

I laughed. "It never really is."

"You said we'd talk after we cleared Zeke."

"I know, Jace. We still will."

He sighed. "You are going to come back, right? This isn't some way to leave me forever with no forwarding address?"

"Come on, Jace. You know it isn't. I said we'd talk, and we'll talk. I just need some time to think about it."

"You know what it is I want, Tess."

"I think I do."

"Okay. I'll wait for you."

"Be careful while I'm gone. Don't get yourself mixed up with any more crooked Pinks. Try to keep your head down." I stepped forward and squeezed his hands. "I want you to be here when I get back."

"I will. I'll try to stick to more mundane news. I always manage to dredge something up. It doesn't always have to do with Sterling Rush."

"Okay."

Jace stepped toward me and pressed his lips to mine. I sighed and wrapped my arms around his neck. It felt nice to be kissing Jace again. It felt right. It would sure give me something to think about on the long, lonely nights out on the range, anyway.

When he pulled away, he wrapped his arms around my waist and drew me into a hug. "Take care of yourself, Tess."

I laid my cheek against his chest. "I always do."

"Hey, Tess!" Vaughn called. "The ship's about to take off. Are you coming or what?"

I leaned my head back and caught the back of Jace's neck to kiss him soundly on the mouth.

"Don't be too long, huh?" he said, and I reckoned he was feeling mighty pleased with himself.

"Tess, come on!" Hazel called impatiently. "We're about to take off!"

I stepped away from my husband. "Bye, Jace."

"Bye, Tess."

I dipped my head and turned away from him to join my friends as they boarded the airship. I was still smiling as I sat between Hazel and Vaughn.

"You think we can stop in Fortune City on the way to pick up Donnie Rio?" Hazel asked hopefully.

We all looked at her incredulously. Then we all thought about it.

"I reckon Lennie can wait a couple more days for me to come get her," Zeke said.

I shrugged. "Why not?"

"I think we deserve a little R&R for all our hard work," Quimby added.

"I reckon I'm not in any hurry to get back to business," Vaughn said.

Hazel pumped her hand in the air. "Hoooeeee! They love me in Fortune City."

"I reckon anything's better than Boston, right, Tess?" Quimby asked.

I glanced out the window at the fading cityscape as we rose gently into the air toward Missouri. "I don't know. I reckon it wasn't so bad after all."

"Aside from all the killings and things."

"Yeah. Aside from that."

Read Book Two in the exciting Tess Mercury Series

Tess Mercury and the Bonny Bandidas

Coming soon from

DC PRESS

www.dcpressbooks.org

About the Author

Eleanor Prophet is an author, columnist, editor, lady of leisure and amateur sleuth. Her most popular works include the Astrid Darby Adventures. When she isn't writing books, short stories, essays and articles of questionable veracity, she is typically enjoying the attentions of Mr Prophet, a dashing international man of mystery and intrigue. Her favourite activities include larking about, rule-breaking, mischief-making and getting to the bottom of things. She often receives fascinating, comical and occasionally disturbing mail to her desk and publishes on her blog for the public's information, entertainment and frequent outrage.

Read Ellie's Blog at:

www.ellieprophet.wordpress.com

www.ingramcontent.com/pod-product-compliance
Lightning Source LLC
Chambersburg PA
CBHW071602180626
46819CB00002B/100